Carol Marinelli recently [...] for her job title. Thrilled t[...] answer, she put 'writer'. Then it asked what Carol did for relaxation and she put down the truth: 'writing'. The third question asked for her hobbies. Well, not wanting to look obsessed, she crossed her fingers and answered 'swimming'—but, given that the chlorine in the pool does terrible things to her highlights, I'm sure you can guess the real answer!

Having once made her home in sunny Brazil, **Luana DaRosa** has since lived on three different continents—though her favourite romantic locations remain the tropical places of Latin America. When she's not typing away at her latest romance novel, or reading about love, Luana is either crocheting, buying yarn she doesn't need, or chasing her bunnies around the house. She lives with her partner in a cosy town in the south of England. Find her on X under the handle @LuDaRosaBooks.

Also by Carol Marinelli

Mills & Boon Medical

The Nurse's Pregnancy Wish
One Month to Tame the Surgeon

Mills & Boon Modern

Rival Italian Brothers miniseries

Italian's Pregnant Mistress
Italian's Cinderella Temptation

Also by Luana DaRosa

Pregnancy Surprise with the Greek Surgeon

Buenos Aires Docs miniseries

Surgeon's Brooding Brazilian Rival

Valentine Flings miniseries

Hot Nights with the Arctic Doc

Discover more at millsandboon.co.uk.

NURSE'S NINE-MONTH SURPRISE

CAROL MARINELLI

FALLING FOR HER MIAMI RIVAL

LUANA DaROSA

MILLS & BOON

All rights reserved including the right of reproduction in whole or in part in any form. This edition is published by arrangement with Harlequin Enterprises ULC.

This is a work of fiction. Names, characters, places, locations and incidents are purely fictional and bear no relationship to any real life individuals, living or dead, or to any actual places, business establishments, locations, events or incidents. Any resemblance is entirely coincidental.

This book is sold subject to the condition that it shall not, by way of trade or otherwise, be lent, resold, hired out or otherwise circulated without the prior consent of the publisher in any form of binding or cover other than that in which it is published and without a similar condition including this condition being imposed on the subsequent purchaser.

® and TM are trademarks owned and used by the trademark owner and/or its licensee. Trademarks marked with ® are registered with the United Kingdom Patent Office and/or the Office for Harmonisation in the Internal Market and in other countries.

First published in Great Britain 2025
by Mills & Boon, an imprint of HarperCollins*Publishers* Ltd,
1 London Bridge Street, London, SE1 9GF

www.harpercollins.co.uk

HarperCollins*Publishers* Macken House, 39/40 Mayor Street Upper, Dublin 1, D01 C9W8, Ireland

Nurse's Nine-Month Surprise © 2025 Carol Marinelli

Falling for Her Miami Rival © 2025 Luana DaRosa

ISBN: 978-0-263-32505-8

05/25

This book contains FSC™ certified paper and other controlled sources to ensure responsible forest management.

For more information visit www.harpercollins.co.uk/green.

Printed and Bound in the UK using 100% Renewable Electricity at CPI Group (UK) Ltd, Croydon, CR0 4YY

NURSE'S NINE-MONTH SURPRISE

CAROL MARINELLI

MILLS & BOON

CHAPTER ONE

An Indian summer in London

HIS INTENTION HAD been to slip away quietly.

Dr Richard Lewis had hoped to be on the late-afternoon train or at least outside the hotel before his absence was noted. Then, when the inevitable texts arrived, asking where he was, he could fire back a one-word answer—Cardiff. Or perhaps a quick line stating that he'd be back on board tomorrow.

It was not to be.

'Richard!'

Unseen, he briefly closed his eyes in mild frustration before turning to see that both Monica and George were making their way across the hotel foyer towards him.

A large medical conference was being held in central London and they were all staying at a hotel here, near Kings Cross. There was a group of eight or so of them who had been side by side at medical school and had remained both colleagues and friends over the years.

Two of them were bearing down on him now.

Monica was now a consultant obstetrician at The Primary, in north London, and was also a speaker at the conference. George, a consultant paediatrician, also at The Primary, had just given a major presentation. Richard was neither speaking nor presenting; he was attending the conference to keep updated, as well as to get his professional development hours up.

His own once soaring career had somewhat stalled, and he currently worked as a locum accident and emergency registrar across several hospitals in London.

'We've been looking for you,' Monica said as they caught up with him. 'We're all meeting at the rooftop bar for drinks...'

'Rafi and Thomas are coming,' George added. 'Though we haven't decided where to go for dinner. Any preferences?'

'Don't make plans around me.' Richard shook his head. 'I'm not going to be here for dinner.'

'You're leaving?' Monica checked, her shoulders drooping, making no attempt to hide her disappointment. 'But I thought you were here for the entire conference?'

'I am,' Richard confirmed. 'I just can't make dinner tonight. I'll be back first thing tomorrow.'

'But we've hardly seen you since the conference started.'

'I've been at every session,' Richard pointed out. 'And I was at the dinner last night...'

'That was a formal function, though,' Monica said. 'And you were late for that—wasn't he, George?'

George flushed a little before responding, 'He wasn't *that* late.'

Richard smothered a smile. He had, in fact, been at the hotel since yesterday morning, helping his old friend prepare for his presentation, though of course George didn't want the uber-efficient Monica to know that!

George fumbled on, trying to persuade him to join them. 'A good night out with the old mob might be just the ticket...'

'It'll be like old times,' Monica urged.

It could never be like old times.

They kept on waiting for the old Richard to come back. For the man he'd been fifteen, ten, five or even three years ago to return. But that version of himself no longer existed.

Richard didn't blame them for not getting it—no doubt he looked much the same. He'd always been the tallest in their group, and at thirty-five his dark brown hair was still neat and regularly trimmed, and he was clean shaven.

Polite and measured, Richard certainly wasn't a rule-breaker. He was predictable…possibly even a bit boring at times—though those traits had been appreciated in their salad days! And he'd always dressed well. Today proved no exception—he wore a smart navy suit, a white shirt with the top button done up, and there was a pop of colour provided by a periwinkle silk tie. Even after five p.m. it remained immaculately knotted.

Typical Richard.

Not quite.

'We'll go out tomorrow night,' Richard promised. 'We could maybe try the hotel restaurant—Spanish-Mexican… I've heard good things.'

George clearly wasn't keen, though he made it about the restaurant rather than admit it wasn't for him. 'I doubt we'd get a booking for all of us.'

'How about Indian, then?' Monica smiled at Richard. 'That's always been your favourite.'

'Sure.' Richard nodded, even though he wasn't sure if Indian was his favourite any more. 'Sounds great.'

As Monica headed for the bar George remained.

'Thanks for not saying anything about yesterday. It was good to have a trial run…'

Despite George's brilliance, he was dreadful when talking in front of an audience and had asked for Richard's help. Yesterday, without the others knowing, they had been locked away in George's suite, ordering room service and going over and over his presentation.

'It more than paid off,' Richard said. 'You did a terrific job.'

'I'm surprised you didn't nod off. You must have heard it twenty times yesterday.'

'I learnt a lot.' Richard meant it. 'I was more than happy to help.'

'Well, it was much appreciated.' George nodded. 'And likewise, if you do ever decide to resume your studies…' George hesitated and swallowed a little awkwardly. 'I'm not trying to push, or anything. I know the others can be a bit much at times…'

Richard chose not to reveal that he was looking to sit the final exam for his Fellowship of the Royal College of Emergency Medicine in May. The decision still felt a little too new to be discussed and debated over dinner, as it inevitably would be.

'They mean well,' Richard settled for saying instead. 'I know that.' He lightly closed the conversation by glancing at his watch. 'George, much as I'd like to stay and chat, I don't want to miss my train.'

'Of course.'

This time he made it as far as the brass revolving door…

'Richard!'

Mr Field, his old boss and mentor, emerged. 'On your way out?' he checked. 'I'd advise against it.' Mr Field was very red in the face and dripping with sweat. 'It's like a damn oven out there…'

'So I've heard.' It was the last week in September, so technically autumn, but England was wilting under a heatwave. 'I believe there are a few colleagues from The Primary up at the rooftop bar if you want to make the most of the unseasonable weather.'

'I'll stay down here with the air-conditioning, thanks,' Mr Field said, and then looked Richard up and down. 'Have you lost weight or grown taller?'

'Taller,' Richard responded good-naturedly. He'd had a few too many comments about his weight this past couple of days, but knew that Mr Field meant well.

'How about lunch tomorrow?' Mr Field asked. 'Don't worry—I'm not trying to fatten you up. I want to discuss something. Just us.'

'Of course,' Richard responded smoothly, even if inwardly he was a touch startled. Mr Field was busy, and in heavy demand at events such as this one.

They made arrangements—or rather Mr Field said that Tara, his secretary, would be in touch. 'Until tomorrow, then…'

Richard took the Tube to Paddington. The station was both busy and familiar. He'd been doing this journey for years, and before purchasing his ticket he stood on the concourse, looking up at the departure board and wondering if he might make the earlier train. But he saw it was just about to leave.

When somebody beside him groaned, Richard could guess why—a few trains on the board had suddenly been cancelled.

Thankfully his own was still on time.

Then the information board was updated again, and as several more trains were abruptly cancelled there was a round of collective moans.

The train to Cardiff was still on time.

Then the board was updated once more and the sign reading 'Cardiff' flipped over.

Cancelled

Richard scanned the board, looking for the later train.

Cancelled

For a second he couldn't hear the loudspeaker system, nor his disgruntled fellow travellers—or rather they all faded into insignificance as a new emotion hit him.

In his oh-so-silent way he analysed the feeling spreading in his chest as he released a long breath.

Relief.

Richard didn't ignore his feelings; he just didn't readily share them. So he had no desire to head to the rooftop bar and reveal this new development in his day, and nor did he feel the need to whip out his phone and provide a group update.

Soon he would head back to Kings Cross, but for now he simply stood there, his face impassive, silently acknowledging his internal response to his train being cancelled.

Relief.

He was relieved not to be going.

CHAPTER TWO

'Excuse me...'

Sorcha Bell's attempt to run up the escalator was once again thwarted—her petite five feet two frame and soft Scottish-accented voice had little effect on the group of people blocking her way.

'Excuse me,' she said, more loudly, and this time they parted enough that she managed to get through.

She ran the last few steps to the top, refusing to entertain the possibility that she might miss her train.

Her long red hair was whipping wildly across her face as she spilled off the escalator and raced across the concourse towards her platform. Though her lilac cheesecloth dress and cream espadrilles weren't ideal running gear, at least there was no luggage weighing her down—just a hefty overnight bag.

Making her speedy way, she was delighted to see that the platform hadn't even opened and people were still lined up.

'Made it...' she breathed, her heart hammering from her rare sprint as she joined her fellow travellers at the barrier. 'I havenae run like that since school sports day...' she said, to no one in particular.

But a breathless lady who had come up behind her laughed. 'Nor me,' she agreed. 'I was sure I was going to miss it. This is the Edinburgh train?'

'It is.' Sorcha glanced up at a Roman numeral clock that had become a frequent fixture in her life in recent months and saw that it was almost five. 'They should let us on soon,' she said, and then wondered out loud if the buffet would be open, chatting easily with the lady as the line moved.

They discussed the sultry weather, both here and at home, as well as a comedy show the lady was on her way to see.

They didn't exchange names; this was just small talk.

While Sorcha might do her best to avoid difficult conversations, when it came to small talk she excelled!

'Was he at the Fringe this year?' Sorcha checked, recognising the name of the comedian.

It was late September, and the Edinburgh Fringe Festival had been held last month. It was definitely her favourite time of the year. She lived a couple of hours out of Edinburgh, and when the festival was on she got there as often as she could.

'I'd have gone and seen him if I'd known he was playing.'

'Not this year. Apparently he—' the lady's response was abruptly terminated as a suited man collided with them, knocking Sorcha to one side.

'Hey!' the lady called out to him. 'Watch where you're going.'

Sorcha righted herself as the gentleman staggered off.

'Cheek of him,' the lady grumbled. 'Too much to drink.'

And that should have been that.

Getting her ticket ready, Sorcha moved down the line. But something was niggling, and she turned around and took another look at the man. He was middle-aged and well groomed. His neat blond hair clashed with his ruddy face and indeed he was staggering. Sorcha watched as he careered into a young man on his phone. He certainly appeared intoxicated, but as an accident and emergency nurse Sorcha knew that blaming alcohol could prove a dangerous assumption.

'Miss...?'

Someone prompted her to move along and Sorcha walked towards the barrier, about to go through. But at the last moment she looked again. The man now stood stock still as others dashed past him, and then he turned slightly and she saw him grimace and clutch his left arm.

'Miss?' a station worker called. 'Move along now, please.'

'That man...' Sorcha started, watching as the man leant forward and moved his hand from his arm to his chest.

There really wasn't time to explain. Leaving the queue, she hastily made her way towards him, hoping she was overreacting.

'Sir?'

The man was doubled over now, but he reached out and grabbed her forearm and for a second almost toppled them both. His grip was tight, and she could feel and see his desperation and panic. Sorcha knew now that she wasn't overreacting. She called out to a passerby for help, but they walked briskly on. She asked another to call an ambulance, but her voice was drowned out by the voice on the loudspeakers.

Glancing back at the clock, she saw it was two minutes after five and knew she was about to miss her train.

It didn't matter now.

'Let's get you sitting down.' She spoke as calmly as she could to the distressed man.

There were chairs a few metres away but, given that he was on the edge of collapse, they were a few metres too far from them. Instead, she managed to guide him to a wall and he leant against it, refusing to sit.

'I'll be okay,' the man insisted, trying to speak normally yet clutching his chest, his face etched with pain. 'Thank you.'

'You need to sit,' she insisted, refusing to be dismissed. 'I'm Sorcha,' she introduced herself, then told him she was a nurse and asked his name.

'Edward,' he told her. 'It's my chest…'

He started to tug at his tie, as if it was choking him, but then gave in. He seemed to accept that he could no longer stand and leant more heavily against the wall. Sorcha helped him slide down to the ground safely, turning her head and calling out as she did.

'I need an ambulance!'

Her voice was loud, the one she might use at work to summon help, but people remained oblivious, just hurrying by, or standing still and looking up at the information boards.

She was about to take out her phone and do it herself, but then the lady from the queue whom she'd chatted with was running over, and the staff member who'd been hurrying her along was coming too.

'What can I do?' the lady asked.

'Call an ambulance,' Sorcha told her, then looked to the staff member. 'Is there an AED…?'

'On to it,' he said. 'And the first aider's been called.'

'Good.'

It helped to know that someone else was on their way, and while Sorcha truly hoped she wouldn't need to use the external defibrillator, she knew Edward could go into cardiac arrest at any given second and it might very well be required.

He was seriously ill.

His face was no longer flushed. Instead it was a ghastly grey colour, and his blond hair was now dark with sweat. He was, she was sure, having a heart attack, right here and now.

'The ambulance is on its way,' Sorcha told him, and the tried to gather as many details from him as she could, such as his medical history and any allergies he suffered from. But there was nothing much she could glean. Edward's concern was for his wife.

'I'm going to have to borrow your pen,' Sorcha said, going into his jacket pocket. 'I'd never find one in my bag...'

She did have paper, though, and wrote down his contact details.

'My wife will be waiting...' He told Sorcha they were supposed to be meeting at Covent Garden. 'I'm always late.'

'It's okay,' Sorcha said, feeling his thready pulse.

'No...' He put his head back against the wall and closed his eyes. 'I'm *always* late.'

His pulse was erratic, and Sorcha could feel her own heart leaping in her chest. She was nervous and doing her best not to show it. Not for a moment did she want Edward to get a sense of her own anxiety.

Sorcha worked in an accident and emergency unit a couple of hours outside of Edinburgh, and though small it had an incredible team and all the necessary equipment. No matter the situation, she never felt alone.

Now, even though a crowd was starting to gather, she did feel alone.

Sorcha considered what best she should do if things took a turn for the worse. If Edward did arrest, she would lie him down and attach the AED when it arrived.

'Always late...' Edward muttered as she undid his tie.

'You've got a very good excuse,' Sorcha said, and then made a little joke as she removed his tie. 'I can write a sick note for you now that I've got your pen.'

He gave a small laugh as she slipped both his pen and his tie into his pocket. As was often the case, even in the worst situations a little humour helped. It didn't just help in making people smile, it drew people closer too.

Edward's eyes opened then and met her own. 'We argued about it last night,' he told Sorcha, and gave her a regretful smile.

Sorcha knew that her face might be the very last that he saw, so she forgot the crowd all gathered around and tried to ignore how scared she was.

'Do you want me to call her for you?' she asked.

'Not yet.' He shook his head. 'She suffers panic attacks.'

He was trying to protect his wife, Sorcha guessed. Trying to keep things normal for a little while longer for the woman he loved.

She heard footsteps, then a male voice. 'Here you go.' It was the staff member from before and he held an AED. Sorcha thanked him, but kept her eyes on Edward. 'The first aider's with someone else,' the man informed her as he put the AED down. 'A passenger with a severely sprained ankle. She asked how bad this is...'

'Get someone else to wait with the sprained ankle,' Sorcha said. The first aider might think this was a simple faint. 'Ask the first aider to make her way here as quickly as possible.' She turned back to Edward. 'I'm going to open your shirt,' she told him.

'You'll stay?' he checked.

'Of course.' She touched his arm. 'You're doing so well, Edward. I know you're in pain.'

How long would the ambulance take?

Glancing up at the platform clock, she was surprised to see only a few minutes had passed; it felt a whole lot longer.

And things were getting worse.

'Edward?' she said as he slumped forward.

He pulled his head up and gave her a nod, then ran his tongue over pale lips.

'Did I tell you my name?' she asked.

'Sorcha.' He nodded again. 'Scottish…?'

'Yes.'

'Our honeymoon…' He couldn't finish his sentence.

'You went to Scotland?' Sorcha said for him. 'What's your wife's name?'

He didn't answer.

'Edward?' Sorcha demanded a response. 'Tell me your wife's name.'

He stirred.

'What's your wife's name?' she asked again.

'Anna.'

She wanted to call out and ask how much longer the ambulance would be, but she didn't want Edward to hear her fear. Also, she knew it was a pointless question. It was on its way. Out of the corner of her eye she could see that the station staff were moving people back and clearing the way. They were being marvellous, really.

She still felt alone, though—especially when Edward rallied a bit and looked at her and told her of his worry.

'I don't want to die here,' he said.

Edward's pale blue eyes met hers and she saw fear. He knew how bad this was.

'I won't let you,' she told him, and locked her green eyes with his.

It wasn't an empty promise—if he arrested, she would

start CPR, and the ambulance would surely get him to hospital in time.

But then his eyes drifted away, and as suddenly things changed.

His head lolled back and his skin turned even greyer. He was diaphoretic—the sweat was pouring off him—and she undid the last buttons of his shirt, ready to attach the AED monitor, all the time speaking to him as she went.

'Sorry to be so bold...' she said, as if it was normal to be urgently stripping off a stranger's shirt. She kept talking, trying to keep the fear from her own voice. 'I'm going to lie you down now, Edward.'

'Can I help?'

She heard a deep, calm voice and looked up to see a man who immediately crouched down on Edward's other side.

'I need to lie him down.'

The new arrival nodded and took the weight of Edward's upper body. He shifted him easily and together they gently laid him on the hard floor. While this lone stranger might not be the paramedic she'd fervently hoped for, there was a quiet command to him, and Sorcha felt as if the cavalry had arrived.

'That's better,' the man said, his fingers moving to Edward's neck and taking his pulse. With his eyes still on the patient, he asked Sorcha what had occurred.

'Sudden onset of chest pain.' She glanced at the time—had it really only been that long...? 'The episode began eight minutes ago...' It truly felt like for ever.

'Has an ambulance been called?' the man asked.

'On its way.' She nodded. 'The first aider's coming, too.'

'Do you know him?'

'No. I just came upon him,' Sorcha explained. 'He was staggering...'

'Okay. Hello, sir,' he said. 'My name's Richard Lewis. I'm an emergency registrar. I work nearby.' He glanced up to Sorcha. 'Can we find an AED?'

'I've got one here.'

'Excellent,' Richard said, reaching for it and starting to attach it to Edward. He asked her name.

'Sorcha,' she told him.

The breathless first aider arrived, explaining that she'd been on the other side of the station.

'Do you have Aspirin?' Richard asked, and she nodded and went to her kit.

'Take these,' Richard said, placing them in Edward's mouth. He declined the bottle of water the first aider offered. 'They're soluble.'

'Water…' Edward gasped.

Sorcha took some gauze from the first aider's kit and doused it, then used it to moisten his lips.

There was little else they could do, yet somehow things were more calm.

Dire, yes.

But since Richard Lewis had knelt down on the other side of Edward, Sorcha had known things were completely under control. This Richard knew absolutely how to handle things, no matter the situation.

'My wife…' Edward groaned as his phone rang.

'They're supposed to be meeting,' Sorcha explained. 'He's worried about scaring her.'

'I'll speak with your wife,' Richard said as the phone rang out. But Edward shook his head, clearly still attempting to protect her.

'She suffers from panic attacks,' Sorcha said, explaining Edward's reluctance to contact his wife.

'Edward?' Richard looked him right in the eye. 'Would she want to be with you?'

He nodded.

'Then give her the chance to be.'

Edward closed his eyes and then nodded again.

'Good man,' Richard said.

'Her name's Anna,' Sorcha said as, with Edward's help, she unlocked the phone to make the difficult call.

As it rang, she handed it over to Richard.

'Anna? My name is Richard Lewis,' Richard introduced himself. 'I'm a doctor, and Edward has asked me to speak with you...' He explained the situation with a mixture of brevity and patience, his eyes never leaving Edward's face. 'It's okay. I know it's a shock,' he said into the phone. 'Take a moment—get your bearings.'

He waited a moment and then the conversation resumed, and though Sorcha knew he couldn't be certain where Edward would be taken, she heard him tell her his best guess was the hospital very close by.

'Maybe start to make your way there. We'll pass on your details to the paramedics.' He was very formal, but quietly kind. 'Yes,' Richard went on, 'he is conscious. Would you like to speak with him?'

He briefly turned away from Edward, and Sorcha heard him telling Anna to reassure Edward and to keep things calm. To let Edward know that *she* was okay.

'That will help him a lot. I'll put him on now.' He held the phone to Edward's ear. 'It's Anna...' he told him.

Edward could barely talk, but with his eyes closed he managed a few words, then added, 'I love you too.'

'She did well,' Richard told him when the call was done. 'So did you.'

All they could do now was wait and, in this awful situation, do their best to give Edward privacy and calm. There was little response from Edward now. Even so, Sorcha kept talking to him, telling him she was still here and that Anna was on her way.

'The ambulance is here,' the first aider said at last, and Sorcha sat back on her heels in relief as she looked out at the sight of the crowd parting and familiar green uniforms approaching, armed with a stretcher laden with oxygen and medical equipment.

'Richard!' one of the paramedics greeted him, clearly recognising him. 'Fancy seeing you here.'

'This is Edward...' Richard introduced the patient and Sorcha stood up to give them space to work. She was a little giddy, and her legs felt numb as she held on to the wall. The paramedics worked swiftly, taking his observations and obtaining IV access, then delivering pain control. The ECG tracing confirmed a STEMI—a serious myocardial infarct.

'They're just letting the cardiologist at the hospital know to expect you,' Richard explained to a now very drowsy Edward as one of the paramedics transferred the tracing and liaised with a specialist.

Sorcha was used to this, albeit from the hospital end of things. The countdown started when they were alerted that an ambulance was bringing in a STEMI, and the aim was to get the patient stented within ninety minutes.

'What time did you get to him?' a paramedic asked her.

'Five,' Sorcha answered, and then recalled checking the time. 'Two minutes past five.'

Turning to look at the clock now, Sorcha was momentarily confused when she saw it was only twenty-three minutes past... She even wondered if the clock was out of order, and that the timing she'd given the paramedic might be wrong, but then Richard confirmed her timeline.

'I arrived shortly after...'

With time of the essence, and a cardiology team waiting to receive the patient, it was an utter relief when a grey-coloured and barely conscious Edward was on his urgent way to hospital. He was still breathing and his heart was still beating.

'Good job,' Richard said to the first aider, and to all who had assisted. Then he nodded to Sorcha. 'Well done.'

'You too,' Sorcha said, smoothing down her crumpled dress and then admitting, 'I've never been so pleased to see anyone.'

'I didn't really do anything,' he said. 'You had things under control by the time I arrived.'

'Oh, no, it's always good to look up and...' She paused, unsure quite what she was trying to convey. She'd had help—the lady who had called the ambulance, and efficient staff doing all they could—but somehow, even with all those people gathered, it had been the moment Richard had arrived when she'd known things would be okay. That even if things got worse, he'd deal with it well.

Confidence?

Presence?

Sorcha decided she would think about that later; right now she had to go and see if there was any hope of making her train or transferring to the next.

'I'd better go...' She glanced up at the board. 'I've no doubt missed my train to Edinburgh, but hopefully there's another...'

'Nobody's going anywhere.' Richard halted her rapid exit. 'All the trains have been cancelled.'

'But I was just boarding...' She looked around and sure enough there was a 'Cancelled' sign above her platform and disgruntled people all around. '*All* the trains have been cancelled?'

'Apparently so.'

'When did this happen?'

'Around the time I heard you shouting for someone to call an ambulance…' He gave her a slightly curious look. 'Sorcha, are you sure you're okay?'

'I'm fine.'

'Do you want to get a drink?'

His invitation was as sudden as it was unexpected, but then she found out the reason for it.

'You're ever so pale.'

'Oh, I'm always pale…' She attempted a joke.

'No.' Richard shook his head. 'Trust me on this.'

The oddest thing was…already, she did.

Richard had seen Sorcha's slight wobble when she'd first stood, but now the colour was starting to leach from her face. Her green eyes were becoming more vivid, and the light dusting of freckles seemed to be darkening against her rapidly whitening face.

'Let's get a seat.'

He took her arm and located a café. Thankfully there was a free table outside, and he suggested she sit while he ordered for them both.

'I don't have any cash.' She took out her phone. 'But I could—'

'Sorcha,' he interrupted, 'I'd far prefer that you sit down than I have to deal with another collapse within the hour.'

'Fair enough.' Thankfully she didn't argue. 'I'll have some water…maybe a white coffee.'

He returned with far more.

'Here.' He put a tray down; there were coffees and bottles of water, as well as two baguettes. 'One's cheese and pickle; the other's chicken and lettuce. You choose.'

She first took a gulp of water, and then chose the chicken. 'Thank you so much.'

He saw she looked better just for sitting down.

'I haven't eaten all day.' She took a very grateful bite of the baguette. 'I was going to head straight for the buffet car on the train.'

'Were you in London for work?'

'No…' She shook her head. 'Just an overnight stay. I came to visit my…' She hesitated for just a second. 'My mum.'

'Doesn't she feed you?' he said, but then he saw her lips tense and realised he'd inadvertently hit a nerve. 'Sorry— that was flippant of me.'

'It's fine,' she dismissed. 'I was helping her paint, and by the time it came to lunch…' She waved a hand. 'She didnae have much in.'

'Pardon?' Her accent was strong, but aside from that he wasn't sure what she meant.

'Food-wise,' Sorcha said. 'Nothing in the cupboards or fridge. So I ended up going shopping for her. That's why I was running late.'

'I see.'

He didn't.

From what he could gather, she'd come down from Scotland to help her mother paint and had nothing to eat. Still, from her rather tense response before he knew better than to probe.

He wanted to, though, and that surprised him.

These days, outside of work, it was unusual for him to want to persist with any conversation, for no more reason than simply because…

'Do you think he'll be okay?'

Her mind was clearly still on Edward, and he dragged his attention back to the reason they were here.

'Obviously you can't say for sure, but…'

'Actually, I do think he'll be okay,' Richard said. 'At least he has the very best chance to be—the hospital is so close to Kings Cross.'

He told her a little about the hospital Edward had been taken to, and their impressive stats—how they aimed for less than ninety minutes from door to stent.

'Hopefully it will be less. I'll go and see him on Monday and find out.'

'Really?'

'Yes. I'm working in A&E there at the moment. I don't usually go onto the wards to follow up, but somehow it's more…' He considered for a moment. 'It's more personal when it happens out of work, isn't it?'

Sorcha nodded. 'It's odd…' She told him how she'd kept checking the clock. 'I honestly thought it had stopped. It felt like time slowed down.'

'When every second counts we tend to notice all of them.'

'Yes. That must have been it—every second counted.'

'You've never come across anyone ill outside of work before?' he checked.

'Never. I was terrified.'

'For what it's worth, you didn't look scared.'

'Possibly because you came along,' she admitted. 'I kept reminding myself not to show how worried I was—that I might be the last face Edward saw.'

The poignancy of her words had the small, good-natured smile Richard was wearing shifting to something more pensive. He knew Sorcha wouldn't have noticed the effect, for she was no longer looking at him, but picking at the crumbs left from her baguette.

She asked him a question.

'Where were you headed?'

'Cardiff. But all the trains from Paddington were suddenly cancelled, so I headed back to Kings Cross to find the same thing starting to happen here too. I'm here for a conference.'

'Is Cardiff not home?'

'No, I live…' He didn't get to finish, and paused as an announcement was made over the loud speakers—it didn't tell them much.

'What do you think the "foreseeable future" means?' Sorcha asked with a slight eyeroll.

'It means that I need to make a phone call,' Richard said.

'Well, I'm going to the ladies',' Sorcha said, and stood. She needed to go, but also she wanted to give him some privacy to make his call. 'Save my seat?'

'Sorry?' he checked, as if he was a little startled, or perhaps not understanding what she'd said.

'I meant I'll be back in a moment.'

'Oh…' He nodded. 'Of course.'

The loos were busy, and as she waited in line, listening in to conversations, hearing talk of a cyber-attack and that all the national railway's computers were one by one being taken down, it became clear she might not be getting home tonight. There was a flutter of panic at the thought of being stuck for the night in London—really stuck. If this dragged on there would be a lot of people looking for last-minute accommodation.

Checking online, she saw that the budget hotel she'd stayed in last night had two rooms left…

Better to be safe than sorry.

The queue took for ever.

Her good-looking coffee companion would be wondering where she'd got to, Sorcha thought as she washed her hands.

And he *was* good-looking.

Her hands paused beneath the stream of water. Now the adrenaline had faded, and now she'd had something to eat—and possibly because now she was well away from him—it dawned on her how very handsome Richard Lewis actually was.

Imagine asking someone as stunning as him to save her seat. He'd probably taken out his phone in the hope that she'd get the hint and leave, now that she was recovered.

She looked in the mirror and saw the blush she usually had while talking to someone as utterly gorgeous as him materialise.

The horror!

Her hair was wild, somehow the dust on the platform had transferred to her cheeks, and her dress was pulled down, exposing the flesh-coloured strap of her bra.

Yikes!

She splashed her face with water and then took out a hair tie and piled her hair on the top of her head. She rearranged her dress and, looking and feeling a little more together, stepped out onto the concourse. She made her way back to the café, determined to be a little more sophisticated this time around.

If he was still there.

She was quite certain he'd be gone.

Sorcha didn't attribute the sudden feeling of dread that descended upon her to his not being there—after all, they'd barely spoken. It was a feeling she was familiar with—as if she'd been given up on…that she wasn't good enough for people to want her around.

It was a general fear of being abandoned.

It was the reason she tended to jump ship first in relationships, preferring to end things before they could be ended.

It was the very reason she was in London, trying to work things through with her birth mother in an attempt to fix herself.

Her eyes scanned the café, saw the empty table, the waiter clearing cups and plates. But just as she accepted that he was gone—the very second she thought she'd been proved right—the waiter moved and she saw Richard stepping out from inside the café. Nodding to the waiter, he retook his seat at the cleared table.

He was still there.

CHAPTER THREE

'Hey...'

Richard smiled as she approached the table and her stomach went tight. How on earth had she sat so casually with him?

'I thought you'd be gone,' Sorcha admitted as she sat.

'Why? You asked me to save your seat.' He pushed a bag towards her and she saw that in it were two almond croissants. 'I got these,' he said, loosening his tie and undoing the top button of his shirt. 'I just spoke with the waiter—it would seem we might be here for a while. Apparently it's a cyber-attack, it's happening nationwide—Birmingham now.'

'I saw on my phone.'

Richard appeared to be relaxing, yet she felt awkward for the first time—not that he seemed to notice, pulling apart a croissant as he said, 'At least you can stay with your mother.'

'I don't really know her well enough,' Sorcha sighed. But then she saw his slight frown as he glanced over and realised how odd that must sound. 'She's my birth mother. We've only very recently reconnected.'

'Oh.'

'It's probably best that I don't land on her. I don't think she'd...' Sorcha halted. This gorgeous stranger didn't need to know the details—he was simply being polite. 'Anyway, I've just booked a hotel.'

'Already?'

'I got stuck overnight in Edinburgh once without accommodation,' she told him. 'It was awful.'

Sorcha knew she was frowning now, watching as he dunked his croissant into his coffee. 'Yuck!'

'I apologise. I usually save that revolting habit for home.' He put down the soggy croissant. 'It's my one vice.'

'Well, don't stop on my account.' She got back to her reason for booking a hotel so fast. 'I didn't want a repeat of that cold night in Edinburgh, so I quickly booked a room at the place I stayed last night.'

'Fair enough—though it's a pity. I've got a hotel room nearby you could have had.'

'Dr Lewis!' She forgot to be awkward and spoke as she would to a friend, interrupting in feigned shock. 'We've only just met!'

'No, no...' He hastily moved to correct the misunderstanding, but in that same second obviously saw the gleam of humour in her eyes. He suddenly laughed. 'What I *meant*,' he said, and their eyes held as he continued, with a smile now in his tone, 'is that I'm in the middle of a conference, so I've not only got my home to go to, but a hotel room.'

'Phew!' she said as if she'd really thought for a second that this very formal man was propositioning her.

'You don't seem too bothered by the delay,' he commented after a while.

'I'm not,' Sorcha admitted. 'At least not now I've got a place to stay. I might even do a tour. I've never seen Big

Ben or Buckingham Palace. I'm only ever here on short trips and always rushing back and forth…'

'And me,' he admitted. 'At least lately.'

'Was it important?'

He frowned at her question, not understanding what she was asking.

'Your trip to Cardiff?' she said.

'Yes,' he said, then swallowed. It was his absolute priority, and had been for the past three years now. But then he thought of the relief he'd felt when he'd seen the signs at Paddington flick over to 'Cancelled'.

Sorcha didn't need to hear about that. As well, he was tired of people trying to say the right thing, and weary of awkward, strained conversations—and that was exactly what this would become if he told her the truth…

Richard liked how they were now.

'I'll get there soon enough,' he said.

It was quite freeing to sit at a busy station and watch the world go by…have a slow, unfolding conversation in such pleasant company.

'Is it a big conference?' she asked.

'Huge. It's taking place over four days.'

'Do you get lots of CPD hours for it?' she asked, her eyes lighting up at the prospect of amassing continuing professional development hours.

Somehow that made him smile.

'Absolutely!' He nodded. 'That was the main reason I agreed to attend, but it's actually fired me up.'

'Worth it, then?'

'Yes.'

They chatted a bit about work, but for Richard the nicest thing was simply sitting there, at times in companionable silence and at other times sharing observations.

They even invented a new game: Phone or Passer-By.

The rules were simple and the unwitting contestants were quietly observed.

'Here comes another one…' she said now, and they both sat up and watched a woman in a smart trouser suit running from the Underground, dashing for the train she clearly thought she was about to miss, just as Sorcha had done.

'Phone!' Sorcha got her verdict in first, even before the lady had skidded to an abrupt halt.

They'd played this game several times now, and whoever declared first gave the other contestant the second choice.

They watched as the lady looked up at the information board, then slowly looked around.

'Damn,' Richard said as the lady went into her bag.

'Told you…' Sorcha said, confident that the woman's first response would be to check her phone.

'Hold on…' Richard warned.

It wasn't quite a World Cup penalty shoot-out, but there was definitely a shared vested interest as they watched the lady, phone in hand, walk towards a group of people.

'Come on…' Richard urged. 'Ask.'

'No, check your phone,' Sorcha said, 'Call someone.'

'Whoa…' Richard said, as at the last minute the lady did an abrupt turn.

They were both wrong. The lady went straight to the line up at the information booth and neither asked a passer-by nor used her phone.

A first.

It was the very nicest of delays.

'I remember that…' Sorcha nodded as a large group went by, the women in pretty dresses, the men in suits, all laughing and chatting.

'What?'

'That Friday night feeling.'

'What feeling?'

'Freedom.' She smiled. 'When the working week is done and there's nowhere you need to be. I used to work in an office.'

'Before you went into nursing?'

'It was awful,' she admitted. 'We ran out of that office on a Friday like it was the end of term break-up for the summer holidays.'

He smiled at her description.

'We miss out on that,' she said. 'Us shift workers. There was something nice about all finishing at the same time as everyone else at work.'

'True...' He thought back for a moment. 'When I was at med school, yes...the weekend was the endgame.'

Their conversation paused often, but they would sit in companiable silence for a while and then easily resume, often picking up where they'd left off.

'There are benefits to shift work,' Sorcha said now. 'Like being able to book dental appointments on a weekday and never being stuck in the rush hour.'

'I'm always getting stuck in the rush hour,' Richard sighed. 'On the Underground.'

'I might find out for myself soon,' Sorcha said. 'I had a couple of interviews last week. I'm hoping to come and work in London—just for a few months. I want to get some more experience living in the big city and all that.'

Another stretch of silence.

Then, 'What about Edinburgh or Glasgow?' Richard asked. 'They're both big and much closer to home.'

'Maybe, but...' She sighed.

Silence.

'I'd like to get to know her a bit better.'

'Your birth mother?' Richard checked, and found he had stopped looking out to the crowd and had turned to face her.

'Amanda,' she told him, and then swallowed, as if she'd surprised herself by how easily she'd told him. 'I actually call her by her name. I just said "my mum" to you because...' She offered a small shrug. 'Well, it was just easier. I didnae know we'd be talking for so long. Well, not properly talking...' She paused. 'I can't really mention her at home.' She shrugged. 'It upsets them.'

'Your adoptive parents?' he checked, and she nodded.

'Do they know you're here today?'

'No.' She shook her head. 'I just find it easier not to say.'

And for Richard it was usually that way too. It was much easier to leave things alone and not delve. Unless he was working, or coming across cardiac patients collapsed at a train station, he generally didn't get involved, and he chose never to prolong conversations. Yet there was something about being suddenly stranded with her, their paths crossing...

Something about Sorcha that made him not merely offer an ear but want to know.

And now Richard was the one who invited further conversation. 'Easier for whom?'

'All of us—my parents don't want to hear about it and I don't want to say.' She gave a small laugh. 'I'm well and truly caught now, though.'

'How so?'

'I'm supposed to be picking up my sister from the airport tomorrow. When I tell my parents I'm stuck in London it won't take them long to work out where I've been.'

'Do you live with them?'

'Gosh, no. I have my own place. They're just...'

He watched the column of her throat as she swallowed, and then she gave an uncomfortable shrug.

'I'll come up with something.'

'Perhaps you could say that you were meeting some guy for dinner before the trains all went down?'

She gave a good-natured laugh at his unhelpful suggestion, but as she looked away he found his breathing had stilled, and he realised he might not just be offering an excuse for her parents.

Was he offering her dinner? With him?

'I'm not sure they'd buy it.' Sorcha turned to him and smiled. 'It's a long way to come for dinner.'

Richard flicked that excuse away. 'Tell them he's good company.'

'Indeed, he is,' she agreed.

'We can go for a drink first.'

'Sounds perfect.'

It was, after all, Friday night.

And there was that feeling...

Freedom. With nowhere you needed to be.

And time was doing that odd thing again.

Every second counted.

CHAPTER FOUR

It was a slice of London Sorcha had never seen before.

Thankfully, Richard knew where they were headed, and soon they were walking down a little lane. Turning off it, they came to a small, very ancient-looking pub.

'I'd never have known it was here,' she said.

It was packed, as well as tiny.

'There's a garden,' he said, pointing to a doorway.

'I'm getting these drinks,' Sorcha said. 'You find us a table. What will you have?'

She carried their drinks outside, to where he'd found a gorgeous table near a tree, and put them down. 'You're a cheap date,' she said, and smiled.

There was icy white wine for Sorcha, and sparkling water with ice and lemon for Richard.

It wasn't a date. Sorcha had to keep reminding herself of that. They were here by mutual inconvenience. Biding their time until the trains got back on track, so to speak…

Yet there was a flutter in her stomach…a giddy, delicious feeling as they faced each other. They were both leaning forward now, Sorcha's elbows on the table, her chin resting on her hand as they chatted.

'So, you worked in an office,' Richard said. 'Doing what?'

'Mainly on Reception.' She groaned at the memory.

'Then they hauled me off of that because I spoke too much to the clients. It wasnae as if I was offering financial advice. It was an accounting firm in Edinburgh, and it was all very conservative and formal. We didn't have a uniform, as such, but we had to wear all greys and navy and…'

'You like fashion?'

'No, it's not that…' She couldn't really explain it. 'It was just very dour; the men all dressed in suits and ties and…' She glanced across the table at him, dressed impeccably in a suit and tie. 'I wasn't implying…' She swallowed.

'Go on.'

'Well, you look very nice in a suit.'

'Thank you.'

'And I'm sure you're not…'

'Not what?'

He'd clearly noticed her blush, and he was smiling at her discomfort, toying with her.

'Conservative.'

'Oh, but I am,' he said happily, owning it.

'All I'm trying to say is that office life wasn't for me, but I had no idea what I wanted to do back then.'

'None at all?'

'Nope.' She thought back. 'A secret agent, perhaps, a spy…' She started to laugh. 'Honestly, I had no clue. My sister always knew she wanted to be a flight attendant…' She rolled her eyes.

'What's your sister's name?' he asked.

'Theresa—she's a year younger than me.'

'And how old are you?'

'Guess.'

Richard shook his head. 'I'm not that foolish.'

'Go on,' she insisted. 'Guess.'

* * *

How old *was* Sorcha? Richard wondered. And he found it was nice to wonder about her.

She'd told him that she'd worked in an office before training as a nurse. Everything pointed towards her being mid to late twenties, but now he looked for visual clues.

Really looked.

She wore no make-up. Her lips were full, and currently parted to reveal a white, slightly toothy smile that was endearing. The blaze of wild red curls which had first caught his eye had been tied up, but stray wisps danced around her full cheeks and the low evening sun brought out the copper and gold tones.

He took in her unpierced ears, then a sweep of his eyes over her face and neck confirmed that she wore no jewellery. His eyes drifted down, taking in her slender frame and the pretty lilac dress. He'd politely ignored the flash of lacy bra when she'd been dealing with Edward, and he very deliberately didn't allow his gaze to go there now—just came back to the green eyes that awaited his verdict.

Beautiful.

Rather than saying that, Richard chose a far more sensible response. 'Twenty-four.'

'I'm guessing you took a couple of years off to be safe?'

He smiled at her perceptiveness. 'Twenty-six, then?'

Those curls resumed their wayward dance as she shook her head. 'I'm twenty-eight.' She took a sip of her wine. 'What about you?'

'Guess,' Richard responded, when usually he wouldn't play such silly games.

It was Sorcha's turn now…

Sorcha, already a little flushed from his slow perusal, now had absolute permission to stare.

His face was elegant, with a very straight roman nose and just a slight shadow on his jaw. His hair was a dark caramel colour, with no visible flecks of grey. She took in the little fan of lines around dark blue eyes, though just for that moment she chose not to linger there. His mouth was perfection, and she tried not to wonder how it might feel to be kissed by him.

She'd never be so lucky as to know, Sorcha was sure.

Even his swallow was sexy, she decided as she watched the bob of his Adam's apple in his long neck. And finally she met the eyes that seemed so kind, and also rather wise, as if those blue depths had seen a lot.

What was the question? Oh, yes…

She hazarded a guess. 'Thirty-five?'

His gorgeous blue eyes widened in surprise. 'Correct.'

'Oh!' She let out a little laugh, and their eyes remained locked, and it was so warm and delicious to be held in his gaze. 'That was just luck.'

Lucky.

That was how she felt tonight.

'Do you have siblings?' she asked him.

'One sister—Gemma. She's a midwife.'

'And do you get on?'

'We do…' He thought for a moment. 'Just so long as we avoid talking about birthing babies. She's all for minimal intervention.'

'I thought about midwifery…' Sorcha nodded. 'That's what first got me into nursing. I wanted to get my general and then do midwifery. But then I did my A&E placement.'

'And you fell in love with it?'

'Not at first. I was terrified to start with—I still am at times. But I loved the variety and the staff. I just knew I'd found what I wanted to do. What about you?' she asked. 'Did you always want to be a doctor?'

'Pretty much, although there were a couple of years when I wanted to be an astronaut.'

'Seriously?'

He nodded. 'But then I turned seven.'

'Oh!'

His humour was so dry, and delivered deadpan. It always caught her by surprise—like a delicious, unexpected treat.

Every time.

The pub garden was filling up and the mood was turning buoyant. Even when the news came through that there would be no trains running till the morning, rather than bemoaning the issue, people were laughing.

It felt a little as if the world had been put on hold.

All plans suspended.

As if the old rules no longer applied.

'I'd better call home and warn them I'm not going to get to the airport tomorrow,' Sorcha said, not bothering to walk away to make her call.

After all, Richard had come up with the lie.

Richard liked how she blushed and crossed her fingers as she lied about her London date.

'Mum, there was no need to tell you. It's just dinner.' She gave him a smile. 'Yes, he's very nice. I'll tell you more when I see you.'

He watched her close her eyes and saw her blush deepen.

'Of course he has a name.' She paused. 'Richard.' She pulled an apologetic face. 'Look, I have to go.'

She ended the call.

'They think I have a mystery man now.' She sighed. 'But at least they don't think I'm here to visit Amanda.'

'It's a shame you can't talk about her with them.'

'I've never been able to.'

He watched as she ran a finger down through the condensation on her wine glass.

'I was always looking for her…long before I turned eighteen.'

He narrowed his eyes in curiosity.

'I used to check everyone.' She nodded to a group of new patrons arriving. 'Like those people sitting down. I used to wonder if one of the women might be her.'

'When did they tell you?' he asked, but then he added, 'Please feel free not to say. I was just…'

'Making conversation?'

'No,' he corrected. 'Enjoying our conversation.'

'And me,' she agreed. 'It's a relief to talk about it. I can't discuss it with anyone back home.'

'What about your sister?'

'No.' She shook her head.

'Wouldn't she get it more than most?'

'Theresa's not adopted. My parents couldn't have children—or they thought that was the case. Until lo and behold, just after they adopted me, Mum fell pregnant with my sister.'

'I've heard of that happening.'

'Well, it happened to them! I'm sure if they'd already had Theresa they wouldn't—'

She halted, closing her lips on what she'd been about to say, although he could guess.

'You don't think they'd have adopted you?'

'Who knows? Anyway, while Theresa's lovely now, when we were little she'd—'

Sorcha stopped talking and gave a tight shrug, about to shut the conversation down. But then she looked up to those beautiful blue eyes that were so patient and present, and she felt safe under his steady gaze.

Safe enough to speak on.

'She'd point out that I didn't look like anyone else in the family.'

He said nothing, and she was grateful for that.

'And when I was naughty…' He smiled a little at that. 'Oh, I was very naughty,' Sorcha assured him. 'Theresa would warn me that if I didn't behave, our parents would send me back.'

His smile disappeared, yet his eyes never diverted from her gaze.

'She was just a little girl. I know that. And if I brought it up now I'm sure she'd be horrified that she ever said those things, and that I remember them.'

'I can see why you might not want to talk to her about your birth mother.' He seemed to consider things for a moment, then, 'What about talking with your friends?'

'They have all known me since I was small. They know my parents too. It would feel disloyal.'

Oh, he got that. So much so that he closed his eyes for a second.

'I feel I'd be letting them down,' she said.

'Yes…' Richard reminded himself that this wasn't about him and opened his eyes. 'I can understand that.' He offered a pale smile. 'So, you give the filtered "everything's fine" version?'

'Pretty much.' Sorcha nodded.

'You're welcome to talk it through with me,' he offered. 'If that might help? Sometimes it's easier to talk to a stranger.'

'Maybe…'

Richard didn't feel like a stranger to her, though.

When he went to get another round of drinks Sorcha thought about his offer. There was something so steady about him—something she'd felt the very moment she'd looked up on the station concourse. She still didn't know if it was confidence, or presence, or quite what it was. She just knew there was *something*, even if she couldn't define it. And there was enough that she found herself wanting to open up for the first time about that which could not be spoken of at home.

Watching him walking back to their table carrying their drinks had her smile as if in a reflex action.

'It's packed in there,' he said, taking his seat opposite.

It felt peaceful out in the garden, though. Oh, there was laughter, and chatter, but little fairy lights were starting to twinkle in the trees and the dusk made it feel even more intimate.

'I don't want to bore you,' she warned. 'And I think you'll be too polite to say if I am.'

'I'm not that polite,' he said, and pointed to a beer. 'I got a pint.'

'You'll stop me…?'

'You'll know if I say I have to get my train…'

Given every train in London was out, Sorcha laughed.

'So…' He took a sip of his drink. 'How did you find out?'

'I've always known. My parents were very good about all that. I was nine months old when they adopted me. I was with Amanda for just a few weeks before she surrendered me. Then I had a short spell in a foster home. She was allowed to write and send cards and such.'

'Amanda?' he checked, and she nodded.

'She never did, though. I tried asking about her as I got older, but my mum and dad would always go quiet. When I turned eighteen, I contacted an agency. It took a while, but finally they put us in touch. We had a few phone calls, and then a meeting was arranged. Amanda lived in Manchester then. My parents wanted to come with me...'

'Did they?'

'Not quite.' She gave a wry smile. 'They just *happened* to be in Manchester that day.'

'You saw them?'

He couldn't help but smile.

'Believe me, James and Jean Bell would not make good spies.' She laughed at the memory. 'I wanted to do it by myself, but even so it was nice knowing they were close by.'

'What was meeting her like?'

'It was odd,' she admitted. 'An anticlimax. There was no rush of love or tears or anything—at least not from Amanda. I wanted answers, but I wasn't brave enough to ask the tough questions. We met a few times, and I thought we were maybe getting closer, but then she stopped taking my calls. She ghosted me, I guess.'

'That must have been hard.'

'I was a mess. But I put it all behind me...forgot about her.'

'*Did* you forget?'

His question was unexpected. Sorcha was used to the subject of her birth mother being avoided rather than probed—treated as something best not discussed—and to hear it addressed so directly had her eyes flying to his.

'No,' she admitted. 'I could never forget.' After years of denial, she found herself suddenly able to be honest. 'I made out that I'd put it behind me. But then earlier this year Amanda made contact, asking if we could meet up again. I decided it would be better not to tell my family. My boyfriend...' She saw a slight question in his eyes. 'At the time,' she added. 'Well, he advised against it.'

'You didn't take his advice?'
'No. We broke up—though not because of that.'

Richard wanted to ask why they'd broken up. He wanted to delve. Only that wasn't what they'd agreed to, and nor was it what this conversation was about.

'I've been coming to visit her once a month or so since then,' she said.

'Have you got the answers you wanted?'

'She's not very chatty.' Sorcha sighed. 'It's quite hard work.'

'Does she look like you?'

'No!' she exclaimed. 'Honestly, not a bit. I think I must take after my father—only she doesn't talk about him. My sister is a mixture of both my mum and dad… I just want to recognise myself in someone.'

'That's something I've always just taken for granted,' he admitted. 'I look like my father.'

'What about your sister? Does she look like you?'

'Yes,' he said. 'Well, she's possibly a bit prettier.'

She laughed, and it felt like a long time since he'd made someone laugh, made a small joke and just…

They were flirting.

Lightly.

He didn't know quite when that had started, but it was mutual and light and so unexpected tonight.

Any night.

Even so, he'd offered to listen, and he was good at that, so he didn't focus on her green eyes or the tiny gap between her front teeth. Instead, he focussed on what was being said.

'I don't want to hurt my parents, but I do want to get to know Amanda some more. The second I mention London, though, they get cross.'

'They're scared, maybe?'

'I don't know why; they're not going to lose me.'

'No, I mean...' He pondered for a moment. 'Are they perhaps worried that you're going to be hurt again?'

'I'm older now, though. I know it's not going to be all rainbows and unicorns.'

'I'd be worried,' Richard admitted. 'If you were mine.'

He hadn't meant to say that.

'If you were mine.'

Richard went to take a sip of beer and found his glass was empty, but he went through the motions anyway. 'If I cared about you,' he attempted, then gave a wry laugh. 'What I'm trying to say, albeit not very well, is that...'

'That I need to careful?' Sorcha finished for him. 'I intend to be.'

'Good.'

'Now I've taken up enough of your time, but thank you.' She reached for her bag, and he guessed she was a little embarrassed at revealing so much. 'You've been a very nice person to be stranded with.'

'How about that tour?' he said, and she blinked. 'We can get dinner afterwards.'

'You don't have to do that.'

'It would be my pleasure.'

They made their way to the Underground.

It was hot—baking hot—and the platform was very, very crowded.

'I need to get my bearings,' Sorcha said, and he steered her away from the masses to a large map of the Underground.

'Where's your hotel?' he asked.

'On the Piccadilly line. How do I get back there from Buckingham Palace?'

He pointed, and while she should have been listening to his instructions—heaven knew she needed them—instead she found her gaze on his hands.

He had nice hands…with long, slim fingers and neat nails. There was the glint of a watch peeking from beneath his cuff.

'Got it?' he checked.

'No,' she admitted with a laugh.

'It's quite straightforward.'

'For you, maybe.'

She looked at the knot of coloured lines and wished she was like the woman who came up next to her now and gave the map a cursory glance. Then, clearly satisfied that she now knew where she was going, she turned and walked off. No matter how patiently Richard explained, Sorcha couldn't get it.

'I was the same as a student,' she admitted. 'We'd all stand around an X-ray, everyone nodding…'

He laughed. 'I'm sure you weren't the only one just nodding along.'

'That's true,' she agreed. 'Where do you live?'

'Canary Wharf.' He pointed to the map.

'Why are you staying at a hotel near Kings Cross, then?'

'To be sociable at the conference,' he said. 'But I changed my mind.'

Richard turned to face her, casually unprepared for the fact that the world as he knew it was about to fall away.

For the first time in the longest time he was exactly where he wanted to be.

Sorcha smiled her slightly toothy smile and he felt the

thump of his heart. It felt as if, after the deepest sleep, his body had returned to life.

He breathed in air that tasted as clear and delicious as if he'd been hauled half drowned from a lake.

He'd known she was gorgeous, and had accepted the physical attraction. Right from the start that had been undeniable—albeit a jolt to his senses. He'd felt dead inside for a very long time, after all. The real surprise was their connection. It was something way more than physical.

He wanted to explain to her just how incredible these few hours had been.

How he felt like himself again.

No matter how others tried, he always felt sequestered from them. But now he looked into green eyes that weren't clouded with sympathy or averted with awkwardness. Instead it felt as if they were looking right into him.

A different him, though. A new him. One who Richard himself didn't yet know.

He didn't do silly things like sit at a train station and people-watch with a woman he'd just met.

Never had.

Until tonight.

And he wasn't one for going to see Buckingham Palace on a whim.

Nor to sit with someone, digging up long-ago dreams of being an astronaut.

And nor did he kiss women on crowded tube platforms. But he was thinking about doing exactly that now.

'I'm very glad I changed my mind,' he admitted now.

For had he gone back to the hotel he'd be eating there now, or out eating a curry, and he didn't even know if that remained his favourite.

* * *

'I'm glad you did too,' Sorcha said.

The whoosh of an approaching tube train seemed to mirror the rush in her stomach.

'We'll get the next one,' she suggested when a packed tube came in.

But Richard just laughed.

'I don't think they'll get any better while all the mainline trains are down.'

Together they squeezed on.

It really was packed, but Richard held a handle, and Sorcha held his arm, and she'd never felt more comfortable with anyone. Only that wasn't quite right. Because when the tube lurched, and so too did Richard, she felt his free hand briefly on her arm, just steadying her, and the warmth of his touch remained long after the source had been removed.

His scent was light, and clean, and he was nothing like anyone she'd been attracted to before or dated.

Not that any of those relationships had worked out.

Sorcha had never allowed anyone close enough.

She really was brilliant at small talk, though. So good that no one could ever guess they were being shut out.

She didn't feel that way tonight.

'Here we are…' Richard said as the train swished to a stop.

As they surfaced above ground her arm was still tingling from that brief touch. And as they walked she had to keep reminding herself that this wasn't a date…that her tour guide was temporary and merely being polite.

'Look at it!'

She smiled at the sight of the palace ahead of them, softly

lit, but nonetheless a strong, solid presence quietly beckoning them closer.

'It's stunning,' Richard agreed. 'I haven't been up this way in years. I think when you live near something you tend to take it for granted.'

'I don't.' She looked over at him and quashed that theory. 'When I'm in Edinburgh, no matter what I'm doing, I look up and see the castle… Or when I'm getting the train I look at it again, as we come in to Waverly…still there, always there. And I just… Well, my heart squeezes. Every time.'

'Really?'

He paused, slowed right down, and for a little while they stopped walking and faced each other.

'Absolutely,' she said. 'Don't you come here for picnics? Or when there's something big on?'

'Picnics?' He shook his head. 'No, I'm always working, or…'

'That's an excuse,' she protested.

He smiled.

'Often I take myself to the botanical gardens and I just—' She stopped. Not because he'd interrupted her, but because there was nothing to say right now. She just wanted to acknowledge the pleasure of being with him on this unexpectedly gorgeous night. 'Thank you for bringing me here.'

Their eyes met, and while she still couldn't work out their exact shade of blue, she felt it was one she already knew.

'It's my pleasure,' he said.

They walked the short distance remaining towards the palace, and then she tripped—possibly because she had three-inch wedges on, or more likely because she was daydreaming and not properly paying attention to her surroundings.

'These shoes…' she moaned.

'Here,' Richard said and offered her his arm.

It was a first for Sorcha.

This whole night was something else completely.

Quite what it was, she didn't know.

He was quiet, as if deep in thought. Was he wrestling with something? Or maybe he was bored with his companion now?

Richard was far from bored.

He was miles from where he'd intended to be, and yet he felt as if he was in precisely the right place.

He looked down and gave her a smile.

Buckingham Palace was everything Sorcha had hoped it would be—beautifully illuminated and bathed in a soft glow. Though unfortunately she had to let go of Richard's arm to get adequately close and peer through the bars. She looked up at the oh-so-familiar building, larger in real life than she'd imagined.

'What time do they change the guards?' she asked.

'I have no clue,' Richard admitted. 'I'm not sure if they do it at night.'

'You're not a very good tour guide,' she teased, and glanced over at him. 'Actually, you're a lovely tour guide—just not very knowledgeable about times and things.'

'Had I known my tour guide services would be required tonight I'd have planned accordingly.'

'Really?' She turned to face him.

'Really,' he confirmed. 'I'll do better next time.'

Their eyes met and she stared up at this very assured man who now seemed a touch bemused—as if he couldn't quite believe they were talking about there being a 'next time'.

'Listen...' he said.

She frowned, but then heard the low chimes that were so familiar from the television.

'Big Ben...' she breathed, and in the still, windless night there were ten chimes.

She heard and felt each one, while gazing into eyes whose colour she still hadn't worked out. And again she felt she knew.

There was another low chime and she realised it was eleven, and that she'd utterly lost track of time. 'I should be pulling into Waverly now...' she said, and he nodded.

'With your heart squeezing?' he said, repeating what she'd said while gazing at her as if he knew that her heart actually was squeezing right now.

She'd thought she must be imagining the attraction, or dreaming and wishing, but every molecule in her body flared as his hand lifted and he brushed her hair back from her face.

To kiss and be kissed felt as necessary to her as breathing. There was no question, no hesitation. It was as if the ache to know each other's lips simply had to be answered.

His kiss was light, and it felt like a stroking deep inside. It felt like a precursor...a little warning that if a light kiss could evoke such a warm stirring, then what else could it do?

She parted her lips to find out, and felt his shiver as he slipped his tongue inside her mouth.

They sank into each other, aching for each other. Her hands moved to the back of his head, not just to feel his hair, or press his face to hers, but so their bodies could be closer.

Their tongues mingled as they breathed in each other and tasted each other and got lost in each other.

She had never thought a kiss could be so delicious. Nor

considered that one day she might stand outside a palace and feel she might as well be in a field, because it was as if the only people here were them.

They both pulled their heads back for a second, their eyes meeting almost in a frown of surprise. Because this really was heaven.

Then they were straight back to deeper kisses, to a slight moan from him, and heat from the press of his hands. And the warmth of the evening was nothing compared to the heat between them.

Then Richard pulled back again, and she knew it was only to stop himself from pulling her indecently closer into him.

She leant her head on his chest and looked up to the palace balcony, where so many kisses had been had. He made her feel like a princess. And this magical kiss told her that something incredible really was taking place.

'What do you like to eat?' he asked suddenly. 'We're probably a little late for a restaurant...'

He halted, because of course food had long since lost its importance.

Sorcha was still leaning on him a little, and she felt him pull her in closer, breathe in the citrussy coconut fragrance of her hair.

'I don't know if I want anything to eat,' she admitted.

It was odd not to be able to locate all her senses. Not to know if she was hungry, or if the ache clutching at her stomach and the craving within her was simply desire.

'Can we go back to your hotel?' she asked.

'Are you sure that is what you want?' he checked, and his hand cupped her cheek.

She nodded. 'Completely.'

CHAPTER FIVE

SORCHA HAD NEVER done anything like this in her life—only it didn't feel reckless. They kissed some more on the Underground platform and then sat on the tube train, staring at their reflection in the window opposite their seats.

Hand in hand they walked to his hotel, with pauses for more kisses along the way and one little stop at a store, because Richard had the forethought to make sure they had protection.

Sorcha stood outside as Mr Sensible went in to make his purchase. Usually, she was sensible when it came to sex, she thought, as a fire engine raced by. Its sirens and lights seemed to match how she felt on the inside. Not even sensible, she reflected. In truth, she'd always found sex a bit underwhelming.

Not tonight.

'Come on, you,' Richard said, and now there was no more stopping for kisses—not with a lovely bed so close by. They speed-walked the last few metres, and then crossed the hotel foyer and reached the elevators.

'Hurry up,' she said, as the elevators slowly descended. 'Or we could always take the stairs.'

'It's here,' he said, and she almost folded in relief at the prospect of being alone with him.

But not quite yet.

The opening doors revealed a dark-haired woman who gave him a delighted smile. 'Richard!' she exclaimed as she stepped out.

'Hi, Monica.'

'I thought you were heading to…?'

Her voice trailed off when she saw Sorcha, and Sorcha felt the cast of the other woman's eyes and saw both the surprise and curiosity in them.

Even standing apart, she and Richard must be so lit with passion that Monica immediately got that they were together.

'Oh, yes, the trains… I heard about that.' Monica wished them goodnight and walked off.

'That was awkward,' Sorcha said when the lift doors had closed. 'I don't think your friend approved.'

'It's fine. She's just…'

Richard had seen the flare of surprise in Monica's eyes, and really, he couldn't blame her for it.

It was most out of character—at least it was for the Richard that Monica knew.

'Just what?' Sorcha asked.

But he pulled her back into his arms and the little niggle was doused by contact.

'Surprised,' he said. 'But there's no need for her to be. We both know what's happened between us tonight,' Richard said, and then kissed her again.

The oddest thing was that his words, to Sorcha, made utter and complete sense.

They both knew that something special had happened tonight.

And they both wanted what was about to happen…

* * *

The suite was large and softly lit, the bed vast, with the covers turned back.

'The fairies have been in,' Sorcha breathed.

And the fairy dust must still be in the air, for modesty was gone, and both of them were stripping off with as much haste and lack of inhibition as they might if a gorgeous lake beckoned.

Only it wasn't a lake. It was a huge white bed and they dived into it together, then lay naked, facing each other, their limbs knotted, still in discovery... Touching, kissing, exploring...

Richard was as exquisite undressed as dressed—or rather, more so. His body was toned, and Sorcha traced a finger over his dark red nipples.

'I'm so pale,' she said, because her areolae were barely visible.

But he kissed them, and sucked them, and it didn't matter if the pink barely showed. His mouth on her breasts was both soft and yet thorough, his tongue, the sucking, the pressure tightening her inside.

'You're perfect,' he said.

She ran a hand down one long arm, then moved it back to his cheek. 'So are you.'

'I want you so much... But I want...'

She was holding his fierce erection and stroking it, wanting to touch him and know him, but at the same time wanting him inside her.

'I know...'

She wanted to linger on the feel of his fingers as he stroked her thigh, and on how they were both beyond waiting for this union, and yet she was desperate to explore, for them to know each other, as if every touch mattered.

Deeply, it did.

Sorcha hated the red curls between her legs. He adored them.

He explored her, stroking her with his fingers, and her lips were reaching for his mouth, suddenly desperate as he stroked her within.

But then he removed his hand. 'I want to taste you.'

'I don't…'

She attempted to protest as he moved and knelt between her thighs. She hadn't thought she could ever enjoy anyone going down on her.

'I'm going to come the minute I'm inside you…you turn me on so,' he said.

And she looked at him, indecently erect, and reached for him.

'And I'm going to come the second you're in,' Sorcha said. Her legs were shaking, and she was taut with desire as she held the velvet skin and stroked him, then ran a finger over his moist tip. 'So you don't have to.'

'*Have* to?' he checked. 'Sorcha, believe me, I want to.'

He moved her hand away, met her eyes as he rolled on a condom. And then, unperturbed, he moved down the bed and lay on his stomach.

'I might have to fake it,' she warned.

He laughed. She felt his breath on her hot, swollen sex, and then that perfect mouth grazed softly upon her.

She moaned as he explored her…fingers, mouth and tongue all concentrated so thoroughly on her. The low noises he made had her weakening. And then his hands took her hips and he pressed her in.

'Oh, God…' Even the soles of her feet were curling on his back as she came to his lips.

A considerate lover would give her time to recover, she

thought as he moved over her. But she preferred him inconsiderate and taking her swiftly, while she was still hot and swollen.

The weight of him was delicious…warm…and he was moving above her and firing her from within. He filled her, stretched her and moved with her, slowly at first. She angled her hips, met his thrusts. She knew he was holding back, as if he was fighting not to come, but she simply didn't care.

Both satisfied and suddenly desperate, she was taut, and tension was building within her again. Richard moved to his elbows, his pace more rapid, and now he was no longer holding back.

She moaned, and it was a sound she'd never made before. 'Oh…' She was urgent, wanting more of this sensation, her every nerve warm and tingling, alive in a way they had never been.

Now their ardour was deeper, and she knew they both relished the mesh of their hot bodies.

It did not feel transient…more like a deepening. They were brand-new to each other, but so in tune, locked into each other. It was as if time had lost all meaning when the cyber-attack had come, and while they might have known each other only for a matter of hours, had shared only a little history, their bodies were old lovers and friends.

Richard sank into sensation, and then looked into her eyes, felt her hand on his cheek. He moved deep within, watching her closely… He saw the way she bit her lower lip and then, when he moved again, saw her neck start to arch. He felt the lift of her hips and the warmth of her tightness around him.

He'd never known such pleasure, nor that he could feel so desperate as he drove her closer to the edge. He upped the tempo, and as her body stretched, arched upwards, she constricted below him and he felt the beckoning of her orgasm, her slight cry as he swelled and released into her.

They lay in the dark place they'd made together, him still on top, her dragging in air and holding his shoulders. He felt disorientated, but nicely so, as if they'd been somewhere and had now returned.

'Damn,' Richard said.

And even as Sorcha fathomed the change to his tone she felt the warm, wet trail as he pulled out and knew why—the condom had torn.

But what could have been a wretched moment was otherwise—as if nothing could invade the bliss they'd just experienced. They even kissed for a moment, still a little dizzy from pleasure, with their bodies still warm and close. So much so that she grumbled when he rolled off.

Sorcha lay still, thirsty for water, but too sated to move.

'Are you okay?' he asked, when the useless condom had been taken care of.

'Thirsty,' she admitted. 'But apart from that…'

He handed her a bottle of water and undid the lid of his own, and now she felt utterly content as they put down their drinks and then lay facing each other.

He addressed what had happened. 'Sorry about that.'

'Please don't worry. I am on the pill.'

'We should have been more careful.'

'We were careful.' She smiled. 'Maybe you should go back to the shop and ask for a refund.'

His hand was stroking her arm, their heads were on the same pillow, and there was so much happiness in the air she felt as if she could reach out and grab a handful.

She had never stared into the eyes of another person so readily.

So blatantly.

Now she knew their colour.

They were lighter than navy.

Twilight blue, if there was such a shade.

They reminded her of the night sky in Scotland at summer solstice…on one of those nights when the sun never really set and light was always on the horizon.

It wasn't a night for sleeping, even though they were so late to bed, so they lay talking and wating for the dawn.

'I wonder how Edward's doing?' said Sorcha.

'I'll call and find out soon,' Richard said. 'I might have to take him some flowers on Monday to thank him.'

Sorcha laughed. 'I should check and see if the trains are running.'

'Hopefully not.'

'You've got your conference,' she reminded him.

'I do. And I'm meeting someone for lunch. A consultant I trained under.'

'Well, you can't miss that.'

'I know. Do you have to go back this morning?'

'I don't know.'

It seemed an odd answer, but her real life felt so far removed from now that she had to cast her mind out to actually recall a world that wasn't just them.

'I'm supposed to be going out with Beth tonight.' They were so close she felt as if he should know these details already. 'She's a good friend.'

'Would she understand if you couldn't make it?'

'She would,' Sorcha agreed.

But the thing was, she didn't quite understand herself. She was lying in bed with a man she'd met only yesterday, cancelling plans, putting everything on hold for more of this.

If felt perfect, though, apart from her stomach growling.

'I need food. That baguette seems a very long time ago.'

'It's all you ate yesterday.'

'I think Amanda forgot I was coming.' She knew he saw the slight pinch of her lips but he didn't say anything. His hand remained on her arm, though. 'Usually I visit once a month—it's cheaper to book in advance—but she asked me to help with some painting.' She frowned. 'Or maybe I jumped in and offered. I just want…'

Sorcha paused, unsure how to explain how she wanted the fear inside herself to abate. How she hoped if she sorted things with her birth mother it might help fix herself. Because she'd never felt good enough—always sure that if anyone got close they'd soon tire of her and leave. Not just men, but friends when she was growing up and her parents and sister.

Yet here she lay, in bed with a man she'd just met, and she was on the edge of baring the darkest parts of her soul.

No.

'I just want to establish some sort of a relationship with her, I guess,' she said instead.

'Fair enough.' Richard nodded.

'What time do you have to go down?' she asked.

'Nine…'

But when she wrapped seductive arms around his neck and pressed her body to his, he unwrapped them.

'Why don't we get room service for breakfast?' he suggested.

There was something Richard needed to share with her. And he knew the conversation to be had should take place out of bed.

He picked up the menu and they ordered a relative feast.

'Freshly squeezed juice? Coffee or tea?' he asked, then smiled. 'White coffee?'

They were starting to know the little things about each other.

When she couldn't decide between granola with the yoghurt or compote, he ticked both. Then there was a full English breakfast for him, pancakes for Sorcha.

He used the bedside phone to call in the order.

'I'm going to have a quick shower,' he told her.

'Can you call the hospital first?' she asked. 'Find out about Edward? I doubt they'd tell me anything.'

It wasn't that straightforward.

The night staff hadn't been involved with Edward's care, but after a few moments he was put through to CCU and connected to someone he knew.

'Judy, it's Richard Lewis...' He explained what had happened the day before, and paused for a moment as Judy spoke, offering to go and find out. 'I'd appreciate that.'

He squeezed Sorcha's thigh through the sheet as he waited, and finally Judy returned.

'That's marvellous news,' he said.

The news was indeed wonderful.

'Edward's currently sitting up in bed having a cup of tea,' he told Sorcha. 'And apparently Anna was there at the hospital when he arrived.'

It sounded as if Judy had spoken with Edward himself before passing the news on, and clearly he was doing incredibly well.

'I'm going to have that shower now,' he said. 'Save my seat.'

Sorcha laughed, knowing he was referring to yesterday, and lay in bed, hearing the shower being turned on. She had not even a tinge of regret. She was just bathed in pure bliss. Sure, there would be plenty of questions from her parents about this mystery man, and she'd have to cancel Beth and she felt bad about that, but for now they felt like little pebbles on a gorgeous expanse of beach.

It was easily the most relaxed she had felt in a very long time—if ever. Excited too, for the day ahead, but so relaxed that when the bedside phone rang, rather than ignore it, or call out to him, she simply answered it, assuming it was the kitchen with a question over their breakfast order...they had ordered rather a lot.

'May I speak with Dr Lewis?'

'Erm...' Sorcha glanced at the bathroom door and could hear the water still running. 'He's not available right now.' It was only then that she wished she hadn't picked up the phone. 'Can I take a message?'

'I really do need to speak directly with him. It's regarding his wife...'

Sorcha almost dropped the receiver. She felt as if she'd been thumped, or as if she'd plummeted from a great height. 'His wife?'

Richard had a wife!

She caught sight of herself in the long mirror opposite the bed, saw her own horrified expression and, worse, saw the bed she sat in, all rumpled from their lovemaking.

She didn't know how to respond to the caller—what on earth could she possibly say?—and so instead of responding she abruptly hung up the phone.

As if she were guilty.

As if she'd been caught.

'No.' She shook her head, as if to clear it, and tried to convince herself that there had been a mix-up, that whoever had called had got things wrong...

Yes. She leapt at that thought, clung onto it. There had to be a mistake, a mix-up—or was she being naïve?

Her eyes lit on his wallet, lying closed on the bedside table. She glanced at the bathroom door and then picked it up.

Trembling, she peeled apart the leather, her heart sinking when she saw a photo. Stifling a sob, she stared into his smiling, lying eyes and then turned her attention to his very beautiful bride, with her clouds of dark hair and velvety brown eyes and a smile on her face as bright as the summer sun.

'Oh, God…'

She pushed the photo down, snapped the wallet closed and stared in horror at the bathroom door. Oh, she'd love to be brave enough to confront him. To rap on the door and barge in, ask what the hell? But the man she'd thought she had met wasn't behind that door.

He'd lied.

Or rather, she hadn't asked the right questions.

Her tendency to avoid the tough questions was damning her now, for it made her complicit.

No, she did not want a showdown. All she felt was guilt and shame, and an utter fool for succumbing to his charms.

It took her seconds to dress.

A minute at the most.

She pulled on her knickers, half did up her bra and tugged on her lilac dress. Then with trembling hands she tied her espadrilles. Certainly, she didn't stop to sort out her hair—just collected her bag.

As she opened the door she saw there was a man there, with a huge silver trolley. Their breakfast was here.

Sorcha held the door open for him, but she couldn't even respond to his polite greeting and dashed for the elevator.

* * *

Richard knew he had to tell Sorcha about Jess.

And it didn't daunt him. Rather it amazed him. Because it was a conversation he'd never expected to have. He'd never expected to feel close enough to another woman to want to share the details of his life.

He stood under the icy water and felt invigorated—not just from the refreshing shower, but from his time with Sorcha.

Last night he'd held back from saying anything. At first because they'd just been talking, and he'd never thought they were headed for bed. And then, as the night had progressed, and as he'd wanted to keep more of her company, he'd wanted to prolong *them*.

He'd just been so sick of sympathy, of suggestions, of being told how to live his life, how he must feel…

But it had been more that.

Last night he'd felt himself.

A new self.

He'd trained himself to live in the present, to deal only with what *is*. And it had worked. Because it was hell to look back, and certainly he didn't know how to look to the future.

He wasn't even doing that now.

For the first time in what felt like for ever he was looking up. As if emerging from the darkest tunnel and taking a breath, looking around. And the world wasn't too bright after all—it was colourful, painted in gold and coppers, and it had smiling green eyes.

Wrapping a towel around his hips, he stepped out of the bathroom and saw that their breakfast was here. There was a serving trolley holding jugs of juice and silver cloches, but he barely gave it a glance as he frowned at the empty bed and took in her absence.

'Sorcha?'

Her clothes were gone. Her bag was gone.

Sorcha was gone.

Only just...

The air stirred, her fragrance lightly swirled, and he went straight for the door, wrenching it open. But there was no sign of her in the corridor.

He wasn't about to chase anyone—and not just because he wore only a towel. Grand gestures and demands were not in his DNA. He was too level-headed for all that.

It was more than unexpected.

He felt as if the world had tipped the wrong way for a brief second and then tipped back. Only now it felt on the wrong level, or the wrong axis...just off-kilter somehow.

Even though he knew she didn't have his number he picked up his phone. Just in case she'd called.

As if in response to his bewilderment it buzzed, and for a second he thought it must be Sorcha. Thought that he was about to get an explanation—find out she'd locked herself out, or...

It was Trefor...

His father-in-law.

'Hey,' Richard said, in a voice that sounded a little off. He was staring around the room, and his feet seemed in two worlds—the one he'd just found, and the one that was the rest of his life, calling him back.

'Jess had a bad night,' Trefor informed him. 'Richard, I think you ought to get here.'

CHAPTER SIX

Fool me once...

London had possibly fooled her twice.

It had been a mistake to come.

It had been an impulse decision, and Sorcha tended only to make them when she was upset.

She'd taken the early-morning train back the morning after her night with Richard, and had leant her head against the window and gone over and over the day before. Searching for clues, for moments when she should have guessed, should have asked or should have known.

Not even the sight of Edinburgh's castle had soothed her. Instead her eyes had filled with tears when she'd thought of standing with him at Buckingham Palace.

She'd forgotten to cancel Beth, who'd wanted a big night out, and she'd sat awkwardly as Beth had been chatted up.

'What wrong wi' your friend?' Mr Awful had enquired as Sorcha had sat there a little stony-faced.

And then, a few days later, her head still spinning from her time with Richard, she'd been offered a job at The Primary Hospital in London.

Sorcha's initial response had been to reject it out of hand. But then she'd looked at things more sensibly... The offer was for a six-month contract and The Primary was in the north of London, close to where Amanda lived. It was not far from where Richard worked, but there was very little chance of seeing him—and anyway, why should she even factor Richard Lewis into her decisions?

She'd started working there at the end of October, but almost immediately after her arrival in London, Sorcha had realised the move was a huge mistake.

Things weren't going brilliantly with Amanda—she'd barely seen her since she'd arrived—and the flat-share she'd found for herself was far from ideal. Thankfully it was a month-by-month rental agreement, and she knew she should find somewhere else. But now it was the middle of November, and the days were markedly shorter. And as she trudged towards her first in a run of night shifts London felt dark, cold and lonely.

Or was it that London could never again feel as it had that night she'd spent with Richard?

Sorcha hated it that she still thought of him.

The good parts, which she'd tried to blot out, still slipped into her dreams, or into her memory if she dared to daydream...

And now she had two weeks on nights in the busy city.

The Primary was a massive hospital, and every time she walked through the entrance it daunted her. It consisted of a central concrete tower with various modern extensions—part spaceship, Sorcha thought, and part rundown housing estate.

Unlike home, where she knew everyone, here there was an endless stream of new staff. And tonight, as she stepped into the changing room, amongst those she already knew there was another set of new faces.

'Hiya.' She smiled. 'I'm Sorcha...'

'Jane—I only work Friday nights.' The woman nodded to a colleague. 'Cindy's a regular on nights too. Who's in charge tonight?' Jane asked Cindy, checking the pockets of her scrubs for pens and such.

'May, I think. And Marcus is second in charge.'

'You know May already?' Jane checked.

Indeed, Sorcha did.

May was the Nurse Unit Manager, and had interviewed her. She was a stalwart of the department. Her Irish accent was soft, but her wit and her eyes were sharp. When she came into the changing room carrying her basket, she gave them all a smile.

'Have you seen that waiting room?' She tutted, opening up her locker. 'You'd think they all had better places to be.'

As Jane and Cindy headed out, May asked them to make her a cup of tea, then turned her attention to Sorcha, who was still changing. 'Are you looking forward to starting nights?'

'I am.' Sorcha nodded as she pulled on some scrubs.

They didn't match—the top was a dark purple, the bottoms lilac—but they were the least threadbare pair on the trolley. Even though they were sized extra small, they were still huge—so much so that Sorcha had left a T-shirt on beneath.

'We'll see if you feel the same in the morning.'

The department was busy, and there was a lot of backlog to clear as well as a constant stream of new patients coming in. Patients and their families were arriving in Reception, ambulances were pulling up, as well as more urgent cases being wheeled in.

'We are in for a night,' May warned as the team gathered at the nurses' station, and then she ran a knowing eye over the huge whiteboard that was constantly being updated. There were electronic boards also, but the staff constantly worked from the central one, updating it themselves, and able to see at a glance which cubicles were taken, who was waiting to be seen or awaiting treatment. Some patients were waiting for review or transfer.

At first it had daunted Sorcha. Everything was on a far bigger scale than at the small unit she was used to working in. She'd stared at the whiteboard in the same way she'd attempted to read the map of the underground. She was still dreadful at that, but she could now make a decent attempt at the whiteboard.

Certainly she wasn't as expert as May, who must surely have a second degree in logistics, because as Sorcha checked the drugs in the resus trolley, along with Teghan, one of the day staff, May was already armed with a marker and an eraser.

She wrote in the name of the SHO who was the junior doctor on duty tonight—Vanessa.

'And Mr Field's on,' she said. Though her smile didn't last very long. 'Who's the registrar?' she called out, for anyone to answer.

'They're trying to find someone,' Teghan responded from over her shoulder, and then added quietly, for Sorcha's ears only, 'Wait for it! May's going to go off...'

'Find someone?' May squawked, and Sorcha couldn't help but smile as May predictably exploded. 'Are you telling me that I don't have a registrar? How, in the name of all that's holy, are we supposed to cover a trauma team? Every blasted weekend. No doubt they'll send someone who doesn't know his—'

'It's a pleasure to see you too, May!'

The smile froze on Sorcha's face at the sound of the dry greeting, delivered in a well-schooled voice which every fibre of her being recognised even while her mind fought for it to be otherwise.

It could not be him!

'Oh, Richard, it's you.' May sounded instantly mollified. 'Thank goodness for that, at least.'

Sorcha dared not turn around.

Quite simply, she could not face him.

Not now.

Not here.

Never.

'Morphine sulphate ten mg,' Teghan said, opening up the boxes so that together they could count the ampoules, and Sorcha forced herself to concentrate.

Somehow she got through the rest of the drug check and signed her name. Thankfully his back was to her as she made her way over. He wore black scrubs, and his arms were folded as he was taken through the board by May.

'There you are,' May said, glancing over as Sorcha approached. 'Can I ask you to go to the obs ward first? I know you want to get stuck in.'

'That's fine,' Sorcha responded quickly, more than grateful for the excuse to hide, and fervently hoping that Richard was too busy looking at the patient info and being updated to notice her.

Unfortunately, there was no reprieve.

He turned then, and she was back in the path of his gaze.

It wasn't so warm as the last time their eyes had met, but just for a slip of a second she was back there…lying with him in bed.

Hurriedly, she looked away.

Richard had had a little more warning than Sorcha—albeit a minute at best. But he would never not recognise that hair.

It wasn't just the unique blend of coppers and burnt oranges, but the curl pattern too… And even though her back had been to him, the way it was piled on her head, and the ringlets that danced on her pale, slender neck were familiar.

Weeks on from that night, and seeing her dressed in faded, baggy scrubs, somehow he still recognised the feminine shape beneath. His body certainly did, and he took a breath, pushing out the sight before his eyes, dousing the physical reaction as he recalled the next morning after that night…

That night…

He'd never been able to envisage another relationship. The agony he'd been through was something he could not bear to repeat. For the past three years he'd been treading water just to survive.

Once, for a few moments, he'd briefly looked up, had almost envisaged walking out of that bathroom and telling Sorcha about Jess, but even then he hadn't really been thinking ahead.

Coming out of the bathroom to find her gone…

The only conclusion he'd been able to come to was that she hadn't booked a hotel after all and had only stayed with him because she'd needed somewhere to stay.

It didn't make sense—but then nothing about their night did.

But this was work, and he wasn't going to let things slip here. Richard knew he had to set the tone, so he greeted her straight away.

'Good evening, Sorcha.'

May did a double take. 'You two know each other?'

'Yes,' Richard said.

Sorcha had heard that 'no' could be a complete sentence. She'd never considered it could also be applied to 'yes' but, having given her a brief nod, confirming they knew each other, he offered no more information to May, and neither did she seek it.

'So, Sorcha, can I ask you to take over in the obs ward?'

'Sure.'

It was a relief to escape and head round to the eight-bedded ward used for the consultant's patients. There were only three patients, but it filled quickly, and Sorcha took the handover, which consisted of two head injuries and a gentleman wating for IV antibiotics.

'You've another patient coming in,' the day nurse told her, and Sorcha was relieved when the doors swished open and the new patient arrived.

She was pleased to be busy with an admission.

There certainly wasn't time to examine her thoughts, and near the end of her stint, when Richard appeared on the obs ward, Sorcha didn't know how to address things.

'You have some charts for me?' he said.

'Just some IV antibiotics,' Sorcha responded, completely unable to look at him and glad of the dim light. 'I think the others can wait.'

'Do they need updating or not?' Richard asked.

'Yes,' she croaked, wishing she could be as polite and detached as him, and wishing his scent didn't have all her senses jumping in recall, like little echoes of their time together. She recalled in intimate detail how it felt to lean on his chest, how it felt to breathe in the cologne on his neck...

She hated him. And hated even more how impossibly attractive she still found him. Her hands were shaking a little as she passed him the IV and drug charts to update, though they didn't shake with nerves, more with anger at herself.

'May thinks we know each other.'

'We do.'

She made a soft scoffing noise, then added, 'You could have been more discreet.'

'We helped a collapsed patient at Kings Cross,' Richard said. 'I was never going to go into any more detail.' He carried on writing and then paused. 'I'll need the desk.'

She frowned, and then realised what he meant. There was a chair at one side, but to sit and write at any length he'd need somewhere to put his rather long legs.

'Of course.' She stood. 'I was going to get a cup of tea.' She just wanted to escape, but attempted to be polite. 'Do you want one?'

'No, thank you.'

She didn't go and get a cup of tea as the phone rang then, and it was either lean over him to answer or take a seat on the chair by the desk.

'He's comfortable,' Sorcha told the relative who was calling, and gave updates as Richard worked away. He was making light work of those charts…hopefully by the end of the phone call he'd be gone. 'He'll be reviewed in the morning,' she said. 'If you'd like to ring at about nine?'

Richard wasn't finished. Instead he had taken out the *British National Formulary*—the bible for all medications—and was checking a drug, and Sorcha had to know if this was going to be a regular occurrence.

'I thought you worked in central London?'

'I do,' he responded. 'As well as here.'

'Often?'

'Depends.'

Sorcha swallowed. She'd been hoping—or rather praying—that this was a rare one-off.

'I wasn't expecting to see you.'

'Again,' he said, and looked over.

Sorcha frowned, unsure as to quite what he meant—

that little addition sounded as if he'd been finishing off her sentence.

'You didn't expect to see me *again*.'

'I hoped never to,' she admitted.

'I rather guessed that when you fled.' He gave her a thin smile then got back to writing. 'Sorry to disappoint.'

'Excuse me—' Sorcha said, because he'd made it sound as if he was the wronged party.

But there was no chance of continuing because May came through the doors just then.

'Sorcha.' She came over. 'I want to talk to you before I finalise the Christmas off duty. Now, you're working… but I am going to try and give you an early Christmas Day, and I'll see what I can do for New Year's,' May said. 'Can you get home?'

'No,' Sorcha said. 'Besides, my parents are away for New Year.'

'What about you, Richard? Are you in Wales for Christmas?'

'Yes.'

'And how is Jess?'

'Fine,' said Richard, and added his signature to the unfinished notes.

Then he looked over to Sorcha—or rather felt the blast of heat from her cheeks. And when he looked up the flash of anger in her eyes told him she knew about Jess.

How?

'Give her my love,' May said.

'I will. Thanks.'

As May headed off Richard remained, though he certainly wasn't going to discuss such personal matters here.

'We'll speak about this after work; there's a café around the corner,' he said.

'I'm not meeting you.' Sorcha didn't so much as look over at him. 'I've got nothing to say to you.'

'Eight o'clock.' He ignored her protest and named a place she'd never heard of. 'If we're going to be working together then we need to clear the air.'

Not a chance.

There was no way she was meeting him.

And there was no way she could carry on working here.

Somehow, she limped through the night, managing to cross paths with him only occasionally. She even put her hand up to volunteer to take patients up to the ward—usually it wasn't a favourite job, but tonight Sorcha happily obliged.

But at four in the morning there could be no avoiding him.

All the trauma pagers were going off and May was calling her to Resus, so she gowned up.

'What do we know?' Richard asked, already gowned and pulling on gloves as he took the head of the resuscitation bed.

May told him the little she'd been told. It sounded very serious indeed.

'Pedestrian versus car—GCS Three…'

Everyone was given roles, and wore stickers to clearly state who they were. Sorcha was monitor nurse, responsible for undressing the patient and attaching monitors, amongst other things.

'Where's Mr Field?' asked Richard.

'With the aneurism…' said another member of the team.

'Okay,' May said. 'Perhaps, Sorcha, you should be the runner?'

'Sorcha shall be fine as monitor,' Richard said calmly.

Did May think she was too inexperienced? Sorcha wondered, but there really wasn't time to think it through as visible through the windows was a flash of red and blue lights and soon the paramedics were swiftly entering.

'Male, query in his forties or fifties,' the treating paramedic said. 'Pedestrian versus car. The driver—the only witness—reports he's been unconscious since impact. GCS Three throughout.'

All this was conveyed as the patient was moved from the stretcher, and from there Sorcha got to work. His jumper had already been cut open, so she swapped over the monitors then set to work on his heavy coat.

There was a smell to it that was familiar, and as she sheared through the thick wool she caught the scent of her father coming home.

Richard was assessing the man, and obs were being relayed. 'I want to turn him…'

The patient was desperately injured. His GCS—Glasgow Coma Scale—was the lowest possible, though he was still breathing.

'Any ID?' May asked.

But there was none.

'He's in his pyjamas,' May commented as they cut off his trousers. 'Do you think he was confused and went wandering?'

Richard didn't answer. He was performing a full trauma screen, and as the patient was rolled he checked his back and for anything missed.

'Query closed head injury,' Richard said at last. 'Let's get Neuro down. CT knows to expect him?' he checked.

'They're ready for him,' May said.

'His respiratory rate is decreasing.'

Richard took the decision to intubate before moving him around, and it was swiftly done.

'Let's elevate the head of the bed to thirty degrees,' he said. 'And why are we doing that?'

Sorcha didn't answer. She knew it was to decrease intracranial pressure, but she wasn't going to put up her hand.

'Sorcha?' May prompted, and she had to answer.

'Correct,' Richard said.

He didn't single her out. He just explained things along the way and asked questions—and really he was a very good teacher, reminding everyone of the importance of maintaining the patient's BP between parameters.

The police had arrived, but they'd gleaned little more information.

'Why would he be out at four in the morning?' May wondered aloud.

Sorcha spoke up. 'I think he might be a baker.'

'What?' May said.

'His coat...' Sorcha had caught the sweet doughy scent of it as it had been cut off. 'My father's a baker, and his coat smells like that, and those aren't pyjamas—they look like the twill trousers he wears.'

'A baker?' May said, and one of the policemen chimed in.

'That fits the location, and explains what he'd be doing up so early. The poor guy was probably walking to work.'

The information helped, because in a few moments a car was being sent to a location near the scene of the accident, and by the time they were getting him ready to go to CT they had a possible name.

'There's a Geoff Billings who works there. He didn't

turn up for his shift this morning and he's usually early. We're sending a car to his house to check.'

'Well done!' May clucked. 'I would never have got that. What are you, Sorcha? A "super-sniffer"?'

'I must be.' She smiled.

But no, she'd know that scent anywhere—and it brought a lump to her throat to think that this man could be her father, just walking to work, with a coat over his uniform and no ID.

'Where's Neuro?' May asked.

'I'm meeting them in CT,' Richard responded. 'Let's get him round now.'

'Well, why don't I come with you?' May asked, and added, 'Sorcha…if you want to clean up—?'

'May,' Richard interrupted, and then rather sharply added, 'We're fine.'

He briefed the member of staff who would be going to CT. 'Marcus, have five mg of Midazolam ready for any seizure activity.'

Sorcha's cheeks were on fire. Not because of the gowns and PPE, more that May clearly didn't think she was up to taking him.

Still, soon they were in the CT room and getting the patient ready for imaging. Sorcha ensured Mr Billings was covered in the warmer, and helped transfer the equipment, and then they all moved into the pod, closing the door and standing behind a glass screen.

'Richard.' The neuro consultant came in.

'Rafi…'

'I didn't know you were here tonight.'

'I didn't know either,' Richard said.

With greetings over they discussed the patient, but the

conversation fell quiet for a long moment as very soon the images came up on the screen.

'Oh, no...' Rafi said, and there were a couple of audible groans. The scans really were dreadful.

The pod fell quiet again.

'Massive midline shift,' Rafi said, then moved to a second screen and scrolled back as the investigation continued.

It was dreadfully sombre, and as the neuro team discussed their findings it was clear that surgery wasn't an option.

May came in then, and Richard spoke. 'He's suffered a catastrophic head injury,' he said.

May looked at the images for a silent moment. 'Poor man.'

'Yes.'

'I have his wife in the family room,' she said. 'Sorcha was correct. He's a local baker, on his way to work...evidently he just stepped out without looking.'

'I'll come and speak to her now.' Rafi nodded. 'Can we please bring him back to Resus and I'll arrange a bed on ICU?'

'Of course,' May said.

'Keep that blood pressure low, and get his head up to thirty degrees as soon as he's out. What is his wife's name, please?'

'Susan.'

'Is she alone?'

'She's waiting to speak with a doctor before she calls her son.'

They brought him back to the department and into Resus, and May allocated Sorcha to care for him one on one. There was a lot to take care of. Geoff was critically ill and ventilated, so was being continually monitored, and Rafi wanted his blood pressure lower than the usual parameters.

'I'll help tidy him up a bit,' said Jane, wheeling in a trolley with a bowl of water and some toiletries.

'I'm just going to clean your face, Geoff...'

Whether or not he could hear her, Sorcha explained what she was doing, wiping off as much blood and dirt as she could before changing him into a fresh grown.

And perhaps just in time, because May popped her head in then. 'Are there any of the neuro team here?'

Sorcha shook her head. 'I thought Rafi was with you.'

'No.' May came over. 'He spoke to Mrs Billings but then had to head up to ICU.'

She took a breath. Her face was flushed and Sorcha knew she was upset.

'How is she?'

'Confused. I need someone to speak to her again.' She pulled Sorcha aside and spoke in low tones. 'The son's on holiday in France, and his mum has just told him his father's going to be fine and not to come...'

'Problem?' It was Richard.

'Not at all,' May said.

Sorcha frowned—because hadn't May just said otherwise?

'Rafi had to go up to ICU, and May needs someone to speak with Mrs Billings again.'

'I can do that,' Richard said.

'You don't have to, Richard,' May countered. 'I might see if Mr Field is available.'

'May, it's fine,' he said.

He stalked off and Sorcha saw May's lips purse.

'I was hoping to avoid that,' she muttered, and rolled her

eyes. 'I'll go in with him.' She went over to Mr Billings and squeezed his hand. 'Your wife will be with you soon, pet.'

Why didn't May want Richard to speak with the wife? Was he too brusque, perhaps?

Sorcha pondered that briefly, though really she was focussed on taking care of Mr Billings. His blood pressure, which had to stay between those strict parameters, kept soaring.

As she checked the drug regime, she could hear loud sobs and shouts, and then a long stretch of silence.

'How is he?' May asked as she came behind the screen, even redder in the face than before. 'He looks very...'

Her mouth wavered, and Sorcha guessed that even close to forty years in the job didn't make you immune from the shock of something like this.

'You've done a nice job.'

Sorcha had found a comb, and also covered up some of the abrasions and cleaned the patient's hands, which were outside the blanket.

'I'll go now and get Susan.'

Only Richard was already bringing in the wife. 'She wants to see him.'

'Of course,' May said.

'Oh, no!' Mrs Billings sobbed when she saw her husband, and May went over and guided her closer. 'Oh, Geoff...'

Sorcha found her a seat, but for now Mrs Billings stood as Richard spoke to her.

'I'll go and ring your son for you, shall I?'

'Please...' She nodded, and when Richard had gone she finally took a seat and held her husband's hand. 'You were supposed to be at work...'

* * *

Apart from a quick loo and coffee break, Sorcha stayed with Mr Billings until the day staff took over.

It was a relief when her shift was over, and she changed back into the clothes she'd arrived in, wrapping her scarf round her neck and heading out.

She saw Richard was at the X-ray finder, and she wanted to turn and walk in the opposite direction—but that would look childish.

'I'll see you at eight,' he reminded her as she went past.

'You won't.'

'You're the one who disappeared without a word, Sorcha. You're the one who ran off without explanation.'

'Why do you think that might have been, Richard?'

'Enlighten me.'

'I found out you were married.'

She walked off—marched off, really—out through the black folding doors and into the corridor, still wet from people bringing in the rain from outside. But even if it was pouring it was a relief to be outside and away from him.

'Sorcha…'

She started at the sound of her name, honestly surprised that he'd followed her out.

'Clearly we do need to talk.'

'Clearly we don't!' Sorcha retorted angrily, but Richard would not relent.

'Look, I'd rather have this conversation away from here. I have no idea how you found out I was married, but believe it or not that morning I was about to tell you.'

'Oh, please…' She was angry with him and ashamed of herself. 'What else were you going to tell me? That your wife doesn't understand you? Or that you have an open marriage?' She felt ill—especially now she knew his wife's name, thanks to May's inadvertent slip. 'How *is* Jess?' she sneered.

'In a coma,' Richard responded. 'She has been for the past three years.'

Sorcha didn't react. She didn't say anything at first—just stared in horror, hating her own poisonous words, so stunned she couldn't think further than that.

'I'll speak to you at eight unless I have to stay back.' He went to walk off, but at the last minute turned. 'I do owe you an explanation but it's a one-time offer, Sorcha—not an open invitation. I try not to bring my private life to work.'

She found her voice then, albeit shaky. 'Or the bedroom?'

Touché, Sorcha thought as she walked off.

But it just didn't feel like a win.

CHAPTER SEVEN

For close to two months, since Richard had come out of the bathroom to find her gone, his thoughts had turned dark when he'd thought about Sorcha.

Now, though, she'd blazed back into his orbit in gorgeous Technicolor—yet the fact there had been a misunderstanding didn't make things easier.

He couldn't allow it to.

Life had already been difficult enough when they'd first met.

It was hellishly complicated now.

He walked in the rain, relieved to be out of the department even while not relishing the thought of sitting opposite Sorcha again.

Or rather, facing the feelings she still evoked.

He pushed open the café door and saw her straight away. She sat twirling a straw in apple juice, and her eyes were wary as he took off his coat and took a seat.

The waitress came over and he ordered a coffee. 'Are you eating?' he asked Sorcha.

'No, thank you,' Sorcha said quickly, clearly wanting this difficult conversation over and done with.

'Just coffee for me, then,' he said, and when the waitress had gone he got straight to it. 'Jess, my wife, is in a care home in Wales.'

'I apologise for what I said before.'

He nodded. 'How did you find out I was married?' he asked. 'Did you go through my wallet?' It was all he'd been able to come up with.

'Not at first,' Sorcha said. 'There was a phone call, on the hotel room phone, and stupidly I answered it. I thought it was about breakfast. But it was somebody looking for you regarding your wife.'

'On the hotel room phone? Why would they...?'

His voice trailed off and he closed his eyes. He swallowed, then his head went back and he sat there for a few seconds.

Then he opened his eyes and met hers.

'I didn't know that they'd tried to reach me at the hotel...' He knew he was making little sense, but the waitress was back, placing down his coffee, and he was glad of the moment to look back. 'I gave them all my contact details—I knew the phones would be off at the conference.' He shook his head. 'They should have called my mobile first.'

'You rang to enquire about Edward,' Sorcha reminded him. 'Maybe the line was busy...'

'It must have been.' He took a deep breath, then pushed on. 'That morning...' He saw a dull blush darken her cheeks and knew she understood the morning to which he referred. 'Jess had taken a turn for the worse, and as it turned out she had pneumonia.'

'What happened to her?' Sorcha asked. 'Did she have a car accident?'

'A horse-riding accident. She suffered severe head and chest injuries.' Her eyes held his and he could see the demand for more information. 'As I said, it's been three years now.'

'It was quite a big thing to miss out while we were talking.'

He gave a wry laugh and saw her look slightly startled. 'I never get to miss it out, Sorcha.'

'I don't understand…'

'You saw how May was last night—and Rafi. Everyone knows, and everyone tries…'

Sorcha looked back on last night with more knowing now. Even though she hadn't noticed anything with Rafi, May had been like a cat on hot bricks around Mr Billings. Or rather, as she now understood, around Richard.

'I was worried May thought I was incompetent.'

'No, that was just May trying to protect me. Look I didn't set out not to tell you…' He called over to the waitress. 'I'm going to get a croissant. You want anything?'

'No, thank you.'

He ordered an almond one, and then carried on speaking. 'I know I messed up, but I wasn't sitting there at Kings Cross, or in the pub, thinking we were going to end up in bed. I was enjoying talking to you—and God knows that's rare these days. Believe me, had I told you, things would have become…'

'Honest?' She finished his sentence for him, but he shook his head.

'I was more honest with you that night than I have been in a very long time.'

She frowned, not understanding what he meant.

'Family, friends…they've been wonderful—I mean that. It's just…' He ran a hand across his brow. 'I honestly don't know where to start.'

His croissant arrived and he dipped it in his coffee.

She asked him a question. 'Why is Jess in Wales?'

'Because…' He shook his head, as if he wasn't going to

answer, but then relented. 'Jess lived in Wales and I lived in London.'

'So, you were separated?'

'No.' He gave her a thin smile. 'We've been together since medical school. From the start Jess wanted to be a GP back in Wales and I wanted to work in A&E in London.'

Sorcha felt her own frown.

'We could never pin down where we were going to live and who was going to make the move. We were on holiday once, and realised that was the only thing stopping us from marrying. On everything else we were on the same page. So we decided to make it official and just...'

'Live apart?'

'We didn't see it that way,' he told her. 'Couples commute all the time.'

'I guess...' She thought about it. 'My uncle works on the oil rigs—he's away for ages at a time.'

He smiled at her attempt to understand. 'Well, it's not quite the same. We saw each other all the time, and always made sure our rosters aligned. But we both got to focus on work and we were studying hard too. It might sound unconventional, but it worked for us.'

'You were happy?'

'Very.'

'And you got together at medical school?'

'First term,' he said, and Sorcha felt her eyes widen.

'You were together since you were both eighteen?'

Richard nodded. 'We got engaged when we were twenty-five and married at thirty.'

'Would you have moved?' Sorcha asked.

'I guess at some point one of us would have.'

'If you'd had a baby?'

'Oh, no.' His response was automatic—the same one he had always given, even before the accident when people had asked about babies. 'Neither of us wanted children.' Richard hesitated, then looked up into the green eyes that had asked him to be honest. 'There was a bit more to it than that, but that's the line we went with.'

'Okay.'

He liked it that she didn't push to know what 'a bit more' meant, just nodded and accepted that there were things he might prefer not to share about his marriage.

'Usually we'd have been together on our days off, but I was about to take the final exam towards my FRCEM when it happened.' Regret flashed across his features and there was a husk in his voice. 'A dog startled her horse.' He put up a hand. 'You don't need to hear all this, but...'

'I'd like to.'

He'd wanted to come straight in, explain as little as possible, and then get out. But he'd completely forgotten how easily they spoke together and the pleasure of sharing conversation with Sorcha.

'I've never told anyone about it from the start,' he admitted. 'Well, apart from medical personnel, of course. But I guess everyone else has lived it with us.'

'Lived it?'

'When the accident first happened and Jess was in ICU people were calling all the time. I ended up sending out group messages. Now I have a group chat for my family, as well as one for Jess's, and another for close friends.'

'Who do you really talk to, though?' Sorcha asked.

'Everyone's been great,' Richard said. 'The thing is...'

She waited.

'They love her too.'

'So you're protecting them?'

'I don't know. I'm probably protecting Jess. She'd hate certain things being discussed. As well as that, I think grief is difficult enough. But because she's still alive… People don't know what to say. Or they say too much.'

'Such as?'

'There are some who suggest I focus on my career, or start dating again. Then there are some who think I should hold out hope, like I did in the beginning.'

He went back to the beginning.

'Jess was in ICU for six weeks, and then for the first year she was MCS.' He realised he was perhaps a little too used to shorthand and said, 'In a minimally conscious state. I was hopeful, though—we all were. Pretty much from the start I knew we weren't going to get her fully back, but Rafi put me on to a rehabilitation place in Europe. I was going to sell my apartment to fund it…we were all on board.'

'All?'

'Her family. She's very close with her parents, and so am I. But then she had a massive bleed. It wiped out all hope—at least it did for me.'

'Not for her parents?'

'No. They clung on, insisted she still had a chance. But…' He shook his head. 'Jess can't regulate her body temperature, so it's hard to know when there's an infection. And that morning, as I said, it turned out she'd developed pneumonia. Trefor, her father, insisted on calling an ambulance, and there was a full resuscitation.'

He watched as Sorcha went to take sip of her drink, clearly not knowing what to say, but her glass was empty.

'With Jess, it's never been as clear cut as with our patient last night. I've tried to maintain shared decision-making— I love her parents. And yet I love Jess more…or loved her.

I know she wouldn't have wanted that. Fortunately, we're in agreement now, so we won't put her through that again.'

'I'm so sorry.'

'Thank you.'

'Did you complete your studies?' she asked.

'No.' He shook his head. 'That shiny career that seemed so important back then has been very much put on hold since the accident.'

'Do you miss it?'

It was a question he'd been asking himself, and she looked at him with green eyes that expected an answer.

'At times,' he admitted. 'I still work, but it's not the same being a locum, and I haven't progressed. I'm in Wales a lot—I work there too. And when I come to London, to be honest, it feels like a break.'

'Well, I'm glad you had that little holiday.'

Richard heard the implication and knew she'd decided he'd been looking for a one-night stand.

'It wasn't like that, Sorcha.'

'What was it like, then?' she asked.

'I don't know,' he admitted. 'But it feels like a very long time ago. How are you?' he asked. 'I've wondered.'

Sorcha nodded. 'I've wondered about you, too.'

Despite herself, even while trying hard not to, she had wondered about him on so many occasions.

The waitress was back and Richard asked for another coffee, and another almond croissant. He glanced at her empty apple juice glass.

'Do you want another?'

She was about to decline, but she did want to speak more rather than dash off, so she nodded. 'But actually...' she looked at the waitress '...I'll have an almond croissant and a tea, please.' She glanced at the selection. 'I'll have a mint tea.'

'What happened to white coffee?'

'If I have one now I'll never get to sleep. I have loud flatmates.' She told him another truth. 'I'm not used to sharing a house. They're probably perfectly lovely—but none of them do shift work and...' She halted, not wanting to be petty about how they pinched her food, the noise, and all the other inconveniences of sharing with strangers. 'Actually, they're awful.'

'That's no good.'

'I'll get through this block of nights and then I'll have to sort something else out.'

'How are things going with Amanda?'

She was touched that he remembered, and also that he asked. 'Not great,' she admitted. 'Still, I'm hoping we can have some time together at Christmas—if May ever finishes the off-duty.'

'How did your parents take the news that you were moving here?'

'They still think I have a mystery man.'

He gave a soft laugh. 'I do have my uses, then?'

'Oh, yes!' She smiled, but it wavered. 'I think they know why I'm really here. To be honest, I wish I'd never come.'

'Really?'

'The flat's dreadful, Amanda's barely home, and—' She looked across the table at him, the latest problem to present itself to her. 'I'm glad we've cleared things up, but...'

He remained a problem.

Now she was no longer hating him, furious at him, she was remembering again just how wonderful their time together had been. How happy and thrilled and content she'd been, all at the very same time.

Now her anger was abating she was somewhat daunted to look into her heart and see the feelings that remained. Those dewy Richard glasses were back on, and she ached to reach for his hand, as she had the morning they'd parted. His jaw was as rough and stubbled as it had been when they'd lain together, and his eyes were still as blue as a northern night.

Their croissants arrived and she took a bite. Instantly she pulled a face. 'That's awful!' The poor waitress glanced over and Sorcha pushed out a smile. 'You have it,' she told him.

'I'm fine.'

'I don't think I can work with you,' Sorcha admitted abruptly. 'I'll work through Christmas, but after that...' She shrugged. 'My friend's only in my flat back in Scotland till the end of January.'

'You're surely not leaving London because of me?'

'Because of a lot of things.'

'You're being ridiculous.'

'I know my limits.'

'Sorcha, things were already complicated when we met. They're hellish worse now. I won't be suggesting we go out to dinner, or fall into bed, or anything else of the sort.'

'I never suggested you would be. But I can't work alongside someone I've slept with.'

'If everyone thought that half the hospital would have to resign!'

'Maybe, but...'

It had come as a shock to find herself still so attracted to him. To sit opposite him again. To look at his pale skin and the shadow on his jaw and to recall how beautiful he looked in the morning.

'Nothing's going to happen,' Richard said. 'I don't know

if I've made things clear, but I can't see Jess getting through this. It could be weeks, months...even years. But now that the decision has been made, I'm going to be there for her.'

'As you should be.' Sorcha nodded. 'But I'm far too insecure to be an occasional lover.'

The depths of her own feelings scared her. She'd glimpsed how much losing him had hurt...to fall further for Richard could prove devastating.

'I'm sorry for all you're going through,' she said. And then without thinking, as naturally as breathing, she reached her hand across the table and touched his. 'And for all that's to come.'

His fingers closed around her own, just lightly, and if it was anyone else she thought she would barely have noticed...would simply have taken her hand back. Except she looked down and stared at her own fingers, curling into his, nestling into them like little purring kittens, nudging to be stroked.

And he reciprocated—or rather he didn't let go.

'I can't be your stop gap,' Sorcha said.

'It was never like that.'

'Yes, it was.' Sorcha was being firm—more so with herself. He still held her one hand between both of his now. His hands were cold, but those fingers were still so beautiful, and she knew she should not prolong this conversation. 'You're about to lose the love of your life and—'

'Please don't,' he interrupted. 'I've got enough people telling me how I should feel and how I should be.'

Sorcha blinked.

'I lost Jess three years ago.'

She looked up then.

'I can tell you the moment I knew she'd gone.'

And now she knew she wasn't getting the amended version, or the group chat version, or anything other than Richard's truth.

'Not here,' Richard said.

And she knew it was not just because half the hospital frequented the café, but more because he could not sit in a public place and voice thoughts that had been kept so long in lockdown.

They walked out into the misty rain and found a little park with gloomy ducks who were huddled under a tree.

'You should have brought your croissant,' Richard said.

'It's bad for them.' Sorcha sighed. 'And it was a bit sickly.' She could still taste the almond. 'It tasted like wedding cake.' She halted. 'Gosh!'

'Stop.' He laughed. 'Please don't be another person who's scared to say the wrong thing.'

'Okay.' She still inwardly winced, but then took a breath and turned and looked at a man she found very beautiful and whose side she didn't want to leave yet.

'How did you know Jess was gone? Was it the scan?'

'I saw the scan, but even then I thought…' He gave a hollow laugh. 'Even then I was still able to override my thoughts. But the neurosurgeon was pretty blunt, and Rafi went through everything for me.'

He sighed, and Sorcha didn't care if it wasn't sensible—she reached over and was soon back holding his hand, telling herself she'd done the same with Mrs Billings, while knowing that it wasn't even close to the same thing.

'It was a couple of weeks later. Trefor was thrilled that she was breathing alone and that her eyes were open, so he and Jess's mother Bronwyn went back home. I think it was the first time I'd been on my own with her since the bleed. Well, I just broke down…'

Sorcha squeezed his hand. Of course she did.

'She didn't react,' Richard said, and he squeezed her hand back. 'Nothing. In fairness, I don't think Jess had ever seen me cry, but...'

Sorcha turned on the bench and looked at him, and she understood now that that had been the moment he'd known.

'There was nothing,' he said again. 'I knew she was gone.'

'And you haven't told anyone?'

'Not really. It feels disloyal.' He looked back at her. 'Do you remember saying you felt like that about your parents?'

'Yes.'

'Well, it's much the same. It's something I've dealt with. How I felt privately didn't change things. I've been working through it, and I'm getting there—albeit slowly. That afternoon, when the trains were cancelled, I was relieved not to have to go.'

He took a breath, as if surprised he'd admitted it out loud.

'I'm never going to divorce her, or stop visiting her, but I think that day I knew I was ready to join the human race again. Things have changed now, though.'

'I get that.'

'I'm mainly based in Wales.'

'You've still got a house in Wales?'

'No.' He shook his head. 'I knew she was never coming back to it, and we had to sell it to pay for her care. I don't think Trefor's forgiven me for that, but it was that or sell my apartment here.'

'You would have sold it for her rehab, though?'

'In a flash,' Richard said. 'But that was when I had hope. I didn't live at the house much when she was alive, but it was hell being there without her. I couldn't live there just to appease her parents.'

'No,' Sorcha agreed.

'Do you still wish I'd told you all this?'

'Of course,' Sorcha said, and then halted. 'I don't know,' she admitted. 'If you had I think we'd have spent the night talking rather than...'

Sorcha blushed and let out a small laugh. How he'd missed that sound. And even on this bleak, grey morning the light, breathy sound brought a reaction, for his lips moved into a soft smile.

'I think that night was perfect just as it was,' Sorcha told him. 'Except for that phone call the next morning.'

'Yes, and except for me coming out to find you gone.' He looked at her lips, tinged blue with the cold, and then up to her eyes. 'I didn't mean to hurt you.'

'I know that now.'

'You're okay?'

'Apart from freezing,' she admitted, and together they stood.

He'd been through so much, thought Sorcha, and she was sure he had a lot more to come. She believed he thought he'd grieved his wife, but it wasn't as straightforward as that.

There was no end in sight and his ties to Jess's family were still strong.

And she liked him far too much.

'How often do you work at The Primary?' she asked as they walked towards the park gates.

'It varies,' he said. 'I've got a shift next week and a couple the week after. It really all depends. Sorcha, please don't think about leaving on my account.'

'It's not just you,' she admitted. 'I haven't really been happy since...' She stopped then, unsure if the blues she'd felt lately had started when she'd arrived in London or when she'd found out about Jess.

Since that night the world hadn't felt the same.

'I think we go our separate ways here,' she said. 'My flat's back that way. Are you getting the Tube?'

'I am.'

It was, Sorcha found, very hard to say goodbye.

After a night wondering how she could avoid him, now she didn't know how to tear herself away.

'Bye,' she said, a little too quickly, and turned and walked away.

'Sorcha...?'

She turned.

'Is everything okay?'

'I just told you.' She shrugged. 'I'm fine. It's just been...'

He walked towards her. 'I meant we had a contraception fail...'

'And?' She frowned. 'I told you—I'm on the pill.'

'You've gone off coffee...' he said.

'I hate the milk here in London.' Sorcha rolled her eyes. 'Richard, there's nothing to worry about in that department.'

'And the croissant?'

'Richard, I'm fine.'

'You look—' He halted in whatever he'd been about to say.

'Just say it.'

'I hate it when people tell me I've lost weight or I'm looking tired,' he said.

'Go ahead.'

'You've got dark circles under your eyes.'

'I have been working all night.' She chose not to tell him

about the many sleepless nights she'd suffered thinking of him. 'Honestly, everything's fine.'

'Good.'

She should turn and walk away. Only if it had been hard enough the first time, it felt near impossible now. And it must be hard for him, too, because suddenly he took her arms and pulled her into him.

'Sorcha...'

'Please don't say sorry.'

'I wasn't about to,' he said.

She listened to the steady thump of his heart and it was the oddest thing... When she should be in turmoil at being back in his arms, it was the calmest and steadiest she'd felt in weeks.

'We should have ended things better,' he told her.

'Yes...'

This felt by far nicer.

And when he lifted her chin so she'd look up at him, it was a much sweeter parting than their last one.

'Your lips are blue...' he said, and then lowered his head to put that right.

He brought her lips to colour and to life, soft and warm, and as their mouths moved slowly she moulded to his body, leant into his warmth.

It was bliss to be kissed by him and to be back in his arms.

Yet what could he offer her?

A day here and there? The odd night.

Or would he ask her to hold on? Because that meant he was waiting for his wife to die before he resumed life.

'Take care,' Richard said.

'And you.'

CHAPTER EIGHT

SORCHA SLEPT THROUGH the days and worked at night, telling herself she didn't miss Richard or want him.

Her final night shift at work was wild. If the department had been busy on her arrival, at midnight it all kicked off—and Sorcha got the big inner city nursing experience she'd hoped for.

Fights and stabbings.

It was a relief not to think of Richard for a while. To be so damn busy that she forgot how much she missed him and how wonderful their brief time together had been.

She was literally running at one point, dashing a patient up to Theatre—a rather famous patient, apparently, not that Sorcha had heard of him.

It was a serious run and she was suddenly all breathless, the lights spinning.

'Are you okay?' the theatre nurse checked.

'Fine.' Sorcha put her head down for a moment. 'I haven't run like that since…' Her mind went back to the moment before Richard had entered her life. Running for the train at Kings Cross. 'Don't mind me.'

To her horror, she found that she was crying.

'Sorcha?' David, one of the porters, came over. 'Whatever's wrong?'

'It's nothing.' She pressed fingers into her eyes. 'I'm just tired.' She waved his concern away. 'You go back. I might go and get a cookie, or something, from the machine.'

It was suitably awful, but sugary and sweet, and Sorcha ate it greedily as she made her weary way back to A&E.

By seven a.m. the sugar rush had long since worn off and Sorcha stood pale and tired and more than ready for bed. Or rather ready to head back to her flat and her noisy, celebratory flatmates, who wouldn't care a jot that she'd been working all night.

She heard May speaking. 'Morning, Mr Field,' she said, greeting the consultant. 'You're early.'

'I'm not.'

'Goodness,' May said. 'Is that really the time? Sorcha, take a marker and help me update the board.'

She read out the names of the medical staff taking over in the morning.

'So, Mr Field…?' Sorcha started.

'When's he retiring?' Jane asked as she cleaned down the trolleys for the morning.

'Not for a while,' May said. 'I think he's here till summer.'

'Who's replacing him?' she asked, but May only shrugged.

'I have no idea.' She got back to reading out names. 'Mr Owen is also on. Hold on…' She sighed. 'No, he's on leave. Maybe Dr Lewis…'

'Might Richard replace Mr Field?' one of the nurses suggested, and Sorcha felt her neck stiffen and her ears prick up to high alert. 'I thought he'd be a consultant by now.'

'He hasn't got his FRCEM,' May said, and Sorcha knew that was the qualification he'd been studying for when the accident had occurred. 'God, but I wish it could be him.'

'He's not exactly fun, though,' Jane said.

'Do you want fun,' May asked, 'or your life saving?

Anyway, he's gorgeous. That voice and those blue eyes... If I was thirty years younger...'

'May!' Jane yelped. 'You can't say those things any more.'

'Of course I can. And if I can't, with a bit of luck they'll fire me.'

It was clear that they all adored Richard, and Sorcha could see he wasn't just a casual locum but a part of the fabric here. He worked here when he could...when his complicated life allowed.

And apparently he was working this morning.

Not until nine, though, and she was relieved that their paths wouldn't cross. She just couldn't pretend to be okay any more.

She'd been so angry with him, but she'd refused to cry over a cheat. Now, since she'd found out about Jess, she felt raw—as if their one night together had occurred just last week. The pain of them being over was as new as if it had happened then.

Perhaps she'd used her anger as a shield?

Now, though, it felt as if that shield was dissolving—as if there was nothing between her and the memory of them together.

'You look dead on your feet,' May commented to her as she brought over the drug trolley keys and then scuttled off to take handover. 'If any journalists call about our famous patient, remember to say no comment.'

'I know.'

'The police are trying to find out about the stabbing. It's an active investigation.'

'I know they are.'

Sorcha sat on a stool at the nurses' station and answered

the phone when it rang, but it wasn't a journalist, and she directed the enquiry up to Theatre.

The next call was a relative of their famous patient. Or she said that she was.

'Is he there?' she demanded.

'I'm sorry, I can't give that information out,' Sorcha said.

It was tough, but the patient had requested confidentiality. His parents were both in the waiting room, and they had told the staff that all relevant parties had already been informed.

'Can't you at least tell me if he's there?' the woman asked.

'I'm sorry, I can't give you that information.'

Oh, she ached for it to be seven-thirty.

'Journalist?' Vanessa checked, and Sorcha nodded. 'Can I just have a quick hand?' the junior doctor asked.

'Sure,' Sorcha said, jumping down from the stool.

'I need to take some blood from a patient, but he's a bit cantankerous.'

She followed Vanessa into the cubicle, where there was a large man asleep and snoring.

'Mr Dennis?' Vanessa said, and the man awoke, startled.

'Hello,' Sorcha said, introducing herself. 'The doctor just wants to take another look at you and get some blood.'

As quickly as that, things changed.

Mr Dennis sat bolt upright and struck out at the junior doctor, and as Sorcha called for assistance he jumped down from the gurney.

Sorcha would have run—she was rather good at that—but her back was to the wall, and the patient was on the other end of the gurney between them.

'Mr Dennis…' She kept her voice calm. Vanessa was

leaning on the wall and holding her shoulder, and David was rushing in to assist. Help had arrived.

This sort of scene unfortunately wasn't unfamiliar, but suddenly, for the first time since September, time slowed down.

Sorcha saw Mr Dennis's hands reach for the gurney. 'No!' she said. But it had already moved. She moved to cover her stomach but she was too late. He slammed the gurney straight into her midriff.

The shock was as searing as the pain—and then everything went white.

The scuffle was over, Security was arriving and already Mr Dennis was compliant. Sorcha sat up against the cubicle wall, unsure if she was hurt or even what had taken place.

Everyone was rushing, and poor Vanessa was being led out, still holding her shoulder, as May came over to where Sorcha sat.

'I'm okay,' Sorcha said. 'I think I'm just winded.'

She attempted to stand, but May was having none of it.

'Stay there,' May told her. 'You're as white as a sheet. Sarah?' she called to another colleague. 'I need a gurney right away.'

'Not for me.' Sorcha pushed up on her hands. 'Honestly, I'm fi—' Except she wasn't, and she sank back down and doubled over. 'I can't get my breath…'

'You're okay,' May said, and she was so calm and reassuring that Sorcha was able catch her breath and take a deep one in. Then another. 'That's it…'

'I'm okay…' Sorcha agreed.

'Come on.'

May helped her onto the gurney and soon she was in a cubicle of her own, being helped into a pale lemon gown.

'How are you feeling?' May asked as she covered her with a blanket and checked her obs.

'I'm okay,' Sorcha said again, and nodded. 'I just feel a bit...'

'A bit what?'

'Nauseous,' she admitted.

'You got a fright,' May said. 'Your blood pressure's a bit low. I might just put a line in...'

'I don't need a cannula.'

'I'll tell that to Mr Field, shall I? When he asks why I didn't put one in when your blood pressure's in its boots.' She turned and smiled. 'Here he is now.'

Mr Field gave her a smile, followed by a sigh. 'Hello, Sorcha, I'm so sorry this has happened.'

He was very kind, and asked if there was anything in her medical history he needed to know, but there really wasn't anything.

And then he examined her.

Thoroughly.

'It's just a bruise,' Sorcha grumbled.

'Indeed, you are bruised.' Mr Field nodded. 'And it's over your spleen. I'm not going to take any chances.' He sat her forward and palpated her back, over her kidneys, and asked many of the same questions he already had. 'We'll get a urinalysis to check for blood, and also a BHCG...'

Sorcha had already told him that she wasn't pregnant, but she knew Mr Field was thorough, and wouldn't send her for an abdominal X-ray without one.

She was left alone then. May had nodded when she'd asked for the curtain to be closed, and it was odd to lie there and hear the sounds of A&E without being a part of the action.

She closed her eyes when she heard Richard arrive, and

could hear him being brought up to speed by the nursing staff.

Very soon the curtain was swished aside.

'Hey...' Richard came in and closed the curtain behind him. 'I just heard. Are you okay?'

'It's nothing,' she said. 'May insisted I was seen.'

'Of course you had to be seen. What did Mr Field say?'

'Not much.' Sorcha shrugged. She felt teary, and that wasn't like her at all, and she felt dreadfully exposed too. 'I'm to have an abdominal X-ray, and I'm on this stupid drip. I think he's just making a fuss because I'm staff.'

'Mr Field is thorough with everyone,' Richard said. 'And you are rather pale.'

'I'm always pale,' she said.

'I heard that the day we met,' Richard said, 'and you were seconds away from fainting then.'

'I'm always like that.' She actually smiled. 'I mean, if anything happens—even just a lack of sleep. I used to always get out of sports at school...'

'I bet.' He smiled. 'But Mr Field doesn't know you like I...' He halted, and then tried to change the personal recollection into a little joke. 'He doesn't know what a sickly thing you are.'

'Peely-wally,' Sorcha said.

'Pardon?'

'That's what we call it at home.'

'Your parents say that to you?'

'Not just my parents.' She smiled. 'Patients say it, and if you worked up there and didn't know what it meant, after a couple of shifts you would.'

'Seriously?' He smiled. 'What does it mean?'

'Pale and sickly. Off-colour.'

'Well, you're definitely looking peely-wally, then,' he said, and took her hand.

She pulled it back. 'Don't,' she said. 'If anyone comes in they'll think there's something going on between us.'

'Because there *is* something going on,' Richard said, almost angrily. 'Hell, Sorcha—'

His voice broke off as May came in, bearing a bedpan.

This was not the look Sorcha had been hoping for!

'I am not using that.' Sorcha was adamant. 'I can get up.'

Richard smiled as he headed out, leaving May to convince Sorcha she was not to get up.

Then the smile faded.

He felt a little peely-wally himself.

The sight of Sorcha on the trolley, and hearing the news that she was injured...

'Upsetting, isn't it?' Mr Field commented as he joined him at the central station.

'Very,' Richard agreed. 'Where were Security when all this happened?'

'They were in the waiting room and at the main entrance,' Mr Field said. 'They can't be everywhere, Richard.'

Mr Field was always fair—he didn't jump to blame anyone—and Richard was usually the same. But this morning his responses felt less rational. 'What's happening now?' he asked.

'I'm going to send Vanessa to the obs ward for a few hours. It's possibly overkill, but she lives alone.'

Richard was doing his best to focus, and to nod in all the right places, but while he was concerned for Vanessa, right now his exasperation and distress was solely for Sorcha, however unfairly proportioned.

It was personal.

But then Vanessa was a colleague also.

He took a breath and knew it was all about his feelings for Sorcha—that despite attempts to dismiss them, to cut them out, they flourished like some untamed garden.

'Surely we can get Sorcha X-rayed now,' he said, irritated that she was presumably having to wait until nine, when the department officially opened. 'I know it's not technically urgent, but...'

'It's not that,' Mr Field said. 'When I was examining Sorcha...' His voice trailed off as May came over.

She gave Mr Field a nod. 'You were right,' May said. 'I don't think she has so much as a clue.'

Richard frowned.

'I'll go and talk to her now,' Mr Field said, but May shook her head.

'It might be better for her to hear it from me.'

'Hear what?' Richard said, and May looked slightly away.

It was just a tiny flash of avoidance, and had he not known her so well he wouldn't have even noticed it. But he did.

'I'm not going to run around with a megaphone,' Richard said, knowing damn well May was protecting her staff member. But he had this gut feeling... Or was it just the thump of realisation as to why the X-ray was being delayed? The possible findings in the routine urinalysis? The pregnancy test Mr Field *always* insisted on in any female patient of child-bearing age?

'Sorcha's pregnant?' he checked, and May gave a tight nod.

'I could feel her fundus,' Mr Field said. 'Ten to twelve weeks, I'd say. I agree, May.' He nodded now. 'It might be better coming from you.'

'No,' Richard said immediately. 'I'll tell her.'

'It's fine.' Mr Field stood firm. 'I think May can break the news more gently—and anyway, she isn't your patient.'

'Sorcha definitely isn't my patient,' Richard agreed and then added, 'I'll tell her.'

And he really could convey a lot with few words, because Mr Field's eyes widened slightly and May went a little pink, her lips pursed as he made it clear he wasn't going in there as Sorcha's doctor.

And possibly his gulp of air and rapid blink had them guessing he was more than a colleague or a friend...

Sorcha was pregnant.

And, as sure as eggs were eggs, he knew it was down to him.

He'd never run away from a tricky situation in his life and he wasn't about to start now.

If Sorcha had to find out she was pregnant at work and deal with people knowing, then so too could he.

'I'll tell Sorcha. If you could give us some privacy, please?'

'Of course.' May's face reddened as she nodded.

'When you speak with her,' Mr Field said, 'can you let her know that I'll be asking the surgeons to take a look and, given her status, I'd like the obstetrician to check her over?' He glanced at the time. 'I'll wait for them to change over.'

'Who's on from Obstetrics today?' Richard asked, and May, who was already in the middle of changing the whiteboard, answered quickly.

'Monica,' she said. 'She's excellent.'

'I know.' Richard nodded.

Monica was the colleague who had seen them that night getting into the lift at the hotel—but, more to the point, she was Jess's closest friend.

He didn't have the capacity to think about that now. He just filed it away as he walked towards the cubicle.

Opening the curtain, he smiled at a rather wan and visibly bored Sorcha, who lay there rolling her eyes as he came in.

'I want to go home,' she said immediately. 'But now I have to wait until X-Ray opens.'

'You're not going for an X-ray.'

'Good,' she said, and moved to sit up.

But the gurney was flat, and it wasn't such an easy manoeuvre—or perhaps her stomach did, in fact, hurt, he thought. Because mid attempt to sit up she lay back down.

'How do you feel?' he asked.

'Stupid,' she admitted. 'I shouldn't have got between the wall and the gurney.'

'It happened,' Richard said. 'There isn't always time to think straight.'

He smiled at the irony of his own words—something had happened that night, and neither of them had been thinking straight then.

'Sorcha, the reason they're not sending you for an X-ray...' He paused, briefly wavering from his usual direct approach, then reminding himself that a long preamble would be both confusing and pointless. 'You're pregnant.'

Her response was immediate. 'No.'

Sorcha's voice was calm, and he looked into her green eyes to see the slight smile on her lips that told him he was mistaken.

'I'm not.'

'Yes.'

She blinked, and he watched as the possibility started to impinge, a tiny frown forming on her brow. And then she hauled herself from acceptance.

'The test must be wrong.'

'It's not just the test,' Richard responded. 'Mr Field already thought you were—he could feel your fundus when he examined you.'

'Then he's wrong,' Sorcha said, in a voice that was no longer calm—instead it edged on defiance. 'This is ridiculous.'

She again went to sit up, but Richard's hand went to her upper arm and halted her panicked response. So she lay back down, her eyes closing for a moment as she wrestled with the facts he'd so calmly delivered.

'Sorcha, if he can feel the fundus, you're around twelve weeks along.'

'I didn't have sex twelve weeks ago,' she retorted sharply.

'Add two weeks.' Richard smiled unseen at her slight belligerence, but he didn't quite know why. Maybe just because he was watching her argue with herself as she lay there. 'And we *both* know you had sex around ten weeks ago.'

Her eyes opened then and met his. He saw for the first time a flash of tears, and understood that she was completely overwhelmed.

Oh, Sorcha was indeed overwhelmed—completely.

She couldn't be pregnant!

Panic was kicking in now.

And if she was pregnant—*pregnant!*—then shouldn't she be finding out alone, not being informed by the damn father?

She hated it that she was at work, and even if she loathed her poky, unfriendly flat, she'd give anything to be there now to absorb these new facts.

'I want to go home.'

It was always her first instinct.

To run.

She knew she was being ridiculous, and Richard's hand was still on her arm. But even before he could halt her from sitting up, she sank back down.

'It's okay,' Richard said.

'It really isn't,' she retorted, then put her arm over her face, shielding herself, trying to fathom it all. Her hand went down to her stomach…to her still-flat stomach. 'I'd know if I were pregnant.'

'You have gone off coffee,' Richard pointed out. 'And you are, as May said after your sleuthing with Mr Billings, a super-sniffer.'

From behind the shield of her arm she gave a half-laugh and thought of all the odd little things that had been happening.

'I am tired,' she admitted. 'I thought it was the move, and not getting good-quality sleep in my flat-share. Plus I suppose I've been more upset than usual.'

'About Amanda?'

'Yes,' she said. And then, because she was too confused to lie, admitted— 'And about what happened with you…' She winced as she said it. 'I mean, I should have got over it, of course…'

'I know,' he agreed, and removed his hand. 'I get that, Sorcha.'

He was being very kind, if a little distant. He let her be quiet for quite some considerable time, and she had no idea if it was his professional persona, or if he was shell shocked too. Or perhaps he just didn't know what to say.

It was then that she thought of his situation.

'What about Jess?'

'Maybe don't think about that now?' he suggested. 'Just think about you.'

'No, but...' She was suddenly all fluttery inside. 'My parents. How do I tell them?' She thought of their disappointed faces. 'Pregnant after a one-night stand with a married man. They'll never forgive me!'

'Sorcha...'

'It's true, though. Even if they understand about Jess, it was still just one night...' She lay silent for a moment and then looked up at him. 'Aren't you going to ask?'

'Ask what?'

'If it's yours.'

'I was there that night,' he said, and even if that didn't make perfect sense, she understood what he meant. That night had been so special—of course this baby was his.

Baby!

'An obstetrician's going to come and review you,' Richard said. 'It might be a while. Sorcha...?' She heard slight discomfort in his voice. 'Do you remember that we met a friend of mine that night, when we were coming out of the lift at the hotel? A fellow doctor called Monica?'

She frowned.

'She's on call today, so it will be her. But I can ask for someone else...'

Sorcha put her arm back over her head and lay silent.

May came in. 'Sorcha,' she said, 'Monica's said she'll be down shortly. She has a paramedic with her—he's on professional development—she's asked if you'd mind him accompanying her?'

'That's fine,' Sorcha said—it was a teaching hospital after all. And then she heard Richard speak.

'May, could we perhaps see if...?'

'It's fine,' Sorcha said, before he could ask for another doctor to take over her care. It would make things even more awkward, Sorcha thought, and anyway, everyone would soon know.

In all honesty, if Richard hadn't told her who she was, Sorcha wouldn't have recognised Monica. She was dressed in a dark navy suit, with her long hair tied back, and she didn't recognise Sorcha.

At least not at first.

'Hello.' Monica smiled and introduced herself, as well as the paramedic who was with her. 'This is Luke.'

'Thanks for this,' Luke said.

'Now...' Monica glanced at the notes. 'You've had two shocks this morning.' She smiled at Richard. 'You think she's around twelve weeks?'

'That was Mr Field's assessment,' Richard responded.

And then his voice went a touch thick. Not embarrassed—Sorcha couldn't quite define it—but he took her hand.

'We think that's right,' he said.

He gave her hand a squeeze, and she watched as Monica did a brief double-take as she realised Sorcha wasn't actually his patient.

Then he looked at Sorcha's red hair and swallowed. 'We had a contraceptive failure at the end of September,' Richard said. 'It must have been then...' He stopped, as if trying to pinpoint things.

With that one statement he'd made them sound as if they were more involved than a one-night fling, and she was grateful for that.

And, when your innards were being served up for several departments in your workplace to pore over, it very much helped to keep some details private. Sorcha gratefully squeezed his hand back.

'Right,' Monica said, back to being steady and efficient

after her earlier very brief falter. 'Richard, could you excuse us for just a moment?'

'Of course.'

'Luke, would you mind stepping out, too? Just briefly.'

'Of course.'

'Sorcha,' Monica said when they were alone. 'I'm not sure if you're aware that I'm a friend of Richard…'

'And Jess,' Sorcha added, so that Monica didn't have to.

'Yes.' She nodded. 'I will understand completely if you'd rather I called a colleague to take care of you.'

'It's fine. I don't need someone else.'

'I will have to ask you some quite personal questions,' she warned. 'Not just now—I have to get back to the unit—but I'll be taking a thorough history and I don't want you to think for a moment that you can't speak freely and frankly. Anything you tell me is confidential. I want you to know that.'

'Yes, I understand.'

'I have to ask my patients about mental health…domestic violence and such.'

'We're not living together.'

'Even so…' Monica gave her a smile. 'Sorcha, I'd like to take care of you. I just want to be certain you're okay with that.'

'Yes.'

'And if you change your mind, that's okay too.'

'Thank you.'

While they were alone, Monica asked if this was her first pregnancy—it was—and if there had been any gynaecological problems or procedures in her past, or anything that it would serve her better for Monica to know.

'Nothing…' Sorcha thought back. 'Except I'm on the mini-pill, and I've been taking it all along.'

'That's fine. It's very common and nothing to worry about.' Monica smiled reassuringly. 'Shall I let them back in now?'

'Yes.'

Sorcha admired Monica for pausing the consultation and confronting the situation immediately, and when both men returned she resumed where they'd left off.

'So, a contraceptive fail at the end of September, then.' She explained things to Luke as she went. 'Sorcha's been taking the mini pill. Have you had any pregnancy symptoms, Sorcha?'

'None.'

'She's gone off coffee,' Richard added, and she was grateful for him mentioning that, as it made them almost sound like a couple. Perhaps it shouldn't matter to Sorcha what people thought, only it did.

It mattered to her, and she rather thought it might one day matter to their baby.

'Any morning sickness?' Monica asked.

'None,' Sorcha said. 'Well, perhaps a bit, but nothing I've really noticed.'

'I'm just going to check your blood pressure,' Monica said.

'It's always a bit low,' Sorcha told her.

'It is,' Monica agreed. 'But it's on the low end of normal. Have you eaten this morning?'

'A giant chocolate cookie...' Sorcha recounted her sins. 'A bag of crisps...'

Sorcha turned as May came in. 'And some mint slices,' May reminded her.

'Okay.' Monica nodded. 'Let's have a look at your stomach.'

Sorcha saw Richard's slight grimace at the sight of her

abdomen and Monica's eyes briefly flashed. 'You're going to have quite a bruise...' She gently palpated the area where the injury had occurred, again explaining things to Luke. 'The mother's health has to come first. We can't just worry about the baby if she's bleeding elsewhere. I'll be putting in another IV—I think that's wisest. With any blunt trauma in pregnancy it's good to have two lines in.'

She smiled to Sorcha.

'Sorry that I'm talking over you, but I'm talking to Luke about a more advanced pregnancy. Your little one is still quite tucked away.' Monica moved her hands further down. 'Yes...' She called Luke over and he had a feel of her fundus, and then Monica smiled and took Sorcha's hand, placing it gently where her own and Luke's had just been. 'Can you feel that?'

There was a little wedge of muscle just above her pubic bone.

'Yes,' Sorcha nodded. 'Though barely...'

'It's just starting to emerge, but I'd certainly put you at ten to twelve weeks...'

She spoke to Luke for a moment, and Sorcha lay with her eyes closed, wondering how she hadn't known.

'Richard, could I ask you to wait outside again?' Monica asked.

This time Luke stayed, though he remained at the head of the bed as Monica performed a gentle internal.

Again she spoke to Luke. 'You'd ask if there was any bleeding, or if the waters had ruptured...check underwear if the patient's unconscious.' They discussed seat belt injuries as Monica replaced the blanket and then removed her gloves. 'Everything seems fine, Sorcha.'

Sorcha couldn't take it in and she didn't know how she felt—let alone fathom how Richard must be feeling.

'It's a lot,' Monica said. 'I was just explaining to Luke that if you were further along we'd put you on a CTG monitor and observe for a few hours.' Monica paused. 'You've obviously had no prenatal care? We'll get some blood work done, the same as I do for all my prenatal mothers, and we'll do a cross match, just in case. For now, we'll get an ultrasound to check dates and the position of the placenta. And I might ask the surgeons to come and take a look—just to check your spleen. I do tend to err on the side of caution. We'll keep you nil by mouth for now.'

'Can't you check if the baby's okay now?' Sorcha said, suddenly desperate to know that the incident hadn't hurt the little life inside her. 'With a Doppler?'

'Sorcha, its heart will be the size of an apple pip. I don't want you to get upset with me trying to locate it. It's better that we do an ultrasound and find out what we're dealing with.'

'Okay.'

'I know my colleague Sandra is on this morning. I was just talking to her about another patient. She's excellent. I'll ask her to take care of you, and she'll let me know.' She filled out a mountain of forms. 'Do you know your blood group?'

'I don't,' Sorcha admitted.

'Okay, after the ultrasound—so long at the surgeons are happy—we'll move you up to Antenatal and I'll come and see you there.'

She smiled at Sorcha and she and Luke trooped out, and then Richard came back in.

'It's all okay,' he said.

'It's not, though.' She heard the shudder in her breathing. 'I don't know what to do.'

'Nothing for now,' Richard said. 'We just need to make sure that you're well.'

There was a flurry of activity as the surgeons came and checked her, and then there was a long lull, but finally she was being moved to Imaging.

'What a morning you're having,' May said. 'And from here they're going to take you up to Antenatal.'

There was so much to think about that Sorcha found she couldn't concentrate on one single thing, so she just watched the ceiling whizz by and then waited in a corridor until a porter came and wheeled her towards a radiography room.

'Do you want to come in?' she asked Richard, who really did look a little grey now. 'I'll get it if you don't.'

'I'll come.'

Richard heard his own rather terse tone and moved to check it, although he actually felt a little ill. Not from lack of sleep, or even the events of this morning…just from being in Imaging, with someone he cared about, ready to find out if all was well with the baby he'd only just discovered Sorcha was carrying.

It was different from what had happened with Jess, of course, but it felt somewhat the same. He pushed that worry aside and made small talk with Sandra, the radiographer, as Sorcha slid onto the examination table.

'We're just checking your upper abdomen first, where the apparent injury is…' Sandra said, and Richard knew they were first checking for anything acute that might need urgent attention.

'I didn't think you'd ever be seeing my spleen,' Sorcha said to Richard.

'Nor me.'

He smiled, but it was a forced one. There were simply too many memories raining in as he recalled looking at the mess of Jess's images and standing behind the glass in a closed-off pod.

'Are you okay, Richard?' Sorcha asked worriedly.

She'd obviously picked up on his discomfort, though he was trying very hard to hide it from her.

'Yes,' Richard answered, reminding himself that surely he should be the one asking Sorcha that. 'How do *you* feel?'

'Honestly? Fine. Just nervous.'

'There's no sign of contusion…' said Sandra, and Richard was relieved that there were no signs of bleeding and everything appeared normal. 'Everything looks fine.'

'I meant…'

He knew Sorcha was worried about the baby. Scared to find out that she was pregnant one minute and then wasn't the next.

The radiographer moved the probe lower, and Richard saw that Sorcha was holding her breath.

Then they heard the heartbeat and saw it on the screen… the baby's heartbeat…whooshing and rapidly galloping.

'Goodness,' Richard said, unable to move his eyes from the screen.

There was a whole other world there…a whole life. It was moving, and perfect—a little cord, and legs, tiny feet and a face.

And while he still didn't know how he felt, the images told him what mattered right now.

He'd always tried to be a good man, but he swore to do better.

As they waited for Sorcha to be moved up to Antenatal he had a suggestion. 'Why don't you stay at mine for a while?'

'Yours?' Sorcha shook her head. 'We don't know each other. We're hardly—'

'Just listen for a moment. You need to rest, and at some point we need to talk. Your flat share doesn't sound ideal.'

'No, it isn't. But I feel that I want to be on my own.'

'I can drive you up to your parents', if you'd prefer—?'

'No,' she interrupted. 'I won't get any rest there.' She gave a weak laugh. 'I love them dearly, but this is going to rock their world.'

'It hasn't rocked mine.'

Richard's voice was steady, and the grey tinge had gone from his complexion. Perhaps a man who had already lost so much dealt with things more calmly. Or perhaps… Her mind darted. Perhaps he didn't really care. Perhaps it was an inconvenience?

'We're going to be parents, Sorcha.'

'Yes.'

'So why don't we try to communicate?'

'I'm not brilliant at that.'

'I had noticed.' He smiled.

'And I don't like arguments.'

'Good, because neither do I.' Then, as he held her gaze, he made another suggestion. 'Stay at mine while you recover from this. I'm not going to demand answers, or police your future. You can stay in your room like a moody teenager if you want. But you're not well, and this is *our* child.'

'Living together, though…?'

'Sorcha, I am not asking you to permanently move in.' He hadn't even fully lived with his wife. 'Just think about it…'

She nodded.

'Do you want me to go now?' he asked. 'Give you some space?'

She didn't know the answer to that question. Did she want to be alone to process things? Right now things felt a little better with him here.

'Thank you for being the one to tell me,' Sorcha said. 'How did you find out?'

'May was looking guilty and trying to speak to Mr Field discreetly.' He gave a smile. 'I think she'd guessed we might not have just met the once at Edward's cardiac arrest.'

'How?'

'We like each other, Sorcha.' He was as direct as always. 'Even if we try not to admit it or show it.'

She was silent, unsure how to respond.

'If you do come to mine, nothing will happen. We will have separate rooms—I can assure you of that. We have too much to sort out without confusing things further.'

'Confusing things?'

'We're not a couple. Other people are going to think that we are, but...' His words sort of punched her in the heart with a velvet glove. 'But we *are* going to be parents. It might be nice to know where we're at before we tell the world.'

Sorcha was moved up to Antenatal then, and placed in a little four-bedded ward. She was too tired to think, let alone think straight.

'Perhaps I would like a rest,' she told Richard.

'Okay. Let me know what's happening later.' Then he clicked his tongue. 'I don't even have your phone number.'

It felt ridiculous for her to be pregnant with his baby and he didn't even have that, but Richard was right. They weren't a couple. Still, they exchanged phone numbers.

'I'll go and tidy the flat in case I have a guest arriving.'

Sorcha wasn't so sure about that. While it would give them a chance to talk, and it would certainly be a more conducive place to heal than her flat share, Sorcha wasn't so sure it was the sensible choice.

She liked him.

A lot.

More than she dared admit even to herself.

And she was having his baby.

When he'd gone, a midwife came and told her she was no longer nil by mouth. 'I've got some sandwiches for you,' she said.

'Thank you.'

'Do you want me to pull the curtains?' she offered. 'Perhaps you could have a little rest? You've been up all night, I hear.'

It was noisy on the ward, but somehow the curtains did block out the world a bit. Sorcha could hear the noise of the department, but for the first time since the gurney had slammed into her she was alone with her thoughts, and grateful that Richard had given her the space to be.

Monica came in and woke her a few hours later, still with Luke.

'Well, the ultrasound was normal,' she said. 'The placenta is nice and high, and the little one is unperturbed. You're twelve weeks pregnant, Sorcha. I know it was unplanned, but you're almost into your second trimester, so if you're considering not going ahead with the pregnancy…'

'I'm not having a termination.'

'Then congratulations,' Monica said. 'Your baby has a due date of June the tenth.'

Then Monica took a thorough history. There were a lot of questions, especially as she explained things to Luke along the way. They discussed everything from her uterus to her mental health and her accommodation.

'I think I'm staying at Richard's.'

'Okay,' Monica said. 'I'll sign you off work for two weeks and see you in clinic before you return.'

'I don't need that much time off—' Sorcha started, but then she sank back into the pillows. Maybe it would be better to have that time to sort things out with Richard. And even though she'd insisted she was fine, the events of today had upset her.

'These things can take a few days to catch up with you,' Monica said. 'You've had a proper fright. Still, I'm very happy with how things are—though you should bear in mind that you're going to be very tender from the bruising, so I want you to really try and rest over the next few days.' She checked her notes. 'I think that covers anything. Do you have any questions for me?'

Sorcha did. Because there was one question that hadn't been asked or answered.

When could she resume sex?

It was an odd question, because she hadn't had sex in ages, and she was only staying at Richard's so they could sort out their cover story, but...

He was still the most attractive man she'd ever met... still the only person who could look right into her eyes and truly see her.

But Monica seemed to think the consultation was over.

Just as Monica walked off, Sorcha met the paramedic's eyes.

'Monica?' Luke said, and Monica turned. 'Sorry...' He was going through his notes. 'I must have missed it...when can the patient resume intercourse?'

'Oh!' Monica came back over. 'Sorcha, I'm sorry—I

thought I'd said that. Sex is fine. As long as you're comfortable, of course.'

'Thanks,' Sorcha said, and the paramedic gave her a smile. 'Thanks,' she said a second time.

Not that she had any intention of finding out.

It was just good to know!

CHAPTER NINE

SORCHA CALLED RICHARD a short while after they'd gone.

'Monica said that the scan was perfect and she's happy. I can go home.'

'That's good. Have you thought about what I said?'

'Yes,' Sorcha said.

She'd thought about it a lot.

'I know it's a dreadful inconvenience…'

'I invited you,' Richard pointed out.

'If I could stay at yours that would be great.'

'Let's just take care of you for now.'

On leaving the hospital, Sorcha immediately regretted her decision to stay at Richard's. As the taxi drove them towards Canary Wharf she desperately wanted to change her mind and go to her crummy flat, or ask that he drive her the six hour journey to Scotland, but soon they were in an elevator.

'I'm on the nineteenth floor,' Richard said, as the lift made pinging noises all the way up, then informed the occupants in an American accent that they'd reached floor nineteen.

'That voice drives me crazy,' Richard said as they stepped out into a hall with subdued lighting. 'I'm in apartment six.' He took out some keys. 'I just got this cut for you; I'd better make sure that it works.'

It did, and just as she was thinking once again that it had been a huge mistake to agree to staying here, the door opened to a view of London that had her breath catching in her throat.

'Welcome,' he said.

And he did just that. He made her feel incredibly welcome.

The view was incredible, but for now she just took in the soft, long leather couch and easy chair, and the low coffee table. It was a large lounge area, yet the artwork and the rug made it feel warm and inviting.

'I can smell polish,' Sorcha said, sniffing the lemony smell of beeswax in the air. 'Did you get a cleaner in?'

'I tried to.' He gave a wry laugh. 'She was booked out today so I had to do what I could.'

'It looks gorgeous.' She smiled.

'You won't be needing to see that for now,' Richard said, pointing towards a very plush-looking kitchen with black work surfaces. And then he gestured to a large study. 'Or that.'

He led her down a long hall.

'That's my room at the end...'

He hadn't closed the door and she could see a large unmade bed.

His bed.

She averted her eyes and he pushed open a second door. 'It's been a bit of a store room until today...'

'It's lovely.'

It really was. She even had her own bathroom which, after weeks of sharing the facilities at her flat, felt like the height of luxury.

'I've put a couple of my T-shirts and things in a drawer. I can go and collect some of your own clothes tomorrow, if you like.'

'I can do that.'

'No, you can't,' he said. 'You're here to get better. Just make a list. Or you can just make do for a few days. Now, what would you like for dinner?'

'I don't mind…whatever you're having.'

He took out his phone. 'I'm not offering to cook.'

'Pasta,' Sorcha said. 'But not loads.'

'Easy.'

He made what might have been awkward and difficult so easy.

'Right,' he said, once he'd ordered dinner. 'We're not talking about anything tonight.'

'You say that now…'

'I mean it,' he said. 'Under normal circumstances you'd have found out you were pregnant first, and then…' He shrugged. 'I don't know. However, you'd have had some time to come to grips with it.'

She nodded.

'So, let's keep to that. Unless you want to talk now?'

'Not yet.'

He'd made her feel so welcome, and now he was making what might have been a very difficult night so much easier.

Soon she was sitting on the sofa as Richard served up two bowls of creamy pasta carbonara, and she knew she wasn't waiting for him to pounce on her with questions.

They watched a spy show…a favourite of his.

'They all look normal,' Sorcha said.

'That's the point.'

It was a very sexy spy show, as it turned out, and watching that was possibly the only awkward moment between them.

'Sorry about that,' he said, taking her plate and rolling his eyes at the very sexy scene that they'd just had to sit through. 'Have you had enough to eat?'

'Plenty.'

'How's your stomach?'

'It's okay. I think I'll go to bed, though. I've hardly slept all day.'

'Of course.'

'I might have a shower first?'

'You don't have to ask permission.' He smiled. 'I got some shampoo and stuff for you.'

He had.

Shampoo for curly hair, and conditioner too!

It was nice to have a shower, but then she caught sight of her reflection as she stepped out and the vivid purple bruise high on her stomach made her breath catch. She thought of the little life within her and suddenly panicked, thinking how different things might have been.

'Don't go there,' she told herself aloud, drying off and then pulling on one of the T-shirts Richard had left for her.

She was so tired that she was certain she'd be asleep the moment she lay down, but instead she lay awake in the dark, with her mind racing back not just over the day's events, but over recent weeks.

How could she not have known she was pregnant?

She'd felt sick, and been dizzy a couple of times, but she'd been upset since that morning at the hotel.

Then she thought about what Monica had said—about it being close to decision time if she didn't want to go ahead with the pregnancy.

Would Richard want to discuss that?

She needed some water, and wished she'd thought to bring a glass to bed. She wondered about drinking from the tap in her bathroom, but that would be stupid when the kitchen was just down the hall.

'Hey...' Richard was standing at the living room window, looking out at the night, as she came out of her room.

'I was just getting a drink.'

'I meant to leave a jug of water and a glass in there...' He turned and smiled. 'My turn-down service isn't up to par.'

She filled a glass and took a long drink, then filled it again and walked over and looked out onto a night that had turned golden.

'Wow, look at all the lights.'

'I know,' he agreed. 'That's what sold it to me. I wasn't so sure—it used to all be offices around here. But the real estate agent was astute enough to bring me back at night.'

'It's so bright.' Sorcha gazed out and tried to get her bearings, looking at the black snake of river. 'Where's the hospital?'

'That way,' Richard said. 'And the palace is that way...'

She could see trains sliding into their stations like toys, and the whole of London was spread out before them.

'My flat in Scotland backs onto a huge park,' Sorcha said. 'The Glen—well, that's what the locals call it. There's just the tops of the trees and the sky...'

'Nice?'

'I could look at it for hours,' she admitted. 'I often do.'

'You miss it?'

'Yes.'

It wasn't homesickness that was troubling her now, though, and as she stared out at the endless buildings she wished she was good at broaching difficult topics.

She wasn't, though, so instead she blurted out what had been keeping her awake. 'You told me that you don't want children.'

He was silent for a moment before responding. 'Jess and I didn't...' He paused. 'Jess couldn't have children.'

'Oh.'

'She had a lot of gynae issues in her twenties.'

'I shouldn't have said anything.'

'Of course you should have. Look, it didn't seem fair to serve up her medical history whenever people asked, so we just said that it wasn't for us.'

'Might it have been? If she could have...?' Sorcha's voice trailed off. She knew her question was perhaps unfair. 'I'll say goodnight.'

'Night, Sorcha.'

Richard had been unsure how to answer that question and was grateful for the reprieve.

He lay on the sofa, looking out at the night, pondering Sorcha's question. Not so much whether he and Jess would have had a baby if they could have had one, but how he felt now that Sorcha was pregnant.

Having his baby.

For so long babies and children had been removed from the equation, and then a few short hours ago all that had changed.

He was going to be a father.

A parent.

How did it feel?

He didn't yet know.

The only thing he could say was that it didn't feel wrong.

Just very, very new...

Her first week at Richard's passed in a bit of a blur.

True to his word he didn't push for conversation about

the pregnancy, but he brought her a mug of tea in the morning and they'd chat…

About how she'd slept.

How she felt.

'Better,' she said today, but then spoiled it by wincing as she sat up.

'Can I see?'

She nodded and lay back and lifted her T-shirt—or rather his T-shirt. It wasn't the first time he'd checked on her injury.

'Today's the worst day,' she said, and pulled the T-shirt down.

'Is it really sore?'

'More that it feels tender.' She shrugged. 'I didn't think it was that bad at the time. I get now why I'm here.'

'And why is that?'

'I'm pregnant with your baby.'

'I'm glad one of us has the answer.' Richard certainly didn't sound glad. 'Sorcha, that's a bit of an insult. I was concerned about you even before I knew about the baby.'

'You feel responsible.'

'I *am* responsible,' he retorted.

She squeezed her lips tight. Clearly he didn't know what he'd said wrong.

'That's actually a good thing, Sorcha,' he went on.

'Is it?'

It was the worst thing, Sorcha thought as she lay on her side, trying not to cry.

He was stuck with her.

As she was sure her parents felt they had been.

'Sorcha…' He came back a little while later and sat on the edge of the bed. 'We'll talk when you're ready. But know this… You're not on your own. You don't have to do this on your own. I know I'm not exactly ideal relationship material, but I will do everything I can to be there for the baby.'

'I know.'

It should help—and in many ways it did.

He was a very decent man and she knew he would do the right thing.

It was another piece of him she wanted, though. But that part belonged to someone else.

The second week brought things into sharper focus.

He collected her things from her awful flat and his silence was palpable as he handed her the holdall she'd been carrying on the day they'd met.

'Thanks.'

She didn't want his verdict on her flatmates and so she went through the bag, delighted to see her computer and all her personal effects.

'Why did you pack my bikini?'

'There's a pool here.'

'This isn't for swimming,' she said.

'What's it for?'

'Holidays,' Sorcha said. 'Lying by the pool.'

He smiled then, that serious face slipping away, and he melted her with the curve of his mouth and the little crinkle at his eyes.

'You're quite complicated, Sorcha.'

'I'm really not.'

'Oh, but you are.' He looked at her. 'We still haven't really spoken…'

'I know,' she said. 'I'm just trying to get my head around things.'

'Are you…?' He paused. 'Are you upset or…?'

'No,' Sorcha said. 'I'm still a bit stunned.'

'Did you ever picture yourself having children?' He gave her an apologetic smile. 'You did once ask me the same question.'

'I did,' she agreed. 'I don't know—and that's the truth. I wanted to sort things out with Amanda. But I'm not good at getting close to anyone, really. I know we fell into bed, but that really was an exception for me.'

'And for me.'

'Come on,' she said. 'You're not looking for anything serious.'

'I wasn't looking, full stop,' Richard said. 'Sorcha, you seem to think I was out on the pull that night?'

'No.' She shook her head. 'But I get it…' She shrugged.

'What?'

'Well, you come to London for a break, and…'

'I come to London to work, and sometimes I catch up with friends.' He frowned. 'You're the only person I've slept with since Jess's accident.' He frowned and she thought perhaps she wore a disbelieving expression. 'Is that so hard to accept?' he asked.

'It's been three years.'

'Three hellish years.' He nodded.

She inhaled sharply 'I thought…'

'Don't think. Ask,' Richard said. 'And when you're ready to talk, we'll do so.'

They did talk—though not about the issue. They spoke about so much, and Richard found himself liking their mornings together. And he was aware of a slight twitch to his lips when she said goodnight and headed to bed.

He'd sworn never to get involved again.

Not just out of loyalty.

More self-preservation.

Yet there was another heartbeat in his home. Two, in fact. And despite it being winter, the world felt warmer. Sorcha returned to work but there was no mention of her returning to her dreadful flat share, and for that Richard was very grateful. Instead, they'd settled into a comfortable routine. Days quickly passed, with both of them working their shifts and spending time together when not at work.

There was colour back in his life…literally.

Sorcha pointed out every rainbow.

'A double one…' she'd say, and he'd come out of his study and take a look.

There were also pastel-coloured knickers and bras tumbling in his dryer.

He came home from a very brief trip to Wales and his heart felt like lead.

No, he did not want to fall in love again.

It bloody hurt.

'What on earth…?'

There was a real Christmas tree in his lounge room, dressed in silver tinsel and red baubles, and there were reindeer on his marble countertops and a gingerbread house.

'Happy Christmas!' Sorcha smiled. 'I couldn't help myself.'

In truth, she'd been antsy all day, knowing where he was.

'How was the visit?' she made herself ask.

'It was okay,' he said.

They cooked pasta together and ate it in the dark, aside from the blaze of London and the twinkling tree.

'Do you have plans for Christmas?' he asked suddenly.

'I'm on an early, and then I'm spending the evening at Amanda's. What about you?'

'I'll go to my sister's on Christmas Eve, and then on to Wales Christmas morning. Are you looking forward to it?'

'I don't know,' Sorcha admitted. 'I want it to be incredible and...' She gave a soft laugh. 'I want her to love me, I guess.'

He smiled at her honesty.

'And not just a little bit,' Sorcha said. 'I want her flat all decorated for me, with mince pies and chestnuts laid out. My parents do all that...'

'Are you maybe looking for love in all the wrong places?'

He made her smile as he addressed the permanent ache in her heart.

'Probably,' Sorcha said, and she looked over to Richard and realised he could be more than a little bit right.

She loved sitting here with him.

As much as she had loved sitting with him at Kings Cross and watching the world go by.

'Are *you* looking forward to Christmas?' she asked.

'I like catching up with my sister and seeing her kids.'

'What about when you're in Wales?'

'We have decorations and mince pies and all this forced joviality.' He thought for a moment. 'I wonder what we'll be doing next year?'

She knew he was trying to broach the subject—to get even a glimpse of what was going on inside her head—but Sorcha said nothing.

'Do you want to go out?' Richard suggested.

'When?'

'Now,' Richard said. 'We can go and see the Christmas lights.'

'It's late,' Sorcha said.

'Next year might be full of teething and babysitters.'

'I would love to see the lights.'

They walked down Oxford Street and Sorcha thought it was wonderful to be in London again. Or was it simply wonderful that she was looking at the Christmas lights with him?

'We'll do the tour,' Richard said.

It was an open top bus tour of London at night, and they sat on the open-top deck. But even with his arm around her and the dreadful woolly hats they'd quickly purchased, it was only just above freezing.

'Look at that...' They saw the London Eye, all lit up in pink, and the Shard, and then they travelled on to Westminster.

They reached Buckingham Palace and she saw the balcony. 'Do you do this every year?'

'I don't do this sort of thing ever. I only like doing these things with you.'

'What things?'

'Silly things.'

They got back to his flat and ate the hot chestnuts they'd bought from a stand, and then on Sorcha's demand he got out photos of him as a baby.

'Gosh, you were born serious!' She laughed, because, honestly, he was almost scowling in all the pictures.

It felt a lot like a first date.

Or a second or third.

But with no kisses.

They were trying, both of them, to take things slowly.

CHAPTER TEN

Christmas Eve

RICHARD WOKE AND it actually felt like Christmas Eve.

He could hear carols playing and Sorcha singing, and something better-smelling than muffins was baking in the oven.

He peeked in and saw there were fat sausages wrapped in bacon roasting. Very possibly it was the perfect breakfast.

He knocked on her bedroom door.

'Wait!' Sorcha said, and he rolled his eyes as he heard her moving things around. 'Okay, now you can come in.'

She was sitting on the bed, wrapping a huge box of candles.

'Does that mean I have to get you a present?' he asked.

He saw the flash of disappointment on her face and smiled. He knew what he'd bought for her, and he was actually looking forward to being back here with her on Boxing Day.

'What time do you head off?' Sorcha asked.

'Late afternoon—traffic will be bad. Are you going to stay at Amanda's today?'

'No.' Sorcha shook her head. 'I'll go there from work tomorrow. I'm just going to drop the presents off now, and the piggies in blankets.

'I can smell them. I was knocking to ask if there were any available for us.'

'They should be ready.'

It was a gorgeous Christmas Eve breakfast, but all too soon it was time for Sorcha to go. And for Richard it felt as if Christmas was over already.

'I'll see you on Boxing Day,' he said.

'You shall.' Sorcha smiled. 'And then we've got a whole week off.'

'I hope it goes well with Amanda.'

'So do I.' She smiled. 'Happy Christmas.'

He wanted to kiss her—but then he always did.

Actually, he would like to cancel Christmas—at least the one that was planned—and haul Sorcha to bed and turn off his phone.

Instead, he loaded the car with presents for Jess and her family, as well as for his sister and the little ones.

The motorway was surprisingly clear for Christmas Eve, but it didn't offer him relief. He felt as if he was hurtling in the wrong direction.

'Richard!'

Gemma was delighted to see him, and it was great to see the kids, but his smile slipped as his sister put her overexcited children to bed and he stared out of the black kitchen window.

'I know.' His sister's hand came on his shoulder. 'It's a difficult time.'

She was offering him support, only it felt undeserved. Her assumption that he was pensive tonight because of Jess was wrong, and he didn't want to milk things. Ever.

'It's not Jess,' Richard said. 'I've met someone.'

'Richard?' He could hear the shock in Gemma's voice. 'I had no idea you were even back out there.'

'Nor did I,' he admitted. 'Her name's Sorcha.'

'And where is she now?'

'Either about to have the best Christmas or the worst,' Richard said. 'And I feel I should be there with her.'

Sorcha was having the worst Christmas.

A text to Amanda had bounced back, and she was having a sense of déjà-vu as she saw the full mailbox at Amanda's flat.

She knocked, and knocked again, and then a man came out with a little dog.

'Amanda's not here.'

'I can see.' Sorcha smiled. 'I just wanted to drop these off. Do you know when she'll be back?'

'She moved out at the weekend.'

Sorcha fired off another text and almost folded in relief as Amanda swiftly responded.

At least until she read it.

Undeliverable.

She'd been blocked.

Again.

It wasn't like last time, Sorcha told herself as she clattered down the stairs. She was older, and she had gone into this with eyes wide open. She'd known there wouldn't be rainbows and unicorns…

But the pep talks didn't help.

And all she knew was that she wasn't wanted.

Again.

It felt as if her heart was a dartboard, with all the little stings of shame, but somehow she got through her shift.

When she let herself into the flat, she didn't even turn the Christmas lights on.

She didn't understand… Why had Amanda got in touch just to do this again?

And what was she, Sorcha, doing here when she had a family in Scotland?

The only reason she was here now was Richard.

And the only reason she was here in Richard's home was the baby they'd made.

She wasn't going to tell him what had happened. Sorcha made her decision as she fell asleep and woke up feeling the same way.

The streets were empty—that was the only good thing about Christmas morning, Sorcha decided. But she smiled and wished everyone Happy Christmas, and pulled crackers with the night staff, and then she dealt with a croupy baby and saw him up to the children's ward.

It was a happy place to be on Christmas morning, and Sorcha smiled as she watched a huge rabbit giving out gifts.

'Isn't that the Easter Bunny?' David, the porter, frowned.

'Shush.' Sorcha smiled. 'He's wearing tinsel.'

It was when she got back to the unit that things fell apart.

'Phone for you, Sorcha,' called one of her colleagues.

'Sorcha speaking?'

'Happy Christmas.'

The voice was unexpected. She'd been expecting it to be the path lab, with some results she'd been chasing, but it was Richard.

'I tried your mobile.'

'It's in my locker.'

'I realised that. Is it busy there?'

'No,' Sorcha said. 'It's actually quiet. How's your day?'

'Quiet,' Richard said. 'How's Amanda?'

'I'm going there tonight.'

'I hope she appreciated the sausages yesterday.'

'Yes.' Sorcha pressed her thumb and forefinger into her eyes. 'She did...'

But she knew her voice was croaky and that he must have noticed.

'Sorcha?'

'She's...'

'What?'

'Please don't ask,' Sorcha said. 'I have to work.'

'Are you seeing Amanda tonight?'

'No,' Sorcha said. 'But I think I knew it was coming. I have to go...'

As terrible Christmases went, it was getting worse...

'It's croup city,' May said, and sure enough here were two more babies, barking like little seals.

'She's okay,' Sorcha said to one anxious mum. 'I know it sounds dreadful...'

'It sounded worse at home.'

'The damp air outside helps.'

The Easter Bunny was still masquerading as Santa Bunny when she took one of the baby seals up to the ward, and there was a puppet show too. She stayed to watch for a few moments and saw the staff making such an effort.

The consultants were wearing Santa hats, and there were smiles on some of the parents' faces as they sat by their very ill children's bedsides, and that made her own problems less.

The gratitude stayed with her. Sorcha even wore her flashing earrings on the way home and then let herself into the empty flat.

Only it wasn't so empty. It smelt spicy and delicious as she stepped in, and the lights on the tree were on.

'Hello?' she called, and was startled as Richard appeared.

'Happy Christmas,' he said.

'I thought you were being burgled.'

'Do you say hello to all home invaders?'

He smiled, and she both cried and laughed as she embraced him.

'What are you doing here?'

'It's where I want to be.'

'Is that a new jumper?' She ran a hand over grey cashmere. 'It's very nice…'

And then she realised she was stroking his chest. And it felt as if her hand had got stuck…as if the cashmere turned to Velcro. And she had to pull it back to remove it.

Oh, she shouldn't have touched him.

She truly hadn't meant to.

He politely pretended not to notice, and handed her a glass of alcohol-free mulled wine. 'It tastes dreadful—be warned!'

It did. But it was instantly her favourite drink.

'Come on,' he said, 'we are going to eat.'

Only he didn't pull out his phone, and there were no signs of recent deliveries as he led her to a beautifully dressed table, lit with red candles and decorated with holly, and laden with slices of turkey, ham, stuffing and all the trimmings.

'Gemma,' he said by way of explanation. 'I went begging.'

'Gemma's the pretty one?'

'Correct,' he said, and then confessed, 'I've told her.'

He pulled out a chair and she sat down.

'What did she say?' asked Sorcha.

'I've been fully lectured,' he said. 'I actually called you

this morning because by the time I got to Wales I felt guilty for teasing you. Of course I'd got you a gift...'

She looked beneath the tree and there was a box. Medium-sized. And, no, she wasn't expecting a ring, but it looked very jewellery-ish, and there was another flat box by its side.

'Which one's mine?'

'Both,' Richard said. 'Sort of.'

'Can I open them now?'

'No.'

They ate, and it was a lot of food when she'd been grazing all day, but it was gorgeous to eat by candlelight.

But there was something she had to know.

'What about...?' She swallowed. 'What did you say to Jess's family?'

'I said I'd been called in to work.'

He knew it sounded a cop-out, and he wanted to explain that he knew decent people didn't ruin others' Christmas Day, but that would only hurt. So he didn't explain...

'What's this?' He looked at a large box that looked rather similar to the gift she'd wrapped for Amanda. 'Candles?'

'Open it.'

Sorcha was blushing, and wondering if she'd got his gift dreadfully wrong.

'A medical compendium?'

'With flash cards and all the bits...' she said. 'I don't know if it will help with your studies, or if I'm pushing...'

'You're not pushing,' he said. 'I'm going to go for it. The exam's in May, then the baby arrives in June.'

'I'm pleased.'

She smiled, and then it was her turn to open her gifts. She reached for the small one…the exciting-looking one.

'Open the other box first…'

It was all ribbons, and she tore at them, and then at more paper, and then she opened the dark blue velvet box inside.

'Oh…'

It was a dress watch, silver, with gorgeous Roman numerals. When she put it on, he helped with the fiddly clip and it actually fitted.

'How did you manage to get my size?'

'Your hospital wristband,' he told her, revealing his devious ways.

'It's perfect.' She would remember them meeting every time she looked at her watch. 'When every second counts you tend to notice them.'

'Yes.'

He made every second count.

She opened the flat box, and found it was a tiny silver frame in the shape of a bell.

'A photo frame for the Christmas tree,' Richard said. 'I thought we could get a picture of us for the baby.'

She looked up.

'Whatever happens between us, our baby will know we mattered a lot to each other.'

'We did.'

She teared up, and then quickly went to put some lip balm on and let down her hair. She moved to take the flashing earrings out.

'Keep them in,' he said, and they went to sit on the couch and took a few photos, capturing their first Christmas.

She lay there scrolling through them.

'That one,' Richard said.

Only Sorcha didn't answer. Because she'd felt something like a little tickle, only stronger.

'It moved.'

'Sorcha—'

'It did.'

'You're only sixteen weeks...'

'Almost seventeen.'

He slipped up her top and looked at her stomach. It wasn't flat, even when she was lying down.

'I know I felt it,' Sorcha said. 'Like a little bird.'

'I can't feel anything,' he admitted. He knew the baby was too small to be felt just yet, but soon...

And then he saw the flash of red hair above her knickers.

And she was looking right at him as his fingers made light circles on her stomach.

And she was willing his hand to move down, just staring at his mouth and watching his lips press together.

And she didn't know that passion could be so instant.

'We agreed,' he said, pulling down her top. 'I gave you my word.'

'Even soldiers get an amnesty at Christmas.'

'We're not at war.'

'Exactly,' Sorcha said. And when he lowered his head and kissed her she felt every fear and every last bit of upset dissolve into nothing. His kiss was so slow and deep it chased everything other than this moment away.

'This isn't sensible,' he warned.

'I don't care.'

It felt right. It felt better than right.

He stripped off his cashmere and her Velcro hands were back, stroking his skin and the fan of hair on his chest. And then she was kissing his neck and his shoulders as he knelt on the floor and she sat up on the couch.

Between deep kisses they slipped out of their clothes, and he traced her newly pink areolae.

He gave her a sensual lover's kiss that made her sigh as his tongue slid in...a kiss that was thorough and faint-making. Their lower bodies were pressing together, his hands digging into her bottom... She could honestly have come just from this kiss.

'Don't stop...' she protested as he pulled back.

And then she realised she was yet to learn there was no stopping this. He pulled her towards the edge of the sofa and exposed her sex and all the gorgeous changes there. She was hot and swollen, and as she exposed him in return, holding him again, her head on his chest, her legs apart, she just wanted to touch the dark crinkly hair for a moment, and see the beauty of him.

Then he took over, moving her right to the edge of the couch, and slid in.

She knew the feel of her, oiled and gripping, must be wonderful for him, because he groaned, and she hovered on the edge of bliss.

They both watched themselves, and it was the most erotic thing she'd ever seen. And then her eyes closed and she put her hands behind her, leaning back, feeling one of his hands pressing into her, the other exploring her breasts. Her thighs were trembling, her calves were wrapped around him, and she felt the warm spread of him, heard the harsh breaths from him.

She buried her face in his neck, almost scared to allow her release. She dared not give in. She wanted to plead and beg him for for ever. There was a desperation rising in her and she knew that she might tell this zipped-up man who had only ever loved one woman that she was completely and utterly crazy about him.

Instead, she gave in to her climax and felt him unleash. And those last powerful thrusts as she came down from her own orgasm almost shot her up there again.

'It's going to be okay,' he told her as he lowered her down. 'Come with me.'

He led her to his bed and they lay there together. He wanted to tell her that there would be no more spare room.

Ever.

But it was too soon for that, surely?

Richard lay there, staring at the ceiling, and knew that if he'd found out three years ago he was to be father to the child of a woman he'd slept with once—or rather, twice now—he'd have laughed at the ridiculousness of the situation.

Now, he lay there and felt the swell of her stomach, inhaled the scent of her hair, and he felt as he had that morning back at the hotel.

It was a feeling he examined as he quietly lay there.

Happiness?

Oh, it wasn't smiling and whistling… It was something more. It was peaceful and yet thrilling. It was a new state of normal that he'd never thought he'd feel.

CHAPTER ELEVEN

AMNESTY WAS EXTENDED to New Year's Eve.

They saved all the questions for later and simply enjoyed each other as they got to know each other.

'We should go out,' Sorcha said. 'Celebrate. We might not be able to next year.'

'True,' Richard said.

'Mexican?'

Sorcha was wearing a clinging mint-green woollen dress and loads of coral lipstick and he thought he'd never seen her go all out like that before.

And he would like to stay in.

'Spanish-Mexican?' Richard said. 'It's a restaurant at the hotel we stayed at for the conference. I wanted to try it…'

'Okay.'

'And there are views…'

'There are views here,' Sorcha pointed out, having possibly read his mind.

But it was brilliant to go out.

To be just another couple and unburdened.

'Happy New Year,' Richard said at midnight.

'Happy New Year.'

They kissed, and then they danced on a tiny dance floor, so small and crowded that there was no other way to dance than to get really close.

So close…

He breathed in her hair, that coconut scent, and he tried not to compare. But therein was the issue.

There was no comparison.

He'd been in love once, and very deeply. It had been a gorgeous, steady, slow burn.

This love—and he was almost sure that was what it was—was like a white-hot flame that danced and flickered and shot life back into his dead heart.

But he would never declare it until he was certain…

The evening before Sorcha's twenty-one-week scan they lay in bed, the world blocked out with his industrial blackout blinds, talking about the next day.

'Do you want to find out what we're having?' she asked.

'I don't mind,' he admitted.

'Do you care what we have?'

'I care,' Richard said. 'Though not about what we have.' He asked her a question. 'When are you going to tell your parents?'

'In a couple of weeks.'

'Good.'

'When are you going to tell yours?'

'I don't know.'

'What did Gemma say?'

He didn't answer. It wasn't just Sorcha being evasive. Gemma had warned him it was all too much too soon. And not to make promises he couldn't keep and rush into commitment. It wasn't just Gemma who'd voiced her doubts—word had spread through the hospital and a few friends had attempted gentle, cautious words…

He didn't want to tell Sorcha all that.

'She said not to rush you,' he told her.

'You haven't rushed me,' Sorcha said, and then took a deep breath. 'But I don't want to be second best.'

She had to ask. Had to know.

'Would we be lying here now if I wasn't pregnant?'

'Would we be lying her now if the trains hadn't been cancelled?' Richard countered.

'It's not the same,' Sorcha said. 'I don't want you to feel stuck with me.'

'What if I want to be stuck with you?'

'Would you come to Scotland?'

He didn't answer.

'The thing is, I don't know if I want to live here,' she admitted as they lay in the dark. 'I have family and friends back home.'

She closed her eyes. It wasn't just that. It was the thought of only having part of him. And she knew there were difficult times ahead. He'd been to Wales again today. Jess was having increasing seizures and that feeling in the pit of her stomach was back.

She was scared that one day he'd look over at her and realise it wasn't the right woman in his bed. Or, worse, he'd think it but be too damn honourable to say it.

But she'd know.

'*Would* you move to Scotland?' she asked.

'Sorcha, it's seven hours on a train from Edinburgh to Wales. We're talking fourteen hours travel in a day...'

'But if I asked?'

'It would mean a lot more of my time spent on trains...' He stroked her arm. 'I'd hoped you wouldn't ask just yet.'

'I see.' She took a breath. 'I know that you and Jess successfully lived in separate places...'

'It's not the same.'

'Is it because of the baby?'

'No.' He shook his head.

'Jess, then.' She breathed out. 'So I'd have to sort my family, my home, my childcare around—'

'Sorcha.' He stopped her from being mean. 'You know those guys who say they'll move heaven and earth for a woman?'

'Yes...'

'They're lying. Because no one can move heaven and earth. But I will do what I can to be there for you if you choose to live in Scotland.'

She wanted the heaven and earth guy, though. Not the logical, honest one.

Richard did not know the right answer. He felt this terrible grip in his chest when he thought of dividing himself between three countries and not being able to get to either of them enough.

No, it wasn't about the baby.

And yet...

Another person to worry about, to love...

'I'm sorry,' she said.

'Don't be. We need to talk.'

'I love my flat in Scotland,' she said. 'And not just the building. I came to London to sort things with Amanda and she's taken off. I've only got you here.'

'Okay...'

'I don't see the point of being in a flat a few miles from here...'

'What about moving in with me?' He turned to her and even in the dark saw her eyes widen.

'We haven't known each other for long enough.' She shook her head. 'That doesn't sound very...'

'What?'

They were both trying to be honest, lying there in bed and trying to sort things out, but they just chased in circles.

Sorcha was trying to hold on to her heart.

Richard was unsure if he was in a place to receive it, let alone if he even had a heart he dared give.

'We could just stay in bed for the next few months,' she said. 'Eat chocolate and make love.'

'That sounds incredible,' Richard said, but then he flicked open the blackout blinds. 'But I have to go to work so I can pay for my rail card...'

She laughed.

And somehow he liked it that he made her laugh even on those difficult days, and in those difficult conversations, and he kissed her goodbye before heading in for his night shift.

'Haemorrhoids,' May told him. 'Cubicle seven.'

'Thank you.'

'Richard,' she said, in that low tone that meant she was about to get personal. 'Can I ask you something?'

He liked May, he really did, but if one more person told him he was moving too fast and that he was heading for a crash, or not to make promises he couldn't keep...

He would never make a promise he couldn't keep.

'Of course,' he said to May.

'I've got blood in my urine.'

He turned. 'How much blood?'

'A lot. I just went to the toilet...' She was teary and flustered. 'A *lot*!'

'Come on,' he said, 'we'll go to Mr Field's office.'

'You're sure?'

'So long as you're not going to faint,' he said. 'You

haven't been eating beetroot, have you?' he teased as they walked around to the offices.

'Jesus!' she said, and started wailing as Richard frowned. 'Why didn't I think of that...?' She started to laugh. 'I had it for lunch—with walnuts and feta.'

She started to laugh, and so did he, and the oddest part for him—the truly new part—was that he couldn't wait to get home and tell Sorcha the story.

It was silly, and funny, and as they headed back all he wanted was to call her...to wake her up just to tell her he missed her tonight.

He got back to work and was mid examination when he heard a commotion outside.

There was the shout of a parent's pure fear that he'd know anywhere, but then he was relieved to hear the sound of a child crying. Vanessa and May were with them, though he kept his ears pricked and heard the parents explaining that their baby had vomited.

'Fainted?' a woman said in broken English.

'She's okay,' he heard Vanessa reassure them, but he concluded his examination and, instead of taking bloods, told the patient he'd be back shortly.

The urgent shout that had alerted him was hard to shake off. 'What have you got?' he asked Vanessa, who was now at the nurses' station.

'Gastro,' she said. 'She's fine. She's had a few bowel actions overnight, and a vomit this morning. She's a little bit dehydrated. I'm going to start an IV... I'm just waiting for the numbing gel to take effect.'

'Perhaps bring her over to Resus?' May suggested. 'Mum's ever so upset.'

'I don't think all that equipment will help her to calm down,' Vanessa countered.

'But from the history the little one might have had a seizure.'

'Fine,' Vanessa said, but with a slight edge that told May she thought she was overreacting.

As May went to move the family, Richard knew he should butt out, but he couldn't.

'If May's worried…' he said. 'If any of the nursing staff are worried…' He breathed in, seeing Vanessa's features pinch, but he didn't get to finish the conversation because it was then that panic returned to the department.

The mother let out another dreadful wail and Vanessa jumped down from her stool, dashing out. Richard followed her, truly expecting to see the baby seizing or collapsed, but instead she was completely fine, patting her distraught mother's cheeks.

'It's okay,' May attempted to soothe the distressed mother. 'We just want to keep a closer eye on little Dina…'

Then the lady's knees buckled. But a very deft May must have seen it coming, because she dealt with it rapidly, as did the baby's father, guiding the mother to a seat.

In the midst of the confusion Richard was left holding the baby.

'Are you going to vomit on me?' he asked little Dina as May helped the mother, who was wearing just a nightdress beneath her coat.

He looked to the father, who was trying to calm his wife down even though he had tears streaming down his own cheeks.

'Sir?' Richard said, and the man looked up. 'Shall we go and talk somewhere else?' When he nodded, Richard smiled at the little girl, who was now openly staring at him. 'I'm going to talk to your daddy…'

'I'll take her.' May held out her arms and the very cute

little girl went easily into them. 'Oh, Richard—she's waving to you!'

'Pardon?'

'She's waving to you.'

He didn't really do the baby thing, but she was exceptionally cute... Or was it that he'd be a father himself soon? Whatever the reason, he gave Dina a wave back, then led the father to one of the family rooms.

Richard introduced himself and asked the man's name.

'Tony,' he said, and cleared his throat.

'You're Dina's father?' he checked—because if the years had taught him anything, it was never to assume. 'You're Dina's parents?'

'Yes,' he said. 'Shula is my wife... Dina's mother.'

'What's been going on, Tony?'

'She went all floppy...'

'Did you see that happen?'

'No, my wife screamed and I ran and got the car...' He was calming down now, and took two rapid intakes of breath, then slowly exhaled. 'We lost our son...'

'How old was he?'

'Six months.'

'When did that happen?'

'He'd be ten now.' Tony gave a helpless, defeated shrug. 'We brought him here, to this hospital...that same room.'

'I'm so sorry,' Richard said. 'I know this is difficult, but I do have to ask you some questions.'

Tony nodded.

'What was the cause of death?'

'Sudden infant death...' he said. 'They couldn't tell us why. I said to the doctor just now, when she asked, that Dina was an only child. I didn't want to upset my wife. You can see how she gets.'

'Yes…' Richard paused. 'We do need to know, though.'

'I was going to tell the doctor away from my Shula.' He looked at Richard. 'Nothing can happen to Dina. We weren't ever going to have another baby; we both swore we could never go through it again.'

Richard nodded.

'When she screamed, I thought it had happened again.'

'Of course.'

'Does Dina have to be in that room?'

'She does.' Richard knew he sounded like a cold bastard, but he wasn't going to stop monitoring the baby just to appease the parents. 'We need to keep a close eye on her. And that means putting her on a cardiac monitor. If you stay calm it will help.'

'Yes.'

He went with Tony back into Resus and the mother gave him a pale smile. Dina was bouncing around on her lap.

'She's looking bright,' he said, watching the little girl who was smiling and utterly without a care. 'We're just going to pop her onto a monitor.'

'No…'

'It's nothing to be scared of.'

Richard took a couple of sticky dots from the trolley and handed one to Dina, who seemed delighted by it, and May soon had them on her chest and her pyjama top back down. He looked at the screen, pleased to see normal rhythm, but still concerned.

He brought Vanessa up to speed on the situation.

'They told me she was an only child.'

'I know they did,' Richard agreed. 'Let's get the brother's notes and see where we're at.'

'Do you think the episodes are related?'

'I sincerely hope not,' Richard said, 'but it's a possibility. I'm worried her electrolytes are out, and maybe that's caused an arrythmia.'

As Vanessa went to see another patient he looked over to the little family. Dina looked up and caught his eye and waved.

He duly waved back.

'Look at you,' May teased, 'waving to babies. I've got the brother's notes for you.'

She was busy trying to get some blood labs back, and she tapped away on the computer as he read through the brother's history.

'I remember him,' May said. 'It was awful.'

'Doctor!' Tony shouted. 'She's vomiting.'

'It's okay,' Richard said, making his way over.

May was straight on it, recording a heart trace and he watched the mother talking to her baby, trying to stay calm as she retched.

'She's okay,' he said again, even when Dina went pale and limp.

He took the baby and placed her on the bed.

'Do you want me to fast-page Paeds?' May asked, but he shook his head. Dina was opening her eyes.

'Hello,' he said to the little girl, who'd now started crying. 'You don't like vomiting, do you?'

It looked like a vasovagal; Dina had been holding her breath as she retched. But with the family history he would have to give his findings to the paediatricians.

He looked over to May. 'Call George for me and ask if he can come down...' George was the paediatric consultant on call tonight, and Richard knew that, if he was able to, he would come straight down.

'You can hold her,' he said to Shula, and she scooped the little girl into her arms.

Richard wrote his notes up by the bed, ordered some bloods and a chest X-ray, and then stood when George arrived.

'Dina's been scaring her parents,' Richard said.

'So I've heard.' George smiled at them and they went through the events of the night and looked at the heart tracing taken during the event.

'May told you about their son?' Richard checked.

'She did.' George nodded. 'Ashrim.'

Richard left the little family in George's very capable hands, and was just heading off to get changed when Mr Field stopped him.

'Richard,' he said, 'have you a moment?'

'Of course.'

It was unexpected—but then life so often was.

Mr Field asked him if he'd registered for the FRCEM exam, and Richard told him he had. 'It's in May.'

'Have you thought about a permanent role here?' Mr Field asked. 'I'm not retiring—it's Mr Owen who is.'

'Oh...'

'Don't listen to rumours.'

'I know.'

'So, is it something that might be on your radar?'

'Absolutely,' Richard said, responding with confidence even if he wasn't sure it was feasible. 'However, I should—'

'Just give it some thought,' Mr Field interrupted. 'It's something to think about.'

'Yes.'

Richard was flattered—especially after the rollercoaster of recent years—and a permanent role at The Primary was more than he'd dared consider.

It wasn't just about him, though.

How could he ask Sorcha to stay here in London when it wasn't where she wanted to be?

He felt the shudder of his heart trying to grind back into life, and didn't see how he could make things work.

He couldn't even ask her to be his wife.

Richard stopped by the ambulance bay and stood there, going through all the reasons it was impossible.

He'd been told by everyone and anyone not to rush things.

Don't make promises you can't keep.

Told that he was still grieving...

'Doctor...?'

He looked over and there was Tony.

'How's Dina?'

'They're going to take her up to the children's ward soon.' He gave him a tired smile. 'Doctor George is quite sure she is holding her breath—cheeky girl.' He smiled again. 'He wants to run some tests, though, and be very sure. I think Shula feels better.'

'What about you?'

'I don't know yet.' Tony sighed. 'Do you have children?'

'No,' he said, and then he did something he usually didn't. 'Not yet, but we're expecting a baby in June.'

It felt odd to say 'we', but he didn't know how else to say that he was soon to be a father.

'Congratulations.'

'Thank you.'

Richard smiled. Tony was the first person to say it.

Everyone else had been shocked, or worried, or warning him to be careful. It was nice to simply be congratulated.

'Do you know what you're having?' Tony asked.

'No, we've got an ultrasound later today.'

And he wasn't one for opening up—not at all—but he

admired this man who stood next to him, who'd been brave enough to risk having a child again—and, hell, he could use some help.

'Can I ask you a question?' Richard said. 'It's personal... you don't have to answer.'

'Sure.'

'You said you didn't want another baby?'

'We didn't.' Tony shook his head. 'Neither of us wanted that pain again. We didn't think we could survive it.'

Richard nodded, wondering if Dina had been an accident.

'Ashrim brought us love and hope and so much laughter...' Tony paused. 'And then suddenly, it was gone.' He paused again, then said, 'We still had love and hope and laughter, but it was very...' His hand moved as he tried to summon the words. 'Not as strong.'

Richard smiled. 'Yes.' He understood that, because after Jess's accident life had carried on, and he had been happy at times, still lived, but it had all felt...

'Diluted?' Tony said. 'My English is not so good.'

'Your English is incredible.'

Diluted was the word that had eluded Richard for three years, but it was the perfect one now. When grief was strong, joy was dimmed, diluted...

But no longer.

Over the last few years he'd looked forward to the escape of work. But now, while still enjoying work, he was looking forward to going home. To finding a treat Sorcha might have left, or to a mug of tea being placed in front of him, or to sitting with her at night, just talking.

There were undeniable problems ahead, though—and he couldn't see a solution.

'Yet you decided to try again?' he said to Tony.

'Not straight away. It was not an easy decision. All our family pressured us… "Have another baby," they said. "Try again." But we both…'

He paused, and Richard found his ears were straining, aching to hear how these people who had lost so much had known it was time to try again.

'We didn't think we could love another baby as much as our first…' He rolled his eyes. 'But you have met our beautiful daughter.'

'Indeed,' Richard said. 'She's gorgeous.'

'I knew,' he said. 'And Shula knew too.'

Richard frowned, the answer still eluding him. 'Knew what?'

'I don't know how to explain it…' Tony apologised. 'We just knew.'

CHAPTER TWELVE

AND RICHARD KNEW.

His life had been diluted.

And then triple-strength concentrated red cordial had come along—or rather Sorcha had—and turned the word as he knew it on its head.

He didn't need all the doubters, or to be warned to proceed with caution. Life was a chance to be taken…

The shops were open by the time he got out of work, and he went for coffee and made a few calls. He was just stepping onto the escalator for the Tube and heading for home when Trefor called.

'Hey…' Richard said. He was halfway down the escalator, his phone starting to cut out. 'I'm coming this weekend—'

'Come now!' Trefor yelled, and his tone was filled with the same shrill panic that had shot his nerves to alert this morning, when Dina had come in. 'Now!'

Richard had known for three years that this day would come, and had prepared for it as best he could. But now, when he heard Jess's latest dire observations, he still felt completely unprepared…

He had run for many trains—knew the schedule almost off by heart. And he spilled onto the concourse, bought his ticket, ran for the barrier and boarded the train for Cardiff.

'Richard...'

It was Jess's doctor on the phone now, and he was calm and brilliant, and by Jess's bedside, talking him through another prolonged seizure.

'We're giving her another five of Midazolam...'

The countryside was zipping by and soon he spoke with Trefor again.

'She's not doing well, Richard. What time will—?'

Then his phone cut out.

Richard stared at the black screen and tried to turn it back on. But then realised it had run out of charge.

Not now.

He asked a lady if he could borrow her charger, but she gave him such a startled look he moved on to the next person.

And he knew he must look like a mad man, because everyone looked away or avoided him.

'Sorry...'

Richard hadn't forgotten the ultrasound, or that he was meant to be meeting Sorcha.

But there were times when there was nothing you could do, and there was no right answer, nothing that could make things right...

This was his life. And it wasn't as if he hadn't told Sorcha how grave things were and how quickly they might change.

Yes, he would miss the ultrasound. He just hoped that Sorcha would understand.

Sorcha didn't understand.

Richard hadn't come home—but then again, his shifts sometimes went way over.

She was early, she reasoned, lining up at the Radiology desk.

'Sorcha Bell,' she told the receptionist.

'Take a seat.'

There were couples sitting together, and women sitting alone. Of course she didn't need him to be there.

She just wanted him to be.

More, she'd thought Richard wanted to be here for this, too.

She fired him a text—a happy, light-hearted one to say that she'd arrived—and then she waited...

Nothing came back.

Her appointment time came and went.

She stared at her phone, willing him to reply to her texts, or for him to call, but there was nothing.

He's an emergency doctor, she told herself. *Delays are to be expected.*

Something must have come up.

It didn't help to think it might be Jess.

The love of his life.

He and Jess had been together for fifteen years before the accident.

Sorcha sat there in the waiting room doing the maths.

For her and Richard to get there he'd have to be fifty and she'd be in her forties, and she felt silly for thinking she could ever come close to what he and Jess had had.

'Sorcha Bell?'

She looked up as her name was called and nodded, then made her way to the cubicle.

'Is it just you?' the radiographer asked, and Sorcha nodded again.

'Yes.'

She was on her own.

And it was time to get used to it.

Her dress was the worst possible choice to wear for having an ultrasound, and she rolled it up and lay there, feeling like a sausage roll that had burst open.

But then an image came on the screen.

'Is that...?'

Of course it was her baby—but it was incredible, seeing the little face and lips, just so detailed, legs that kicked and tiny slender feet.

Richard should be here!

What was the point of her being in London if he couldn't be here for moments such as this?

'Do you want to know what you're having?'

'No.' Sorcha shook her head. 'We wanted it to be a surprise.'

'Look away, then, because the baby's moving.'

She turned her head away and stared at the wall, but suddenly she was tired of uncertainty.

'Actually...' She changed her mind. 'I would like to know.'

It was a wonderful moment, and she cried out in surprise. She would have loved to reach into the screen to hold her little one. But that sweet moment was over too soon, and she was back on the busy London streets, and she had to double-check the map to make sure she was going in the right direction for Canary Wharf.

Suddenly she was tired of being a little bit lost in London.

Fed up with chasing people who didn't fully want her, or couldn't commit.

She took a breath. She knew Richard wouldn't appreciate being lumped into the same category as Amanda... Right now, though, he was. And she had to preserve her heart and be strong for her little one.

She put a hand over her not so small bump.

'We're going home.'

* * *

Jess was okay.

Not well, but not as bad as Richard had envisaged on the hellish journey there.

He knew the day was coming, though.

It might be tomorrow, it might be in ten years, but he would be there for her—as he'd promised.

'You gave us a fright,' Richard said gently, holding Jess's hand. 'But it's all okay now. Get some rest.'

He glanced up as Trefor came in and gave him a pale smile.

'How's she doing?' Trefor asked.

'She's resting.'

'Is your phone working now?'

'It is. They're charging it at the nurses' station.'

He'd seen the many missed calls and had fired Sorcha a text, explaining that Jess had been taken very ill…

But he knew something had to give.

'I'll have to head off soon,' he said.

'Already?'

'Yes.'

He could blame work again, but that had been a Christmas lie, and he loved Trefor and Bronwyn too much to have them inadvertently find out. They deserved far better. And even though he would do anything not to hurt them, life had already taken care of that.

'I'm just going to speak with your dad,' he said to Jess, and then kissed her hot forehead. 'I'll be back soon.'

He motioned to Trefor.

'What's this all about?' he asked as Richard headed to one of the small sitting rooms.

'Trefor…' Richard took a seat, but Trefor stood. 'I haven't

told anyone apart from Gemma, but I don't want you to hear this from anyone else.'

'What's that, then?'

'I've met someone.'

Trefor shot him a look. 'I could have saved you a confession. We knew you were seeing someone at Christmas, when you legged it out of here before lunch.'

Richard let that one go. 'We're having a baby.'

His father-in-law's reaction was just as swift and below the belt as the last. 'Well, you didn't waste much time, did you?' Trefor sneered.

Richard let that one go too, and chose not to mention that it had been three years, because he knew his father-in-law well and could already see there were tears in his eyes.

'Oh, God...' Trefor suddenly sobbed. 'A baby...'

Trefor sat down then and wept, and Richard stayed with him. 'I know it's hard...'

'You don't know!' he said, then relented. 'Of course you do.' He was a mess. 'Will you still come and see our Jess?'

'Trefor...' Richard did not let that one go. 'Look at me.' He waited until Trefor did so. 'Do you need to ask?'

He'd known Trefor since he was eighteen and Trefor had known him.

'You know that I'll still be coming here, but I'm telling you now because I'll need to be there for Sorcha too.'

'You're right.' Trefor was blowing his nose and sniffing, calming down. But this man had almost lost his daughter today. 'Oh, Richard. You a father!'

'I'll be back here in a few days,' Richard said. 'But if you need a bit of a break from me, I'll understand. We need to honest.'

'Yes.' Trefor nodded. 'I appreciate that.'

* * *

Sorcha had got Richard's text, but it felt too late for all that. She ran up the escalator at the station and this time around there wasn't a single person blocking her way.

She got a ticket in moments and there were no cancellations...

Nothing to stop her from heading straight onto the train and home.

Except the baby was kicking—real kicks—as if in protest, and it was those little kicks that had her slowing down and drawing in breath.

She didn't want to go, she wanted to stay, but more than that she wanted Richard's love.

Wanted to be the love of his life.

It was hard to accept he'd already had that when she was head over heels in love with him.

But maybe love really did make you brave, because now she did something she'd never thought she would.

Sorcha took out her phone, drew in a breath and called him.

'Hello?' he said.

'How's Jess?' she asked.

'She's stable now...just resting,' he said. 'Did you get my message?'

'About two hours after I had the ultrasound I got one that said your phone had died.'

'How did it go?'

'It went well,' she said, but didn't elaborate. 'Where are you now?'

'About half an hour from Paddington. Where are you?'

'I'm already at Kings Cross.'

'What time's your train?' he said with an edge. 'I assume you're leaving?'

His question had tears pricking her eyes.

She knew that Richard had been up all night working, and it sounded as if he'd had the most dreadful day. Sorcha knew she was a good nurse—but possibly not the best support to have at times like this…

'I can get a refund…' She sniffed. 'Richard, can we talk?'

'Yes.'

'I've got so many questions.'

'I know you have.'

'I'll wait here at the station.'

'Thanks,' he said, and rang off.

He watched the night close in as the train approached London.

And when he eventually arrived at Kings Cross, he saw her straight away, with that mane of hair he'd recognise anywhere.

She was sitting at the café where they'd passed all those hours away, and she'd been crying.

Sorcha didn't do tears very often, and had splashed her face with water and even put on some concealer.

Then she saw him.

He had on his big grey coat and black jeans, and somehow, even after being up for more than twenty-four hours, he still looked suave. Her heart soared when she saw him.

'Hey.'

He didn't play games, or sulk. Instead he gave her a kiss on the cheek and took a seat.

'I overreacted,' she said.

'You're pregnant, in a different country, with a guy who—'

'I adore,' Sorcha told him. 'But…'

'Say it.'

'I can't...'

'You can.'

She shook her head.

'I am sorry I couldn't let you know what was happening,' he said. 'I'd finished work, done a bit of shopping... I was just coming into the Underground when Trefor called. I was talking to him and Jess's doctor on the train when my phone died.'

'What happened to Jess?'

'Seizures,' Richard said. 'Prolonged.'

'I kept telling myself that something must have come up...that maybe you'd been late leaving work, or Jess... I just didn't understand why you couldn't call.'

'Sorcha,' he said. 'Next time—and there will undoubtedly be a next time—instead of trying to work out why, tell yourself that I love you and that there must be a good reason.'

She started when he said that, and her eyes shot up to warn him. 'Please don't just say that.'

'I do love you, though.' He stared at her with those gorgeous blue eyes. 'I would never say it unless I was certain, and I wasn't certain until today...but I love you.'

She swallowed. 'What happened this morning?'

'I just knew...' he said. 'I know you've been through a lot, and I know things are very up and down in my life. I had to be sure.'

'So all those times we made love you didn't know...?' She stopped, but only because he'd smiled.

'I thought I might...then I was sure I did...' Then perhaps he saw her frown. 'I've been in love,' he said. 'I thought I knew what it was. I didn't realise it could be so different.'

'We're different.'

'Not just that...' He shook his head. 'I didn't believe people who said they fell in love in a matter of days. It doesn't make sense to me. Or it didn't. But I think we fell in love that first night. I just took a few weeks to realise it.'

'A lot of weeks!'

'Sorcha, I dated Jess for seven years, I was engaged to her for five...'

He didn't want to compare, but he was finding out that was the bewildering beauty of love, and he chose to try to explain it.

'Falling in love with Jess was like...climbing a mountain together.' He watched Sorcha's lips pinch in jealousy. 'Falling in love with you was like bungee jumping.'

She actually laughed.

'Or diving off a cliff.'

'You really love me?'

'Yes—and it feels selfish. I'm not in a position to marry you... I can't promise my phone won't go and I'll have to rush off again...' He leant forward and took her hands. 'I *can* promise you that I'd do the same for you.'

'You already have,' Sorcha said. 'On Christmas Day.'

'Yes.' He smiled. 'You had questions...?'

He looked at her eyes, felt them scanning his, and even with all the questions she must have he could see the deep well of understanding waiting to emerge, and he gave her time for it.

She took in a shaky breath.

'Ask anything...' he invited, as he always had.

'I'm scared you'll feel stuck with me.'

'Like you think your parents feel?' He was possibly being too direct, but it had to be said. 'Because I happen to disagree. I think they love you. A lot.'

'You haven't even met them.'

'I've heard you talking to them, and it sounds like a pretty great relationship. And they came to Manchester that time...' He looked at her. 'I think they're worried about Amanda hurting you. I know I am.'

'I'm not just talking about my parents.'

'About Jess?' he asked. 'No.' He shook his head. 'I never thought I'd come close to feeling happy again, but I am. And if you knew how I felt when I met you, you'd know how deep the love I have for you is.'

'I know how much you love her...'

He nodded.

'And I keep thinking...' She clearly didn't know how to describe it. 'What if we'd met when Jess was okay?'

He frowned.

'If Jess had been at the conference and that thing with Edward had happened...' She swallowed. 'What would have happened to us?'

'Nothing.'

She stared back. 'I feel guilty,' she admitted.

'Please don't.'

'I still remember how dreadful I felt that morning, thinking that I could have broken up a marriage.'

'Not mine,' he said. 'Sorcha, you're not the first beautiful woman I've seen, and I'm not going to pretend like some guys that I don't even notice, but nothing would have happened between us.'

'You sound very sure.'

'Because I am sure,' he told her. 'I'll tell you exactly what would have happened. I'd have taken you to this table, bought you some drinks and snacks and made sure you were okay, and then I'd have gone.'

She nodded. 'Would you move to Scotland if I asked you?' she asked.

'I'd hoped you wouldn't ask me that again.'

'I'm asking if you would.'

And he looked right into her green eyes and knew she was challenging him, and he didn't blame her one bit. He was asking her to give up her life there because of his own chaotic life.

'No.'

He watched the column of her throat as she swallowed and knew that might have sounded harsh, especially as she was pregnant with his child, but it had been written on his heart long ago.

'The only way I can explain it,' he said, 'is to say that if the same thing happened to you—God forbid—I wouldn't move a ten-hour journey away.'

And it might be the wrong answer for some, but for Sorcha it was perfect.

'Sorcha, if you do need to be close to your family then I'll make it work... I'll commute, and then later...'

His voice husked, and she knew what that difficult pause meant.

'When it's just us, then I'll move up to Scotland...'

When he gave his love it really was for ever.

Not just in good times, but right to the end, and for someone who had been so badly let down from the cradle it meant the world.

'Come on,' he said, and stood.

She thought they were heading for the Underground, but he led them out of the station.

'Where are we going?'

'Guess...'

It was the hotel where they'd gone that first night, and where they'd welcomed in the New Year.

'Why are we here?'

'Because I want you. And the Tube would take too long to get us home,' he said, carrying her holdall as they walked through the crisp winter night.

The foyer was almost empty, and there was no one jumping out on them at the lifts—just dark and quiet and tranquillity.

'Sorry about this,' he said, picking up his phone as they stepped into the lift. 'I've got a lot of people asking after Jess. I'll just send a message.'

She watched as he put his day into a few lines.

'What are people going to say about us?' she asked.

'I think most of my friendship group knows. I've been getting a lot of messages asking how I am.'

'What about your family?'

'Gemma knows.'

'Jess's family?'

'I told Trefor today.'

'How was he?'

'He'll get there,' Richard said assuredly. 'I know he will.'

She looked over at him and thought she had never known someone as strong and yet as kind as him.

He swiped the keycard in the door of their hotel room and she saw the fairies had been in—a different lot.

There were candles in hurricane glasses, a silver tray with chocolate truffles and flowers, and an ice bucket filled with bottles of sparkling water.

'I didn't really bring you here to ravish you...' he started.

'That's not fair,' Sorcha said, and she put her arms around his neck and kissed his tired mouth.

He shrugged off his coat, and then there were her boots

and scarves. He unwrapped her like a parcel and kissed her down onto the bed.

They didn't even get in it.

They rolled together, kissing and turning, finding the tender places they needed to be, their legs scissoring each other's, taking their time to explore the other.

'Lucky me,' Sorcha said—because that was how he made her feel every day.

It was a delicious climax, watching each other, driving each other to the edge, and then just lying locked together afterwards.

Richard was on his back and Sorcha on her side, one leg over him and her coconut scented hair tickling his face. He smoothed it away.

'Stay still,' Richard said, and she frowned. 'I just felt the baby move…'

Just this little nudge…and he really wasn't imagining things.

He rolled her onto her back and, yes, their baby was moving. He felt the little kicks, and asked again about the scan.

'It was incredible,' she said. 'They're going to send us the films.'

'I can't wait,' he said, and frowned as Sorcha rolled off the bed.

Even if she was the most comfortable she'd ever been, she did have a surprise for him.

She went to her bag.

"I've got something for you…'

She pulled out the image and handed it to him.

'Meet your son.'

'You found out?'

'I did.'

'He's beautiful…'

And she knew that wasn't just a proud father speaking. It was the most incredibly detailed image…tiny nails and beautiful lips.

He stared at the image for a very long time, looking as entranced as she had been.

'I'm sorry I wasn't there.'

He wasn't so much apologising, but he was sorry to have missed it, she knew.

'I know,' Sorcha said. 'Next time.'

'Yes…'

He put the image down.

'Sorcha, you've ruined my plans.'

'I know. Nappies all the way now.'

'No, I meant for tonight. I booked the room this morning.'

'I thought it was a last-minute thing?'

'No.'

It was Richard's turn to roll from the bed and she watched as he reached into his coat.

'This morning, before it all kicked off, I went to the jeweller's where I got your watch…' He pulled out a box, and though it was her third box in only a few months, this one was little, and velvet, and if she hadn't known his circumstances she might have thought he was about to propose.

'What is it?' she asked.

'Open it and see.'

Perhaps he saw her nerves. 'It's not an engagement ring, Sorcha,' he said. 'We'll do all that when the time is right.'

Earrings, she decided, and vowed to love them even before she'd prised open the velvet lid.

She gasped when she saw a ring, and its glittering diamonds. He took it from the box. It was a semi-circle of diamonds, in silver or platinum—whatever metal it was, Sorcha didn't care. It was simply the ring she needed from him...

'It's an eternity ring,' Richard said.

'Yes...' She watched it blurring through her tears.

'I chose it because it means for ever. And, yes, it's unconventional to start with that, but...' He looked at her and she knew he told her a truth. 'I want yours to be the last face I see...'

They were the words she'd used on the day they'd met.

'It's beautiful...'

She looked up to the eyes that always steadied her. It was in the gaps, the times in between, when he wasn't there that the old fears surfaced, the constant terror of being left. But moored in his gaze she felt safe.

His love was a gift.

This really was a for ever love.

'Tomorrow,' he told her, 'I'm going to introduce myself to your parents, and we're going to tell them about the baby together.'

It was a blissful night, and in the morning they took the train to her home.

In a few hours they'd be official.

Well, they already were.

But for a moment it was still a lovely secret, waiting to be shared.

'Have you told them we're coming?' he asked.

'I have,' Sorcha said, and she could not stop smiling.

As the train pulled into Waverly she saw the castle, proud and looming, and she felt the gorgeous sense of being overwhelmed it delivered every time...

'Heart squeezing?' he checked.
'Always.'
'Let's go and meet your family.'

EPILOGUE

EXAM DAY DAWNED.

And it was a day that had been missed or cancelled too many times.

That would not be happening today.

Richard came out of the shower on a puff of steam and started to get dressed, but his eyes were watching her, as if he knew she was not being completely honest with him.

'Sorcha...?'

'Mm...?' she responded, taking a sip of tea, pretending she didn't know what he was asking as he clipped on his watch.

'Is everything okay?'

'Of course it is.'

Sorcha refused to be in early labour.

She wasn't having contractions—just a little tightening now and then. Braxton Hicks, she was completely sure. But she knew if he got even a hint, he wouldn't leave.

He came over and sat on the bed, put a hand on her stomach.

'What are you doing?' she asked, all affronted.

'You're acting strange.'

'I am not,' she said, and put the mug down. 'I'm nervous for you.'

She put her hand up and felt his gorgeous smooth jaw,

then wiped a tiny bit of shaving cream from his ear and willed her uterus to behave.

'He's awake,' Richard said, as they both watched the performing circus that was her stomach.

'Very,' Sorcha said. 'Richard, you really do need to go.'

He nodded, and removed his hand from her stomach. He gave her a light kiss goodbye, but then lingered in her embrace.

'Good luck,' she said.

He pulled away and then stood. 'You'll call me if anything changes?'

The flat felt very silent after he'd gone, and she lay down for a while, relieved she hadn't told him, because really nothing was happening.

For once the gorgeous view of London didn't distract her, even on a bright blue May day, and she found she kept checking the time. At eleven, when she knew the first exam would have started, she wandered into his study.

She picked up a heavy paperweight and then replaced it, then turned and looked at the photo of Richard and Jess. There were several of Sorcha and he around the apartment, but his wedding photo was here, not prominent, or looming over their bed or anything awkward…

Jess had died in March, with her husband and loving family around her and her closest friends…

All as it should have been.

Sorcha had gone home for a few days rather than sit alone in the apartment, and she'd spent some time with her mum…found out a few things.

Her mum had cried when she'd found out she was pregnant with Theresa. 'You were such a cheeky wee baby… we just didn't know how we'd manage…'

Her own baby was being a bit cheeky…

She took a deep breath and felt the hard rock of her stomach.

That wasn't a Braxton Hicks.

Oh, God…

She went to call Richard…to tell him that, actually, he ought to get here. But then she looked at the time. The second exam would be starting…

First labours last for ages, she told herself, and checked her book.

She lay on the bed, but then another pain came, and so she started to time them.

She rang the midwife.

'They're quite irregular,' she told her, but no, her waters hadn't broken.

And then they did—just as she was on the phone to her mum.

Her mother was a little dramatic with her advice, she thought—to Sorcha, it was almost a code violation for an A&E nurse to call an ambulance for herself. You had to be actually dying or…

Giving birth.

'I think it's coming,' Sorcha told the controller. 'I might be wrong…'

She went back to the view, resting her head on her forearm, just too deep inside herself to think of answering the ringing phone. She stared at the streets and the stations and knew that somewhere out there Richard was making his way home.

Relief rushed over her when she heard the elevator, then the thud of footsteps.

'Hello?' She heard a female voice. 'Ambulance—where are you?'

'Through here.'

She looked up, then did a double-take—because walking behind the lady was an oddly familiar face.

'I know you...' he said.

'Luke!'

It was the paramedic from that day at the hospital.

'How are you, Sorcha?' he asked, then told his partner how they knew each other.

'Richard has exams today. I'm scared he's going to miss the birth.'

'How far away is he?'

'An hour or so?'

She wasn't certain—but she rather thought she saw Luke and his partner share a small smile.

'I think,' the treating paramedic said, 'that he has every chance of making it. Do you think you can walk to the elevator?'

'Walk?' Sorcha gave an incredulous snort.

Richard made it in plenty of time!

'You knew,' he scolded, taking her in his arms.

'I didn't.'

She swallowed and just breathed him in, simply relieved he was here.

'I had the tiniest twinges... Nothing really happened until you were on your way home. Football players have to do it,' she said. 'They have to play in the final and things...'

The midwife nodded. 'And the military.'

'I'm not a footballer—nor in the military.'

It was a very quiet birth.

Sorcha went right into herself and pushed life into the world, and Richard was there, kind and constant.

And he was so calm that even Sorcha, who knew him better than anyone else on the planet, saw nothing in the glance he shared with the midwife as she checked the baby's heartrate.

'I can't do this…' she said at last, shaking her head. 'It's been hours.'

'It's not much longer now,' he said.

'You keep saying that!'

'Sorcha…'

She looked up in surprise to see Monica, tying on an apron as she read the CTG.

'Is everything okay?' she asked.

'Baby's not liking the contractions,' Monica explained. 'So when the next one comes I want you to really push.'

'I already am!'

'I know you've been working hard, but when the next contraction comes you're going to push for England, Sorcha. Got it?'

'I'm Scottish,' Sorcha snapped, masking a slight panic that something was going wrong, but Monica seemed unfazed, the midwife too, and Richard was his usual measured self.

She felt that certain feeling of calm that always descended when she met his gaze.

Confident.

Safe.

He wouldn't let her fall.

'You've got this,' he told her, and that took away her fear. And somehow she was free to do what she had to.

She pushed for more than Scotland or England. It felt as if she was pushing out an entire globe.

'Save your breath,' Monica warned when she shouted out. 'One more push.'

And then he was here.

Sorcha glimpsed big eyes and brown hair, and a very affronted look... He was long and tall and delivered high onto her tummy, and she pulled him to her chest, where he shivered and let out a husky cry.

A blanket was placed over him and she saw Richard's finger stroking his cheek. Then his hand was pulled away, and she looked up and saw his fingers were pressed into his eyes.

She'd never seen him cry.

Oh, Sorcha had guessed a couple of times that of course he must have, but now she saw this beautiful man surrender to emotion for a moment. And when she touched his cheek he gripped her hand. Today he didn't cry alone.

Life was precious...every second of it—even the storms that swept you away only to bring you back in.

'He's a mini you,' Sorcha said, already utterly in love, stroking her baby's straight brown hair and watching it fall into perfect shape. 'He looks like he's just been to the barber's.'

'Look at those eyes,' he said as they opened—they were almond-shaped, like Sorcha's. 'They're yours.'

'They *are* mine...' She nodded, fascinated to see a part of herself in her child.

'Baby Lewis,' the midwife announced. 'Born at five minutes past twelve.'

Sorcha looked up at the clock and saw that it was just after midnight.

And that felt right.

It really was a brand-new day.

'Do you have a name?' the midwife asked.

'James,' Sorcha said, because it was her dad's name— her real dad...the one who had raised her.

Or perhaps because it was the only name they'd been able to agree on.

'Nice and conservative,' Richard had pointed out.

And Sorcha was more than content with that.

* * * * *

*If you enjoyed this story,
check out these other great reads
from Carol Marinelli*

One Month to Tame the Surgeon
The Nurse's Pregnancy Wish
Unlocking the Doctor's Secrets
The Nurse's Reunion Wish

All available now!

FALLING FOR HER MIAMI RIVAL

LUANA DaROSA

MILLS & BOON

CHAPTER ONE

SOMEHOW THIS HOSPITAL was exactly the same. Granted, Allegra didn't have the experience of serving in many hospitals. Counting her most recent departure from San Francisco General, and the hospital attached to the med school she had gone to, Palm Grove Hospital was the third hospital she'd worked at. A part of her had thought she would lead the emergency medicine department at SF General for the rest of her life. That had been before her marriage had come down around her in a flaming ball of chaos.

Her phone had buzzed as Allegra had stepped into Palm Grove Hospital, her new home for the foreseeable future, and Lewis's name had lit up the screen along with the instruction *Do Not Answer!* As if her past self had thought she needed a reminder not to give her ex-husband any more of her mental space. The second their divorce had been finalised a few weeks ago, she'd accepted the first job that took her to the other side of the country so she could leave San Francisco behind once and for all. Their divorce had been contentious enough that she'd initially needed to stay close for all the meetings with lawyers and accountants. Another tactic from Lewis to exert power over her. Just as he'd done with her job at the hospital, he'd grabbed every opportunity available to delay their split to punish her. To remind her he held that power.

It was the same reason he kept calling her now, even though she hadn't answered a single one of his calls or texts.

Allegra shoved the thoughts of her ex away, focusing instead on the tour of the emergency room and the curious glances the staff shot her way as she strode in. Curious and...apprehensive? She kept her face neutral, not wanting to let on any of her thoughts. Of course, the staff would feel cautious about a new leader. People hated change, and she represented a big part of that. Still, the tension in the air was palpable, and she had to admit that she was hoping for an easy adjustment. Going by how conversations cut out as she walked past clusters of people and the whispers erupting afterwards, there would be at least some contention to deal with.

If Eliza Bailey, Chief of Medicine of the Palm Grove Hospital, noticed any of the glances she received, she didn't let it show. No, the older woman happily prattled on as she spoke about the funding the ER received from the federal government, as well as some charities run in the Homestead area.

'There are some excellent substance abuse recovery facilities that we work with in the area,' she said as they rounded another corner that led them to the nurses' station.

'I assume you have noted those facilities in the binder? Along with any other charities we're in regular contact with?' Allegra asked as she patted the binder she'd tugged under her arm earlier.

The woman had certainly prepared enough documentation for the handover, which she appreciated. Allegra had approached leading the emergency room at San Francisco General with a similar approach to detail, having a plan in place for every single contingency. She'd had to come in strong when she'd first started because of Lewis's and his family's stake at the hospital. As his wife, she'd been scrutinised far more than someone else would have been, with the accusation of nepotism never far from people's lips.

But Allegra wouldn't think about *that* right now. Or ever. There was a reason she was here, in a new hospital. Where, going by the continuing looks from her colleagues, she would have to start all over again. Not the easiest thing for the woman referred to as 'ice queen' by the people who had liked her ex better.

Allegra never deigned to repeat the less flattering nicknames.

'Yes, you can find everything you need in the binder. But I'll also introduce you to the person who put most of the information in there together,' Eliza said, and Allegra gave her a sidelong glance before forcing her expression back into an impassive mask.

The chief hadn't been the one to put together this information? It probably shouldn't surprise her. A chief of medicine would be far too busy to put together such extensive records. But if someone working in this department could provide her with such a detailed plan on how to run this ER, why weren't *they* running it?

Eliza approached the nurses' desk, where one was typing away behind her charting computer while the other one stood by the side, holding a white phone to her ear.

She gave the chief a broad smile that dimmed considerably as Allegra approached.

'*Dónde está* Jamie?' Eliza asked the nurse at the computer, who turned around in her chair before shrugging and saying something too fast for Allegra to understand.

'I'm here, Chief,' a bright voice from behind them said, in English this time, confirming what Allegra had suspected Eliza had asked.

The woman approaching them stood out from her environment for all the wrong reasons. Her hair was cropped short at the sides while remaining a few fingerwidths long at the top. Just long enough to run her fingers through them and tug her closer.

The thought popped into Allegra's head out of nowhere and she pushed it away before she had a chance to examine it. The last thing she needed was an entanglement with a colleague.

Still, Allegra couldn't help but run her eyes over the doctor smiling at her. Her lab coat was—thankfully—white, but her scrub top didn't match the colour of the trousers. Her bottom half was dark blue, while the top one was a powdery green. Allegra's eye twitched at the lack of uniformity.

Had this Jamie person somehow heard of her and chosen this outfit because Allegra had a reputation? She wasn't entirely sure if she would call her reputation fair, but, then again, she didn't really care what people thought of her as long as her emergency room performed to the high standards she envisioned. And reaching that standard usually involved a lot of pushing and arguing to the point where she ended up being the bad guy.

Allegra's assessing gaze travelled up to Jamie's face.

Her features were soft, with round cheeks and full lips that were parted in a smile. A *genuine* smile, judging from Allegra's involuntary reaction to it. Because that smile sent a zap of electricity racing down her spine and before she could even think about it, she was smiling back at the woman.

'You must be Dr Tascioni, yes?' Jamie asked and her voice skittered across Allegra's skin. Her eyes flared for a second as Jamie matched her welcoming smile with an equally warm spark in her eyes.

Silence spread between them as Allegra stared at the woman, blinking several times to try and shake off the mesmerising effect of her amber eyes.

She cleared her throat to find her voice again. 'That's correct. It's nice to meet you, Dr...?' she said, stepping forward and offering her hand to Jamie.

'Dr Rivera,' Jamie supplied, and Allegra fought the impulse to immediately pull her hand away when Jamie's fingers closed around hers. The point where their skin touched flared up with a spark of heat that left her itching beneath it. She balled her hand into a fist to not rub it against her thigh to relieve some of that strange feeling. Because that would look rather rude and, though she'd only just arrived here, Allegra knew she began her journey here on thin ice.

Except with Dr Jamie Rivera. She seemed quite happy for Allegra to be here. At least that was the vibe she got from the woman.

Was that out of the ordinary for Jamie?

'Jamie is one of our most senior ER physicians and a local to the area. So she knows not only how our emergency room works inside out but also our surroundings and the cases we tend to get here,' Eliza said, looking between them with an expression that looked a tad pinched. Was there trouble between the two women?

Before Allegra could contemplate that, the chief continued, 'I suggest you two spend some time together. Give Dr Tascioni everything she needs to get started, Jamie. We have some aggressive goals to achieve to keep the board of directors happy. Allegra, they want to see you take charge here from day one to bring up the throughput of the emergency room. They are also our investors, after all, and want to see their money at work.'

Ah, there was the word Allegra hated to hear in healthcare. *Investors.* People who knew nothing about what it meant to run an ER. All they cared about were the numbers in a spreadsheet, even though something like providing adequate healthcare should not be decided on wealth factors. Whose idea had it been to commodify healthcare?

Jamie shifted from one foot to the other, some of the brightness in her eyes wavering for a split second before it appeared again. Did she not enjoy the mention of investors, either?

'I'll have a look at the file once I've had a tour of the facilities. It's too early to tell how realistic any targets are without understanding the current state of the emergency room. I know the board wants to see results but I can't promise anything at this stage,' Allegra said, knowing full well that it wasn't the answer Eliza wanted, but she cared little for that. Though she hadn't asked the chief outright, she suspected Eliza knew who Allegra used to be married to and that she might have hired her because of the weight Lewis's family name carried in the medical community across the country. If that was the case, the woman would soon face the disappointment that would come with the knowledge that Allegra had completely severed ties with her ex and her family by marriage.

Eliza's smile dimmed, but she was wise enough not to challenge Allegra right now. Instead, she motioned towards Jamie. 'Jamie will give you a tour right now, won't you?' The last words were directed towards Jamie, who nodded with the same smile still on her lips.

No, wait. That wasn't true. There was a slight edge to it as Jamie looked at the chief. One that disappeared as she shifted her eyes towards Allegra. So there *was* some contention between the two women. That would be a fun dynamic to figure out.

And by fun, Allegra obviously meant tedious. Interpersonal relationships were the last thing she wanted to concern herself with at *any* job. It was the entire concept of mixing work life and home life that had ultimately forced her out of her old job. Because none of her *friends* had picked the ice queen over her 'life of the party' husband. No, when the dust of their divorce had settled, Allegra had found herself alone and abandoned by the people in her life. Because they'd never been her people but rather Lewis's friends and Lewis's family. She was a single child with parents that were enjoying their retirement on a different Caribbean island every month, and the people that Lewis had brought into her life had been the only ones she'd known. And they had all stayed with him while she got to move across the country to escape.

'Of course, Chief. Leave it to me,' Jamie said, and yup. She *definitely* had a problem with Eliza. Her words were far too sweet to be genuine. Nobody who worked in these high-pressure environments had time for overt friendliness. The ER had the habit of grinding that out of you early on. That or doctors changed specialties because they couldn't cope with it.

'If you'll follow me, Dr Tascioni. I'll give you a quick look around so you can get situated,' Jamie said as she turned to her, and Allegra gave the chief another courteous nod before following the other woman.

'I'll take you to your office so you don't have to carry that binder around the ER,' Jamie said as she led Allegra towards a small room tucked away at the far end.

The familiar noise of the Palm Grove ER buzzed around her, filling Jamie with the itching need to get involved. She knew exactly how many people were on staff right now and how there weren't nearly enough to service a hospital of this size. Thankfully, they didn't stumble upon any patients being treated in the corridors as Jamie ushered the other woman along. Despite everything Eliza had—or rather *hadn't*—done for this hospital, Jamie still didn't *want* Allegra to see how their entire ER was coming undone at the seams. It wasn't her fault, and she'd worked far too many hours trying to fix things that were outside her responsibilities as a mere senior physician at the hospital.

Sure, she could have fixed things if Eliza had picked her to be the head of the ER instead of Allegra. Jamie knew all the holes that needed plugging and where the emergency room was the most vulnerable. But Eliza hadn't picked her. No, she'd gone with some expensive West Coast doctor that probably cost triple what Jamie made while also not knowing this hospital the way Jamie knew it.

She pushed those thoughts away with a shake of her head. Nope, that thinking right there was exactly what she had vowed to avoid when Eliza had announced that Jamie hadn't got the job. Because no matter how much it stung, it wasn't Allegra's fault. She probably didn't know how much of a mess she was inheriting. Well, she would know soon enough. With the chief of medicine being as absent from the ER operations as she usually was, Jamie knew Eliza hadn't cracked that binder open even once. If she had, she would have no doubt told Jamie to make the contents sound more flattering.

Well, flattery wouldn't help the hospital or Allegra. Or Jamie, for that matter.

'Thank you,' Allegra said as she lengthened her stride to keep up with Jamie's pace. The heels of her shoes clicked across the floor, blending in with the general noise of the ER drifting towards them. Jamie's much more sensible clogs squeaked with every other step, contrasting the difference between the two women's dress codes.

Who wore heels in the ER, anyway? A strange choice to make, even if it gave her hips a delicious sway with every step she took. Jamie knew that because Allegra had yet to receive her lab coat and so she was walking next to her in tight trousers and a button-up blouse that hugged every dip and curve of her body, infusing Jamie with a strange flavour of self-consciousness over her own outfit.

Because what on earth was she supposed to wear during her ER shift when she was literally jumping from one fire to the next for twelve hours straight? She had just about enough time to shower and sleep before the cycle began anew at Palm Grove Hospital.

Jamie stopped in front of the closed door to her

office—*Allegra's office now*, she reminded herself—and pushed the door open. She'd come in moments before Eliza had paged her to let her know she and Allegra were coming by, so she'd barely had any time to tidy up the space and—

Damn it, those were her *favourite* shoes lying in the corner. How could she discreetly extract them without making it seem as if she'd been squatting in an office that had never technically been hers to occupy?

'Here we go. *Tu segunda casa*,' Jamie said, spreading her arms out to indicate the fairly sparse office.

The computer was from this century, but that was about it. The beige furniture hadn't been updated since the eighties, resulting in the deep brown carpet clashing with it in the most hideous way. Jamie would have redecorated if she'd got the job. If there were room in the budget for it, which she knew there wasn't.

Allegra tilted her head, a line appearing between her brows. Jamie stared at her, waiting for a response, when she realised what the confusion was about.

'Do you speak Spanish?' She'd assumed yes, but...

Allegra shook her head. 'No, I don't,' she said, and Jamie swallowed the exacerbated sigh building in her throat. Of course, Eliza hadn't hired someone who actually understood the language most of their patients spoke. Because it wasn't as if the head of ER was supposed to be treating patients. No, it was an admin position that should be more concerned about the board of directors and budgets rather than saving lives.

That was the reason Jamie hadn't been tapped for this role—at least according to Eliza. But that woman was so full of her own nonsense, Jamie wasn't sure what to believe on any given day. She wasn't surprised to learn that Eliza had apparently gone out and hired a mini her, either.

Though Allegra almost immediately forced her to reassess that thought when she said, 'When I researched the hospital, I noticed the predominant demographic seems to be Hispanic. So I downloaded an app to practise, but I'm afraid the vocabulary's not great for a medical setting.'

Huh. That was…surprising. And also weirdly adorable. An app wouldn't be nearly enough to teach her what she needed to know, but at least she was trying. That was all anyone could expect.

'Yes, most of our patients are Latine. English is fine for most people and a large part of our staff speaks Spanish. If you need any help, you can just page me and I'll translate. Though I don't expect you to encounter much Spanish in the paperwork.'

Allegra nodded, then looked around the office, her sharp gaze noting everything. Then she sat down on the office chair. When she gestured at the chair opposite hers, Jamie took a seat, not without looking at her watch, though. Something that caught Allegra's attention, because she said, 'I appreciate you have to go back to attending the ER, so let me make this as brief as I can.'

Jamie gave her a thin-lipped smile. 'The shift is changing over and they'll expect me to run point.'

'Great segue into the one request I have for you.' She paused, for dramatic effect no doubt, because when she continued, she said, 'Tell me how big of a mess the ER is.'

'Pardon me?' The words came out of her mouth as more of a reflex than anything else. Jamie was too stunned by Allegra's *very* forward question. In the back of her mind she sensed her hackles rise at her hospital being called out like that when Allegra had spent only five minutes there. But the ER was a mess. A *gigantic* mess.

'What—?'

'What makes me think it's a mess?' Allegra hoisted the binder onto the table and laid her hand on top of it. Jamie watched as her short nails tapped against the plastic cover.

'The binder?' There was no way she had already read it. Hell, even Eliza hadn't read it.

'A well-run ER needs ten pages of instructions at best. So I'm guessing everything in here details what currently sucks about working in this emergency room.' She raised her eyebrow at Jamie, as if seeking confirmation, and it took Jamie a minute to realise the pause was exactly for that: to give her the chance to put it in her own words.

She would have liked to have given Allegra a few days to settle in before she dumped all this on her, but if she was asking for it who was Jamie to deny her that?

'We are severely understaffed. With the amount of through-put the chief expects from us without the wait time ballooning, it's been stretching everyone very thin. We have fifty beds, but the staff for twenty.' She paused before adding, 'On a good day.'

If Allegra was shocked to hear that, she didn't let it show. She only nodded as she looked down at the binder. 'So basically everyone is doubling up on their patient roster?'

Jamie nodded. 'Each one of us handles far too many patients and works longer than we are sometimes allowed to.'

She wasn't sure how smart it was to admit that in front

of the new department lead, but Allegra had asked for honesty, and even though Jamie was bitter she hadn't got the job, she desperately needed *someone* to fix things. Because even though she was angry she'd been passed up for a promotion that was by rights hers, Jamie loved this place, loved the people she worked with.

After years of struggling—first through her parents' continued substance abuse and then through countless foster homes—she'd finally found a place that was hers. She had found people with whom she could let her guard down occasionally. The need to please—to put on the sunshine face even when she wasn't feeling it—sometimes still broke through even with the staff here that she now considered family. But every day she felt herself soften and get more comfortable.

Fighting the need to change herself because she'd learned that was how she survived in foster homes.

The amount of side-eye Allegra had received as they'd walked around the ER showed how protective the staff felt over Jamie, too. She sensed they wouldn't make it easy for the new lead to do her job just because they were as annoyed as Jamie that she hadn't been promoted.

Another problem to solve, though a petty part of Jamie wasn't sure if she should intervene at all. Eliza had made her bed, she could lie in it. Except the ire wouldn't be directed at the chief. It would land squarely on Allegra's shoulders and, even though she had stolen Jamie's job, she was innocent in all of this. Or at least, that was what Jamie assumed when she was feeling charitable.

'I see.' Allegra hummed, and Jamie's eyes darted towards the other woman's mouth when she raised her long finger up to it and tapped at those pillowy lips. The strange wish for it to be Jamie's finger surfaced inside her, because then she'd be the one touching Allegra's lips and—

Wait, what?

'Dr Bailey mentioned you were the one who put this binder together. When you can spare the time, I would like to understand what the high-level issues are outside staffing so I can prioritise everything,' Allegra continued, her eyes darting left and right as if she was making a mental list.

Then she suddenly stood, catching Jamie off guard, who remained seated and found herself face to face with Allegra's torso. More specifically, Allegra's breasts and the way the tight fabric of her blouse accentuated her waist and highlighted her curves in all the right ways.

Jamie's fingers twitched in reaction to the unbidden attraction bubbling up within her and she pushed down on the heat uncoiling in the pit of her stomach. Where was that coming from? Knowingly or not, this woman in front of her had stolen *her* job, so ogling her wasn't just inappropriate because they were colleagues, but she should—and did—resent her presence here.

Was Allegra even into women? If Jamie's short hair and love for flannel weren't enough of an indicator for other women to know to approach her, they could still fall back on the various rainbow items she kept on her even when she was in scrubs. Only a colourful bracelet and an unobtrusive pin in the lapel of her lab coat. She did it mostly to set at ease patients who might need the attention of a queer doctor for more personal matters.

Though she loved living here, the area was on the rougher side. Every so often, she'd encounter a queer youth in the emergency room who needed discreet assistance without alerting their parents.

'If you wouldn't mind walking me back to the emergency room, you can get the shift change started while I'll walk around and observe,' Allegra said, looking down at Jamie, who still had her butt planted in the chair.

She blinked at Allegra, then stood and cast one more longing gaze at the shoes in the corner before stepping out of the office.

CHAPTER TWO

Jamie sipped her black coffee, her eyes still bleary from far too little sleep. Yesterday's shift had turned from bad to worse when a car crash had coincided with a nearby shooting, putting the entire staff both under pressure and on edge. Gunshot wounds meant dealing with the police in the ER, since they had to report every single one of these incidents to the authorities, and that only heightened the tension among the staff. The time and effort that went into filing police reports would be better put into actual patient care.

When she'd seen some of the blue-clad men loitering around the patients, Jamie had sighed as she'd realised dealing with the officers would once again fall to her. Juggling three critical patients as she had been, she hadn't really had time to deal with anyone. But then an already familiar tapping of high heels against the floor had swelled in the air and Allegra had popped out from one of the rooms, approaching the officers and ushering them into an area where they weren't so intrusive.

Some nurses and residents had cast a glance in Jamie's direction, as if they'd been looking for her to form their own opinion about Allegra. Not wanting to give the staff any indication, she'd just shrugged. Though Jamie had been more than happy to see the new head of ER walk away with one task that would have fallen on her instead.

In the week since Allegra had arrived, the two women hadn't spoken much. Every now and then, she'd seen a glimpse of Allegra's auburn locks disappearing around corners or behind doors while leaving a distinct trail of wild vanilla orchid in the air.

'Yah, I saw her leaving the hospital at almost midnight,' a soft voice said in Spanish, and even though Jamie's spine stiffened ever so slightly, she didn't turn around to see who was talking.

'That's late. I wonder if it's a tactic to impress the chief. We were drowning in patients all evening so she definitely wasn't helping there,' another voice replied, male this time. The resident who had started his second year here after switching from another hospital. Jamie tried and failed to recall his name.

Were they speaking about Allegra? She took another sip of her coffee, pretending to scroll on her phone as she listened.

'She was actually on the floor quite a lot, but I don't think she knows what she's doing. She kept offering to help run some of the trauma rooms, but we handled things all on our own. I mean, who does she think she is to walk in here and pretend like she's the boss now? This bruja got the job instead of...'

The voices trailed off, leaving Jamie alone to unpack them. Of course, everyone instantly disliked Allegra, yet it still bothered Jamie. It wasn't her fault.

Because she couldn't help herself, she'd looked up Allegra and her old hospital online. She'd told herself she was simply inspecting her to make sure she would keep the community's best interests in mind. But a part of her knew she wanted to know more about the woman underneath the heavy leadership crown. No matter what time of day Jamie glimpsed the other woman, she was always put together impeccably, as if she'd just walked in. Unlike Jamie, who more often than not had to run a comb through her hair as she changed into her scrubs.

'Where is the resident running the trauma room?' A familiar voice floated towards Jamie from down the corridor. She was sitting at the nurses' station to drink her coffee in peace before her shift started. There was a tension in Allegra's voice that set something off within her.

'Realmente tengo que explicarle la rotación de turnos a la jefa del departamento?' said Catarina, one of the senior nurses working the day shift, followed by some mumbled things Jamie couldn't hear. 'Dr Lopez is only scheduled to start in a few hours. We don't run this room until all the staff members arrive for their shift,' she then continued in English, keeping her tone more professional than in the previous sentence.

Uh-oh. More unrest within the staff. Allegra probably didn't even know what kind of hornets' nest she was walking into. Time for Jamie to swallow her pride and show up for the new department lead. If they saw that Jamie herself accepted their new boss with no hard feelings, hopefully that would signal to everyone that they could back off. While she appreciated the gesture, she didn't need them to haze Allegra because of the chief's decision.

Guess her shift was starting early. Pushing herself onto her feet, Jamie tucked her travel mug behind a monitor at the nurses' station and then began moving towards the voices.

'I understand that. But there's a patient in there with only an intern to look after them. We can't have interns doing this kind of work unsupervised,' Allegra said, and the quiver in her voice was one Jamie was familiar with. She'd worked with enough difficult people to know when someone was doing their very best to repress a surge of anger.

Hell, she probably did that daily.

Jamie stepped into view as Catarina told the intern in Spanish to ignore Allegra and prepare the patient for a chest tube. Allegra, on the other hand, stood with her arms at her sides inside the trauma room and scanned the patient with a critical eye.

'Tubo torácico,' she mumbled under her breath, and then looked up. 'Thoracic tube—chest tube?'

Catarina's eyes widened, her lips thinning, and Jamie knew the nurse was about to say something when she cut in. 'Dr Tascioni, if you have some time to spare, we would appreciate you helping out this morning. One resident hit their weekly working limit, so we are down a couple of hands,' she said, giving Catarina a meaningful look to back off.

Allegra's eyes widened at her intrusion, and Jamie hoped that Catarina's little stunt hadn't annoyed her enough to pull rank in this situation. Because it was quite obvious that Allegra had attempted to do exactly what Jamie now suggested: help run one of the trauma rooms because they were short-staffed. She'd probably been the one to receive the message that one of her residents wouldn't be coming in because of working-hour limits.

'Of course, I'm here to help,' Allegra said with a nod, and Jamie swallowed the sigh of relief building in her chest.

Situation defused. Good. Jamie's heart squeezed at the fierce loyalty the staff of Palm Grove Hospital showed her. When she had been passed around from foster home to foster home, *no one* had ever been loyal to her, causing her to feel adrift all her life. Until she'd landed a job here and found her people.

And now, strangely enough, she had to protect from those very people the woman who had accidentally stolen her job. She could think of only one easy way: showing everyone the work Allegra was capable of doing inside the ER and not just as an administrator but as a doctor.

The monitor beeped in a steady rhythm as they stepped through and Jamie stayed behind Allegra to let her assess the situation, even if everything inside her was pushing to take charge of the situation.

The intern, Colin, stood over the patient with his stethoscope pressed against the patient's chest, his eyes growing wider with every passing second.

'What are you hearing?' Allegra asked, clearly coming to the same conclusion as Jamie. She focused her attention on the intern, who stood up straight with his stethoscope still in his ears.

'I can't hear anything on the left side and hardly anything on the right,' Colin said.

Jamie's eyes darted between the two as she watched Allegra take in the situation.

Allegra's mouth thinned into a tight line as she scanned the vital signs on the monitor. 'Give me a rundown of the patient and what you've done so far,' she said, her eyes darting down to the ID card hanging from the intern's lab coat. 'Colin,' she added.

'Patient arrived with decreased lung sounds after a motor vehicle accident. According to paramedics, he was on the passenger side. No signs of internal bleeding after palpating the stomach.' He rattled off the information, his voice growing in steadiness. Clearly he hadn't wanted to deal with all of this on his own, either, despite the nurse trying her best to stop Allegra from involving herself.

After a week basically locked inside her office—and a week of trying to figure out budgets, staffing and whatever else Eliza expected of her for their investors—Allegra needed a change of scenery. So when one resident had called in to tell her that because of an incoming emergency last night he couldn't come in due to hitting his weekly hours limit, Allegra had jumped at the opportunity to help.

She hadn't expected to encounter such resistance from the staff. So the dirty looks following her around weren't a figment of her imagination. That, at least, was reassuring, even if she wasn't sure what she'd done to deserve this hostility. Allegra wasn't oblivious to workplace politics and knew as a newcomer she had to prove herself. Which was another reason she'd jumped at the opportunity to take a shift in the ER today.

A shrill beep cut through the air and all the eyes darted to the monitor, where the patient's vitals ticked away at a steady rhythm. Then Colin snatched his beeper from his belt, looking at the text crawling over the screen. 'There's another ambulance coming into the bay,' he said, looking uncertain.

Allegra didn't hesitate as she said, 'Go help them out. We've got this.'

Then she turned back to the patient, putting her stethoscope to the chest and listening for the decreased breath sounds.

Jamie, standing at the other side of the patient, scanned the chart. 'Paramedics performed a needle aspiration but weren't able to reinflate the lung.'

Allegra frowned. Lung sounds were only decreased on one side and the monitor didn't show any tachycardia. This patient was unwell but not critical. Maybe they could avoid the chest tube and rely on less invasive oxygen therapy despite the needle aspiration not working.

'Do we have images already? X-rays?' she asked, putting the stethoscope down and looking up at Jamie.

Jamie shook her head, looking at the chart still in her hands. 'That should be the first thing we ordered when the patient arrived. Let's get the portable X-ray machine in here and see what's going on in that chest,' Jamie said, hanging the chart back onto the bed and then stepping towards the nurse, Catarina, who still wore a deep scowl on her face.

As Jamie passed her, she mumbled something in Spanish to the nurse that lightened her expression, if only a fraction. The clattering of wheels filled the air and then the portable X-ray machine appeared in the doorway. Together, they set it up and left the room to take the films before stepping back in.

'I'll set up the screen,' Jamie said as she moved to the display hanging from the wall.

'Sir, my name is Allegra. We're still noticing decreased sounds in your lungs,' Allegra said to the patient, looking down at him with a reassuring smile. Each of his blinks was slow, his breathing shallow and the pain etched into his features. 'As soon as we figure out our next steps, we will see about pain medication.'

The patient mumbled something. Allegra bent down to put her ear next to his head and when he spoke again, she stood up straight. He'd just spoken Spanish to her.

Shoot.

When Jamie had mentioned that speaking Spanish was beneficial to their work here, Allegra had quietly hoped that it wouldn't hold her back. But that hope had eroded over the last week. Whenever she'd walked around the ER, most of the staff were speaking Spanish to each other, too.

She made a mental note to look into classes. If this was going to be her new home, then she needed to speak the language everyone else spoke. It was only right that she met the community of Palm Grove where they were and didn't make them communicate in a different language because *she* didn't speak it.

The chest X-rays flickered to life on the screen as Allegra stepped towards Jamie. 'Everything okay?' the other woman asked as she shot her a sideways glance.

Allegra tamped down on the instant reaction that shot through her body. A reaction that was becoming far too familiar whenever she saw Jamie and one she needed to cut out. Allegra's life was messy enough as it was and moving to Florida had been her escape from a tumultuous marriage that had apparently ended because *she* had spent too much time at the hospital working her butt off to provide her and her ex with the life they were accustomed to. It definitely hadn't ended because she'd found him in bed with another woman. That would imply that he carried at least part of the blame, which wouldn't have helped him paint Allegra as the ice queen he'd needed her to be to gain the sympathy of family and friends. Not that he'd had to work hard for their sympathy. They'd been his friends, after all.

Never hers.

She shook the flash of memories off and gave Jamie a tight nod. 'I think the patient prefers to speak Spanish,' she said, her eyes flittering over the X-ray. The stark contrast of black and white hues revealed the interior landscape of the patient's chest. A dark, crescent-shaped area on the right side of the chest cavity stood out like an inky void. 'There's the pneumothorax.'

Jamie nodded. 'No signs of broken ribs, which means we're not dealing with any punctures,' she said and Allegra heard her counting underneath her breath before she continued, 'We go in on the fifth intercostal space?'

'Sounds like a plan. Can you update—?'

Jamie's smile cut her off as the woman looked at her and nodded. 'Already on it,' she said, stepping to the patient and introducing herself before launching into an explanation of the procedure.

As Jamie's murmuring voice filled the room, Allegra turned away with a hint of trepidation pulsing through her that she pushed down into the same space where the strange tendril of warmth for Jamie lived. Neither of those feelings would get her very far in a hospital where the staff seemed determined to hate her.

'Please prep everything we need for the chest tube,' she said to Catarina and even though the nurse's jaw was still set, she simply nodded and walked out of the room.

Allegra stepped back to the patient, listening as Jamie spoke to him in a low voice. Reaching towards the gloves, she put them on and by the time she'd prepped the lidocaine for the local anaesthetic, Catarina had appeared with a cart containing everything they needed to proceed.

'Can you translate as I explain the procedure?' Allegra asked Jamie, who nodded and looked at her with an encouraging smile. Or at least Allegra thought it was encouraging. There was something about Jamie that made her hard to read. As though the smile radiating gentle warmth at everyone around her was somehow carefully crafted. Not fake, but not entirely real, either.

'There's a build-up of air or liquid in your pleural space that is pushing on your lung tissue,' she began, and then she paused to let Jamie convey her words. 'To make it easier to breathe, we'll have to insert a chest tube to help drain what's in there.'

Allegra listened and caught the words *'tubo torácico'* again. Reaching for the tray Catarina had brought in, she lifted the chest tube to show it to him. His face contorted, and he said something to Jamie.

'I informed him that the main thing he will feel is pressure, but that it's likely he will interpret it as pain. We are good to start,' Jamie said, and, next to Allegra, Catarina nudged the tray forward so it was within easy reach.

Taking a deep breath, Allegra injected the lidocaine into the patient's skin around the insertion point and kept narrating what she was doing as she grabbed the scalpel and cut a horizontal incision in the fifth intercostal space. Catarina held out the forceps as Allegra put down the scalpel and she nodded with a grateful smile before getting to work on dissecting the subcutaneous tissue and intercostal muscle until she could reach the pleura.

'We're almost there, hang tight,' she said when a spasm went through the patient's muscles, no doubt a result of holding tension in anticipation of the procedure. Even with explanations, it was hard to conceptualise what was happening to someone if they couldn't see things.

Inserting her gloved finger through the tract she'd created, she confirmed she had a path to the pleural space. Satisfied, she guided the chest tube into place and secured it with sutures before passing it on to Catarina, who connected it to a drainage system hanging from the side of the gurney.

The second her hands came off the patient, his expression relaxed as the pressure in his chest eased. She watched as Jamie gave his arm a squeeze and then looked up at Allegra with a smile.

A real one. It was absolutely dazzling and her stomach swooped, giving her the sensation of falling through a weightless space.

Not good. Not good *at all*. Whether the zing in her veins was from attraction or something else, there was no room for that. She was the head of the ER now. A leader to the people here. And there was a chance Allegra was simply lonely and latching onto something innocent. Her move—or rather the divorce—had removed her from the only group of friends she'd known for eight years.

She cleared her throat to shake those thoughts off before saying, 'Let's get another X-ray done to confirm proper placement of the tube.'

Her eyes only briefly met Jamie's as she said that before stepping out of the trauma room and back into the bustling of the ER. Some of the staff glanced her way before turning their heads back to whisper, but there was something different about their voices. Even if she couldn't understand the words, the tone had shifted.

When she glanced over her shoulder as steps sounded from behind her, Allegra got a vague idea why. Because Jamie was still sporting that smile that set something within her loose as she gave her an encouraging nod.

Definitely not good.

CHAPTER THREE

THE GRUMBLING AND gossiping from the staff lessened as they saw Allegra getting involved in the shift. Just as Jamie had hoped they would. Lessened, but it didn't quite disappear. She'd still have to keep an eye on it to ensure everyone was playing nice. Why exactly that had become her job when she was actually the wronged party in all of this, she didn't quite know. But even if it would fill Jamie with untold pleasure to watch Eliza Bailey's plan unravel and bite her in the rear, she couldn't let her pettiness get in the way of the work they did here. Neither could she let the staff act out on their pettiness either, though that would be an entirely different challenge.

Now that everyone had seen Allegra rolling up her sleeves and working alongside people, they would have a harder time finding fault with her. At least that was what Jamie hoped.

Her problem wasn't with Allegra. Or rather, as far as the job was concerned, she didn't have any beef with the woman. Working with her, however, was an entirely different thing. One she didn't want to contemplate too deeply.

Not when every time she let her thoughts wander, they focused on Allegra's soft, floral scent, and her capable hands that Jamie had watched far too closely throughout the entire procedure, wondering what they would feel like without gloves sliding over skin. *Her* skin, specifically.

Nope. Not going there again.

It didn't help that during yesterday's online stalking session she'd discovered not only Allegra's accomplishments at her old hospital but also some photos of charity work she'd done as the head of emergency medicine at San Francisco General. More specifically, Jamie had found articles written about the hospital's efforts to reach out to LGBTQ youths and provide them with educational and sexual health materials in a judgement-free space.

Allegra had spoken about her experience as an LGBTQ teenager and how the unravelling of her own sexuality without a support system had inspired her to launch this initiative.

Which wasn't *conclusive* evidence that Allegra was into women, but it was as close to a confirmation as Jamie would get without actually hitting on her. That, of course, would never happen because Allegra was her boss and Jamie had experienced enough instability in her formative years that she didn't need to invite more of it into her adult life.

Love and work better remained separate. At least, that seemed to be the prevailing sentiment online. Jamie wouldn't know. Her entire love life consisted of one-night flings without any attachment—acting on a very basic sense of attraction to fill a shallow need within her. Anything else was too permanent for Jamie. After spending her life with her luggage stowed away underneath her bed so she was ready to bounce whenever her latest foster family decided she wasn't worth the effort, she'd concluded that permanent connections simply weren't for her.

At least not *human* connections. Palm Grove Hospital had shown her that places were different. As long as she had her own space, being tied to a singular place hadn't been half bad. Her colleagues were exactly the surrogate family she needed—staff turning over frequently enough that it didn't feel unsettling for someone who was used to people moving in and out of her life. She found that even comforting, at times. It signalled clearly that people never changed, and that she was right for never getting attached. The few exceptions, like Catarina, only proved her points, and she didn't care how little sense that might make to people. They weren't living inside her head and didn't have to deal with what she'd had to grapple with all her life.

Jamie glanced at the clock on the wall, then looked around the ER. Her shift had ended a few hours ago, but things hadn't calmed down until now. She still needed to catch up on some charts and sign the release forms to transfer patients before she could call it a night. Time to find a quiet corner and get through it as fast as possible. There was a staff room at the end of the emergency room that was never used. It was too far from the main area and took people too long to get back if there was an emergency. That would do.

But when Jamie pushed the door open, someone was already in there. Despite her tired appearance, Allegra still looked perfectly put together. Her braided hair remained neatly in place, with not a single strand displaced, and Jamie couldn't see any signs of the day they'd had on Allegra's lab coat or scrubs underneath. Only the slightly slumped shoulders as she bent over her laptop showed the strain she'd been under today.

A thrill went through Jamie as adrenaline surged at the sight of Allegra. She'd come here to be alone and get her work done quickly. Allegra's presence stood in the way of that, but as she stepped into the room, she found something inside her had hoped they would get to catch up. There wasn't even anything in particular that Jamie wanted to talk about. She just wanted to talk to her, get to know her.

'Why aren't you in your office?' Jamie asked, making the other woman look up.

Allegra blinked those big, light brown eyes several times as if she was finding her way back into the present from wherever her thoughts had gone. Was it weird that Jamie wanted to know that? Definitely. But she was too tired to question it right now.

'I'm here because…' Her voice trailed off, her eyes darting down at the screen of her monitor. Jamie could see subtle changes in her expression. Was she debating how much she wanted to tell her? Of all the things Jamie could have asked, she'd thought this was the most harmless question she could come up with.

Allegra shook her head with a quiet laugh. 'I asked the maintenance staff to turn the office into another patient room. It's too big for me alone and I can catch up on all the admin stuff like this.' She lifted her hands, indicating the surrounding space. 'But it seems this break room isn't as secret as I thought it was. You're the first person to find me here all week.'

Now it was Jamie's turn to blink, her brain wrapping around what Allegra had revealed. One week at the job and the first change she'd made was to give up her office so they could make it into another patient room? How was Jamie only hearing about this now? Even a few more beds meant so much in the dire situation they were in.

Allegra seemed to read the question in Jamie's eyes because she said, 'It's not ready yet. Maintenance ordered all the furniture we need and they also need to figure out some electrical work. But the room should be ready to go next week. Which reminds me.' She got off her chair and Jamie's eyes followed her every move as Allegra walked over to the row of cupboards and opened one above her, pulling out a tote bag and handing it over to Jamie.

When she opened the bag—she noted it had the letters *SF Pride Parade* stamped on it—she stared down at the light brown ankle boots she had left in the office. Her head whipped up, looking at Allegra as gratitude mixed with confusion. 'Thank you. These are my favourite shoes,' she said, even though other questions popped into her mind. Mainly: how had Allegra known these were hers?

A small smile spread over Allegra's full lips. 'I figured the person who was holding the ER together before my arrival was probably the owner of these shoes. After seeing you interact with the staff and considering how much effort you put into the binder, I'm pretty sure that you are the one who's been keeping people going.'

Jamie clutched the bag to her chest when a strange sort of heat trickled through her from her head to her toes. Allegra had guessed these were her shoes simply by observing her throughout the week. The thought of Allegra keeping an eye on her over the last few days caused the heat to flare as it reached her stomach.

But before Jamie could say anything, Allegra continued, 'I also appreciate you stepping in today. I've had to endear myself to members of different teams before, but I've never had as hard a time to win the staff over as I have here. Their scepticism of a newcomer makes sense to me, but it's on a far different level than I expected.' She paused as she sat back down on the chair, the light of the screen illuminating her face. 'I want to say it's been marginally better since we worked together on that patient. Which makes me think you are more to them than just a senior physician in the ER. Are you maybe the leader they actually wanted?'

Jamie couldn't detect any animosity in Allegra's voice, but she froze for a split second as she considered her options. Allegra had drawn this conclusion from observation alone, hinting at a keen eye for people. So even if Jamie wanted to pretend that she hadn't coveted the job—and that everyone in the department hadn't rooted for her to get it—chances were Allegra wouldn't believe her. Or would even think of her as a liar.

What was she trying to avoid by not being honest with her?

'That's one way to put it,' Jamie said when she couldn't come up with an answer to her own question. 'The previous department head, Dr Hartman, left maybe six months ago. Even before his departure, many of us realised he wasn't coping well with the stress and the general state of the ER. So I started helping wherever I could. Organised shift rotations and took care of any holes in the coverage. Eventually he abdicated more and more of the responsibility to me, to the point where I was doing everything.'

When Jamie paused, Allegra nodded and extended her

hand, indicating the chair across from her. Jamie sat down and heat pricked at the back of her neck when their knees bumped against each other as she stretched her legs out.

'I realise now I shouldn't have made any assumptions. I mean, I'm a doctor. That's kind of the rule for us. But with how many hours I spent in the ER and with me fielding all of Dr Bailey's requests, I honestly thought the job was mine. I put the hours in, after all.' Jamie cringed at how desperate the words sounded, even though they rang true within her. Telling someone else so openly felt like laying her naiveté bare.

But Allegra only nodded, sympathy softening the set of her mouth. 'You ran the ER by yourself and when Dr Hartman left, you acted on a logical conclusion. So did everyone else on staff. Otherwise, they wouldn't be giving me such a hard time.'

'Yeah, I'm sorry about that. Nobody means to be rude. They are just very protective of their own. Seeing us work together should get them to back off a bit,' Jamie said.

Allegra looked at her screen, her eyes darting over whatever was written on it. Then she lifted her head again, and a fiery zing went through Jamie, burning the ends of her nerves. What kind of reaction was that? They were talking about Jamie's failure to secure herself a promotion, yet somehow her body reacted as if they'd been exchanging whispered secrets in the dead of night.

'It's okay. It shows that the staff care about the ER and what happens to the people that come here seeking help. I'd be more worried if they were completely apathetic, which could easily happen if pushed too far. In my experience, such people are much harder to win over because they don't care.' Allegra shrugged but the smile spreading over her lips didn't quite hit as the other one had. Something about it was practised. Almost uncanny.

Was that a glimpse into life at her last hospital? Had Allegra left there because the staff didn't care enough about their work? The question hovered on Jamie's tongue, but then a ping from Allegra's phone interrupted her.

She picked up her phone, a line appearing between her delicate brows. Jamie hadn't realised she was someone who paid particular attention to eyebrows, but now that she was looking at the arch on Allegra's, she found a strange appreciation for the symmetry she found there.

Wait, why was she staring at her boss's brows? Even without her scent invading her thoughts all day, that was a weird thing to do.

'Sorry, I have to take care of this,' Allegra said under her breath, seemingly talking more to herself. Her eyes sharpened when she looked up at Jamie. 'Your shift ended—' she glanced back at her phone '—seventy-two minutes ago.'

Jamie opened her mouth to protest, but Allegra shook her head. 'All the late-shift residents have already checked in to their shift. Get out of here.'

This time the smile was genuine and warm and far too brief, for Allegra was out of the door before Jamie could even process how her heart had sped up at the glimpse of white teeth before she'd disappeared.

And by the time she was halfway home, Jamie realised that somehow Allegra had known when her shift had ended to the exact minute.

Odd.

CHAPTER FOUR

THE POUNDING OF her feet against the pavement blended with the electronic house music blaring in her ears. With the beats per minute increasing, Allegra cranked up her pace until she could feel the burn in her muscles as she continued down the path leading out of the park. Two weeks had passed since she'd left San Francisco for Homestead, Florida, and it was the first time she'd found the time to go out for a run.

The hospital had kept her tied up since her arrival, and after working non-stop for all fourteen days, she needed to spend some time on her own. Allegra could have kept normal hours if she'd wanted to. Her verbiage in her contract allowed her to spend most of her time behind her desk to focus on how to 'maintain high standards while increasing throughput to fill funding gaps'.

Apparently, Dr Bailey—and the board of directors— seemed to think that the ER was running at a high standard. It was, Allegra had to concede, but the price the staff was paying was far too high already. If they had to accept and manage even more patients, they would probably lose all the nurses and more experienced residents.

They might lose Jamie.

Allegra fell out of step as the thought popped into her

mind. She caught herself before she went flailing into the dirt path and slowed her jog down.

It didn't matter to her that if she couldn't fix the issues in the hospital Jamie might be leaving—something that she also based only on her own assumptions. It wasn't as though the woman had expressed any thoughts about leaving the hospital. And why would Allegra be bothered about that? She hardly knew her. Sure, they had spent quite a few hours going over the binder and working side by side in the emergency room. Allegra was grateful to the other woman for standing up for her, even though she now knew that she'd inadvertently stolen her job.

That had been the main reason Allegra had worked just as many hours as the rest of the staff since her start two weeks ago. They needed to know that she was on their side and that she was here to help them and not some greedy directors who thought commodifying healthcare was a good thing.

Her phone buzzed, and Allegra frowned as she read her ex-husband's name. Declining the call with a huff, she pushed her phone back into her pocket and forced her legs to move faster to rid herself of the unpleasant shiver Lewis and his incessant calls caused.

The path under her feet changed from gravel to asphalt as she left the park and jogged along the sidewalk. Glancing around, Allegra didn't recognise the street she was on. She'd spent a year trapped in San Francisco to untangle their lives, to the point that when she'd finally been able to leave she hadn't even looked for an apartment, opting instead to live in a hotel until she could find the time for a property hunt. So she knew the way from the hotel to the hospital, but outside that she hadn't really had the time or energy to explore Homestead.

Something she'd decided to change this morning as she'd set out for her jog.

The early morning sunlight filtered through the lush green canopy of trees that lined the streets of Homestead, casting dappled shadows on Allegra's path as she jogged. The gentle rustling of leaves accompanied her steady footfalls, creating a soothing rhythm that matched the beat of her music. She passed by cosy cafes with tables spilling out onto the sidewalk, the rich aroma of freshly brewed coffee mingling with the scent of blooming flowers from nearby pots.

There weren't many people out this early on a Saturday morning. But the people she encountered sent her tentative smiles as she jogged past them, none pausing for more than a second before resuming whatever they were doing.

Was it strange that this street in this Miami suburb already felt far more welcoming than her neighbourhood in San Francisco had? Even though she had spent the last eight years in that house, with that man, pretending his life was hers because she'd thought that was the only way she could show her love to him?

Of course, Homestead already felt more like her own place than San Francisco ever had. Because he and his mistress weren't here every day, taunting her with the awful choice she'd made by marrying Lewis in the first place.

Leaving the street, Allegra went down a quiet side alley, shaking her head as the song changed and the beat slowed down. Her lungs burned as she came to a stop, her breath sawing in and out of her. She pulled her phone out again, swiping away Lewis's message without reading it, and was tapping on it to select a new playlist when a cluster of people appeared a few paces down the alleyway.

Two people were carrying a third person between them to the building in front of them. Allegra lowered her phone when she noticed a flash of bright red spreading over the limp figure's abdomen.

Allegra's heart leaped into her throat as she registered the urgency of the situation before her. Without a second thought, she broke out into a jog again, her emergency physician brain kicking in. The injured person seemed to be losing blood rapidly, their pallor alarming against the stark red seeping through their clothes.

They hauled the patient through a door into the building just as Allegra reached them, and she opened her mouth to offer help. The words didn't come out when a familiar face glanced up from the group to look directly at Allegra.

Jamie Rivera stood in the building's entryway, talking to the group of people in a low voice. She stopped as she recognised Allegra. Her lips moved as she remained frozen in place for a second, and it took Allegra a second to realise the music was still blasting in her ears. Yanking the earbuds out of her ears, she stuffed them into her pocket. Low moaning immediately filled her ears.

'Damn it, I don't have time for this,' Jamie muttered under her breath and then turned back to the patient, ushering the group through another doorway. She pointed at something beyond Allegra's view and as Jamie was about to close the door, she fixed those amber eyes on her. 'Are you going to help or not?'

As she stepped into what looked like a small, makeshift clinic, Allegra's eyes darted around to take in all the details. This space used to be a storage facility, by the look of the unpolished concrete floors and the amount of chips and scratches visible on the metal shelves lining the walls. Medical supplies were scattered around haphazardly, and the scent of antiseptic tried in vain to mask the underlying mustiness of the old building. Allegra's focus quickly zeroed in on the patient laid out on a cobbled-together stretcher, his face contorted in pain.

Jamie grabbed a pair of scissors from the shelf and began cutting the fabric of the shirt away to uncover the underlying skin and find the source of bleeding. The heart-rate monitor continued to beep, showing an elevated pulse and blood pressure, but not to the extent Allegra would have expected with the amount of blood covering the shirt.

'What's your name, sir?' she asked as she circled around to the other side of the stretcher and grabbed a pair of latex gloves from the box sitting on the shelf.

The patient's eyes shifted to her, and she noted the alertness with which he scanned her. But then he looked at Jamie, uncertainty rippling over his expression.

'You can talk to her. She's a friend. *Lo prometo*,' Jamie said, her eyes flicking towards Allegra for only a fraction of a second before she focused back on peeling the rest of the shirt off the patient's body.

'Miguel,' he said and then winced when Jamie pressed down a large square of gauze onto the wound.

'What do you see?' Allegra asked, this time looking at Jamie, who pressed down on the gauze using her bodyweight.

'A large laceration across his abdomen, but it looks superficial,' Jamie replied, and something about her phrasing set off additional alarm bells in Allegra's head. There were a lot of questions she planned on asking Jamie once they stabilised the patient.

'What type of wound is it? Knife?' She looked at Miguel. 'Were you stabbed?'

Miguel winced again when Jamie shifted her hands, pulling out more gauze from behind her on the shelf. Then she nodded at his feet. 'There should be some cushions to elevate his legs.'

Allegra followed Jamie's nod, grabbing the cushions and stuffing them under the patient's legs before returning to the injury. Jamie lifted the blood-soaked gauze to inspect the wound, granting Allegra a better look at it. The edges appeared ragged, with slight bruising already visible on the blood-covered skin. She fought to keep her face impassive, but couldn't help a sharp glance at Jamie, who returned it with an equal fierceness.

This was a gunshot wound. A shallow one and as Jamie cleaned it with the antiseptic solution, Allegra let out a breath of relief when it turned out to be only a graze.

'This is going to need sutures. Do we have everything we need here?' she asked, pushing away any thoughts of potential explanations.

Jamie nodded, turning around and grabbing a box from the shelf. Pulling the lid off, she set it onto a rickety tray at the end of the stretcher and pulled out the vacuum-sealed needle, forceps and thread to suture the wound.

The needle gleamed under the harsh overhead light as Jamie threaded it, her fingers moving with practised precision. Allegra observed in silence, her eyes flickering between Miguel's abdomen and Jamie's focused expression. The sterile scent of the antiseptic hung heavy in the air, mixing with the faint metallic tang of blood, making it hard to breathe.

Despite that, Jamie worked fast, pushing and pulling the needle with the forceps until the wound was closed with a tight line of stitches running about three inches. When she put the instruments down, Allegra grabbed the sterile dressing, putting it on top of the freshly closed wound, and together they moved Miguel to wrap the bandage around his waist to keep any dirt and debris away.

Jamie stepped back to one of the shelves, sticking her hand into a container and rummaging through it. When she drew her hand back, she held a blister pack with some pills already missing. Then she nodded at the box still sitting on the tray at the end of the stretcher.

Allegra took out some spare dressing and bandages and handed them over. The small smile spreading over Jamie's lips as she received them sent a flutter down her stomach.

'Here's what you need to switch out your bandages. Change them every day or if you see any discharge seeping through them,' Jamie said as she handed him the items. Then she put the blister pack on top as she said, 'These are strong painkillers. Do not take more than two a day. I'll also need to see you in a few days to take the stitches out. Call me on Wednesday to tell me how you're doing.' Miguel grabbed everything with a tired nod.

Then Jamie shifted her eyes to Allegra. 'Could you give him some water and the first dose of the meds while I speak to his friends?'

Allegra nodded, stepping past the two anxious-looking people, who began speaking in hushed Spanish as Jamie walked out of the room with them.

Jamie looked up when the door to the patient room opened and swallowed a sigh when Allegra stepped out with an unreadable expression. After getting the details on how Miguel and his friends had got shot—apparently a stray bullet from an unrelated shootout had caught Miguel across the abdomen—she'd sent his friends away to come back in a few hours after Miguel had had some rest and quiet. The last thing they needed was to be stopped by the police because Miguel was shaky on his feet. The whole reason they'd come here rather than a proper hospital was because they didn't have documents.

Allegra's arrival had complicated an already nightmarish situation into a dimension Jamie could hardly grasp. But an instinct had told her to trust the woman—to invite her to handle the incident with her. When the one person showed up that you didn't want to see and caught you breaking the rules, you had to think on your feet. In Jamie's case, she'd ended up dragging Allegra into her mess. And she was about to find out whether that trust would pay off.

Sinking onto the floor next to Jamie, Allegra rustled through the plastic bag Jamie had brought in with her this morning and took out a can of iced coffee, holding it out to Jamie. Their fingers brushed as she took the drink. The heat of that minuscule touch was a stark contrast to the cold aluminium of the can. Another reason Allegra showing up here was a bad thing. Jamie's reactions to the woman were inappropriate. Unthinkable, really. For the good of the ER, she'd got over the fact that Allegra had all but stolen her job, but that still meant that she was in charge of the emergency room, in charge of Jamie.

There was no reasonable scenario in which the low hum of attraction coming alive inside her whenever she saw Allegra was a normal reaction that she could feel comfortable following. Or acting on. Or anything, really. If only that soft scent of vanilla weren't already imprinted into her brain from working with Allegra so closely. Even here, in the staleness of her makeshift free clinic, the woman's soft smell filled the air, piercing through her thoughts with an ease that should worry her. *Did* worry her. Or was the worry the result of the conversation she knew they were about to have? Jamie wasn't oblivious to the mountain of trouble she could be in if her trust in Allegra was misplaced. What she'd done here today—and many days before that—wasn't just against hospital regulations. There were state laws and the medical licensing board to consider, too.

'Thank you for jumping in,' Jamie said when Allegra remained quiet. 'As unexpected as your appearance here was, it's appreciated.'

Allegra took a sip from her own can, her eyes dropping down to it as she twisted it in her hands. Drops of condensation ran down her hands and Jamie pushed down the urge to reach out and trace the water, catching it with her own hands. *Inappropriate*. The woman next to her could fire her right on the spot for what she'd witnessed today and all Jamie could focus on was the string of tension winding tighter and tighter as she looked at Allegra, feeling a draw to her that should best be left unexplored.

'I think you know what I'm about to ask,' Allegra said, and Jamie's stomach bottomed out. She wanted an explanation. That was a good start, at the very least. She hadn't dismissed her outright, but rather wanted to hear what she had to say. Would Allegra—as an outsider—understand the reasons that had led Jamie down this path, why she would have to continue with this, no matter what the consequences?

'Sometimes during the weekend or whenever I have days off, people come here to get some minor medical needs fulfilled. It's rare that people need the support we gave Miguel today, but it happens. The right people in the community know my number and will call me if they need anything.' Jamie kept her answer deliberately vague, giving herself an out if she needed it. If Allegra decided she wanted to cut her loose, she didn't want the woman to have too much information about what she was doing here.

'And you do all of this in your free time out of this storage unit?'

Jamie didn't miss the unspoken question coming through her words. *Why aren't you doing this in a hospital?*

'Some people don't have the means to go to a hospital. Especially not people like Miguel.' Jamie didn't dare to say the word dancing at the edge of her tongue. A word that described Miguel's status as much as her own conduct here. But she couldn't expose him like that, even though she doubted Allegra would do anything rash that would target their patient. Nevertheless, trust was hard to come by in this community and she could only say so much to someone who was hardly more than a stranger.

Allegra's brows furrowed. 'Federal law dictates that we cannot turn people away from the ER regardless of their insurance status.'

'True, but doctors and nurses aren't the only people frequenting the emergency room. With someone like Miguel, we would have to report the gunshot wound to the right authorities. That might lead to questions that are hard to answer,' she said, raising her eyebrows ever so slightly to bring her point across. She did not know how often Allegra had dealt with undocumented people in her previous hospital or what her attitude towards them was.

'He should still be able to—oh…' Allegra's voice trailed off as realisation dawned in her eyes. Jamie watched as a myriad emotions flitted across Allegra's face: surprise, understanding, and a glint of…respect?

Hope flickered alive in Jamie's chest—both that she might not be losing her job today and maybe also that she could be making a new ally in this endeavour.

'I see,' Allegra finally said, her tone softer now. 'There are people here who need our help but have to work outside the system.'

Jamie nodded, relieved that Allegra seemed to grasp the complexities of the situation. The tension that had coiled within her unwound slightly, though she remained cautious. That was until Allegra nodded, her hand tightening around the can as she said, 'If these people need help then it is our job to help them. Tell me what needs to be done.'

* * *

Seeing Allegra sitting across from her in the small cafe around the corner of her makeshift clinic was an unusual sight. One that was compounded by the fact that, instead of scrubs, she was wearing a skin-tight tank top and leggings that clung to her legs like a second skin. Perfectly normal and acceptable attire for someone who'd gone on an early morning jog—one that had somehow led her to Jamie's location by accident—yet for Jamie the visual was electrifying. And distracting. *Very* distracting.

'How did you end up running that place?' Allegra asked once their coffees had arrived and the waiter was busy serving other customers.

'I'm usually the one who volunteers for the first-aid tent at any parades or neighbourhood events around here. People know what I do for a living and my story isn't so different from theirs,' she said, taking a sip of her flat white and relishing the heat of the beverage along with the zing of caffeine hitting her stomach.

'Were you born here?' Allegra's fingers wrapped around her own iced latte served in a tall glass and, not for the first time since the woman had arrived at Palm Grove Hospital, Jamie found herself distracted by the sight of those long, delicate fingers with the perfectly manicured nails trimmed down to a length that were perfect for—

'No, I moved here a few years ago. I grew up in Texas.'

Allegra's eyebrows shot up. 'Texas? Where in Texas?'

Jamie took another sip of coffee to buy herself some time. There wasn't one specific place she'd called home there. She'd lived in Pasadena for the first few tumultuous years of her life, learning to be on her own whenever her parents were out working or just out of it in general. Then, thanks to the foster system, she'd been carted around from town to town, never really finding a permanent anchor spot until she'd aged out of the system.

But that wasn't something she could tell Allegra. Her colleagues didn't even know that side of her, and the people at Palm Grove Hospital had got as close to resembling a family as Jamie had ever let happen. A large part of why she hadn't told anyone was the deeply rooted fear that, at any point, all of it could be ripped from her again. Just as it had been before, far too many times to count.

'Pasadena, but I haven't been there in a long while,' she said after putting her cup back down, sticking to the truth that had served her well so far in her life and hoping that Allegra wouldn't dig any deeper.

'I'm originally from Seattle, but I went to med school in Austin,' Allegra said, and Jamie latched onto the bit of information that let her steer the conversation away from Texas and all the hurt that was so tightly wrapped up in that place.

'You must have enjoyed the weather if you went from Texas straight to California,' she said, remembering Allegra's career history from looking her up.

Allegra let out a low laugh that skittered across Jamie's skin looking for a way to burrow further down. She wouldn't let it. It hadn't been appropriate before their encounter this morning. Now, after Allegra had seen what Jamie did in that storage-space-turned-clinic, it would be beyond foolish to let her attraction to this woman run wild.

Only problem was that with Allegra offering her help—rather than threatening Jamie's livelihood for breaking the rules, as she'd expected—she had kicked the slightly ajar door open, and Jamie couldn't stop her curious nature from peering through.

'I guess then coming to Miami really cements my reputation as a sunshine girl. I'm not sure the weather has ever been a consideration whenever I contemplated a new job, but I can't deny a pattern when I see one.' Allegra laughed again, sending it after the one already racing down Jamie's spine.

When had Allegra become so *likeable*? Jamie had never had anything against the other woman—outside the misplaced annoyance that she'd snatched up *her* job—but she hadn't ever seen Allegra so relaxed. Whenever they saw each other, it was usually during some kind of incident where they had to work fast to save their patient's life.

Seeing her casually sipping on an iced latte with a small smile curling those pillowy lips that looked as delicious as the rest of her—

Whoa. Where had that come from? How often did Jamie have to remind herself that these thoughts had to stop?

'Though I'd say California wasn't my fault. I moved there with my husband to be near his residency spot,' she said, and that just about managed to banish the rising heat in Jamie.

Husband. The word sank inside her like a stone.

That didn't have to mean anything. Bisexual people existed. Just because Allegra was married to a man didn't mean she had no interest in women and that Jamie had completely misread the subtle vibes pinging back and forth between them.

Except, of course, *she was married to a man*. She'd said 'husband'. Not *ex*-husband. Not *estranged* husband.

A question popped into her mind and Jamie didn't stop to think before she asked, 'Did he move here with you?' She hadn't heard of another doctor starting at the same time as Allegra, but anything outside the emergency room didn't really capture her interest.

Allegra's eyes dropped to the tall glass of coffee-flavoured sugary milk—there was no other way to describe a latte, in Jamie's opinion—and she gave the liquid a stir with her straw, the ice cubes clinking against the glass. The smile on her lips faded, and Jamie regretted asking. But, at the same time, something inside her chest unfurled, a tiny glimmer of...what? Hope? Wasn't that a bit dramatic just for the mention of a husband?

'Ah, no. We recently finalised the divorce. I guess I should say *ex*-husband, since I haven't lived with him in a year.' The smile she gave Jamie was a paler version of the previous ones and regret stabbed at her for bringing it up in the first place. Why had she even needed to know Allegra's exact marital circumstances? That information wasn't relevant to her life and there wasn't anything she'd do with that knowledge.

Was Allegra maybe just an ally? Jamie thought back to the article she'd seen, the Pride tote bag that seemed so out of place for Allegra and—no. Jamie took a fast sip of her coffee, focusing on the heat running down her throat to keep her grounded in the moment. She wouldn't jump to any conclusions, but even if she did, it didn't matter. Because she wasn't—*shouldn't*—be interested in her like that. Sleeping with colleagues was already a big no-no. Double that for colleagues who were also technically your boss.

'If you aren't originally from here, how did you end up in Miami?' Allegra asked, blissfully unaware of the chaos she was causing inside Jamie's head.

Another question that trod far too close to spaces that she wanted left undisturbed. But there had also been a glimpse of vulnerability in Allegra's eyes when she'd said the thing about her ex. As if doubts had grabbed at her for sharing her story—which was something Jamie didn't want to leave hanging in the air. If Allegra regretted sharing things about herself, then she might never do it again and Jamie wouldn't get the chance to know her better. For what purpose she *wanted* to know her better was better left unexplored.

The only thing she could think of in that moment was to offer up a piece of herself. Information for information. An equal exchange.

'Mostly coincidence? I had to rely on scholarships to get me through college and med school. Still ended up graduating with significant debt. So when it came to my internship placement, I went with whoever wanted me. The only factor for me was how much the placement could afford to pay and how cheap the area was. By default, that meant most of the more prestigious hospitals were out of the question.'

The glimpse into her inner life was shallow, yet Jamie saw something in Allegra's gaze spark alive as she absorbed the information. As though she hadn't expected her to reply the way she had and her appreciation was apparent. What caught Jamie on her back foot was the flash of *something else* in her eyes—hunger. For more? For Jamie herself?

Before Jamie could react, or even make up her mind about what she'd seen, Allegra continued, 'And yet you've grown close to the people in the community here. Close enough to risk your job and your medical licence for them, at the very least. That's quite extraordinary.'

Jamie blinked at her and then burst out laughing at the sheer absurdity of the conversation. 'Extraordinarily stupid, did you mean to say? Because I know well that if I had any sort of self-preservation skills, I would stop right this second and pretend none of it ever happened.'

Allegra nodded, and Jamie's stomach fluttered when her teeth sank into her lower lip, leaving a small red mark along her lip line when she released it. The sight was mesmerising, pulling all of her attention to that one spot. So when Allegra said something else, Jamie looked up at her.

And blinked again.

'Sorry, what?'

If Allegra realised what had her distracted, she was kind enough not to draw attention to it. 'I asked why you do it if you know how dumb an idea it is?' She exhaled a laugh and added, 'To paraphrase your words.'

If Jamie actually had any qualms about what she did for the people in this neighbourhood, then this question would keep her up at night. But she did what she had to do with conviction and purpose—even though she knew it carried a huge risk.

'Because someone needs to do it. The public health system of this country has let people down. Nobody should be denied healthcare because of who they are— including their immigration status.' Her voice dropped low as she said the last two words, casting a look about to make sure nobody was listening. 'Hospital policy dictates that I have to call the police for certain things and it doesn't leave any wiggle room for when calling the authorities puts my patient in danger.'

Allegra had already agreed that she wanted to help, which Jamie hadn't expected. When she'd turned up behind her emergency patient, Jamie had hoped that showing her what she did in her makeshift clinic would get her to shut up about it. No part of her had ever considered Allegra might want to help.

'I'm glad I happened upon you today, Jamie. Because I agree. Our hospital procedures should not be something our patients are ever afraid of and if they are currently not seeking us out because of a material fear for their lives, then that's something we must change.' Allegra paused, giving her drink another stir. 'There must be something I can do in my position to help. Even with mandatory reporting laws, there has to be something more we can do.'

Jamie's heart squeezed at the determination shining through Allegra's words. Before she could think about it—or consider which impulses to suppress and which to give in to—she reached across the table and wrapped her hand around Allegra's. Their fingers brushed against each other as Jamie slipped her palm against Allegra's and then gave her hand a firm squeeze.

The spark created by this small touch was instant. Heat raced down Jamie's arm, setting ablaze any nerve endings it encountered before wrapping itself tightly around her stomach. Across from her, Allegra's lips parted in a near-silent gasp that somehow still reverberated through Jamie's entire body.

Their hands lingered as they locked eyes and both women became suspended in the moment of this strange touch that had transformed into something new the second their skin had connected.

'Thank you.' Jamie willed the words out of her throat to end this moment and reclaim her hand. But they remained like that for a few more seconds, neither of them ready to sever the connection.

So Jamie really hadn't misjudged—

The waitress bumped her shoulder as she moved between the tables, mumbling her apologies as they were ripped out of whatever had transpired between them. Allegra's hand fell to the table and Jamie pulled her own hand back, laying it flat on her thigh and willing the tingling sensation away.

What had just happened?

CHAPTER FIVE

THE PIERCING WAIL of sirens sliced through the steady hum of Palm Grove Hospital as Allegra stepped out of the common-room-turned-office and hurried down the corridor towards the main part of the emergency room. A page had gone out to every available doctor, asking them to triage their patients according to their prioritisation protocol and help with the incoming incident: a bus crash leaving several passengers and bystanders injured. Serious enough that they'd paged every person, including her.

The end of this week marked her one-month milestone working at Palm Grove Hospital and even though Jamie's interventions throughout the month had helped Allegra find her feet with the staff, they still regarded her with a healthy—or unhealthy, depending on where you stood—amount of suspicion. She tried not to blame them and understood that a newcomer would be difficult to trust. Especially since she knew the history with Jamie now.

The woman turned out to be far more intriguing than Allegra wanted. Intriguing was *not* good when she was still trying to get her life back on track after the divorce had left her without a home, a family, or friends. Allegra hadn't ever thought that her reliance on Lewis would come back to haunt her. But now she was reaping the fruits of that by having absolutely no one to rely on as she built her new life.

And then there was Jamie, playing dangerous games with the concept of 'no one' that Allegra had just got comfortable with after so many years of living in a co-dependent marriage. She didn't want—or need—anyone close to her. Not when the people she'd thought were friends had shown her that their relationship hadn't been as precious to them as it had been to her.

This was what gave Allegra pause as her thoughts wandered to Jamie. She'd helped her out with Miguel and planned on working within the hospital's policies and state laws to ensure people like him could seek help without the fear of deportation. Not because she had anything to gain here, but because it was the right thing to do, another way for Allegra to defy the people who had put their greedy fingers into the healthcare system and twisted it into something that served the rich better than the poor.

Jamie's gratitude—and Allegra's reaction to it—was the wildcard. Their hands had lingered on each other for far too long, and the heat from her touch still ghosted over Allegra's palm whenever she let her thoughts wander back to that moment at the cafe.

A connection had sprung to life between them. One that she couldn't easily ignore when her work involved seeing Jamie on a near-daily basis. Even when she shut herself into the break room to work on the board report, Jamie's voice echoed down the corridor whenever she opened the door.

Organised cacophony enveloped Allegra as she entered

the emergency room, with the staff already executing their plan for high-volume patient intake. Jamie had put the protocol together, as noted in the binder, and Allegra took a second to admire how seamlessly it was being integrated into the situation at hand. Everyone knew exactly what they were supposed to do and how to triage the patients.

Allegra looked around, searching for the familiar dark brown hair. It had grown out a bit since their last encounter at the cafe and was now long enough that some strands flopped into Jamie's eyes whenever she moved her head—like right at this moment. Jamie stood beside the screen showing the current admissions, talking to each doctor or nurse that approached her and sending them away with specific instructions. Every now and then, she pushed her hand through those short strands of hair, pushing them to the side only for them to fall back to the front.

The motion was mesmerising, keeping Allegra rooted into place for several seconds as she imagined what Jamie's hair between her own fingers would feel like. A stretcher with a patient zipping past her unfroze Allegra, and she pushed those thoughts away before approaching Jamie.

'Dr Rivera, I got a page to come and help. Where do you need me?' she asked, and forced herself to meet Jamie's eyes despite the heat crawling up her neck.

'Allegra.' Her name, one she'd heard probably a million times at this point of her life, still hit her somewhere warm and squishy when Jamie said it, making the next breath harder to swallow. How could her own name sound as if it were Jamie's to wield whenever she pleased?

She only realised how casually Jamie had addressed her when the two interns standing in front of her exchanged looks, with one of them giving a one-shouldered shrug. Jamie noticed too, for her spine stiffened and she cleared her throat before assigning the interns their work.

A shiver crawled down Allegra's spine when their eyes met, the spark between them hot enough to singe her nerve endings. A reaction neither ideal nor appropriate for the situation they were in. How come Allegra had to remind herself of that every time Jamie was near her? Not even while working with Lewis had this been much of a problem.

'Where do you need me?' Allegra repeated, ripping them both out of their stupor.

Jamie cleared her throat again, and Allegra wasn't sure if that was a flush creeping up the other woman's neck or if the fluorescent light of the ER was playing tricks on her eyes.

The doors behind them leading down to the ambulance bay burst open with two paramedics pushing a stretcher towards them. 'Another passenger from the collision. John Doe, potential crush injuries on the leg. The firefighters had to cut parts of the car open to extract him,' one paramedic said, looking first at Jamie and then at Allegra.

'This one is for us. Let's go.' Jamie put her hand on the stretcher, guiding them to one of the trauma rooms where a nurse was already waiting to connect their patient to the vital monitors. The second the leads were placed, the machine started to beep and Allegra scanned the numbers.

'Vitals are dropping,' the nurse announced just as Allegra reached the same conclusion.

'Let's get him intubated while we get a visual on the wound,' Allegra said, nodding towards Jamie.

The other woman moved around to the end of the stretcher and Allegra heard the clattering of the tools along with Jamie's muttering as she worked on freeing up the airways of their patient.

With the help of the nurse, Allegra cut away the clothes around the injured area, letting out a low hiss as she beheld the devastation. The limb was mangled, with compound fractures and torn flesh. Blood oozed from the gaping wounds of one of the worse injuries she'd seen in her years of ER experience. She'd saved patients in similar situations, but the odds were against them in this case. Allegra knew they had to act incredibly fast if they were going to save this man.

'I need lap sponges here,' she called out. The nurse placed a stack in her hands and Allegra pressed down firmly to stem the bleeding. She looked up and met Jamie's eyes as she finished connecting the breathing tube to the Ambu bag and handed it over to the nurse assisting Allegra, gesturing at her to come and take her place.

'This isn't something we can solve here. He needs surgical intervention,' Allegra said as Jamie stepped up to her side. Judging by the frown pulling on her lips, Allegra could guess how slammed the surgical department was with the unexpected influx of cases.

Then Jamie nodded, picking up the phone hanging on the wall and pressing a number. Holding the receiver between her shoulder and her ear, Jamie stepped back to the patient and put her hands on top of Allegra's. 'I'll keep applying pressure while you get a large-bore IV started.

We need to get a blood transfusion going before we can move him safely and—yes, this is Dr Rivera.'

She stopped mid-sentence and Allegra took the opportunity of her momentary distraction to pull her hands away from under Jamie's, pointedly ignoring the tingles flashing through her fingers as she pulled free from her touch. The nurse handed Allegra a fresh pair of gloves, avoiding eye contact with the blood-spattered ones she'd just removed. Allegra disposed of them in the biohazard bin and prepared to insert an IV for the blood transfusion.

Allegra worked with practised precision as she inserted the IV into the man's uninjured arm. Then she connected the tubing to start the transfusion, watching as the nurse hung a bag of O negative from the IV pole. They had to replace what he had lost and get his pressure back up before he could endure the stress of surgery.

'We'll send him up shortly,' Jamie said into the phone and then raised an eyebrow at Allegra. Understanding her non-verbal cue, she took the phone receiver from Jamie and hung it back on the wall before turning around to look at her.

'Blood pressure is stabilising,' she said, and Allegra nodded, both of them staring at the monitor to their left. 'Do you feel confident in transporting him?'

'If the ER is ready, then now is as good a time as any. We can't stop this bleeding with sponges alone,' she replied, and knew from the hum leaving Jamie's throat that she agreed.

'Okay, let's get him moving. There are more patients to come and interns needing our help,' Jamie said before kicking the brakes on the wheels of the stretcher down and together they moved the patient to the elevator bay leading up to the OR.

The hours zipped by after they delivered the patient to the OR. They'd split up after their initial case together, though throughout the day they kept bumping into each other as they transferred patients or pushed around diagnostic equipment. There had been no time to stop and breathe, not until the wailing of the sirens finally stopped and the evening shift rolled in to take over.

Now the ER was back to its usual capacity, and as Allegra found her way down the near-empty corridors, she pushed away the disappointment building inside her whenever a staff member she encountered turned out not to be *her*. Not that she was *actively* looking for Jamie. That would be ridiculous. With her divorce having unravelled her life so thoroughly, she would never agree to a workplace romance again—regardless of how curious she was about what Jamie's fingertips would feel like as they skated down her spine. Or how good a certain someone smelled.

'—took over. It's been one change after another,' a voice grumbled, the resentment in the words biting.

Allegra froze in her step, her stomach clenching as she realised who they were talking about: her.

'We got by well enough without some hotshot doctor from the west coast needing to tell us what to do,' a second voice chimed in, and Allegra knew she should step away and let the staff have their grievances. She'd been in that situation herself, had she not? Where she'd needed to vent to someone about leadership, regardless of how fair it was. Maybe that was the part that kept Allegra's feet glued to the floor, so that she could hear more of what they said.

Because it *wasn't* fair. The processes she'd introduced to shift changes and staffing were there to ease the crunch times of the ER. Allegra had spent her evenings poring over reports of their throughputs in the emergency room, analysing when the patient intake peaked and when it evened out. Without more in the budget to hire people, she had to get creative with how to use the existing staff.

It had worked so well today, yet she wasn't that much closer to winning the staff over. To be fully accepted. It bothered her more than she'd thought it would.

'She was helpful enough today, but I'm not convinced this isn't just an opportunistic act. Have you ever actually interacted with her outside work? There's such a coldness to her.' The first voice shivered, and it struck Allegra.

Because the accusation was one she was familiar with. This wasn't the first time people had called her cold or unapproachable. Ice queen had been the nickname whispered in her old hospital along with sympathetic whispers for Lewis. As if it was no wonder he'd cheated on her because who wanted to come home to a pillar of ice?

This was the moment to leave. These words wouldn't have bothered her back in San Francisco because the people there hadn't been hers. If they had been, some of them would have reached out by now and checked in on her. No, because Lewis had been the driving factor for her to even be working at that hospital, she'd never evolved to become more than Lewis's wife. Had never aspired to more because it hadn't been necessary for her to do an excellent job.

But things here were different. This was a place she

had chosen for herself, where she wanted to make her new life, find new people. People who wanted her here because of who she was and not because of who she'd married. Yet despite the effort she'd put into this role over the last month, the staff still talked behind her back. Allegra was still the ice queen. Maybe this was a defect inside her and she wouldn't be able to change that, no matter how hard she tried.

She was about to leave when footsteps echoed down from around the corner and something about the cadence was familiar, though Allegra couldn't explain how. The second she heard the next words, she realised what had triggered that sense of familiarity.

'*Cállense*, both of you.' Jamie's words sliced through the air, and even though Allegra couldn't see them, she could almost hear them stand up straighter. 'Dr Tascioni has brought far more order into our chaotic ER than you give her credit for. I know that because she's worked with me every step of the way to ensure she's made the right decisions for our team. She's not this intruder you make her out to be, and you won't see anything improve if you keep fighting the person trying to bring about the changes.'

Allegra held her breath, hidden just out of sight, as stunned silence followed Jamie's words. The silence stretched, taut as a wire pulled too tight.

'Maybe you don't see it, but hiring her might have been the one smart thing Eliza Bailey has ever done,' Jamie continued. 'So, back off and show some respect. She's doing a better job than I could have done if the chief had picked me.'

A low muttering replaced the previous derision, and

when the shuffling of feet grew louder, Allegra finally moved. The last thing she needed after what she'd just heard was to be caught eavesdropping.

The echoes of Jamie's defence of her reverberated through her. Somehow, the words made each breath harder to take than the one coming before. A reaction so out of the norm for Allegra, she didn't know what to do with it. She didn't know why the initial words had struck her, because, at the end of the day, she *was* the ice queen. Allegra knew that about herself. Not because she didn't care, but because her life experience had taught her that most people simply didn't understand her brand of caring.

Jamie did. Otherwise she wouldn't have stood up for her the way she had. What other reason did she have other than seeing the work Allegra had been doing in the background and appreciating it for what it was?

Her heart thudded against her chest in an uneven beat as her mind shifted towards Jamie—towards the snap of attraction between them. Though what had just happened was more, was it not? Jamie had shown her this unexpected act of loyalty, and Allegra found herself disarmed.

Uncertain what it meant.

The steps around the corner grew louder again. Allegra retreated further into the hospital, tracing her steps back to the common room she'd made into her office. The day had brought up far too many things within her and she needed some time to think.

To build back that wall of ice Jamie had been slowly chipping away at.

Jamie's legs felt like leaden pillars as she navigated the maze-like corridors of Palm Grove Hospital, her mind fogged by the relentless toll of the shift. She had been an automaton of triage and treatment during the bus crash, getting involved in whatever trauma rooms had needed her most.

Throughout the shift, Allegra's auburn locks had popped up in the periphery of her vision, Allegra dealing with each emergency that came their way with the kind of competence anyone working in the emergency room would wish from their head of department. So when she'd heard a group of junior doctors complaining about Allegra, Jamie hadn't been able to stop her sharp tongue from slicing into them.

Though the words coming out had surprised her. One month. That was how long it had taken Allegra's influence to show in the way the emergency room ran. Only four weeks to see the difference between before and after Allegra. Not just in the ER, but also…

Jamie let go of that thought as her leaden feet carried her along until she got to the room she hadn't realised she'd been looking for until she stood in front of it: the break room at the far end of the emergency department. Allegra's makeshift office and also the sanctuary they had carved out for themselves where the buzz of the ER couldn't reach them. It had been here where she'd shown Jamie the new protocols to help with staffing and where they'd begun setting their plans for how to treat undocumented people without risking their deportation.

Her hand hovered over the door handle, hesitating. They'd also spent hours here in companionable silence, neither feeling the urge to fill the space between them with words. A tentative friendship had formed between them, underpinned by the moment Allegra had helped her save Miguel's life. And the moment in the cafe.

There hadn't been another moment where they'd touched deliberately. The only times were when they worked together and had to hand things over. The thrill of her hands brushing against Jamie's remained even in the high-stakes environment of an incident, though she'd tried her best to ignore those tingles. And the lingering stares. And the thick tension coalescing between them whenever they spent too much time around each other.

It would be better if Jamie spent less time with Allegra. Though she was convinced the attraction wasn't one-sided, she also knew that it couldn't lead anywhere. Even if they weren't working in the same department, Jamie wasn't about to risk the one place where she'd finally found belonging for the first time in her life. The feeling was so precious—and so fragile—she would do anything to protect it.

Taking a deep breath, she pushed the door handle down and stepped into the dimly lit break room. The door clicked behind her as she closed it and Jamie's heart stuttered in her chest as her eyes fell on the woman who had dominated her thoughts since she'd arrived at this hospital.

Allegra sat slumped in a chair, her eyes closed and her breathing deep and measured. Jamie hesitated again, not wanting to wake her up if she was sleeping.

'Hey,' Jamie said, her voice quiet enough to not be too intrusive.

'Hey, yourself,' Allegra replied without opening her eyes, a wisp of a smile playing on her lips.

'You look like you've been through a war.' The words

were a blatant lie because even after eleven hours of relentless emergencies pouring into the ER, Allegra looked nothing short of radiant. But Jamie wasn't about to tell her that. Instead, she relied on the usual platitudes ER doctors threw at each other after a long shift.

Allegra opened her eyes, the brown colour somehow darker today as she gave Jamie a once-over. The corners of her lips twitched, brightening her smile until Jamie saw a flash of white teeth. 'Not everyone can look as good as you after eleven hours of chaos,' Allegra said, and with that threw out Jamie's entire tactic of professional distance.

Her pulse skittered to the surface of her skin, pounding hard enough that Jamie could hear the blood in her ears. One compliment—one that was as blatantly untrue as Jamie's words had been—and she was reduced to a mute version of herself. When was the last time someone had slipped under her skin just like that? The answer came to Jamie without much effort: never. Because of the instability she'd experienced as a child, her relationships—if she could even call them that—had been transient, with Jamie being the one not wanting to stick around. Not wanting to risk the rejection she'd lived with all her childhood.

Realising she was still leaning against the door as stillness filtered through the break room, Jamie took the seat perpendicular to Allegra, pointedly ignoring the heat flaring alive right behind her navel as their knees knocked against each other. Their legs still touched as she settled down and Jamie held in a breath as she waited for Allegra to pull away. She didn't.

Instead, she levelled a contemplative stare at her, lashes

fluttering against her cheeks with every blink. Jamie forced herself to sit still and not squirm under her eyes, even though the longer it lasted, the more exposed she felt. She was about to ask about Allegra's thoughts when the other woman spoke again.

'Thank you for standing up for me today. I heard what you said and I...' Her voice trailed off and Jamie tensed as she detected a hint of a wobble in Allegra's voice. She'd overheard the staff talking about her? The knowledge dropped a boulder into her stomach.

For the first time since she'd met Allegra, she could see some cracks in the woman's armour. When she'd helped Jamie out with Miguel, her compassion had shone through, but even then she'd remained distant, not letting Jamie see below the surface level. The wavering in her voice at the end sent a jolt through her. She acted before she could debate whether she should follow the impulse bubbling up inside her.

Her hand slipped over Allegra's, her fingers wrapping around hers and giving them a squeeze. When Allegra lifted her eyes to hers, the colour deepened further and the flutter of Jamie's pulse against her throat went berserk.

'I didn't know you were there,' she said, forcing the words out before they could morph into something wholly inappropriate like, 'I would really like to kiss you.'

'I was around the corner and stopped to listen when I heard their voices. Probably shouldn't have, but now I'm glad I did. How else would I have known what you really think of me?' The smile spreading over Allegra's lips was slow. Tentative. As if she still wasn't sure that she wanted to share it with Jamie.

Jamie's heart thudded against her chest in an uneven rhythm. There was no way the truth was a good thing to say, yet Jamie couldn't stop herself. 'On a professional level, I believe you now know exactly how I feel.'

Allegra's eyes flared as Jamie's words registered. Then they narrowed as she said, 'And personally?'

Jamie shivered, her inhale shaky and filled with the alluring scent that was Allegra. That was a trick question, wasn't it? Because there was no way Allegra—her boss—could be encouraging what Jamie thought she was hinting at. She'd asked about her personal feelings because she wanted to lure Jamie into some kind of trap.

But that thought was absurd. She'd never given Allegra any reason to doubt her integrity. Quite the opposite. Jamie had come into this working relationship thinking it would be contentious. Dr Bailey had passed her over, after all, and, in Jamie's mind, the only reason for that was because she'd found one of her minions to take over the ER. Because Jamie knew Bailey thought her too softhearted and agreeable to make tough choices. Little did the chief know Jamie was kind and bubbly *because* of the decisions she'd been forced to make throughout her life. Because that was the part of her personality people in the ER agreed with the most.

Did Allegra somehow know this about her? Was that why she was asking about Jamie's personal feelings for her? Or was it because Allegra sensed something, too? Her fingers flexed underneath Jamie's hand, and when her index finger traced a small arch across her palm, the resulting shudder shook loose the words Jamie was trying her best not to let out into the world.

'I suspect on a personal level you also have a fairly

good idea how I feel.' Her fingers tightened around Allegra's as she said that and the other woman took a deep breath. Jamie's eyes dipped lower, watching her chest rise and fall before darting up to her face again.

Then everything seemed to slow down while also all happening at once. Their fingers wove together, palms pushing against each other and sending sparks down her arm and across her body. Allegra's scent enveloped her as she leaned closer and Jamie's eyes dropped to her lush lips—suddenly so much closer to her than they should be.

They were also too far away to kiss. That needed to change. Because even though Jamie wasn't sure whether this was a good idea, some other, more primal, part of her brain had taken over calling the shots and that part needed to know what Allegra's lips would feel like against her own.

Jamie leaned in, closing the gap between them until Allegra's breath grazed her cheek. She lifted her free hand up to Allegra's face, her fingers tracing her jaw bone with a slow gentleness, giving Allegra the opportunity to pull back if she wanted to.

She didn't. Instead, she leaned her head to the side and into Jamie's palm and the connection rocked through her, pushing all the remaining breath out of her—along with the slivers of restraint she'd hung onto until this second. This was all the encouragement she needed.

Her fingers slipped down to Allegra's neck, threading through her hair until she cradled the back of her head. When she pulled her closer, Allegra didn't resist. Her eyes were alight with a fire that leapt into Jamie's body when they met in a tender, explorative brush of their lips.

The softness of her mouth was exquisite, her breath hot

against Jamie's cheeks. And her *scent*. God, how could she still smell this good after eleven hours in the emergency room? Jamie inhaled deeply, letting Allegra's smell overwhelm her senses as she pressed closer. Her teeth sank into Allegra's bottom lip and the throaty moan she got in response threatened to overwhelm her.

Until this moment, the idea of Allegra—of *sleeping* with her, more precisely—had been a purely intellectual pursuit. There were so many things standing between her and the low simmering desire that Jamie hadn't even thought about coming on to her. They were colleagues. Allegra was her superior, and from what little she'd shared about her personal life she'd just gone through a divorce. The implication here being that Allegra was the settling-down type.

Jamie stood at the exact opposite of that spectrum. Her relationships hadn't ever lasted more than a few casual nights together, and that was by design. That way, she got the physical release without having to deal with the heartbreak that inevitably followed.

Something she should probably have brought up before she fell mouth first in Allegra's direction, but it was a bit late now and a large part of her also didn't want to think about it. Wanted to simply enjoy this feeling she hadn't had for quite some time. With how important the hospital had become to her and how much time she spent here, there hadn't been any time for ages to find someone for quick releases.

But when Allegra's hand brushed against Jamie's waist to pull her closer and deepen the kiss, her thoughts scattered along with any reservations of how difficult things could get by sleeping with a colleague. All of Jamie's attention narrowed on where their lips met, where fingers pulled on fabric to find the skin beneath in a frantic chase of release they were both craving enough to forget anything else.

Or rather, *almost* anything else. Neither of them could ignore the shrilling sound coming from Allegra's belt. She gasped into Jamie's mouth and hands that had been exploring now pushed her away. Jamie complied immediately, even though the emptiness Allegra's mouth left when it lifted from hers was jarring.

Her mind still struggled to process what had happened between them when Allegra dug the pager out of her pocket and looked at the code crawling over the display. A line appeared behind her brow as she reached for her phone, reading whatever message had accompanied the page.

'Damn, what could possibly be important enough to request at this hour?' she mumbled, more to herself than to Jamie. Then her thumbs flew over the phone, typing up a reply.

Jamie meanwhile stared at Allegra, at the now puffy lips and the small red marks her own teeth had left on them. Then her eyes dipped lower, watching the rise and fall of Allegra's chest slow down, and Jamie mirrored her own breathing to match it, coming down from the frenzy that had overcome them.

And then what she'd done sank in.

Who she'd done it with.

When Allegra put her phone down and looked back up, that piece of information seemed to catch up with her too—her eyes flared wide, blinking at Jamie several times, her lips slightly parted.

'I...um...have to go. Bailey. She—' Allegra stopped mid-sentence as she got to her feet. Grabbing her laptop, she moved to the door and froze on the threshold, looking back at Jamie. 'This isn't me fleeing because of...well, this. I need you to know that. Maybe we can talk after the thing tomorrow?'

Jamie blinked, her mind still half dazed from the roller coaster that had been the kiss and the sudden withdrawal from Allegra. The thing? Her mind was far too hazy to remember any specific things outside her name and that she needed to have Allegra's mouth on hers again. Whatever thing—

'Oh, the first-aid tent. Almost forgot about it.' After Allegra had witnessed some of what Jamie did for the community, she'd asked to be included in whatever else she did. In this case, be the first-aid person at a street festival in her neighbourhood to celebrate Hispanic Heritage Month.

The prospect of spending time with Allegra in an enclosed space was now somehow both more daunting and more appealing than it had been when she'd first invited her. Especially since Allegra wanted to *talk*. Not something Jamie was used to doing. Unless the talking she referenced was filthy. Then she was all for it.

Jamie cleared her throat as the rogue thoughts bubbled up in her and gave Allegra a short nod. 'Yes, we'll talk tomorrow,' she said, voice still husky from the desire the kiss had exploded through her.

Allegra nodded, the hint of a smile tugging at her lips as she gave her one last glance before walking out of the break room and leaving Jamie to figure out exactly what kind of mess she'd put herself in.

CHAPTER SIX

THE BLEND OF laughter and spirited conversations melded with the vibrant beats of salsa music, enveloping Allegra in a tapestry of festivity as she navigated the crowded street. Miami's Hispanic Heritage Month had transformed the thoroughfare into a pulsating artery of life, each heartbeat marked by the flutter of colourful flags and the rhythmic sway of dancers moving wherever music spilled into the streets. Which, by the looks of it, was everywhere.

Aromatic tendrils wafted from food carts stationed at every corner, vendors praising the taste of their freshly prepared empanadas and tamales. The air itself seemed to shimmer with the sheer joy of the occasion. Allegra wanted to get lost in the exuberance and soak up the celebratory vibes, but each step that brought her closer to her destination wound the string inside her tighter.

Because waiting for her at the first-aid tent at the edge of the festivities was Jamie. When the woman had first told her about volunteering for this event, Allegra had jumped at the opportunity to help out. The different communities of Homestead would be the people most likely landing in her ER.

She'd hired a Spanish tutor to teach her at odd hours

of the day. With the unpredictability of her schedule, it was sometimes hard to find the time to actually sit down and study. But if she was serious about her place at Palm Grove Hospital—and she *was* serious—then she would have to learn the language, even if it was little by little.

Though was she really allowed to claim she was serious when she was making out with her subordinates in clandestine areas of the hospital? Granted, the area was only clandestine because people seemed to have forgotten it existed. Allegra hadn't sought it out because it was secluded, but so they could use the space they had more appropriately. She'd never planned on that room becoming her and Jamie's own little oasis in the middle of the chaos that was the ER.

How exactly had she let things go so far? Allegra had no idea. Her attraction to Jamie had surfaced early on and, with Jamie having held the emergency room together before Allegra's arrival, she'd had no way of avoiding her even if she'd wanted to. Which she knew she hadn't. No matter how much she might want to claim otherwise, the magnetism drawing her to Jamie had been far too powerful for her to resist.

Allegra had waved it off as a silly infatuation with a woman she worked with in close proximity. Jamie was objectively beautiful and outgoing, the veritable sunshine in an otherwise stormy emergency room. In fact, Allegra could see she hadn't been the only one to succumb to Jamie's charm. The whole reason the staff had been giving her such a hard time had been because they thought Allegra had stolen something from Jamie: her job.

Which created another layer of complexity in an already complicated situation. Because Allegra had done the whole office romance once before and it hadn't ended well, with her marriage not being the only collateral damage in the entire divorce saga. That was the reason she was here now, rebuilding her life and career at Palm Grove Hospital. Even a year later, the damage to her life continued. Because no matter how much she knew her life was different now—that it should be new and hers alone—a part of her remained back in her old life. To remind her of the mistakes. What would happen if she got too wrapped up in someone else's life instead of building her own.

Lewis had taken everything from her and now wouldn't even leave her in peace to start over. Not that Allegra was doing particularly well with that, considering the ghosts of her divorce and departure from her old life were still haunting her.

She really wanted love to be a part of it and could feel the hollow the trauma had left in her chest. But never again with a colleague. That was a lesson she didn't need to learn more than once. So the kiss with Jamie had been an ill-advised slip-up. They would talk about it after this event, would agree that, in the position they were in, whatever attraction floating between them was best ignored and then they'd go back to their peaceful—even if sometimes mind-numbingly hot—co-existence as colleagues and friends.

Maybe that was the right thing to focus on. Jamie wasn't just a competent doctor that Allegra wanted to have by her side. Throughout figuring out the staffing situation, their internal policies and navigating the expectations of the investors sitting on the hospital's board, Jamie had become a resource to lean on. Someone to learn from. Someone who understood the struggles and shared them with her.

Wasn't that feeling far more important than some flights of fancy or potentially hot sex? And by potentially, Allegra of course meant that it would be *very* spicy. At least if their kiss was anything to go by.

By the time the bright red tarp of the first-aid tent appeared, Allegra was flushed in the face and batting away the intrusive fantasies coming at her unbidden. Hadn't she told herself that these things *weren't* worth risking their budding friendship? Somehow, the two sides of her brain had become disconnected.

Even though she braced herself as she stepped into the tent, she still wasn't prepared to see Jamie. Or rather, her mind had concocted so many outlandish fantasies about Jamie that heat surged through her body, deepening the red streaking over her cheeks and leaving Allegra without speech for a few seconds.

All she could do was trace Jamie's shape with her eyes, stopping at the round curve of her hips before wandering further up her body until she came to another halt at those talented and soft lips that had twisted her mind so much. Now all she could think about was what they would feel like on other parts of her body. Specifically the lower, softer parts of her body where—

Nope. This was definitely *not* how friends thought about each other.

'Hey,' Allegra pressed out, catching the attention of Jamie, who sat on a stool with another person's foot in her hands.

She looked up from the female patient, the earrings lining her right shell jingled at the jerky movement, and when a smile unfurled across those damn kissable lips, Allegra's breath stuttered out of her in an uneven staccato.

'Hey, yourself,' she replied, mirroring the interaction they'd had yesterday but in reverse, and Allegra couldn't fight the smile appearing on her own mouth.

'You've sprained your ankle, but it's not too bad and won't require any follow-ups. Just stay off your feet if you can for a few days and take over-the-counter pain medication to regulate your discomfort,' Jamie said to her patient, then looked at the man standing next to her with a worried look on his face. 'You two okay getting home?'

The man nodded and then helped the woman up from the little exam table. Jamie smiled at both of them as she followed them to the tent entrance, and the flutter in Allegra's stomach went into overdrive as the other woman's scent enveloped her. It shouldn't be such a familiar smell. Yet here she was, breathing in those floral hints and shivering at the warmth it brought to her bones.

Meaning when Jamie turned around to greet her, she was in a complete daze and staring at her. Her hands twitched with the need to reach out and touch her. To push her fingers through her short hair and feel the silkiness of the strands against her skin. To pull that mouth onto hers again and let their passion play out with no interruptions this time.

Allegra almost gasped when Jamie's eyes narrowed on her, her gaze tipping to her mouth and remaining there for far longer than a cursory glance would—as if she was thinking about the same thing. The thought turned the heat running through her veins higher and she wasn't sure if the sweat she felt on her neck was real or imagined.

Neither of them moved for a loaded second, each woman waiting for the other one to make the first move.

'I like your—' Allegra began.

Just as Jamie said, 'You look lovely.'

Allegra's eyes widened, and she looked down at herself as if she hadn't spent the morning agonising over what to wear. Not something she usually struggled with. For the last several years of her life, she'd lived at the hospital, meaning she'd hardly ever had reasons to update her wardrobe. It hadn't been as if Lewis and she had had much of a life outside work. Ironic how he'd cited their lack of connection outside work as the reason he'd cheated on her when his mistress had been working in her department.

Now that lack of interest in anything that could look pretty or sexy on her had come to bite her in the butt. Because, for some reason, she'd really wanted to look her best today. No, not for some reason. For a very specific reason—*person*. Only just a few moments ago, she had vowed not to let herself drift any closer to those burning feelings for Jamie.

So she'd put on a 80s rockabilly-inspired dress while making a note that she should go out shopping soon.

'You don't mean that, but thank you anyway,' Allegra said, rubbing her palms on her thighs. Why were they sweaty? She had dealt with situations far more daunting than this one, yet somehow this had her flustered beyond all comparison.

Jamie's eyebrow quirked up. 'Of course I mean it. Why wouldn't I?'

Allegra looked down at herself again, as if her once-over hadn't sufficed to take stock of her outfit. 'I guess because this is one of the few things I have in my suitcase that isn't hospital attire, and I see it very much as functional clothing.'

She had no idea why she was sharing the word salad tumbling around in her mind verbatim, but here she was, doing exactly that. To her surprise, Jamie let out a low laugh that filled the space between them with an electric current.

'How long has it been since you came to work here? You can't seriously still be living out of your suitcase.' Jamie took a step towards her. The noise from the crowd outside dimmed as Allegra focused her attention on her rather than on the rapid pitter-patter of her heart.

'I just passed the one-month mark. And yes, I'm still living in a hotel out of my suitcase. I haven't looked for an apartment yet,' she replied, her own feet shuffling her closer and she couldn't tell if that was against her will or because she really wanted to be closer to Jamie.

'Do you need any help with that?' Jamie asked, and somehow her voice had dropped even lower. 'I can ask around and see if anyone is moving and looking for someone new.'

How could this possibly be suggestive? Jamie was offering her help, as any friendly colleague would do. Yet another flash of heat crawled up Allegra's neck as the words washed over her as if Jamie had told her all the different ways she wanted to see her undone.

And why was it that this was the first thing Allegra's mind grabbed at? They had shared a brief kiss, hardly more than a brush of their lips against each other, and somehow that had led her brain down far too many filthy roads.

'I have to find some time to sit down and do it. With how understaffed the hospital is and how much I need to do for the board while also doing patient work, it just felt overwhelming to put moving into an apartment on that list. Especially since the hotel is so close to the hospital.' Again the truth tumbled out of Allegra's mouth with no filter. Something about Jamie seemed to bypass the icy exterior she usually kept such a tight grip on.

Jamie nodded and for a second Allegra could see the light of the same fire she'd seen in that dark gaze yesterday and her fingers twitched, wanting to reach out and trace the edge of her jaw. Memorise what she felt like, because Allegra knew she couldn't have her, but maybe that one taste would be enough.

The tent moving had both women shaking off their stupor and then Jamie rushed over to the entrance to help the woman holding her arm gingerly against her chest. Behind the woman, another street-fest patron came in, one eye half shut from the swelling.

Jamie and Allegra locked eyes again, though this time there wasn't a hint of the attraction between them but rather the silent and efficient way they communicated with each other during incidents in the hospital. She didn't need Jamie to tell her where she needed her to be as she moved to the man with the swollen eye and escorted him to the back of the tent while Jamie looked at the woman's arm.

Over the course of the street fest, the first-aid tent remained slightly busier than Jamie had expected. With the amount of sprains, dizziness brought on by dehydration or alcohol, and an allergic reaction as well as the occasional scraping wound from falling over—at least that was what she chose to believe—Jamie was glad she'd asked Allegra to join her. She'd done that primarily to show her the type of work she did here for the community, even though she knew Allegra already cared enough to want to help her by changing some of the emergency room policies.

There were enough people that they didn't have any time to talk. Or to discuss anything that had happened between them. That 'anything', of course, being their kiss. Thinking of it as an insubstantial 'anything' made it easier to compartmentalise and push away. Something she'd had to focus on throughout the day whenever Allegra's voice floated through the air or she glimpsed a flash of those auburn curls as she walked around the tent.

'Make sure you keep drinking lots of water,' Jamie said to Alejandra, an older woman who lived on the same street as her. 'And I mean water. Not coffee, okay?'

Alejandra shook her head while clicking her tongue. 'There's water in coffee,' she replied as she shuffled onto her feet and waddled towards the tent exit where her grandson was already waiting for her.

Jamie rolled her eyes while Alejandra's eyes were still on her but couldn't fight the chuckle bubbling up in her chest. People like Alejandra filled her with a sense of comfort that was both soothing and frightening. Because even though she'd been here since her internship six years ago, a part of her still refused to settle down—to fully let herself sink into the comfort of knowing that she'd found a place she could call home. Turned out eighteen years of instability were hard to shake, even though the last decade had let her take charge of her own life.

'What has you smiling like that?' Allegra stood a few paces to her left, and when Jamie turned her head, the electric current zapping back and forth between them snapped back into place at the eye contact. The tension had been here the entire day. With the hectic atmosphere of the first-aid tent, it had been easy enough to ignore. But now the music from the street had wound down, the sun dipping below the horizon an hour ago and bathing their secluded place at the edge of the festivities in a rosy light.

'The street party is one of the nicer things I get to be a part of,' Jamie said, focusing on the familiar warmth that thinking about her community brought to her. Not the raging inferno that tried too hard to take over whenever her eyes met Allegra's.

'You must care a lot with everything that you do here in your spare time. Considering how much time you spend working at the hospital, that's quite the commitment,' she said, the air filled with a soft patter as she began moving things around the tent.

Jamie joined in, folding away the cot they'd used as a makeshift exam table. 'Palm Grove Hospital is where I did my internship and residency. After leaving Texas, I didn't know anyone. Which wasn't much of a change to Texas, if I'm honest. It wasn't like I left much behind,' Jamie said, keeping her eyes on her hands as she said that. Those weren't words she had said out loud before, but something inside her compelled her to explain her motivation to Allegra. She wanted her to understand her on a deeper level.

So when more words bubbled up, she continued, 'Still, there was a sense of displacement in moving halfway across the country. The street festival happened on the first weekend I arrived here and the noise of the celebrations drew me in. At first, I didn't know what to do, but I think my cluelessness showed on my face because it didn't take long for a group of people to just sweep me up and take me along with them. As if I had always been a part of them. Up until that point in my life, I'd only ever known belonging as a vague concept. But after arriving here, I began to understand what it really meant to me—what I'd been missing my whole life.'

Jamie could feel Allegra's eyes on her, trailing up and down her body, and not for the first time in the month that they'd known each other this one thought popped into her head: did Allegra like what she saw?

If yesterday was any sign to go by—and Jamie seriously hoped that it was—she knew Allegra was into her enough to have a far too brief make-out session with her. They had yet to talk about it in detail, but Jamie knew that conversation was about to happen. Maybe that was why she had shared so many of her thoughts, far more than she ever had before. Because the longer she spoke, the longer she would avoid the inevitable conversation: the one where Allegra told her last night was a mistake and that they'd best remain at a professional distance.

Because even after six years of calm, Jamie knew people left. It was simply what they did. Her parents hadn't cared enough to pull themselves together and show up for the daughter they'd created. None of the many homes she was put in had gone beyond the bare minimum to sustain her. The impressions—the hurt—ran deep enough that, even now, Jamie had a packed duffel bag in her closet with all the essentials she needed in it.

That habit had never died because even though the

sense of belonging to this place was there and she genuinely felt it, a tiny part inside her still couldn't let go.

So it was better they had this conversation now than three months down the line. That way, her silly infatuation wouldn't get any air to breathe and morph into something else. Something far more hurtful when it would all come tumbling down on her.

'What do we do with the tent?' Allegra asked, and Jamie glanced over to her side where everything was neatly stacked into piles. Looking back at her own side, it was in a similar state. They were all done cleaning up.

'It belongs to the organisers, along with everything else in here. They'll come pick it up when they're ready, but we don't have to wait around,' she replied, even though a part of her wanted to tell her they needed to guard the things. Allegra hadn't shared anything of her own. Hadn't even commented on Jamie opening up.

They also hadn't talked about their kiss, even though Allegra had said she wanted to. Had she changed her mind? Jamie hoped she had, while another part of her would even take that disappointing conversation over not talking to her at all. That was the state Allegra had her in after their kiss.

As if Allegra had caught her thoughts on some unconscious level, she said, 'Are you in the mood for a walk? The park bordering this street seems nice and there's still some warmth left in the air.'

Jamie nodded, thrown off by how easily Allegra had asked her the thing she'd agonised over in her head. Why was it so hard for her to talk to this woman? Making shallow connections was easy for Jamie. A lifetime of rejection had taught her to read people's moods to the point where she knew exactly how she needed to be to get on someone's good side. But somehow Allegra threw that entire concept into disarray.

How?

The faint noises of celebrations underlined the quiet of the park. With the city permit only allowing them to play music outdoors up to a certain point, most of the street party had been moved to the various restaurants and bars of the neighbourhood. Which served Jamie well, as it gave them a nearly deserted park to amble through.

'I appreciate you helping today,' Jamie said as the quiet went on, not sure if she wanted to have the conversation about the kiss now or if she should try to stall with some unrelated topics.

Next to her Allegra smiled, her head swivelling around as she took in the quite limited sights. There wasn't anything overly intricate or unusual about this park. It had the usual playground along with winding paths lined with trees and other shrubbery. Jamie herself had attended some neighbourhood cookouts here but no more than that. Yet somehow Allegra was taking it all in as if it were her first time enjoying the quiet of a small park.

'I have to thank you for inviting me along. Community service isn't something I'm familiar with from an emergency room perspective. At my old hospital, we had quite a few programmes dedicated to drug rehab and homelessness charities. I've always collaborated with them to the best of my abilities, but it never actually occurred to me I could—*should*—get involved myself,' Allegra said after a beat of silence.

'Don't let this convince you that this is a Palm Grove

Hospital thing, because it's not. I do this to give back to people who were so welcoming to me when I needed it the most,' Jamie said.

'Still, I think this is an ideal to aspire to for anyone running a hospital in such a close-knit community. It was such a different experience from San Francisco in some ways when I think about it. Sure, we had some regulars that we saw in the ER, more often than not, but even with those people I can hardly recall their names.' Allegra stopped in front of a bench and gestured towards it in a silent question. Jamie nodded and sat down, leaving a deliberate chunk of space between them. She could feel every inch of that space even though she tried her best to ignore it.

'Was your hospital much larger than Palm Grove Hospital?' Jamie asked, to distract herself from the tendrils of heat beckoning her to touch Allegra.

Her auburn hair tumbled across her shoulder when Allegra tipped her head to the side with a contemplative hum. 'Not much larger. We had more beds in the emergency room but not enough that I'd say it made a huge difference. But the hospital was in downtown San Francisco, where most cases coming in were drug-related or medical needs related to homelessness. With their transient nature, we saw many faces only once.'

'Do you miss working there?' Jamie wasn't sure why she wanted to know, only that she did. Her voice had a wistful quality that she couldn't quite categorise as positive or negative. The sensation was just…there.

The incredulous laugh shouldn't have felt as relieving as it did. 'God, no. The hospital itself wasn't as bad overall, but the people…' She paused to let out a shudder.

Jamie couldn't help but laugh. 'That bad, huh?'

Allegra joined in with her laugh, though her voice remained strained. 'Ah, not all the people. But even a few can make it unbearable. Far too cliquey for my taste now that I look back on it. Lewis, my ex, was part of the surgical team there, along with a large part of his family. His father is the chief of surgery there, so when we got married, it was a given that we had to move there for his residency once we were done with med school. I worked hard to show everyone I earned my place at the hospital, but when your last name is Kent at SF General, they kind of assume you got there because of your family connections.'

Jamie paused, considering. Though their experiences sounded similar, she wasn't sure if it was true. The staff—in the emergency room at least—were all close to each other, a necessity when you worked in a place like the ER. But even though they were close, Jamie wouldn't call them cliquey. Though as that thought bubbled up, she remembered how she'd had to intervene more than once on Allegra's behalf and downright order people to get off her back.

The motivation—the why—behind their actions had been different, but the result looked indistinguishable from what Allegra had experienced at her other hospital. 'I'm sorry people have given you a hard time here,' Jamie said, keeping her hand curled into a tight fist so she wouldn't reach out to Allegra.

The other woman gave her a one-sided shrug. 'I understand caution at a place like Palm Grove Hospital. With leadership more concerned about throughput and having enough money left over to pay dividends to investors, anyone coming in should be regarded with suspicion. Bailey also thought she was hiring someone who would do what she needed without much care for the staff.' She paused, then tilted her head to look at Jamie with a small smile that was powerful enough to set her heart aflutter. 'Don't worry about the staff at Palm Grove. After being cheated on by my ex with a woman on my team and then also being blamed for the fallout, I've grown a thick skin. Their hesitance is downright refreshing, actually. At least they are protecting one of their own and not some obnoxious nepo baby publicly cheating on his wife.'

Jamie stared at Allegra, blinking a few times as she absorbed the information the other woman had shared. Processing the glimpses of her that Allegra had granted her. She'd said it with such detachment that it sounded as if it had happened to another person altogether. A different Allegra.

'He was sleeping with people in your department while you were married?' That was the bit of her story that her brain couldn't let go, and it became another source of validation for Jamie's decision to never give someone that kind of power over her. Everyone left at the end, after all. So had Allegra's husband, and, even worse, he had forced Allegra to carry the emotional burden of his actions.

Why were people like this?

'Not his finest hour. But at least that gave me the guts to leave. We were unhappy before that. Hardly seeing each other... Barely talking.' Allegra shrugged again though this time Jamie could see the tension rippling through her. 'He said because I spent so much time working, he had to look for closeness elsewhere. That my long hours and commitment to the hospital were so present in our life together that he couldn't help himself when someone showed him some kindness. Never mind the fact that the only reason I was even working so hard was because, unlike him, I needed to prove myself worthy of *his* name. But because he spent his entire life just getting what he wanted, he didn't realise—or empathise—what it's like for other people.'

The words kept coming, each one sharper than the other, and halfway through Jamie got the impression that these words had never seen the light of day before. Not until now, sitting on this bench. Even her iron will couldn't stop her hand from unfurling and reaching across the gap between them to lay her palm flat on Allegra's thigh. The tremble she sensed going through the muscle beneath almost had her retrieving her hand again, worried she'd overstepped, misread the situation.

But then Allegra slipped her hand over Jamie's as she turned towards her with an uneasy smile pulling at her lips. Her mouth opened, and Jamie leaned in, not wanting to miss a single word she had to say. But then Allegra sighed, shaking her head. 'Sorry, I don't even know where this came from. That's a lot to put on you.'

'Why?' Jamie could come up with a hundred reasons on the spot. They were co-workers. Allegra was in charge of the department in which Jamie worked. They still hadn't addressed this *thing* between them. But that didn't mean any of them were true for her.

'Because despite—' She halted, then skipped whatever she'd been about to say. 'You don't really know me well enough for me to trauma-dump my failed marriage all over you.'

Jamie couldn't contain an amused snort at that. 'Is that

what we're doing here? Trauma-dumping?' She looked down to where Allegra's hand covered hers and twisted her wrist so their palms lay flat against each other. 'And here I thought you were finally opening up and letting me see more than just a sliver of the woman behind the head of emergency medicine mask.'

To her surprise, Allegra's lips kicked up at one side in a half-smile. 'Yes, I guess the not really knowing me well is by design. I thought I was close to my colleagues at SF General, but when Lewis began his affair, so many people covered for him. People I thought liked me because of me rather than my marital name.'

Jamie nodded, understanding her point even though her heart squeezed inside her chest for Allegra. 'Past experience has taught you to keep a professional distance, so that's what you do. I understand that.' Though Jamie was quite friendly with everyone around her, her own life experience had taught her similar things. Mainly how to hide herself so, even though she was friendly, no one could really know her. If no one truly knew her, no one could reject her by leaving.

Something lit up in Allegra's eyes, a fire unlike the one she'd seen before. The one that woke up a deep-seated hunger within her whenever she saw it. That craving had been the reason she'd even given in to the impulse to kiss her yesterday. An impulse that was rearing its head again as Allegra's gaze bore deep into her.

Jamie expected Allegra to ask her about her experience and braced herself to answer as vaguely as possible without killing the conversation entirely. But instead, Allegra huffed out a laugh while shaking her head. 'I was doing just fine on my own, I thought. The staff would see the quality of my work eventually and get over themselves. Plus, I didn't need them to like me. It's probably better if they didn't because then I wouldn't get attached. But you turned that thought on its head.'

Allegra flexed her fingers, intertwining them with Jamie's. The steady pulse of heat that had started with their palms pressed against each other increased to a jolt of electricity that ran down Jamie's arm, singeing her nerves as it went down and through her body. 'You judged me by my actions, by my plans. My intentions. Not by some arbitrary thing like my name. Even though I came as a stranger into this place you have chosen as your family.'

Jamie's breath whooshed out of her, her heart slamming against her chest in a ridiculous attempt to escape. They shouldn't be having a conversation like this, yet she was powerless to resist. Especially when Allegra's gentle warmth radiated through her and her lashes lowered in a look that sent gusts of heat billowing through Jamie.

She needed to feel those lips moving against her mouth again. Nothing else mattered in this delicate moment of shared vulnerability. Consequences were nothing more than a triviality when Jamie put her other hand on Allegra's waist and pulled her closer.

The space between them grew smaller as Allegra shifted closer under Jamie's touch. Except for their clasped hands, their skin wasn't making any contact yet the liquid fire racing through her veins stoked up as if she were sitting naked in front of the other woman. A thought that turned her insides into goo, her heart skittering at the fantasy. Would it be as good as her imagination—and the occasional hint of a touch—made her believe?

Despite it being a terrible idea, Allegra wanted to find out. She couldn't remember any of the reasons *why* this was a bad idea. Granted, she wasn't trying very hard to remember anything. Couldn't, really, because all her brain's processing power was preoccupied with mapping the gentle slope of Jamie's jaw as Allegra cupped her cheek.

She'd come here to clear the air and regain some semblance of their professional boundaries. Instead of telling her they needed to take a step back, Allegra was drawn into her orbit. *Wanting* to crash land because how was anything else possible under their circumstances?

Allegra's fingers grazed the earring hanging from Jamie's earlobe and from there they crept further up, touching and counting each stud and ring as she moved.

'I like your earrings.' Her breath hitched as she said that. A smile tugged at Jamie's lips and she leaned closer until their noses touched. Until Allegra's mouth was angled perfectly under Jamie's, waiting for the gap to close.

'Thanks. I don't usually wear them for my shifts at the hospital,' she replied, her lips close enough to hers that Allegra shuddered at the sensation of the phantom kiss ghosting over her.

She had noticed the spots around Jamie's ears where the jewellery was missing whenever she saw her at the hospital, and had wondered what it would look like. Her imagination hadn't done it justice. Probably never could when it came to Jamie. So much of that woman just seemed out of reach. Smooth edges where Allegra's were sharp. Sunshine that melted away the icy exterior she'd crafted so carefully to protect herself from any kind of attachment that could hurt her as it had in the past.

'Probably wise, though I'm sad I won't get to see them more often,' Allegra said, her fingers moving back down the shell of Jamie's ear to trace her jawbone.

Jamie let out a huff that was either a laugh or a moan. Either way, the sound raced through Allegra in a bolt of lightning, igniting everything it touched. 'What's stopping you from seeing them more often?' Jamie asked, her breath feathering over Allegra's heated cheeks.

There were no thoughts left in Allegra's mind to reply to that. She had no answer. What *was* stopping her? This morning she'd had enough to fill a page in a notebook with all the reasons why getting closer to Jamie was a bad idea. But apparently those reasons were as solid as papier mâché, disintegrating under the lightest touch.

Because there was nothing left in her brain, Allegra didn't say anything. Instead, she closed the remaining gap between their mouths, surging into Jamie in a repeat of yesterday's kiss.

Except this one was nothing like the first. There wasn't a hint of hesitation from either of them as their lips touched, no tentative probing. This wasn't even close to what she'd planned for this moment, but the words—her refusal—had disintegrated underneath Jamie's heated touch, leaving her with nothing to grasp at. Nothing but Jamie. Would she regret it again when they parted?

Had she even truly regretted the first kiss?

Jamie's hand slipped to the small of Allegra's back, pulling her closer until she was nearly sitting on the other woman's lap. She draped one leg over Jamie's, the other woman's thighs falling open to let her leg dangle between hers. Even though they were fully clothed, that little gesture sent a prickling wave of need through Allegra that had her breath sawing out of her.

The rustling of leaves, the quiet mumbling of people an undetermined number of steps away, and the whispers of the music of the still ongoing party—it all dimmed into nothing until all Allegra could hear was the blood rushing through her ears and the low moans coming from Jamie's throat as her tongue swept into her mouth.

Or were those her own moans? Their bodies blended together as the kiss deepened, making it harder to even see the lines between them. All her attention narrowed to the point where they touched, so when Jamie's hand found its way underneath the hem of her dress's skirt and rested on her bare thigh, her entire skin lit up from head to toe. The need to feel her own hands on Jamie became an urging force within her and she grasped for the other woman, finding anything to hold onto. Her fingers tunnelled through Jamie's short hair, relishing the feel of the buzzed sides as they merged with the slightly longer strands on the top of her head.

The gasp tearing from her lips was involuntary when Jamie reared her head back, gulping down air in big breaths. All at once, the sounds of the park kicked back in. The shrieking and giggling of children playing grew louder, so did the music filtering through the trees from the streets beyond. An icy breeze hit Allegra's flushed skin, and she blinked several times to acclimatise to the sudden absence of Jamie's mouth on hers.

Why had she pulled away? Her heart raced, pulse pounding in her ears and against the base of her throat. Second thoughts? Allegra couldn't even parse that possibility, her stomach falling through her body, thinking how close she'd just got to something she really, *really* wanted and hadn't known she did until this very second.

Her nerves eased when Jamie huffed out a laugh. 'Sorry, I was about to do some very pornographic things to you. Considering we're sitting on a bench in a public park, that's the only word that feels accurate enough.'

Jamie's grin was wicked, her face entirely transformed by the thing that had come to pass between them in the last few minutes. Gone was the ever-sunny expression Allegra was used to seeing, replaced with something raw and alluring. A side of Jamie no one ever got to see. No one but Allegra.

The thought vibrated through her, sending a shiver clawing through her that settled down right behind her bellybutton in a low and pulsating heat.

Pornographic really was the right word, even if it sounded downright vulgar. Because all Allegra could think of was how much she wanted to explore the depths—the implications—of that word together with Jamie. While she could still pretend that none of this would ever catch up with them. While she didn't care. Something about Jamie had slipped right under her skin, not letting her escape, melting the carefully cultivated icy exterior Allegra had adopted. Strange how that protection was already failing her. Or was it strange how little she cared?

She leaned back in, her leg still dangling between Jamie's, and drew the woman into another, somewhat more subdued kiss. Her teeth sank into Jamie's lower lip, applying just enough pressure for her to gasp. When that sound turned into a growl, Allegra's insides dissolved into molten lava.

'There's a place nearby that is a lot less public and therefore more appropriate for…pornographic things.' She said the word slowly, unsure if she was stumbling over it or savouring it. Probably both.

One of Jamie's eyebrows shot up. 'What place is that?' she asked.

Allegra's entire being vibrated as she parted her lips and committed to the thing they had started by saying, 'My hotel room.'

CHAPTER SEVEN

THE CLICK OF the door falling into its lock behind her was like the starting signal Jamie had been waiting for the entire walk to the hotel. It was near the hospital and only a few minutes away from where the street party had been. Yet those minutes had been akin to hour upon hour as need ratcheted higher within Jamie with every step.

She would have done filthy things to Allegra right there on the bench. That was how little control she had over her reactions when it came to that woman. In fact, she'd been so close to sliding her hand all the way up her thigh because she needed to know how turned on Allegra was. How keenly it matched Jamie's own desire and how ready she was to have this. Have her.

Something had shifted inside her after they'd sat down on the bench, probably even before that. As they'd been packing up and Jamie had let slip far more information about her history in Homestead than she normally would. Had told her how she'd left nothing behind in Texas. And when the disappointment of Allegra's quiet had settled in at the bottom of her stomach, she'd realised that a part of her had opened up to Allegra because *she* wanted to know her, too. Forming connections was still so foreign to her, Jamie had figured the way to do it was to put herself out there first.

Turned out she'd been right. And now she was getting a lot more than she'd aimed for. Which suited her just fine. She might not have expected it, but, by the tightness winding around her core, she knew how much a part of her had wanted this.

Her hands found Allegra's waist and tightened around it as she pushed her against the hotel room door she'd just closed behind them. Allegra's gasp turned into a muffled moan when Jamie's mouth crashed into hers, pulling her into the sort of kiss that wasn't appropriate for a public park. One that was deep and frantic, with tongues and teeth clashing as they both established their non-verbal agreement where this would end. Only thing left to establish was what Allegra liked. Jamie planned on spending the next few hours figuring out all the different ways to make Allegra come. Because that had been the one thing going on in her mind since things had got heated between them.

Jamie's hand slipped down the other woman's body until she found the exposed skin of her thigh again. Her lips traced the strong jawline Jamie had been admiring from afar for weeks now, her teeth nibbling at flesh and drawing out delightful little gasps from Allegra. God, did she even know what she sounded like? As though she'd never known pleasure as intense as what Jamie was doing by simply kissing her?

One thought gripped Jamie as her lips danced over Allegra's collarbone, her tongue darting out to lick at her skin, savouring the taste. If those were the sounds she made now, what would happen if—?

Her thumb brushed over the front of Allegra's underwear. The response was instant. Her hips bucked at the featherlight touch and her head fell back, giving Jamie access to her neck. Access that she greedily accepted, moving her mouth across the sensitive skin there.

'You taste exactly how I imagined you would,' Jamie whispered against her skin, letting slip how often she'd thought about Allegra in this very position in the last few weeks. Even if she had said nothing, her actions were proof of her desire for this woman. There wasn't any way to deny it any more, even if she'd wanted to.

Not that she wanted to. No, what Jamie wanted was—

'This…' She breathed the word against Allegra's skin as her fingers slipped under the piece of fabric covering Allegra's core and Jamie couldn't stop the moan falling from her lips as her fingers brushed over her, relishing the wetness she found there.

Allegra slumped even heavier against the door, as if several bones inside her body had suddenly disappeared. Good. That was exactly the type of pleasure she wanted to bring to her.

Jamie's fingers slipped up and down, teasingly dragging her fingers over Allegra's hot, wet centre. She breathed in deeply, taking in the sweet scent of arousal that filled the room. A room she'd taken no note of—and didn't plan on until they were done here. Which could be many, *many* hours from now.

'Are we really—?' Allegra's sentence was lost in a huff of air when Jamie traced a line down Allegra's neck with her tongue.

'We are,' Jamie said, her fingers drawing lazy circles across Allegra's inner thighs before returning back to where she knew Allegra wanted her. *Needed* her. 'Unless you have second thoughts. Say the word and I'll leave.' Jamie would, even though it would break something new and fragile inside her. Hearing the sounds from Allegra as she touched her, tasting every inch of her skin... She wanted more of it.

Allegra shook her head, her breath coming out of her mouth in uneven pants as she pushed her hips against Jamie's hand in a silent plea. Or probably more command than plea, the way she knew Allegra.

'Is that how it'll be tonight? You're still the boss of everything, even here?' Jamie asked, each word forming a kiss against Allegra's heated skin. 'I'm to please you right here, against the door?'

Before Allegra could say anything, Jamie's finger pressed against her, rubbing gently at first.

Seemingly beyond speech, Allegra nodded and then gasped as Jamie pushed inside her. The tightness as she clenched around her fingers almost pushed Jamie over the edge. Somehow, this moment transcended any other she could remember. Although there weren't many because being close to Allegra seemed to wipe any coherent thought from her brain. All she could focus on were the moans and gasps leaving Allegra's mouth as Jamie moved inside her, finding and cataloguing how she reacted to speed, pressure and location to map out what drove her wild.

The way she moved against her hips showed just how desperate she was for release, bucking whenever Jamie brushed her thumb over the bundle of nerves. Jamie smiled against her skin as she shifted position to kneel between Allegra's legs, parting them wider so she could see everything she had been fantasising about for so long.

Her fingers trembled—with excitement or with nerves, Jamie wasn't sure—as she pushed the skirt of Allegra's dress up until the woman was exposed. She breathed her in, the alluring scent enough to weaken her knees. Jamie glanced up as she hooked her fingers on each side of her underwear and watched the desire light up Allegra's eyes as she dragged the lace down her thighs, lifting one leg and then the other one before both feet sank back into the carpet.

Not that Jamie noticed any details about the carpet or Allegra's feet. Not when she was so close to *her*. So close to fulfilling all those distracting and vivid fantasies that had been haunting her ever since Allegra had set foot in the hospital with her alluring curves and that scent that Jamie would recognise anywhere.

Jamie's lips grazed the inside of her thigh, kissing and nibbling her way up to her centre. There she paused for but a second to even out her breathing. This moment would be special. Unique. There were so many things unclear between them, so much to discuss. Jamie wasn't even sure if this was a one-time thing or if it could happen again.

And though they weren't even halfway done, she knew that she would jump at the opportunity to do this again. To have Allegra in countless different ways. The implications of that hung heavy in her mind and she pushed it away.

One thing at a time. Right now it was time to claim what she'd yearned to have for far too long.

* * *

Jamie's hot breath hit Allegra's sensitised skin, rippling over her and giving her a preview of what it would be like to have her mouth right there, licking and—

Her core muscles contracted when Jamie parted her with one long, luxurious stroke of her tongue and sent waves of fire racing down her veins and across her entire body. The moan ripping from her throat sounded so foreign, it took Allegra a moment to realise it wasn't just her own voice she was hearing but Jamie's too as she licked and kissed and suckled in ways that made Allegra's head spin with pleasure.

Her eyes rolled back in her head, unable to focus as Jamie's tongue flicked out and teased at the sensitive bundle of nerves. She wanted more than anything to grab onto something, to hold onto this sensation, but with the door behind her and no support for her hands, she was left pinned in place by desire itself.

Her fingers clutched the fabric of her own dress, its skirt bunched up around her waist while the bodice still pressed into her chest. Though that wasn't the reason each breath was hard fought as she gulped down air like a drowning person. No, her struggle had to do with Jamie and her skilful tongue swirling and nipping at her most sensitive parts.

Release already gathered at the base of her spine in a searing ball, ready to throw her down into the starry abyss. Only she didn't want it to stop. Allegra's thoughts were incoherent as her muscles clenched when Jamie slipped her fingers back inside her, and she didn't know why she never wanted her to stop—only that she didn't.

On the off chance they would never start again if they stopped now.

'Jamie.' Her name was a plea on Allegra's lips as she fought against the tidal wave of pleasure pressing against her from every side.

The sound of their heavy breathing filled the room, mingling together in a harmony only they could hear. It was intoxicating. Addictive.

'You're ready for me already?' Jamie said as she pressed an open-mouthed kiss to the inside of her thigh. 'But I barely got to taste you.'

She paused, her hands digging into Allegra's backside as she moved one of her legs over her shoulder.

'Please,' Allegra whimpered softly between gritted teeth, arching into the touch as Jamie's finger traced up and down her folds, hitting all the sensitive parts.

'Okay, let's compromise. You want to come. I want to continue licking you senseless. How about I make you come, but then I keep on going?' Jamie's nose traced over her skin near her centre as she said that—taunting her into the answer she wanted.

Not that Allegra had much of a choice. She would have agreed to absolutely anything just to have Jamie continue what she was doing. Consequences were an insubstantial concept that didn't apply to her in this position. At least that was what her need-addled brain wanted her to believe. So Allegra nodded, her 'yes' coming out garbled when Jamie's tongue hit the right spot once more, her fingers working their magic. A few more strokes and Allegra plunged into the pleasure erupting through her body thanks to Jamie's touch.

Each spasm pulled another moan from her lips as

Jamie kept going, not slowing down in her pursuit to bring her pleasure. Allegra clenched around her fingers, holding onto the last dregs of the release as she tried to come back down—if only Jamie would let her. But as promised, she didn't relent until Allegra felt herself clench and drop all over again.

The door behind them creaked as her muscles gave out, forcing Jamie to tighten her grip so Allegra wouldn't fall over into a heap of melted bones.

When Allegra could finally speak, she managed to croak out a 'thank you' between breaths. She turned her gaze down at Jamie, finding those amber eyes locked onto hers with an intensity that threatened to reawaken every nerve ending once more. How could she possibly want to continue when she could barely stand up? Allegra didn't know how, only that she could.

'I should have done this a lot sooner,' Jamie whispered against her skin, voice rough with desire, before moving up to capture Allegra's lips in another deep kiss. This time it was slow and exploratory, their tongues dancing together in a tangle that sent more pressure straight to her core.

A lot sooner. The words echoed through Allegra's hazy brain, rubbing against a soft spot inside her. Jamie had been looking at her like that for a while? The same way *she'd* been checking her out? Allegra wasn't sure why she was surprised by that. Somewhere during the period of her marriage, she'd stopped viewing herself as a desirable woman—and as a woman with her own sexual desires.

Seeing Jamie breathless and completely undone by *her* pleasure...

Allegra gasped when Jamie wrenched her mouth

from her lips and grabbed her by the waist, spinning her around. The sound of a zip being pulled down filled the air and cold air hit Allegra's skin. Twisting her head, she tried to lock eyes with Jamie. The other woman tightened her grip around her waist, pinning her against the door. One of her hands slipped under the peeling fabric of her dress, her fingers grazing over Allegra's stomach before coming up to palm her breast.

Jamie's other hand went back down to her thigh, not even giving Allegra a second to catch her breath before her fingers found her entrance again.

'What are you doing?' Allegra asked with a surprised laugh that turned into a moan when Jamie's fingers pumped into her again.

Jamie pressed herself against her back, closing the gap between them. Her soft scent enveloped her and along with the deft fingers brought Allegra close to another orgasm. Feeling the flutter of her walls, Jamie hissed behind her before pressing a kiss to the back of her neck. 'I told you I would keep going until I've had enough. And I don't think I'm even close.'

They lay on the bed in a tangled mess of limbs, and Allegra wasn't sure where her body began and where Jamie's ended. Didn't care about that, either. This moment had no business feeling this perfect, yet here she was with her eyes closed as she listened to Jamie's even breathing. Allegra's fingers skated over the other woman's stomach, appreciating the softness of Jamie's skin and memorising every curve and dip that she'd spent the last several hours exploring. Her fingertips followed the slightly raised stretch marks on her lower abdomen before stopping just as her fingers grazed over a small patch of hair.

Allegra should be spent after this night. Jamie hadn't been exaggerating when she'd said she'd continue until *she* had been satisfied, though at some point Allegra had managed to make her way on top of her and showed her that she could give just as good as she got. When she'd felt Jamie's first orgasm on her tongue, she too had seen a firework of stars explode behind her eyelids, understood why Jamie had said what she'd said. After experiencing that, Allegra didn't relent either. Couldn't.

In the early hours of the next day, with the fire still burning but with less of a frenzy, Allegra waited for the regret to set in. The panic of far too many boundaries crossed and potential mistakes looming on the horizon. She knew the consequences of her actions were right there in front of her: she had slept with a subordinate at her hospital. That alone would be enough reason to fire her on the spot.

But the concern—and her deeply ingrained habit of switching into 'fix it' mode—hadn't kicked in yet. Maybe because even on a good day Eliza Bailey had no idea what was going on in her hospital's emergency room. Whenever Allegra met to talk to her about changes, the chief of medicine was only ever concerned about the numbers. If their throughput matched against their staffing while cost remained at an acceptable level for the investors.

So even if she ever found out what had happened between her and Jamie tonight, would she care enough to do something about it if it didn't affect the bottom line? Allegra doubted it.

Unless this wasn't the one-night thing she was currently treating it as. Granted, Allegra had precious little experience with affairs—illicit or otherwise. She didn't even know if people still referred to affairs as illicit. Or if that was what they had done. Maybe this was simply a one-night stand? Though she didn't believe that those went on all night long and ended with a cuddle session that had her core tightening again.

Her hand drifted away, grazing over Jamie's legs before coming up her hips and relishing the softness of her skin there. One night hardly seemed enough time to explore everything that was Jamie, even if she restricted it to a purely physical sense. Considering she hadn't been with anyone since ending her marriage and before that…

'Are you freaking out about this?' Jamie's voice shook her out of her contemplation, and Allegra blinked several times until her eyes focused on Jamie's face.

She'd turned her head to look at Allegra, her eyes heavy-lidded and sleep still clinging to her. Her smile was soft, not reflecting any of the, well, overthinking that Jamie was apparently able to pinpoint even half asleep.

'Maybe freaking out is putting it a little too strong? I'm…concerned about the implications of all of this.' Allegra had always been someone who appreciated order and labels and definitions ahead of time. It was the only way to navigate the chaos of an emergency room. With broad plans for all kinds of eventualities they could fall back on, they never had to stop in the middle of an incident to think about the next steps.

Something that would have been useful to Allegra at this point, even though she knew relationships didn't work that way. Or should she rather say interpersonal incidents? *Relationships* sounded so rigid, so *official*. What if—?

'I can see the wheels turning in your head, Allegra,' Jamie said, then untangled their legs as she rolled onto her side to face her. The loss of Jamie's legs mingling with hers hit her almost immediately, and something inside her urged her to reclaim the space.

Only before she could talk herself out of this nonsensical notion, Jamie hooked her foot around Allegra's calf and drew her closer to her until their noses almost touched.

'Tell me what's going through your mind.'

Allegra laughed. Not because the question was funny, but because it was so simple. Straight to the point, when her own thoughts were a tangled mess of unrealised consequences and searing desire trying to find a compromise she knew very well probably didn't exist.

But then Jamie's lips ticked up in a small smile, her still sleepy gaze warm and holding space for Allegra to unravel. So she did.

'I like order and procedures. As a doctor working in emergency medicine, I think people tend to lean either one way or the other. You either regiment your entire life with plans and processes to keep as much space free as possible for the chaos that is the ER. Or you ride the waves of chaos, go with the flow and see what happens. There isn't really an in between for people like us.' Those were far too many words to fling at a woman she'd just slept with for the first time only a few hours ago. Then again, Jamie had asked, and at this point she should probably know what really went on inside her brain.

Jamie listened without comment, her hand finding

Allegra's under the covers and weaving their fingers together. Then she pulled her hand towards her chest, nestling their clasped hands between her breasts. She tilted her head, placing a soft kiss on the back of Allegra's hand before looking back up at her.

'You try to balance out the unpredictability of life with order,' she said, something in her gaze shifting. As if she was somehow familiar with that concept. Though the way Jamie had approached things so far led Allegra to believe she stood at the opposite end of that spectrum. That she was someone who rolled with the punches, accepting the chaos of life for what it was.

Something delicate shifted between them—a fragility that didn't belong inside the constructs of this affair. Vulnerability was for people who had discussed it, had agreed to it beforehand. The thought that she might have forced this conversation with her rambling bubbled up inside her and she needed to set the record straight. Correct any misconceptions that could arise in this undefined space between them.

But the words stalled when Jamie squeezed her hand, searching her face with a veiled expression. Allegra's mouth snapped shut when Jamie exhaled a throaty laugh. 'I used to look for order in chaos, too,' she said, shaking her head at a dim memory she'd yet to share with Allegra.

'Growing up, I...' She halted, her grip on Allegra's hand loosening. That vulnerability Allegra had sensed a moment ago expanded, enveloping them and filling what little space was left between them. 'I grew up in the foster-care system after my parents one day didn't come home. They struggled with addiction, and I guess one of our neighbours noticed I was alone at home at far too young an age. Every few years they would place me with a new family, after the old one got tired of me or couldn't figure out how to deal with a scared child who had lost control of her life and actually just needed someone to show her some stability.'

Jamie's eyes slipped out of focus, examining a particular memory only she could see. Her voice grew fainter, becoming more detached from the words she spoke as she continued, 'So I had to learn to live with chaos because pushing against it—trying to control it—only ended up in me landing with yet another new family.'

An instinct to comfort Jamie took over, and Allegra reached out with her free hand, putting it on the other woman's hip. Her fingertips connected with the soft skin there and she forced herself to ignore the zap of lightning travelling down her arm as she focused on the words Jamie had said. Was she sharing them because…?

Jamie shook her head, her eyes coming back to focus. When they connected with Allegra's again, she caught a glimpse of the walls that had come back down a moment ago. 'What I'm trying to say is that I understand your need for control. In a different life, I think I would have been the same way.'

She paused, licking her lips in a way that drove a spear of heat right to Allegra's core. It would be so hard to forget what these lips had done to her throughout the night when she'd still see them every day at work. See *her* and all the complicated things they had just summoned into their working relationship. In her mind, Allegra knew that 'bad idea' didn't even begin to cover it. But even with that knowledge, the regret—the need to take it back and pretend nothing had ever happened—didn't settle in.

Not until Jamie sighed and said, 'I'm not telling you this to…open up, or anything. I know that's not what either of us wants out of this. Right now, I've found a way of life that works for me, with Palm Grove being as much of an attachment as I can handle.'

Allegra tried to ignore the stutter of her heart at those words. They made sense, after all. She wasn't looking for an attachment, either. Especially not at the hospital she was working at. With one of her subordinates. That was a recipe for disaster and not remotely what she needed. The sinking feeling in her stomach was the by-product of an unexpected rejection. No matter how much sense it made, things like that were bound to sting.

'Yes, of course. I couldn't agree more. This was…' Her voice trailed off because she didn't know how to finish the sentence. A one-night, multi-orgasm event? A casual fling to call upon during lonely nights?

Jamie pushed forward until the tip of her nose brushed over Allegra's before pressing the suggestion of a kiss onto her lips. 'It was fun. Like, a lot of fun. And I'm definitely keen on having more fun if you're up for it. I want to make sure we both know where we stand with this.'

The sinking feeling at the bottom of Allegra's stomach intensified when she should be nothing but relieved. This thing between her and Jamie had come out of left field, catching her completely off guard. Her divorce had only now been finalised, finally letting her leave San Francisco behind. She wasn't emotionally ready for something new, anyway. So where was this jittery feeling coming from when she knew she should agree with everything Jamie had said?

Allegra knew only one thing: that she didn't want

this to stop. She wasn't sure what *this* was. Only what it was not.

'Casual is good. With work anything more would become too complicated. We'll have to be discreet.' The smart thing to do would be to leave it at one night and not dwell on this connection further. Thoughts of her divorce, of how Lewis's affair had played out in the public eye for all her colleagues to witness and take part in her humiliation, made her flinch internally. It would be far safer for her to stop now.

But even with all the doubt and past hurt swirling around in the pit of her stomach, she couldn't help herself as her hand cupped Jamie's cheek and drew her face closer. Their lips met again, the kiss twisting from a gentle, reassuring brush into something hungrier.

There was no good explanation for why Allegra wanted her as much as she did and a lot of reasons why she shouldn't. But none of that mattered as she slipped her hand lower, finding the dampness between Jamie's legs and shivering at the eager moan leaving the other woman's lips as she brushed over her.

It would end, but until then, Allegra would have her in whatever way she could.

CHAPTER EIGHT

THE SUN HIT her skin as Jamie was walking down the sidewalk to the address of Catarina's house when a white Prius slowed down until it stopped a few feet away from her. She raised an eyebrow and continued walking until the door swung open and a familiar figure stepped out of the car. Shaking out her auburn locks and patting down her dress, Allegra looked as if she'd just come from a perfume advert shoot. Or maybe some fancy medical magazine that liked to put gorgeous and accomplished doctors on the covers, though Jamie wasn't entirely sure why. Doctors were already a small subsection of the entire population, so the audience of those magazines was already limited. Did they really need to sex it up to sell more magazines?

Wait, why was she thinking about that when Allegra stood right in front of her, lips curled in a small smile? Small for the uninitiated. After a month of fooling around in the hospital, sneaking kisses—and sometimes more—between shifts and ending up every night at either her or Allegra's place, Jamie had learned all the other woman's mannerisms and how she expressed herself.

Like that tiny twitch of her lips, which meant she was

happy to see Jamie. A feeling Jamie returned with her own grin splitting her lips wide.

'You came,' she said as she approached her, and her hands found their way to Allegra's hips all on their own. Heat bloomed at her fingertips, racing up her arms and running through her entire body like a bolt of lightning. Pulling Allegra closer, she rubbed the tip of her nose against her cheek before closing the remaining distance for a kiss. One that turned from innocent enough to passionate within two heartbeats when Allegra's hands tunnelled through her short hair, finding purchase there and pulling Jamie closer to her. Allegra's lips parted and Jamie groaned when their tongues met, filling her mouth and nose and body with the taste and feeling of Allegra.

Was the urgency ever going to fade? Jamie wasn't sure any more. By now she would have thought the feelings—the attraction, to be precise—would have fizzled out and brought their affair to its natural conclusion. She knew her own pattern, after all, and things never lasted, because she didn't want them to last. Didn't want to put any effort into relationships she already knew were going to fail. But somehow Allegra had spun that theory on its head. Every time she saw the woman, she braced herself for the feeling to lessen—as if a part of her was scared that it *would* lessen—but it hadn't so far.

No, quite the opposite. During the quiet hours they spent together, Jamie had convinced herself that if she reached out for this life and grabbed it, she might be allowed to keep it. Sure, there were some rules and hospital regulations to figure out, but that would be the easy part. The hard part had been finding each other.

Though whenever Jamie let her thoughts wander down

that path, she pulled back. This wasn't what they'd agreed on and just because, in a fantasy version of their lives, Jamie could maybe see it happening didn't mean it could work in *this* life. Did Allegra feel the same way? They had both insisted on keeping things purely physical, yet she found herself powerless to resist those thoughts and to wonder if maybe Allegra scented it, too. If she did, she didn't let any of it show. Whenever Jamie considered asking the question, her courage faltered until it disappeared. Hadn't she been the one to insist this could never be anything serious? How was she supposed to take that back now?

Allegra huffed out a laugh when their faces finally came apart. 'You certainly know how to make me come,' Allegra said, her voice low and containing a promise that filled her with a heady sensation.

'Dr Tascioni, you really have a filthy mind and an even dirtier mouth to accompany it.' Before Allegra could say anything, Jamie closed the gap between them with another kiss. One that took another great effort to break apart.

'You bring out the worst in me,' Allegra said, and that small smile tugged at her lips again, turning Jamie's insides into liquid fire. There was simply no way she would ever grow less attracted to this woman. Which was a problem she wasn't ready to face now.

Or ever.

Whatever was going on between them lived in a fragile bubble that relied on neither of them poking any holes in it by asking questions or talking about their feelings. They'd spent the last month sleeping with each other and doing the delicate dance of avoiding topics that would bring them closer to the end of this affair.

Jamie wasn't sure if similar thoughts crept into Allegra's mind, but when this kiss ended, she took a step back so there was an arm's length between them. Then she looked down at herself, her hands brushing over the fabric of her floral dress and smoothing out the already perfectly pressed skirt.

'Do I look okay? I didn't know what to wear to a garden party filled with people who can barely tolerate being around me.' Her expression was neutral, trying a bit too hard to appear deadpan. But Jamie hadn't just catalogued Allegra's smiles, but also all her other expressions, and knew the signs when she was tired or stressed or—

'You're worried about causing a scene?' Jamie phrased it as a question even though she knew already that this was what was swirling around in Allegra's mind.

A crack appeared in the ironclad facade, showing Jamie that she'd read the situation right. The rush of satisfaction coursing through her was hard to ignore and shouldn't really feel this good. What would she do with all this very specific Allegra knowledge once their affair had run its course? They couldn't continue indefinitely because...

In the last couple of days this sentence surfaced in her head whenever she stared at Allegra for too long, her brain stuttering to a halt as it searched for the words to end it. They wouldn't come.

A frown tugged at Allegra's lips. 'I have no intention of causing a scene. But I do need to acknowledge that even though I've made some progress with the staff, some are still not happy about me coming in.'

Jamie nodded. The way the ER staff treated Allegra now was like day and night from when she'd first started at Palm Grove Hospital, and Jamie had made sure to set anyone straight who was still running their mouth about their new department lead. But it turned out that people thought she was just being nice to the newcomer because that was her nature. In their minds, Jamie was nice to everyone, whether they deserved it or not. They didn't realise that this was a coping mechanism from a lifetime spent moving from family to family and adopting whatever personality traits gave her the highest chance of survival.

Only Allegra had seen beyond the construct and was still here, looking at Jamie as if she meant something to her.

'Once you can announce the changes to the ER policy we've been working on, they'll realise that you're on their side. That there are actions behind your words,' Jamie said, raising her hand to Allegra's cheek and stroking it with her thumb. 'Plus, you did get invited by Catarina. She asked you to be here.'

That Jamie had mentioned Allegra to Catarina and how much she would appreciate an invitation didn't need to come up in this particular conversation. If Allegra believed that she was building trust with the staff enough to get an invitation, Jamie wouldn't destroy that. Plus, she *was* building trust. Jamie could see that. A bit more time and some further changes would shift the staff's opinion in due course.

The line between Allegra's brows smoothed out as she considered that piece of information and the light coming into her gaze was worth the small deception. Even though that forced Jamie to acknowledge the complexity of her own feelings for Allegra. If this was just sex, and she was willing to walk away from it all tomorrow, would she really care that much about smoothing things over at work? Would she want to help so much that she continued to jump into conversations between their colleagues at work unprompted?

'I guess that's true,' Allegra said on an exhale, tilting her head so she was pushing against Jamie's palm. A thrill went through Jamie at the small gesture and she found it increasingly hard to push those moments away. If they weren't supposed to be permanent, then she had no reason to enjoy anything beyond the sex.

But the vulnerability she glimpsed in Allegra's eyes did something to her insides that she had no control over. It drove her to pull the other woman closer, wrap her in her arms and then hold her hand as they walked down the street until the noise of the garden party grew louder.

Allegra's fingers flexed against her palm and, for a wild moment, Jamie wanted to throw caution to the wind and walk in while still holding her hand. Declare her intentions for this woman in front of the entire emergency room so there could be no questions about her choice, that she wanted to *be* with Allegra and not just sneak around in the hotel or meet her after dark. After all the instability, all the strife that had led Jamie to this place here in Homestead, she was ready to believe that maybe she could have it all.

But then Allegra took her hand back, and that feeling of wholeness vanished as fast as it had bubbled up, leaving behind a hint of tension as Jamie unlatched the garden-fence door and they stepped into the bustle of the party.

Allegra really wanted to believe Jamie's words, and for the first hour of the party she did. She trailed behind Jamie as she led them through the crowd to say hello to Catarina, their host—who was also the first person to hint at how Allegra might not be as welcome as she'd wanted to believe. The nurse raised an eyebrow when she spotted her behind Jamie before asking whether they'd arrived together.

Before Jamie could say anything, Allegra jumped in to say, 'We just bumped into each other outside.'

Which was, of course, the truth. Kind of. She'd texted Jamie when she'd left her place—which at this point was still the hotel room she'd been occupying for two months now—and told her when she'd be here in hopes of seeing her before she stepped into the party. The thought of having an anchor, someone to hold onto while she navigated the still fragile relationships within the emergency department team of Palm Grove, soothed her. Or rather, had soothed her until her brain had finished the thought and realised what impression she might be leaving if she clung too closely to Jamie.

Wasn't that part of the problem already? That she relied too much on Jamie to smooth things over with the rest of the staff? Though it had meant a lot to Allegra to hear her stand up for her, she knew that alone wasn't enough. The changes she'd wanted to see at Palm Grove's emergency department were slow, needing multiple rounds of revision and buy-in from the board of directors. When all they cared about were profits and how to squeeze the most out of a still understaffed ER, she needed to bring the right arguments to the table to convince leadership to sign off on things.

They didn't care that protecting the most vulnerable that came to them looking for help was the right thing to do.

Which, in turn, made Allegra look as though she didn't care. Her grand aspirations for the emergency room meant nothing if she couldn't show people that she was working on their concerns. Words were cheap, and she currently lacked in the 'action' department. But she *needed* this to work. This was so much more than just another job for her. It was the first time Allegra had stood on her own, without her ex-husband's name attached to her position. She was here because she'd been the best of the applicants.

With how much influence the Kent family wielded in different medical fields, she needed to build up her own reputation independent of her past. That would be the only way she could withstand any of Lewis's interference. Allegra reminded herself that she couldn't risk that for a relationship, not even for one that felt almost real.

She suspected that this was the reason she was hovering at the sidelines of the party while watching Jamie flutter from group to group with a bright grin on her face. Maybe it wasn't the quality of her work or the inability to get the board of directors to approve her changes. What if it had to do with who she was at a very fundamental level? Because as she looked at Jamie, drinking in the sheer beauty and positivity radiating from her, she struggled to see how it was *not* related to her icy exterior.

Her lack of approachable energy had been a common criticism people liked to bring up to point out that she hadn't actually deserved her last position and that her former last name had had much more to do with why she'd been hired. The rational part of her knew her own accomplishments and that she'd left San Francisco General in a better state than when she'd arrived. But those achievements were so much harder to recall when she'd caught heat from both sides for different reasons.

And then there was Jamie. The calm centre of the swirling unrest surrounding her.

Would Jamie have walked in here holding Allegra's hand if she hadn't pulled back? A part of her hadn't wanted to untangle herself, had yearned to see what would happen if she simply accepted the thing brewing between them as her new reality.

Allegra's phone vibrated, and she scowled at the screen when she fished it out of her pocket and saw the notification. Lewis.

I signed everything you wanted me to sign. Please, pick up the phone.

It was as if her thoughts had conjured him into existence. She opened the message, gaining not a small amount of satisfaction from giving him the 'read' notification without ever replying. Not for the first time since she'd left their marital home, her thumb hovered over the 'block' button to finally and truly have this man out of her life for ever.

It would be so easy. All their conversations went through their lawyers, anyway. They didn't have any reason to stay in touch. No children, no shared friends or family to haggle over in the divorce. Because when they'd got married, Allegra had been more than happy to slot into his life while abandoning the few friends she'd found during med school. He was a Kent, a dynasty in neuro surgery. She was lucky she'd even caught his attention—as people had never tired of telling her. Enough that, over the years of marriage, even she'd begun to believe it.

Wouldn't it be the same if she let this thing with Jamie go any further? Allegra scanned the crowd, looking for her. Though her professional achievements wouldn't be under scrutiny, she'd still be in a similar position: relying on someone else's reputation to smooth over any friction.

Her phone buzzed in her hand again and Allegra swallowed a groan when she read the name on the screen and *Do Not Answer!* Lewis. That was the problem with her pettiness in wanting him to know that she'd read his messages and chosen not to reply.

'What's bringing your mood down?' Allegra pressed her phone against her chest at the sudden sound of Jamie's voice next to her ear. Swiping the call away, she dropped the phone back into her bag before turning sideways.

'I was looking for you,' Allegra said. Another thing that was technically true, even if it didn't really mean what she was implying. She'd wanted to see Jamie, but she also hadn't gone out of her way to actually find her.

A line appeared in between Jamie's brows accompanied by a frown tugging at her lips. Two signs she rarely saw in the other woman and out of character enough for Allegra to brace herself.

'Are you okay?' The frown on Jamie's lips deepened as she leaned her shoulder against the pillar next to where Allegra had been standing while watching the proceedings of the barbecue from afar.

Allegra blinked several times. It took her a few seconds to understand the interaction and what Jamie was hinting at. An involuntary smile spread over her lips. 'You're worried about me?'

Jamie's eyes darted up and down her face. 'You say it as if it's something surprising. Of course I worry about you when you lurk around in the shadows of a party while everyone else is having a blast.' She looked around, emphasising the isolation Allegra had put herself in by drifting further to the side. 'We can leave if you're not enjoying yourself. I'll make up some emergency and get us out of here.' Her voice dropped a register lower as she added, 'My place isn't far. I'll make sure you feel better within seconds of your back hitting my mattress.'

Allegra shivered as heat bloomed in the pit of her stomach, unfurling into long, searing waves that crashed through her. There was no denying that Jamie's appetite matched her own. Something that still caught her by surprise. Though Allegra certainly wouldn't call herself prudish and she'd been aware and accepting of her sexual preferences since late high school, she'd never been overly adventurous in her sex life. Things with Lewis had been electric at the beginning but had then quickly waned, leaving her with a warm satisfaction she'd thought was normal in relationships.

With Jamie, the need to feel her mouth all over her

body only seemed to increase with each encounter—making the offer almost irresistible. Who wouldn't rather want to have an orgasm than stick around at a party where most people didn't care much for her at best, and actively disliked her at worst? But...

'I don't want you to miss out just because I'm still in a weird place with the staff. They clearly like you.' She gestured to the clusters of people gathered around as fragments of conversations in both English and Spanish floated through the air. 'I also don't need to give them another reason to be suspicious of me. We would have to leave separately so they don't think we're together.'

That would be the final nail in her reputation. Allegra wasn't sure what exactly members of staff would think if they realised that she'd been sleeping with Jamie, but she could only imagine it would end poorly. Accusations of impropriety would be the least that were said.

Jamie let out a sigh at that. 'Is that what you're worried about? That they'll find out? What would be the worst that could come from that?'

Allegra, who had been scanning the crowd in front of her still and noting the furtive gazes cast their way now and then, whipped around to look back at Jamie. 'What would be the worst thing that could come from everyone finding out we're sleeping together?'

Was Jamie being serious right now? What potential benefit could she see that would negate the negativity they would no doubt be on the receiving end of if their situation became a topic of conversation at the hospital? Maybe this wouldn't have a big impact on Jamie, but Allegra... She was already fighting against the current as it was.

Jamie frowned. 'No, what I meant...' Her mouth snapped shut with an audible sound, the rest of her sentence trailing away.

The tension in the air between them rose and, coupled with the already hostile vibes she was getting from the people here, Allegra suddenly felt as if maybe she'd overstayed her welcome. For a few weeks, she'd thought that perhaps she would be able to settle here. Jamie had compounded the feeling that she could belong somewhere, even though the staff situation wasn't improving by much. But as she stood there, still not a part of this—still alone—the feeling crept in that maybe this wasn't going to be the new beginning she had hoped for.

Allegra waited for Jamie to finish her thought. A muscle in Jamie's jaw feathered as the silence stretched on with neither of them saying anything else. Because there was no way Jamie was genuinely suggesting that they make their affair public knowledge when they themselves hadn't really talked about what this thing between them was. They'd both agreed this would be a casual fling because, realistically, what else could it be? They worked together in the same ER and in a power imbalance. The appropriateness of their situation was already questionable, even though they were both willing participants, and they could be in trouble if anyone found out.

Allegra knew this also wouldn't help endear her to anyone on staff. They would probably see it as an abuse of power. How else would the ice queen sweeping into the emergency room from a land far away end up with the sunshine among them?

Whatever Jamie was trying to tell her, Allegra knew this couldn't be it. She wasn't looking for some kind of public declaration because what they had was comfortable and easy and…not that serious.

That last part sank inside her as if it had been weighed down with a bunch of stones, settling in the pit of her stomach with a heavy *thunk*. Was Jamie about to poke a hole in the idea of their casual state? That thought shouldn't be half as thrilling as it currently was. Because she couldn't keep her. There wasn't a single version of this fling that would end up with them together. With their work situation, it wasn't possible and entertaining the thought would only lead her down paths she shouldn't go. The whole reason they had agreed on something casual had been to get the tension to snap between them without doing anything stupid—anything messy. Allegra had lived through enough mess with her divorce, only finally coming through the worst of it now while her belligerent ex still called her almost every day.

This was supposed to be her fresh start, her opportunity to focus on her career, on her reputation in the medical community. On herself. 'I might be reading into this situation, but I've already been through the whole workplace romance with my ex-husband and it didn't end well. I had my abilities and my merit questioned, and heard people theorise how much easier it must have been for me to get the job simply because of who I knew.'

Saying the words out loud sent a shiver clawing down her spine as the need to speak pushed against the deeply ingrained habit of keeping things to herself. Even though that, too, was probably part of the reason she struggled to connect with everyone here. Everyone except Jamie. Allegra hadn't even encountered an ounce of resistance from her as they'd got closer and started their fling.

Jamie glanced over her shoulder at the buzzing of the party and then nodded towards a shed a few paces away. The noise died down somewhat as they slipped around the corner and faced each other. Allegra's eyes roamed over Jamie as she leaned her shoulder against the side of the shed, drinking in all the details up close that she'd been cataloguing from afar already. Something about this woman defied all of her previous expectations of herself, her obsession to know things about her bordering on something that had less to do with a physical attraction and more with—

No, she absolutely couldn't go there. So she chose the words that would reflect that.

'We agreed this wasn't anything more than a physical connection and that neither of us was looking for more. You were the one to be very clear about that boundary,' Allegra said and even though her voice was low, her words factual, hearing them still sliced Jamie in a place she hadn't expected.

Because the truth of her own feelings had come out without her input or her desire to share. Just like almost every other aspect of her entanglement with Allegra. Jamie had finally found her footing here at Palm Grove Hospital after years of feeling adrift, and the last thing she needed in the middle of that was a complicated affair where unbidden emotions were emerging. Especially when she knew she couldn't keep it going.

Because she *knew* she couldn't. Hadn't she been the one to say that emotional attachments had no place in her life? How could she defend her position like that when she'd been the one to make her boundaries clear from the very beginning? Allegra was right to call her out like that and yet…

'You don't have anything to say to that?' Allegra asked, her expression not giving a hint as to any of the thoughts lurking beneath the surface.

'I have plenty to say,' Jamie began, even though she knew it was ill-advised because her control on her thoughts had slipped the leash when she'd first seen Allegra on the sidewalk outside this house. 'But I don't know if I should. Don't know if you want to hear any of it when it already feels too close to a space you're trying to avoid.'

It sounded more accusatory than Jamie had intended, and the second the words drifted into existence between them, she wanted to reach out with an invisible hand and snatch them right back. 'That didn't—'

'I'm trying to avoid things? You were the one who insisted that attachments weren't her style. It was one of the first things *you* said to *me* before we could discuss anything else,' Allegra said, her brows drawing together. 'If I've been avoiding a specific space, then it's because you told me under no uncertain terms that I don't belong in that space.'

The hurt in her tone struck Jamie and her hand came up of its own accord, stretching out to touch her but stopping just above her arm. Allegra looked down, seeing the place where they weren't touching, and for a few seconds they both hovered there. Then Allegra took a step back, taking a deep breath as she glanced down at her feet. When she looked back up, Jamie paused as a different version of the woman she'd spent the last few weeks with stared back at her.

This was the exterior of the ice queen so many of the nurses and doctors in the ER talked about. The face of Allegra Jamie had somehow never really got to know. Whether it was by accident or because something in their connection had been genuine, somehow she'd skipped a few steps of the 'warming up' period and had instead found the real Allegra.

That was, until this moment.

A heat different from the last few weeks rose within her, one tinged with the familiar taste of her experiences, reminding her of the reasons why she didn't seek out any attachments in the first place. How had Allegra made her forget about that? She'd come to this party reminding herself of their agreement, of what this fling was supposed to be to both of them, and yet when she'd seen Allegra surrounded by her people, something had clicked into place. A long-lost piece of a puzzle finally slotting into place and completing a picture that had remained blurry until this moment.

They were supposed to be the same. Allegra had struggled to find herself again after her marriage and Jamie had seen herself in that struggle, and knew what it was like to recover after being lost for far too long. Hell, this was still a work in progress for her, with some days that came easier than others.

If she wanted to keep this picture in her life, she needed to be brave. Needed to risk the pain of losing something over the fear of abandonment that gripped her whenever she let her guard down.

'You've never changed your mind before?' Jamie asked quietly, letting whatever words that wanted to come out flow. She had no idea where she was going with this, only that her chest became lighter with every syllable spoken. 'You never found yourself in a situation that forced you to evaluate everything you thought you knew about yourself? And that's all because this person stepped into your life and threw everything you knew into disarray and chaos?'

Jamie took a step towards her, putting herself within Allegra's reach even though she knew she shouldn't. It wouldn't help the rising temper in her to inhale Allegra's scent with every breath, but the urge to be close to her was overpowering. Even if she knew that this was only going to end poorly. Things like this had never lasted in her life. Why should this time be any different just because something inside her begged for it to be more than it was?

'Jamie…' Allegra breathed out her name, and it ran through her like a current of warmth, its heat increasing until the ends of her nerves burned. Jamie's eyes dipped lower as the other woman took a shaky breath in, her lower lip vanishing between her teeth for the fraction of a second. Cracks appeared in the facade of the ice queen.

It shouldn't thrill her as much as it did. But if she was going to be brave, it would be now or never. So she pressed on. 'I see something rare forming between us. Something I couldn't have anticipated when we first met. Yes, I was the one to tell you I needed things to be casual between us. But seeing you here, in the middle of a group of people I care about, and not being able to grab your hand…'

Her words trailed off as she took another step towards Allegra. Allegra's eyes flared at her words, but then her expression shuttered once more as she retreated back inside her fortress—this time without Jamie.

'You're missing the point of this. Or maybe you don't care all that much about your reputation because you're already the popular one. So you're not risking anything by revealing an illicit affair with your superior. Meanwhile, I'm already in a tricky situation trying to appease the staff while also bringing in the results the chief and board of directors want to see. Two concepts that are oftentimes at odds with each other.'

Allegra's eyes narrowed as she spoke, prompting Jamie to take a step back. 'Not to mention, I've told you about my ex, about the damage he's done to my career. I count myself lucky to be here right now, having secured this job when I know his family has been whispering poison about me in the ears of anyone willing to listen. With how much is at stake for me, I can't just follow my feelings in an act of blind trust. I *can't*. I've already lost everything once and I've only now started clawing it all back. The last thing I would do is risk any of that on a whim.'

A weight dropped into Jamie's stomach as she processed her words while still grappling with the truth about the depth of her feelings for Allegra revealed in this explosive conversation. Because Jamie had meant it. There was something between them and it had struck her to see Allegra surrounded by the people who had become Jamie's friends over the years—when she had finally dared to let them come close.

And she was now hoping that Allegra would take up that dare with her, too. Add another piece to the mosaic of her life that Jamie was painstakingly putting together after getting torn apart by grief and loss and displacement at far too young an age. Didn't Allegra understand how hard—how rare—it was to find something like that? Something as insubstantial as a reputation meant nothing in the grand scheme of things, right?

'This is not a whim. I don't understand how you could even call it that. Were we not living the same moments together? I can solve some of these things if you stick with me and let us try this. Let me deal with the staff like I've already been doing for the last few weeks while you focus on Bailey and the board. Can't you see that together we have the qualities we need to not only make this emergency room a success for the board but also improve the lives of the people who work there with us?'

Jamie wasn't blind to the reality of Allegra's ongoing struggle with the staff and a part of her wanted to believe that if they went public with their relationship, their colleagues would come to see her in the same light that Jamie had been doing all this time. But because Allegra was trying to please so many people at once, she was falling short.

Meanwhile, Jamie knew exactly how to win them over. She needed some trust from Allegra. The assurance that she wouldn't leave because their relationship had morphed into more than casual. More than physical.

Allegra shaking her head pushed all the air out of her lungs.

'Have you even been listening to a word I've said over these last months?' she scoffed, and the sound sliced through the air and into Jamie's skin. 'You can't have, or you would know that the last thing I want is to depend on someone else vouching for my abilities as a doctor and a leader of my department. It's exactly what gave Lewis far too much sway over my life, and I refuse to conveniently slot into some predefined space again.'

That was what Allegra thought she was suggesting? Jamie tried to recall the words—the actual words, not the sentiment behind them she'd tried to convey—but before she could, Allegra continued.

'This isn't a conversation we should have like this. That wasn't part of the plan. Of the…agreement.' Allegra let out a sigh, pushing both hands through her hair. Her auburn locks cascaded through her fingers and Jamie yearned to feel the silky touch on her own skin. To ground herself in a moment that was unravelling right in front of her eyes. That wasn't what she'd planned—or even intended—when she'd come over to talk to her.

None of this had been in her mind. It had just…tumbled out.

Allegra was right, of course. This wasn't the time or the place to have any kind of serious conversation and if Jamie had a better grip on her impulses, she might have managed to stir the conversation smoother. But once again, her deficiencies led to people leaving her without a second thought. It had happened before and, because it hadn't happened in a while, somehow she'd let herself believe that maybe she'd finally got the hang of making a permanent connection.

Except there was Allegra—the woman she'd been about to spill her heart out to, to ask her if she would consider being more than this absurd casual construct that had been doomed to fail from the very beginning—

taking steps to the side so she could slip out while giving Jamie the widest berth possible.

Just like that. She'd once more become disposable. Replaceable.

The thoughts blazed through her and fuelled the next words coming out of her mouth. 'Of course this isn't part of the plan. Because there *is* no plan. As an emergency medicine physician you should know that. Situations change and you need to adapt as you learn new information. You think that doesn't apply to life as well?'

She had to get out. Because if Jamie was actually going down the road Allegra thought she was, Allegra had no idea how she would react. A traitorous little part inside her wanted to hear those words again, wanted to hear Jamie confess her feelings—and wanted to say it all back.

But that wasn't possible. It *wasn't*. She had laid out all the reasons why they wouldn't work, and why the best course of action would be to sever their connection now before it could become too messy. Before she could be persuaded to give in and try when she knew it would end as her marriage had.

Allegra had set out to rebuild her life and prove to people—and to herself—that she was worth her merits. That she hadn't 'married up' in med school and since then received all her achievements because of a name that hadn't even been hers. That could not happen again.

And Jamie... That look of hope mixed with hurt was almost enough to bring Allegra to her knees. To ignore all the warning bells in her head and go for it and see what would happen. Except whenever she thought about what the worst thing could be, pictures of her failed marriage flashed in front of her eyes. How could she recreate one of the biggest mistakes in her life when she couldn't guarantee that this time it would be different? Wouldn't she just be once again slotting into someone else's life here in Homestead, using Jamie's credibility—her likability—to assert herself as an authority with the still sceptical staff?

Relying on Lewis had left her with nothing the second he'd decided she wasn't worth his loyalty, and the lessons she'd learned there had been too painful to repeat.

'This is not what I agreed to, Jamie,' she said, forcing herself to take another step away—towards the exit.

'So that's it, then? Because we came up with only the one way that this relationship could work means we are not ever allowed to change our minds? My feelings for you are not valid because this started out as a no-strings thing? You won't even hear me out when I say that I'm—'

'Stop!' The word left her throat with an intensity that had both women flinching in equal measure. Allegra because she hadn't meant to shout, and Jamie... The hurt on her face was undeniable. She was trying so hard to put herself out there, but Allegra couldn't let her. Didn't know how to deal with it in fear of repeating the same pattern in her life over and over again. How could she claim to be both free of the influence of Lewis and a capable physician—an effective leader—if she couldn't get the staff on her side without someone else's help?

The pressure in Allegra's chest increased when Jamie's flared eyes slowly narrowed and her expression turned to stone. This was it, then. The end that had been inevitable from the very start, yet somehow Allegra had convinced herself it would never come. That they could go on like this for ever in their vague bubble that didn't require explanations. Where they had just been allowed to *be*.

'Jamie, I think we shouldn't...' Allegra didn't know how to end that sentence. Talk about this here? Continue this conversation because she was this close to falling in love with her despite knowing she shouldn't?

Jamie set her jaw and took a deep breath that came out in a shudder that broke Allegra into pieces. A part of her screamed to take it all back. Pretend this conversation had never happened and go back to how things had been before she'd come to this garden party. But how could she pretend things hadn't changed between them after what Jamie had just said? After pointing out all of Allegra's shortcomings and offering to fix them *for* her rather than helping her figure it out for herself? Was she really only ever going to be a project for her romantic partners to fix? And when Jamie realised that she couldn't fix it for her, would she seek out someone else—someone easier—just as Lewis had?

'I get it, yeah. You don't feel...' The rest of the sentence turned into a sigh, and Jamie shook her head. Allegra's eyes darted to where Jamie's hands contracted into fists before releasing the tension. A steady rhythm of tensing and releasing her fingers—and a clear sign of her internal struggle.

Allegra wanted to step in, soothe the woman who'd become far too important to her in the past months they'd spent together. First by working side by side and then slipping so much deeper than that. So much further than she should have let herself go. All of this wouldn't have happened if she'd been more careful.

Her fingertips tingled with the need to reach out to

Jamie and feel her skin on her palm. But if she touched her now, her entire resolve—the reasons why she needed to step away—might crumble under the weight of her genuine feelings for her. And that would lead her down a path she wasn't ready for. Might *never* be ready for.

'I—should go,' she pushed out as she took the final steps that would sever her from Jamie. She couldn't watch her reaction, not when she felt so fragile that a strong breeze might tear her apart.

This wasn't the ending she'd imagined, but then again, how else had she thought this would end?

CHAPTER NINE

THE BREAK ROOM was so quiet Allegra's voice echoed loud enough that she dropped her speech into a whisper as she recited the presentation she would give to the board of directors in a few days.

She stopped her pacing to look at the screen of her laptop with the open presentation on it outlining how changing the internal policies on mandatory reporting would help the staff with safety, anonymity and how it would increase the amount of vulnerable people they could serve that currently relied on illegal back-alley clinics to get their needs sorted. The board didn't need to know about her personal involvement in one of those clinics, though having witnessed how they had to make do with unsafe conditions had Allegra all the more determined to get these people into her ER.

Reaching for the keyboard, she skipped to the next slide and her stomach dropped as she scanned the content. Jamie had typed out the words on the slide, talking about not just the statistics of undocumented people in their city but also the rate of fatalities because they didn't have adequate access to the hospital. How Palm Grove Hospital could not only play a vital part in upholding the welfare of the residents of Homestead but also ensure that they were standing up for human rights.

Allegra knew that the board wouldn't care about human rights or their place in it. Some people would pretend it was an important aspect in their decision, simply because they would feel far too awkward disagreeing with the importance of upholding people's right to medical care. But these people were in the positions they were in because they were skilful masters of twisting their words to make it seem like they cared about helping people, while all they actually cared about was the number at the bottom of the financial statement. More precisely, that it was a positive number.

A lump appeared in her throat as she read Jamie's words, recalling the many evenings they had spent together working on this—among other things. It was those very specific *other things* that brought a heaviness to her chest whenever she let herself think about what they'd shared for the last weeks. How it had ended.

She could hardly believe that the garden party had been only last week. Since then, time seemed to have slowed to a crawl, not letting her escape the hurt the memories brought back each time.

Her resolve had softened in the following days, leaving her open and vulnerable to the creeping doubts winding their way into her brain. Had she really made the right choice in moving on from their entanglement? What would the alternative have been? Neither of them had gone into this looking for a relationship and even if her feelings about Jamie had changed, it didn't automatically change her ideas about relationships.

Jamie, to her credit, had been nothing but professional

towards her whenever they crossed paths in the emergency room—which thankfully wasn't that often. If anything, Allegra had been the one avoiding her by choosing to stay in the break room turned makeshift office. Not that this room provided much of a refuge. She and Jamie had spent far too much time here. First working on future improvements to the hospital, like the plan detailed in the presentation. But as they'd grown closer, they had moved on to other things under the pretence of collaboration.

The memories brought an equal amount of pleasure and pain, the good times they'd had always chasing the way it had ended. How Allegra had brought it all down around her.

She jumped as her phone rattled over the table and the one name she didn't want to read flashed over the screen yet again, as it had so many times before. Picking it up, she glared at the name of her ex-husband. The pleasure and pain inside her twisted into something sharp and ready to slice. All she needed was a target that wasn't herself.

Her thumb hovered over the red decline button, her heart beating against her chest as she switched over to the green side. Before she could contemplate the wisdom—or the very obvious lack thereof—of answering the call, she pressed the button and held the phone to her ear.

'Stop calling me, Lewis. I know you're a smart man, so I don't have to tell you that eighty declined calls over the span of two months means I *really* don't want to talk to you. How is that message not getting through to you?' Allegra had no idea where she was going with this, but somehow seeing his name as she was experiencing an even lower point than his blatant cheating had caused had set her off. If he was too obtuse to understand she never wanted to see or hear from him again, then she would have to spell it out.

A large exhale sounded from the other line, followed by some static, as if he'd shifted the phone from one ear to the other. Allegra glanced at the clock on her laptop. It would be six a.m. on the west coast in a few minutes.

'Sorry, I didn't think you would pick up the phone so I didn't really prepare anything to say,' he said, and Allegra picked up on an all too familiar grogginess in his voice. Had this man really just woken up and decided to harass his ex-wife, who hadn't spoken to him without a lawyer present for the last year?

'Only you could have this much audacity to call me without actually having anything to say,' Allegra said, barking out a humourless laugh. 'Or maybe you still haven't got over your sense of entitlement. Because you believed I somehow owed you for my job and my career and my life, really. Apparently, that hasn't changed even after I left you.'

'No, that's not true at all, and even before all the lawyers got involved, I was trying to tell you…' His voice trailed off and Allegra heard the rustling of sheets coming through the phone.

She rolled her eyes, even though she knew he couldn't see it. Leave it to Lewis to wake up with the intention of harassing her. For some reason, this was worse than if he'd at least made the effort to get out of bed and have a coffee before ruining her day.

No more of that.

'I didn't pick up the phone to talk to you. I'm sick of you filling up my call log and my voicemail with incessant pleas to call you back. Especially since you apparently don't have anything to say to me,' Allegra said, praying that her voice remained steady as she tore into Lewis.

'I just need to talk to you. After you left, I— There are things I wish I'd done differently, and I realise now what I did to you. To us.' More rustling in the background and Allegra hated that she could hear the shift in his voice.

Even after a year of separation and their divorce finally done, so much useless knowledge about this man remained in her system. There'd been a very specific time in recent weeks where Allegra sometimes couldn't even remember ever having been married. Almost able to forget what a detrimental effect Lewis had had on her life. Until Jamie had brought up helping her—letting her borrow her influence in the ER—to achieve her goals rather than helping her learn how to stand on her own two feet. And everything had come rushing back.

The feeling wasn't the same, though. Not even close. This conversation alone reminded her how much Lewis had always relished throwing the weight of his name around. Enough that even now he felt entitled to her time, to just call her out of the blue. Meanwhile Jamie had respected her choice to distance herself.

'I think you should discuss the regrets you have about how you wrecked our marriage with a professional. A therapist. Not with me when I've done my best to move on,' she replied, and a part of her urged her to pull the phone away from her ear. Hang up and block his number the way she should have done the second their lawyers had got in touch with each other.

She hadn't though, and even now she wasn't sure why

not. Why she had inexplicably kept this door propped open when she knew that calamity was the only thing waiting for her behind it. No, that wasn't true. She knew why she hadn't blocked him and had kept a close eye on that feeling inside her—how it had slowly and surely diminished ever since she came to Homestead.

The last flickers of the painful doubt that came with ending a long marriage were gone. Certainty was all that remained inside her.

Lewis sighed again and she could almost see him sitting at the edge of the bed, hair ruffled and the frustration clearly written on his face. She also found that the image brought up nothing within her. No longing, no wishing things had gone differently.

'You're telling me to go to therapy when you refused to go to couples' counselling with me? I get that I messed up here and I keep calling you because I need you to know that I *want* to make things better. But I can't do all of this by myself. We have to do it together.'

Allegra tipped her head up to look at the ceiling. 'This again? I'm not interested in helping you fix what *you* broke. Especially not after you broke it with impunity. You thought I owed you everything—my career, my home, my life. And I'll admit where I went wrong: I let you do all of it. I was happy to slot into your pre-existing life and be the wife you needed me to be. But guess what?' She didn't give him a chance to say anything before she continued, 'I'm fine without you. Sure, the people working in my department now aren't making my life easy, but at least when they do turn around—and I *will* win them over—it will be because of what I did. Not because of my last name.'

'You're struggling with your new team?' The question sounded innocent enough on the surface, but Allegra's defences immediately rose. She wasn't sure if she was determined to think the worst of him at this point, but was there a subtle gleeful tone to his voice? Allegra cursed herself for revealing that detail. Why was she still on the phone with him?

'Lewis, I'm hanging up. Don't ever—'

'Your chief is Eliza Bailey, right? I'm sure I met her at one of the foundation's galas. If you're having trouble, I'm sure we can have a chat,' he continued, right over her, and Allegra would have snapped at him if she hadn't been so shocked at hearing the chief's name out of his mouth.

Alarm bells rang inside her head. Was he seriously suggesting that *he* would intervene on her behalf to smooth over the difficulties in her job? Even after a year and more apart, he thought he had the right to walk into her life uninvited and *fix* her.

A low simmering fire erupted in her stomach, reaching all the way up to her throat. It honed each of her next words into sharp blades designed to finally sever a connection she'd been carrying around with her for far too long. 'As I was saying before you interrupted me, don't *ever* call me again. Lose this number and forget that you even had a wife. Because I've certainly forgotten all about you.'

It was a truth she was manifesting as she reminded herself how far she'd come to escape his influence and find her own self-worth. He had never loved her but rather the idea of the medical power couple that would continue *his* legacy, without ever caring about what that meant for her. Even the calls she'd been declining hadn't truly been designed to reconcile with her but had been an attempt to snatch back control.

His reaction vindicated all the thoughts tumbling through her. 'You had nothing when we met. All the connections, all the experience you gained throughout the years, were thanks to me and my family's name. Don't even pretend anything you did—'

Allegra moved the phone away from her ear and pressed the disconnect button. Then she tapped on Lewis's name and blocked his number before he could get over his shock and redial her to harass her some more.

With a sigh originating from the deepest parts of her bones, Allegra plopped down on her chair and buried her face in her hands. The words spoken, the emotions still churning through her, whipped themselves into a storm that raged around her strongly enough to scatter her thoughts. She'd thought she'd been done with Lewis after the ink had dried on the paper, but somehow the connection with him had remained as long as they were moving in the same circles. So she'd packed up her life and moved to the opposite side of the country, wishing to have as much distance between herself and her ruined life as she could get.

A fresh start.

But clearly she'd still been holding onto too much of the emotional burden. Why else had she felt compelled to answer the phone and rip into him? She was already at her lowest point since the divorce and then seeing his name had brought up some unresolved things.

Well, they were done now. All that was left for Allegra was to pick through the ruins and formulate a plan for how to rebuild her life. Or rather, how to continue this journey. She'd envisioned Palm Grove Hospital as that fresh start, letting her find her feet and confidence in herself that her career achievements had been hard-earned. But now this place was looking more like a temporary stopgap rather than the one where she could truly shine.

What had happened between her and Jamie probably wouldn't help to endear her with the staff. Jamie hadn't seemed particularly sullen towards her on the very few and all too brief occasions they'd crossed paths in the ER since last week. But she knew Jamie had friends among the staff. They might guess what had happened.

When she glanced at the presentation again, the boulder from earlier appeared back in her stomach. This was not how she'd envisioned things between them ending. She hadn't thought about the ending at all because it had seemed so…far-fetched? Like, how could their bubble ever pop when everything between them had clicked?

Things couldn't have been more different in her marriage. When Lewis had officially introduced her to his family, the expectations of her had risen to an alarming level. As the woman he'd chosen to be a part of the Kent dynasty, she'd realised there were certain things required of her. She'd followed his lead because that was what you did for someone you loved, was it not? You helped them make their dreams come true, and they did the same in return.

They could be large things like when she'd put herself second so Lewis could pick the hospital of his choice for his residency—the one his parents had already invested a lot of money in to gain an advantage. Only she knew if she were still with him, she would still be waiting for him to care about what she wanted.

Or they could be small things, like spending hours putting together a presentation. Encouraging her to find creative ways of packaging her solutions so she would have a better chance at pushing those changes through. Standing up for her when Allegra didn't even know she'd been listening.

Allegra's chest tightened and she slammed the lid of the laptop shut.

She tried to recall the indignant anger at Lewis and his conduct—his sheer entitlement—and to hang onto that feeling. But it was as if the final dregs of him had disappeared when she'd hit the block button, leaving nothing but the gaping hole caused by someone else.

Allegra had seen herself in the same situation last week and baulked. But what if the situations weren't the same because the people were different? Jamie hadn't demanded that they go public with their relationship. She had just asked a question.

What would be the worst thing that could happen?

Apparently, the answer to that was Allegra.

Pushing herself to her feet, she gathered the laptop and slipped her phone into her pocket. At this point, she'd so royally messed things up with Jamie, she wasn't even sure if the other woman would attend the meeting with the board next week. When they had worked on the presentation together, they'd planned on doing it together, just as they had intended to do so much more with the ER as partners.

Would that still stand considering how Allegra had pushed her away? She doubted it as much as she now questioned her place here at Palm Grove Hospital. Maybe her time here wasn't the new beginning she'd been looking for after she'd left San Francisco, but rather the final step she needed to take as her old self.

CHAPTER TEN

'You should talk to whoever transported the patient to the surgical floor where the rest of the fingers are. We sent them up along with the patient,' Jamie barked into the phone, rolling her eyes as the surgical nurse went on a rant about proper procedure.

She waved at one of the interns walking past her, covering the receiver as she said, 'Go and retrace the steps up to the surgical floor. The patient we just sent up came with a cooler box containing most of his fingers, and apparently *we* lost it on the way up.'

The intern's eyes grew wide, and only when Jamie had waved him away did they move in the direction of the ORs. With a sigh, she got back to the nurse. 'I'm sending someone up to help with the search, but I highly doubt we were the ones who misplaced it. No, I'm not kidding about that. With how many patients we transport up, I don't think we need a reminder of the process.'

Catarina walked up to her, eyebrows raised and an amused smile playing around her lips. Tensions between the ER and surgical staff were in a constant state of push and pull. Because emergency medicine was so unpredictable, they had to work closely together and most of the time their relationship was frictionless. But then sometimes a cooler full of severed fingers mysteriously disappeared and, as she was the most senior doctor around, it fell to Jamie to smooth over the edges such incidents created.

Conflict resolution used to be one of her greatest strengths. After all, she just needed to figure out which version of Jamie would get the other party to calm down the fastest. Though she had enough psychiatric training left from med school to know that this was maybe not the healthiest coping mechanism, it had served her well in settling interdepartmental disputes.

Until today. Or maybe a bit longer? Jamie hesitated to look too far into the past because she knew exactly what she would encounter there: a sharp pain she'd been plastering over for the last two weeks.

A slicing edge that wound its way through her as the nurse on the other end began talking again and said exactly the words Jamie *didn't* want to hear in this moment.

'Sure, you go ahead and tell Dr Tascioni whatever the hell you want. I have no doubt she'll be thrilled to have her time wasted by *your* staff breaking the chain of custody for severed limbs and this won't at all end up biting you in the ass.' Jamie brought the phone down with a loud clatter and pushed out a deep breath in a futile attempt to push out the tension winding around her chest.

'I always admired your ability to de-escalate situations,' Catarina said with a smirk that stood in direct contrast to Jamie's foul mood.

'You shut it,' she replied with a glare, crossing her arms in front of her chest. Then she uncrossed them, head slumping forward as she added, 'Sorry, that was uncalled for. I'm just frustrated.'

Judging by Catarina's low laugh, she didn't think much of the sudden outburst. Unlike Jamie, who had to remind herself to keep it together. Her life wasn't any different now from how it had been a fortnight ago. *Nothing* had changed in any real or measurable sense. She was still in the same space, leading the same life, just with no sex. And companionship. And her true self slipping further away from her.

Okay, so things *weren't* the same. But surely similar enough that it shouldn't matter. How could the impact on her life be so significant when the amount of time she'd spent with Allegra was so short?

Too short.

Catarina leaned her shoulder against the wall next to where Jamie stood, looking her up and down. 'So…are we going to talk about it or are you just gonna continue antagonising people?' she asked, switching their conversation into Spanish.

'What do you mean?' The question was out before Jamie could consider the plausibility of any denials she might utter. Even though she had spent years at this hospital and grown close with the staff, her default approach to anything personal was to remain at a surface level. That was where it was safe. Where she had the most control over how people saw her and, therefore, could give people what they wanted to set them at ease.

'Don't give me that, Jamie. You know what I'm talking about and I'm insulted you would even try to wiggle out of this conversation.' Catarina levelled a stare at her that still sparkled with some humour. Her words were meant to jolt her out of her usual pattern, but Jamie wasn't sure if she wanted that.

Wasn't entirely sure what was stopping her, either. It had been six years since she'd started here and the people—her people, as she'd described them to Allegra—had stuck around. Catarina was sticking around *right now*, even though she had snapped at her a few moments ago.

Still, the knowledge of that didn't make the words any easier to get past her lips. She wouldn't spill the tea on what had happened between her and Allegra standing in a corridor of the hospital. If they had been a one and done thing, maybe that was the right approach. But they weren't. Or rather, they hadn't been. Now they were nothing. Not even friends.

Because you couldn't fall for your friends and then go back to the way things used to be. At least not immediately, and the way Allegra had retreated from her, Jamie wasn't sure she wanted to be more than strangers any more.

'I know I've been a bit more agitated at work than usual, and I promise I'll do better. Things are…complicated for me right now. I don't know if I want to get into the specific things right now.' It was as much as she was comfortable revealing and even that tiny amount of insight triggered an immediate defence response in her that she pushed down.

A frown pulled on Catarina's mouth. 'And that agitation has nothing to do with our ice queen in residence, right? Just *things*.'

Jamie's defences gave way almost instantly. Not because she was any closer to confiding in her friend, but because hearing anything negative about Allegra hit a spot inside her that *no one* was allowed to touch—regardless of any history they might have.

'Don't even get me started with this now, Cat. For weeks you've been hazing Allegra and making life so much harder than it needed to be for *everyone* involved. Despite you all knowing that she didn't make the decision to pass me over for the promotion. Bailey did.' She pushed off the wall, needing to move to get rid of the energy coursing through her.

Next to her, Catarina shook her head. 'We weren't any harder on her than we are on *any* new person. You know what it's like when people join here. The stress is high, the hours are long, and the pay is not worth all the trouble. But we do it anyway because people depend on us. That's why we're also hard on new people. They need to know that this is no joke.'

'And you think Allegra has once treated this as not serious?' The very suggestion was preposterous. She'd risked her job—her licence—to help strangers she didn't know get treatments in the tiny space Jamie called a clinic.

'I'm saying that we're careful with who we trust. Why is this an issue? Things are different if you're sleeping with this person, huh?' Catarina eyed her knowingly and stuck her chin out at Jamie.

Busted.

Though Jamie couldn't find it in her to feel sheepish about it—neither for what she and Allegra had found together nor being called out on it. Because it had never been about them sleeping with each other. That hadn't been something Jamie had aimed to do as she grew closer to Allegra. No, it had been the result of the trust they'd built through helping the community and planning and long nights spent together figuring out what changes they could make to the hospital that didn't cost much but would still make a difference to the workload.

How was it possible that she'd been the only one to see how much value Allegra had already added to the hospital when everyone had benefited from Allegra's hard work?

'The difference is that Allegra showed up for all of us—not just in the ER whenever we needed her but also in the boardroom, where she pushed for changes that would help us. Not a single thing she's done so far was to please the board of directors, even though that was what we assumed when she came in here.' The words twisted a painful spike into Jamie's chest, but she forced herself to go on. 'I know you were all rooting for me to get the promotion, and I'll admit that my pride was hurt when I realised Bailey hadn't picked me. Turns out for once the chief was right in the choice she made because I don't know if I could have ever achieved as much as Allegra has.'

Catarina's eyes flared, her mouth closing with a snap. Silence spread between them. Neither of them was in any hurry to fill it. She'd wanted to know why they should treat Allegra differently—like one of them now—and she'd got her answer. *Everyone* had got their answer because Jamie knew it wouldn't be long before the word spread. Hopefully people were more interested in what Allegra had done rather than in their affair.

Although Jamie wasn't exactly sure why she was still so eager to work towards Allegra's acceptance when she hadn't even hesitated to call things off between them at the first sign of trouble. Even though her heart was broken from the woman who she'd fallen in love with rejecting her, she could still admit that Allegra was doing—and would continue to do—right by the hospital.

Though going by the next words coming from Catarina, she had picked up on the wrong message in Jamie's impassioned speech in Allegra's defence. 'Oh, no, *querida*. This think between you two isn't more than a fling? I thought this was casual,' she said, pressing her hand against her chest.

'It *was* something casual,' Jamie replied and knew that everything she didn't say weighed heavy in her voice.

Catarina frowned, reaching out and putting a hand on her crossed arms. The admission was enough to drain the tension left between them and something inside Jamie settled into place. Speaking the truth out loud wasn't going to fix things, but it could be the first step out of many that would let her move on.

At least she'd thought she needed to move on until her friend threw a new curve ball her way. 'You know, this makes so much more sense now. I can't believe I didn't consider the option that she was more than just a bit of fun. But she's in love with you.'

The snort was out of Jamie's mouth before she could stop it, along with a shake of her head. 'She's not. The whole reason I'm snapping at OR nurses is because *I* wanted more and she didn't.'

Granted, Jamie hadn't thought the entire interaction through before she'd confessed—correction, *tried* to confess—her feelings to Allegra, but she knew that if the woman had felt the same way, they wouldn't have ended up in the place they were now.

Catarina waved her hand in front of her face in a dismissive gesture. 'I do believe that she has the emergency room's best interests at heart. We are coming around to her, we just aren't doing that at the speed you want. Or rather, wanted. But anyway, that's not the point I'm trying to make.'

Her gaze drifted away from Jamie, examining a point behind her. When she spoke again, Catarina's voice was lower. Contemplative. 'I heard some people talking about the board meeting today and that Dr Tascioni had a big presentation prepared for it.'

Jamie nodded. 'She wants to introduce a way to report certain things to the police anonymously—like gunshot wounds. You know how undocumented people sometimes have to work outside the system? This policy would give them better access to the hospital. It won't be hugely popular with the board since it will probably end up costing money if we're treating uninsured people.'

That was the reason they had spent so much time workshopping that pitch. If the directors could see a benefit from somewhere else, they wouldn't object to the change in policy. Jamie's eyes darted to the digital clock hanging on the wall. Allegra had asked her to be part of the meeting today, but after what had happened at the garden party, Jamie wasn't sure if she still wanted her there. A part of her had wanted to talk to Allegra and figure out where they stood on that. But she knew that not a small part of that was pretence, looking for a reason to talk to Allegra simply because she missed her.

God, she missed her.

'I knew about that one. All the questions she's been asking the staff in the last few weeks pointed towards such a plan,' Catarina said, shaking her head. 'But in the last few days, the questions have changed. She's asked a lot about leadership, about what the future of the emergency room should look like and...'

Her voice trailed off and her gaze flitted away from Jamie's face.

'And what?' she asked when the silence continued, the uncertainty in Catarina's face setting off a brand-new set of alarm bells.

'Well, she was asking about you,' Catarina finally said.

Jamie paused. 'Me?' It didn't make a lot of sense to her when Allegra had been so buttoned up until the very end. Had she gone around talking to the staff about them? Or her specifically?

Seeing the confusion play on her face, Catarina continued, 'Not by name. She never actually mentioned you. But she was asking about what leadership qualities we were looking for before she'd joined. Who we thought would have been a good person to pick up the mantle if she hadn't been around. I thought she was trying to figure out how to be more like you or maybe somehow find some info she could give to the board.'

That didn't make any sense to Jamie. How was that information related to her meeting with the board today? Asking covert questions wasn't really her style. Allegra had never been interested in the politics that Bailey had wanted her to get involved with. So if she was asking questions like that...

Jamie's thoughts screeched to a halt.

'You think she's leaving?' Allegra wouldn't do that just because of Jamie, would she? The reason Jamie had kept her distance these last two weeks had been because she hadn't wanted to push her into something she wasn't ready for. Wanted to respect her decision for a clean break between them and let the dust settle. Even if said dust made her choke whenever she thought about it.

Catarina looked uncertain for the first time in their conversation. 'I haven't heard anything to confirm that. Just my gut feeling after talking to her and asking other staff members what they thought about it.'

A low buzz crept into Jamie's ear, making it harder to hear Catarina's words.

'Allegra would leave like that…? When she knows…?'

A frown appeared on the nurse's face, and Jamie realised that she'd spoken her thoughts out loud rather than wonder quietly to herself. Allegra had her in such a state that she'd let too many of her real thoughts slip out. Even after so many years of working together, she'd never felt truly relaxed enough to let people catch more than a glimpse of the woman beneath the carefully constructed sunshine persona that had helped her survive years of rejection.

Somehow Allegra had not only found a way around that without Jamie noticing. Now she was bringing down her defences without even being here.

'I wouldn't claim to know what was going through her mind when she questioned all of us, but maybe she realised your respective positions in the ER would always lead to conflict and she's taking steps to change that? She can't get involved with her subordinates, you know that,' Catarina said, but her explanation made too much sense for Jamie to consider it.

Which was strange, because Allegra was definitely the sensible one between the two of them. If it had been up to Jamie, they'd probably still be sneaking around until a solution dropped into their laps. Or they got caught. Because even though Jamie didn't want to listen to Catarina, she was right to point out that for their relationship to work, one of them would have to give up their place in the emergency room—for good.

No, it just *didn't* add up. 'She said she didn't want to be with me. Why would she even contemplate leaving her job to remove this conflict when she already told me that?' Jamie said, ignoring the flare of panic at sharing herself again. At this point, she'd revealed so much to Catarina, she might as well go all out.

Catarina tilted her head to the side. 'When was that?'

'At your barbecue.'

'That was two weeks ago. People do change their minds, especially if they've had some time to sit on their feelings. I'm not guaranteeing she feels any different now, but if you find her behaviour in the last two weeks strange, maybe there's something new to learn.' Jamie followed her gaze, both of them looking at the blue digits of the digital clock hanging on the wall. 'Weren't you supposed to be there for the board meeting?'

With how much time she and Allegra had spent locked away rehearsing, everyone knew they'd had a big plan for the meeting. Changes they had been excited to introduce to everyone.

'She ended things between us after I told her I could help her turn things around for her with the staff. That with her experience in running large-scale operations and my relationships throughout the emergency room, we would be in the perfect position to enact change—if she accepted my help.' Jamie had thought back to that moment a lot, going over everything she'd said, everything Allegra had heard.

Jamie understood now that she'd moved too fast. Allegra's past with her ex still weighed heavily on her and informed how she'd seen Jamie's intentions when she'd made her offer. The last thing on her mind had been to force a decision on the woman who meant so much more to her than she'd thought would be possible from the very outset. So even though she hadn't meant to cross a line, Jamie had accepted that, in Allegra's eyes, she had and so she needed to stay away from her—as hard as that had turned out to be.

Could it really be that she'd changed her mind? The hurt Allegra's rejection had carved into Jamie's chest still throbbed alive with an overwhelming fierceness whenever she thought of that moment. Even though she'd made a conscious effort to understand and empathise with Allegra, she couldn't deny the pain of having her intentions misunderstood. That Allegra would think she could ever do something that wasn't to Allegra's benefit or act in her own self-interest…

The beeper clipped to Catarina's waistband emitted a low sound, and she grabbed it. Jamie watched as she squinted at the display before letting out a small sigh. 'They need me to sort out something,' the nurse said as she put the beeper down.

'Anything I can help with?'

Catarina looked up at her with a sheepish smile. 'You might not know whether she wants you at the meeting or not, but there seems to be a simple solution to that. One that might also lead to more answers.'

Jamie frowned when the nurse walked past her, turning to call after her, 'What solution is that?'

Catarina paused for a second, sending her a look over her shoulder. 'You should just ask her.'

CHAPTER ELEVEN

ONCE AGAIN ALLEGRA found her resolve disintegrating. Her heels echoed in the otherwise empty corridor as she walked up and down, waiting for her turn with the board of directors. Even though she'd told herself repeatedly that she was doing this alone—that her decision was final—she couldn't help but look up whenever someone approached, hope that *she* would be here seizing her heart each time.

She knew she shouldn't hope for that. Not after Allegra had been the one to tell Jamie to stay away from her. That she was now doing alone this part of a journey they'd taken on together from the very start was her fault and no one else's.

And now she was too late. She'd rejected Jamie in her moment of vulnerability, not even letting her finish her thought before accusing her of trying to wield too much influence over her with her relationships in the hospital.

Even though her call with Lewis had been frustrating, at least he'd helped her figure that part out—even if it was too late to change anything. He had the most things to feel sorry about, to want to reconcile with her. But when she'd confronted him on his surface level of regret, he'd instantly turned on her again and showed his true colours. The same ones that had finally convinced her to leave him.

That wasn't what was happening to her right now. Jamie hadn't been that way and it pained her to realise this only now. Her suggestion to use her excellent, well-established relationships to help Allegra out in the ER had come from a place of caring. Of wanting them to be successful as a team.

Together.

From afar, these two things had looked the same, spooking Allegra into making the wrong decision. Now she didn't know how to take it all back. Because spending the last two weeks alone with her thoughts and the presentation on her laptop, she'd realised that she didn't actually *want* to leave this hospital. Work continued to be tough and the people on staff here weren't easily convinced. But she liked that. Winning them over and delivering on the promises she'd made would be that much sweeter when it all finally panned out.

Despite hating the tension and yearning to get to a place where things were okay between her and Jamie, she didn't want this to be the last step she'd be taking in her journey as the old Allegra. No, she wanted to claim this win with the ER and its staff. She wanted to see her changes implemented.

She wanted to be with Jamie. Because she was in love with her. Stupidly in love.

The last thing was the trickiest piece of it all and the one filling Allegra with the most sense of trepidation. A part of her had hoped that Jamie would show up to this meeting, sending her a signal that her regret—her advances—wouldn't be unwelcome. But wasn't waiting for such a sign just another form of her avoiding doing the hard thing?

It had been Jamie who'd always put herself out there, talking about her evolving feelings and asking the question that still popped into Allegra's head every day.

After the garden party, she'd spent a lot of time imagining the worst-case scenarios of an ill-considered relationship with Jamie. They could end up hating each other, or Allegra could end up leaving again. She still wasn't certain she had fully unravelled herself from the marriage to Lewis. What if she got completely wrapped up in Jamie rather than taking the time to find herself?

These had been all the reasons she'd clung to so her actions wouldn't sting so much. The justifications she'd kept reciting to herself over and over again. With each repetition they grew more hollow, and now she was at a point where she was certain she hadn't ever really believed them. Or if she had, they had only served as a shield because she was too scared to let herself be happy.

And even though she realised that now, she still hesitated to seek out Jamie and tell her how wrong she was because… What if it was too late? The hurt would slice through her all over again.

The door of the conference room swung open and a man in a suit stepped out followed by a familiar face—Dr Eliza Bailey. She mumbled something to the man, then shook his hand and watched him trot down the corridor away from Allegra.

Her spine stiffened when Dr Bailey turned back and their eyes locked. A deep breath calmed the roiling of her stomach as she remembered the purpose of her meeting with the board today. Not to dwell on the most recent series of regrets she carried around, but to represent the needs of the emergency room. Allegra might not be certain of her future here at Palm Grove Hospital, but for now she was still in charge of the ER and needed to convince the board to go along with her plans.

Allegra took a step forward when Dr Bailey approached her, stretching out her hand. 'Thank you for your time today, Dr Bailey.'

The chief nodded, her smile fraying at the edges. 'I asked to take a short break as we move on to the next agenda items. Been stuck in that room all morning. But they'll be ready to hear your proposal imminently.'

Something in Bailey's tone shifted, too subtle for Allegra to decipher, before she continued, 'All the department leads are presenting their progress today, and the board is keen to see what has been happening in emergency medicine.'

There was that tone again. Allegra frowned and the familiar sensation of the ice queen facade spread through her chest. 'I have no doubt they will be satisfied with the state of the emergency room. Our mortality rate is down, so are staff absences, while staff satisfaction is improving.'

The last point had brought a flutter to her chest when she'd received the number from the staff surveys. No matter how she felt about her reception among the staff, the numbers were indisputable: staff satisfaction had increased since Allegra had arrived.

Chief Bailey gave a non-committal shrug. 'Is it true that you gave up your office to put more beds into the ER?' The astonishment in her voice spoke volumes as to what Bailey thought about that idea. Though Allegra couldn't really judge the chief of medicine for not understanding giving up her office. The chief's job had very little to do with treating patients.

Still, Allegra couldn't keep the frost out of her voice. 'The expected throughput of the emergency room wasn't achievable without either more budget or more beds. Since I didn't get an increase to hire more people, I had to think creatively.'

That was the one thing the chief had noticed about Allegra's tenure at Palm Grove? That she didn't have an office? No wonder the hospital's goals seemed misaligned to her across several departments. Leadership had more regard for profits than to make medicine more accessible for the community they served.

A head poked out of the meeting room. 'We just called for a coffee refill. Once that's arrived, we'll be ready to continue.'

Some of the professional detachment she'd summoned within her gave way to nerves and she looked over her shoulder, scanning the empty corridor behind her. Bailey noticed the gesture as well, lifting one eyebrow. 'Waiting for someone to join you?'

'Dr Rivera was the one who put the binder together in the first place, helping me figure out what holes to plug in the ER. She's been instrumental in my work here and I was hoping to have her speak to the board as well.' Allegra wasn't sure why she'd chosen this moment to be open with the chief. Even if Jamie didn't show up—which seemed more likely with each passing second—she couldn't let everyone believe that the achievements and ideas she'd be presenting today were hers alone.

Bailey's lips disappeared into a thin line. 'Dr Tascioni,

there's a reason I hired you to lead the emergency room. If I'd trusted Dr Rivera to take over operations and bring us the numbers we need to see, I could have given her the role. Don't get too friendly with your subordinates or they might influence you in an adverse way. Jamie Rivera has had an agenda for the emergency room ever since she started and, since she didn't get the role, she might be using your friendliness to her advantage.'

Allegra couldn't stop the snort of derision from escaping her throat. Bailey's eyes widened as the sound echoed through the otherwise empty corridor. Before the chief could say anything, Allegra said, 'I mean no disrespect, Dr Bailey. This is simply one of the more ludicrous things I've heard from leadership since I started here. You are doing your entire emergency medicine department a disservice by underestimating Jamie. Not only was she keeping the entire place together before I joined—and I suspect also for a significant amount of time while my predecessor was still here—but she's also an almost endless source of energy everyone draws from. Including me.'

She knew that, tactically, this wasn't the smartest choice right before an important meeting. But Allegra didn't care. There was a time when she'd watched her words in front of an authority like Eliza Bailey. She'd been taught to respect legacies and important names within a hospital's hierarchy by Lewis and his entire family. But staying quiet when she disagreed—when she had far superior ideas—had also been the thing that had kept her glued to her ex's side for far too long.

Allegra would not let that happen again.

From the way Bailey's eyes widened and her mouth

hung open, she had the impression that the other woman had rarely had her opinions challenged. Or maybe the shock came from Allegra doing it—a person the chief had believed to be firmly planted in her square.

Silence stretched between them for a few seconds before Bailey stood up straight and plastered on a fake smile. 'Disregarding my warnings will come around to haunt you, Dr Tascioni. Do not think for a moment that the board will be impressed by any hysterics.'

Allegra opened her mouth for another ill-considered retort when a different voice cut in. 'True, the board is all about promises of profits and how much we can squeeze out of both patients and staff before you have to deal with people's "hysterics".'

Both their heads swirled around to face Jamie coming down the corridor, and Allegra couldn't keep the relief from showing on her face. Didn't want to hide any of her feelings as Jamie looked at her with a gentle softness that almost brought her to her knees.

Allegra said nothing—just swallowed the sigh building in her throat—as Jamie stepped next to her and they both faced the chief, who crossed her arms as her gaze darted between the two women.

'This lack of diplomacy is exactly why you didn't get the job, Dr Rivera. Running a hospital costs money. As a department lead you should know that. We can't go around giving away treatment for free. I'm pretty sure your precious staff members would be the first to admit that if their pay cheques were delayed.' Her voice turned into a low hiss, and Allegra's eyebrows shot up as she learned of this new side to Eliza Bailey.

She'd never been a fan of the woman, knowing her

type from her time at San Francisco General. But even though they all knew that profits were the only thing she cared about, to have her so blatantly admit to that was a revelation. How did someone go into medicine as a profession just to turn out like that?

Bailey turned her gaze on Allegra, her frown deepening. 'I thought you understood what needs to be done around here to provide an adequate service while also ensuring that the hospital comes out ahead. But apparently that impression was misguided.'

Allegra returned her frown with her own icy expression. 'I never believed in commodifying healthcare and I'm surprised that this is the impression you got from me during the recruitment process. Seems like we both need to adjust our expectations going forward, don't we?'

The message behind her words was clear, but it surprised even her as she said it: Allegra was here to stay. Of course, the chief had the choice to replace her, but by the line appearing between her brows—the frown deepening—Bailey had also just remembered the early termination clause in Allegra's contract and that it would cost the hospital far more money to get rid of her than to go along with her plans.

The rattle of dishes clattering against each other floated through the air as a service trolley laden with coffee carafes and other snacks appeared around the corner, heading towards them. Bailey turned her head towards it and when she looked back, the fake smile had reappeared on her lips.

'We're about to start. The board may be inclined to approve your plans, but don't think even for a second that I'm not keeping a very close eye on you.' She made a point of looking at both of them before turning around and stalking back into the meeting room.

Tension flowed out of Allegra's body as the chief disappeared. 'That was—'

The rest of her words got lost in Jamie's mouth as the other woman covered her body with her own, pushing Allegra against the wall and sliding her lips over hers in a kiss that lit up every exposed nerve ending inside her body.

All the thoughts inside her fell away, leaving only space for Jamie and her mouth on hers and how much she'd missed her throughout the last two weeks. Yes, she had made the decision to step away and distance herself, yet the longing for Jamie hadn't lessened. Maybe even the opposite. Somehow, the need exploding through her was even fiercer than before.

After the spectacle with the chief, Allegra had no idea how the meeting would end. But whatever would happen, at least one decision had become clear: she could fix what she'd broken between her and Jamie.

And she would do whatever was needed to fix it.

Allegra's delicious scent drifted up her nose, bringing back the memories of nights spent entangled in bed together. Jamie breathed her in, relishing the closeness and the energy the kiss awakened within her. As if the world had faded into dull sepia tones and only Allegra's presence in her life could bring out the full spectrum of colour that was now normal to her.

The high of finally kissing her again hit her bloodstream immediately, carrying her away on a cloud of desire and affection—pent-up feelings she'd tried to forget about for far too long. So when the reality of where they were and what Jamie had done hit her, she pulled back immediately and held her hands up.

'Sorry, that was… I shouldn't have done that.' She swallowed, her heart bouncing so forcefully against her chest, her breath came in short pants. What on earth had possessed her to act on the impulse to kiss Allegra? No matter how much she wanted to, she couldn't go around kissing the woman who had told her in no uncertain terms that they were done. At least not before she took one last shot and shared her feelings with her.

Allegra's chest rose in a matching rhythm, her lips slightly parted from the abrupt start and stop of that kiss. Jamie searched her expression for fury, or any other hint of her touch having been unwelcome, but her expression remained steady and veiled, not letting Jamie guess her thoughts. Then she shook her head and a small chuckle escaped her.

Jamie held her breath as Allegra reached out, taking her hand and giving it a squeeze. 'I was hoping you would show up here. I have to admit, I wasn't sure if you were going to.'

'I wasn't sure if you wanted me to be here,' Jamie replied, which earned her another chuckle, though this one was strained with an underlying pain.

'I don't blame you after what I said. How I pushed you away.' Allegra dropped her hand along with her gaze, in a gesture that was so unlike her that Jamie's chest tightened. Allegra had hoped she'd come here, but did that mean her kiss had been welcome? Or was this a purely professional wish?

Reaching out, Jamie slid her fingers underneath Allegra's chin, lifting her head so their eyes locked. 'I went about it the wrong way. I saw you struggle, but all I focused on was how to help you rather than listen to you and let you find your own way. You are amazing and I should—no, I *have* full confidence in your abilities. The last thing I want is to be a reason you doubt yourself.' She swallowed the lump in her throat. 'I'm sorry.'

A brittle smile appeared on Allegra's lips, still so timid. The desire to fix things, to shield Allegra from everything that could ever hurt her, wasn't necessarily a bad thing. But that protective instinct, honed through the rejection Jamie had faced all her life, had snapped in too tight, not leaving Allegra any space to manoeuvre. If this was going to work—and Jamie hoped against hope that this was where this conversation was leading—she needed to deal with her fears without making them Allegra's burden. And she would. If Allegra gave her another chance, she would do whatever it took.

'It was— *I* need to apologise. Lewis and I have been separated for more than a year at this point but I didn't realise how much of my marriage's ghost I was still carrying around. Still *am* carrying around right now.' Jamie slipped her hand from Allegra's chin to her cheek and let out a shaky breath when Allegra leaned her head into the touch. 'I'm a work in progress and there will sometimes be things that freak me out for no good reason. But if you can deal with that then I want to try this. Us.'

Allegra smiled again, but this time it was bright and soft, causing Jamie's knees to weaken, her breath to catch. 'Because I'm in love with you, and I don't want my own fear to stand in the way of something that could change my life in the best way imaginable.'

Somehow, the already quiet corridor grew even more silent. Or maybe that was due to the ringing in her ears that started the second Jamie heard the words coming out of Allegra's mouth. The words that she herself had kept close in her heart, ready to burst out on that fateful day two weeks ago. Allegra hadn't wanted to hear it back then and Jamie had thought it was because she'd misread the signs. That she had given their connection more credit than it deserved. But that hadn't been it at all.

'You've been fighting these feelings? That's why you pushed back?' she asked, tracing her thumb over Allegra's cheek. Warmth spread through her fingertips, trickling down her arm and sending a delicious shiver through her. Was this really happening?

Allegra pressed her lips together, then nodded as she took a deep breath. 'I thought I was seeing all the red flags I had missed during my marriage now being repeated with you. But that wasn't true. The red flags I was seeing were my own hang-ups, and I was holding onto them too tightly for fear of repeating my mistakes.'

'Allegra.' How was it possible that Jamie felt so brittle and yet invincible at the same time? The energy within her defied logic, yet she knew it was true—both her feelings for Allegra and that she felt the same way.

Her other hand came up to frame Allegra's face, and she leaned her forehead against hers, taking a deep breath and relishing the scent enveloping her. Looking at Allegra, she couldn't fight the grin spreading over her face as she said, 'I love you, too. I don't know how it happened or how we got here. But for the first time in my life, I found someone who just gets me. The real me. Not a carefully curated version—not sunshine Jamie—but me. I couldn't resist you because you slipped into my heart long before I realised it. That's what you do to me, Allegra.' She pulled her face closer, brushing against her lips in a gentle kiss before withdrawing again. 'I have my hang-ups, too. So let's promise to hold a space for each other, even when things suck. Together, we can figure things out.'

Allegra nodded, letting out a deep sigh that turned into a laugh halfway through. 'Wow, this was more nerve-racking than preparing for this leadership meeting now.' She glanced sideways just as the trolley full of refreshments was wheeled out of the room again.

During all of this, Jamie had kind of forgotten where they were having this conversation. Or what was to come next. 'We'll still have a problem with Bailey. If she finds out we're dating, she'll throw the book at us. She already dislikes me and with this, she'd have a reason to get rid of me.' Jamie knew Bailey didn't like her style and that it had been part of the reason she hadn't picked her for the job. But the chief wasn't dumb and had realised that Jamie was the glue keeping the entire emergency room together. But if she attributed all the recent success to Allegra, maybe she wouldn't hesitate any more to fire Jamie.

Allegra's smile turned sheepish, and Jamie raised an eyebrow. 'What are you cooking up in that beautiful brain of yours?'

'Okay, don't freak out,' Allegra said, taking a step away from the wall to put some distance between them.

Jamie narrowed her eyes. 'Always suspicious when things start like that.'

Allegra breathed out a laugh. 'I had a lot of spare time

to think in these last two weeks. I—well, I finally picked up the phone and told Lewis to lose my number.'

Jamie's jaw tightened at the mention of her ex-husband and the many calls he'd subjected Allegra to. Whenever his name had appeared on her screen, Jamie could feel the tension radiating from her. A part of her had wanted to tell Allegra to block him—that calling her incessantly even though it was abundantly clear that she didn't want to speak to him had just been another way of controlling her. He might not have been able to talk to her, but he'd made sure he knew she was thinking about him.

Because they hadn't been in a romantic relationship, Jamie hadn't felt justified to give her advice on how to deal with a personal situation, even though she could see the struggle on her face. Though when she'd imagined Allegra finally giving her ex the boot, she would have preferred her to block him rather than answer the phone. What good could possibly come out of giving the guy who had looked down at her skill and competence as a wife and doctor more airtime than he deserved?

Allegra seemed to read her thoughts, for she shook her head. 'It wasn't to hear him out. It was so that I could finally tell him a few things that had been playing on my mind since I moved out of our shared home. I'm glad I picked up the phone so I could witness the sheer entitlement with which he still treated me, up until that call.'

Despite the gap between them, Jamie reached out, even if it was to only briefly run the back of her hand over Allegra's cheek.

The other woman took a breath before she continued, 'You said it before and, even though I agreed, I thought him knowing I chose not to speak to him somehow made it better. What I didn't realise was how much space I was giving him inside my head by not fully excising him from my life. When I pushed you away—that was when I let my fear make decisions for me. I thought maybe coming here was the final step the old me needed to make. I was ready to move on with my life.'

'Move on?' The words stung far more than they should have. Allegra wasn't leaving. She wouldn't stand here and admit to that if her plan was still to walk out. But the thought of never seeing her again—of how close she'd actually got to that reality—struck a searing spike through Jamie.

The apologetic smile spreading over Allegra's lips calmed Jamie's nerves. 'As I said, don't freak out. I'm not leaving. It took me a while, but as I thought back on Lewis and his calls—and my reaction to you—I realised I didn't want to leave.' She paused, the small smile turning into a wolfish grin. 'When planning my exit, I came up with a way of forcing the board to accept you as my replacement—by tying it to something they couldn't refuse.'

'Me?' Jamie's eyebrows shot up. 'How?'

'Well, I—'

The assistant's head appeared in the doorway. 'They're ready for you now.'

Allegra nodded, brushing her fingers against Jamie's as she turned to walk into the room, bidding Jamie to follow her into the meeting just as they had planned in what felt like another lifetime.

'Wait, what's the plan now, if you're not leaving?' Jamie whispered as she caught up. Her replacing Allegra as the department lead for emergency medicine didn't solve anything.

'I'm going to demand that they make you co-lead,' Allegra said, her grin so wicked, Jamie wanted to press her back against that wall and devour her whole.

She pushed that impulse down and followed Allegra into the conference room, where they faced six pairs of eyes staring at them with varying degrees of scepticism.

'Sorry, you want to *split* the responsibilities of the department lead?'

Allegra nodded, a small smile playing on her lips. She knew this was a done deal. The numbers she presented spoke for themselves. Without any increase in budget, she had managed to increase the hospital's throughput while lowering staff absences and turnover. Nobody could deny that she was doing exactly what the chief and the board had asked of her.

When she'd presented the policy changes she and Jamie had been working on since that day at Jamie's makeshift clinic, the board hadn't done more than nod and deem the changes sensible for the service of the community even if it might annoy local law enforcement. Allegra had watched Bailey closely in that moment and searched her expression for any displeasure at how easily they'd been able to introduce it. But the woman's constantly annoyed face didn't really give many hints to work with.

Figuring out what the tension between Bailey and Jamie was would be one of Allegra's next projects—once she'd dealt with this part of her plan.

'Yes, that's right. It's a similar approach to what I did at San Francisco General before coming over here. One lead for the day-to-day operations and on-the-ground support for the staff—in this case that would be Dr Rivera—and one lead to function as the administrative head, keeping everything that needs to happen in the background going so that the staff can clear their heads of anything not helpful to their daily tasks.'

She went back a few slides to point at a graph showing the increased throughput over time through a steady budget number at San Francisco General. 'This increase in productivity was thanks to introducing a dedicated lead for the staff. Not only does it help to have the final decision maker on the floor with them every day, it also uplifts staff morale while keeping mortality rates low. People like to see their leaders committed to their work.'

Allegra didn't mean to sound insulting, but she could still see a few of the board members who were also physicians bristle at the call-out. Not that she cared much if her words forced them to examine their own motivations. As long as she got the answer she wanted.

Of course, Bailey was the first person to speak up. 'This is unprecedented and has never been done this way at Palm Grove Hospital.'

Ah, exactly the kind of denial Allegra was more than prepared for. The flimsier the arguments from the chief were, the easier a time she'd have convincing the rest of the board to go along with her plan. By the thoughtful expressions on most of their faces, she knew she had already planted the right seeds earlier in the presentation.

'Just because something hasn't ever been done before, doesn't mean that we shouldn't consider this change if it could be transformative for the hospital,' Jamie said from next to her, going down exactly the same road Allegra would have with her argument. They were already the kind of team she wanted them to be. All they needed was the approval of the board.

To think two weeks ago she'd been ready to leave all of this behind. How close she'd come to making the worst mistake of her life.

Bailey's eyes narrowed on Jamie but she continued, undeterred. 'As the most senior doctor, I was already acting as the lead for the department during the previous lead's tenure, doing exactly the things Dr Tascioni describes in her proposal. Our staff have been accepting and appreciative of the guidance they have received every day. Formally acknowledging this function also serves to show them we care about their needs.'

Allegra suppressed a smile as she shot a glance at her girlfriend—and soon to be co-lead. Jamie had barely had five minutes of lead time on Allegra's idea of making them co-lead, yet she'd picked up on her strategy as if it had been her own idea.

They still had some way to go before they could become an official item at work, but the fact that they were already setting plans into motion calmed a part inside her still bruised by her treatment in her marriage.

How she could have ever thought Jamie and Lewis the same was beyond her. Whatever demon had possessed her in that moment would hopefully stay far, far away after witnessing the acts of love and affection they had shown each other. Even if this plan didn't work out, Allegra knew they would find some other way to be together. They were *both* all in. Equal partners in everything they did.

The members of the board looked at each other, and

Allegra could see them giving the idea the merit it deserved. Then Bailey piped up again. 'And I imagine this official title comes with a big bump in compensation? Don't tell me that's something you haven't thought about at length.'

Jamie's eyes widened, and she blinked several times before looking towards Allegra. It was almost disappointing how predictable Bailey was with her rebuttals. None of them actually hinged on the benefits the hospital could derive from this solution and were all about her personal dislike of Jamie.

The shock on her girlfriend's face was another thing Allegra had counted on because even though the thing between them was fresh and their relationship still developing, she knew this woman already. Being a leader in the hospital and helping people—it had never been about money to her. Something the board now also realised as they looked at Jamie's befuddled expression.

But Allegra wasn't going to let Jamie sell herself short. 'The salary of a department lead does come in at a different point from that of a senior doctor. But if you look at it as an investment into the emergency room, you can see where a small bump can lead you.' She pointed at the chart again, showing off the steep curve upwards of the second line—the one showing the budget she'd worked with at SF General—and let the information settle. The board members exchanged glances, some nodding appreciatively, and Allegra could feel them buying into her plan.

All except one, of course. 'This isn't a decision we can make with just your word, Dr Tascioni. I'm sure the members—'

'You can have the money to create this role, Dr Tascioni. With that we hope to see great things from you at Palm Grove Hospital,' one of the board members, Dr Michelle, said, cutting off Bailey.

Allegra nodded, forcing her expression to remain neutral despite fireworks popping off in the pit of her stomach. 'You can expect nothing less from both of us,' she said, including Jamie next to her with a hand gesture before taking the board's quiet murmuring to each other as a dismissal.

Though she couldn't resist shooting Eliza Bailey a self-assured smile before stepping out of the room and back into the corridor that had changed her entire life not even thirty minutes ago.

They walked next to each other in silence and only once they'd turned the corner did they stop to look at each other. Jamie's eyes were still wide, and Allegra knew they would both be processing this victory for a while. But one thing was clear.

'We did it,' she said with a smile that mirrored Jamie's grin.

'We really did,' Jamie replied.

She stepped closer, her face hovering close to Allegra's, and Allegra braced herself as longing thundered through her.

But then Jamie stepped back and started down the corridor again, her shoes squeaking against the floor with every other step.

'Wait, where are you going?' Allegra's heels clicked in an urgent staccato as she caught up to her.

'Some place where I can devour you without people walking in on us. Maybe a quiet space that is just for us leads?' Jamie's voice dropped low, sending a searing flash of heat down Allegra's spine and she bit down on her lip to stop herself from moaning in anticipation.

'Not what I had in mind when I came up with this idea on the fly,' she replied, though the heat staining her cheeks would show Jamie exactly how she felt about it, even if it was unexpected.

'Well, then… Lead the way, Dr Rivera,' Allegra said as she shot Jamie a glance that conveyed the need coursing through her.

Her co-lead. Her girlfriend.

Her equal in every way.

* * * * *

*If you enjoyed this story,
check out these other great reads from
Luana DaRosa*

Hot Nights with the Arctic Doc
Pregnancy Surprise with the Greek Surgeon
Surgeon's Brooding Brazilian Rival
A Therapy Pup to Reunite Them

All available now!

MILLS & BOON®

Coming next month

SECOND CHANCE IN SANTIAGO
Tina Beckett

Vivi tried on a fake smile.

'Hi! I didn't know you were at Valpo Memorial. At least not until I saw you in the operating room.'

That dark gaze stared her down for a minute or two. 'Didn't you?'

Cris's words took her aback and she frowned. 'I'm not sure what you mean by that.'

'Surely my name was on the list of hospital staff when you came here looking for a job.'

He made it sound like she'd been desperate or something.

'Actually, I didn't 'come here looking for a job.' I saw a posting at the hospital where I was *already working* as a scrub nurse and applied. I didn't scour the website looking for familiar names.' She threw in, 'Besides, I might not have even recognized your name if I'd seen it.'

That was a mistake, and he knew it because one side of his mouth curved. 'Oh really? I got a few letters that seemed to indicate otherwise.'

Yes, she had written several long pages of prose that reiterated what she'd said the last time she saw him...that she would love him forever. That she would never ever forget him.

Her face heated. 'I was a child back then.' And she didn't talk about the fact that he hadn't written her back because she didn't want him to know how soul-crushing it had been that he hadn't cared enough to respond.

The way she'd never responded to Estevan's texts? No. That was not the same. She was convinced that he'd never really loved her—or he wouldn't have been able to jump into another relationship so quickly. It seemed she was forever doomed to love men more than they loved her. But not anymore.

'It seems we both were.' His face turned serious. 'And now we're both adults, so I assume we can both work at the same hospital—the same *quirófano*—without it causing a problem, correct?'

Continue reading

SECOND CHANCE IN SANTIAGO
Tina Beckett

Available next month
millsandboon.co.uk

Copyright © 2025 Tina Beckett

COMING SOON!

We really hope you enjoyed reading this book.
If you're looking for more romance
be sure to head to the shops when
new books are available on

Thursday 19th June

To see which titles are coming soon, please visit
millsandboon.co.uk/nextmonth

MILLS & BOON

FOUR BRAND NEW BOOKS FROM
MILLS & BOON MODERN

The same great stories you love, a stylish new look!

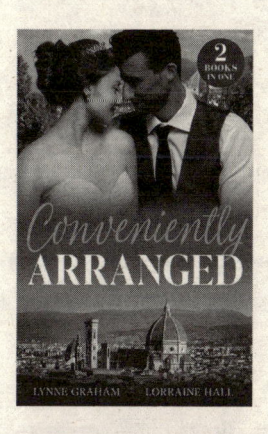

Conveniently ARRANGED
LYNNE GRAHAM — LORRAINE HALL

WANTED: HIS HEIR
MAYA BLAKE — DANI COLLINS

DEFIANT Brides

THE BILLIONAIRE'S LEGACY
ABBY GREEN — NATALIE ANDERSON

OUT NOW

Eight Modern stories published every month, find them all at:
millsandboon.co.uk

afterglow BOOKS

Afterglow Books is a trend-led, trope-filled list of books with diverse, authentic and relatable characters, a wide array of voices and representations, plus real world trials and tribulations. Featuring all the tropes you could possibly want (think small-town settings, fake relationships, grumpy vs sunshine, enemies to lovers) and all with a generous dose of spice in every story.

♪ @millsandboonuk
◎ @millsandboonuk
afterglowbooks.co.uk
#AfterglowBooks

For all the latest book news, exclusive content and giveaways scan the QR code below to sign up to the Afterglow newsletter:

SCAN ME

afterglow BOOKS

NOT SO FAST
He's on track to win her heart...
KAREN BOOTH

Much Ado About Hating You
They're enemies at work...but can love write their happy ending?
Sarah Echavarre Smith

- 🎾 Sports romance
- 🔥 Enemies to lovers
- 🌶 Spicy

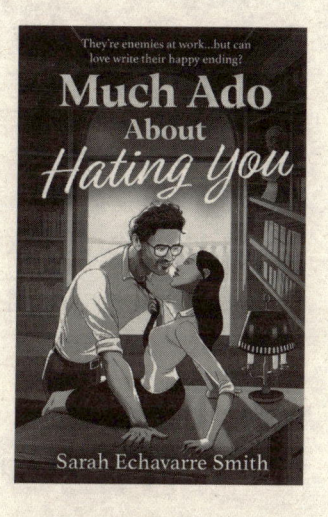

- 💻 Workplace romance
- 🚫 Forbidden love
- ☯ Opposites attract

OUT NOW

Two stories published every month. Discover more at:
Afterglowbooks.co.uk

LET'S TALK
Romance

For exclusive extracts, competitions and special offers, find us online:

- **f** MillsandBoon
- **X** @MillsandBoon
- **○** @MillsandBoonUK
- **♪** @MillsandBoonUK

Get in touch on 01413 063 232

> For all the latest titles coming soon, visit
> millsandboon.co.uk/nextmonth